COUNTER CURRENTS

A STORY OF SMUGGLERS, RIVER PIRATES, LOVE, WAR AND FREEDOM FIGHTERS IN 1838

By Shaun J. McLaughlin

ISBN 978-0-9879035-2-5

Counter Currents
Copyright © 2012 by Shaun J. McLaughlin

Published by Raiders and Rebels Press
www.raidersandrebelspress.com

No part of this book may be used or reproduced in any manner whatsoever without the prior written permission of the author, except in the case of brief quotations in reviews or scholarly works.

This novel contains some adult content.

Cover design by Amelia Ah You

This novel is dedicated to

my late father,

John Clifford Thomas McLaughlin,

who encouraged me to start writing and shared with me his love of the outdoors

and to

my late friend,

Dirk Peter Vanderlee,

who encouraged me to keep writing and taught me never to give up.

Contents

Rebellion's Casualty	1
Winter's Pupil	20
Spring's Refugee	34
Indian Summer	49
Smuggler's Apprentice	65
Pirate's Helper	76
The Firm's New Partner	100
Queen's Suitor	122
Secret Society's Novitiate	142
Captain's Aide	156
Colonel's Recruit	168
War's Attendant	186
The Road's Fork	212
Trial's Pawn	233
Fort's Inmate	253
Letters	280
Epilogue	289
About the Author	290

Author's Notes

While a work of fiction, *Counter Currents* respects the history it borrows. Of all the named characters, only the protagonist Ryan Lone Pine and six others are fictional. Any character presented with a Christian name and surname existed in the occupation and location at which this story places them (to the best of my knowledge). Where I had a physical description of them, I gave it. None of the major historical events and institutions is an invention. The names of towns and places are those used in 1838, and several names have since changed: Abel's Island (Picton Island), Bytown (Ottawa), Hemlock Island (Heart Island), Lower Canada (Quebec), Pakenham Mills (Pakenham), Upper Canada (Ontario), Van Diemen's Land (Tasmania), Wells Island (Wellesley Island). Depot Island is a fictional name for Lindoe (a.k.a. Lyndoch) Island.

I owe a debt to historian W. J. Wraith, a man I know little about and never met. Under the name of John Northman, he wrote the only biography of "Pirate" Bill Johnston. Published in one hundred and twenty installments in the *Watertown Daily Times* from 1938 to 1939, *Pirates of the Thousand Islands* provides details found nowhere else about Bill Johnston and his family. Wraith interviewed Johnston's grandchildren, great nieces, nephews, and cousins, as well as elderly men whose fathers knew Johnston. Wraith also viewed Johnston's *lost* scrapbook, an invaluable collection of his personal notes and newspaper articles. Wraith's work has disappeared. No online anthology or historical work I've read cites it.

Besides Wraith's work, I consulted numerous primary and secondary sources written in the 19th century and early 20th century. Several veterans of the Patriot War of 1838 wrote books about their experiences. Three Americans who raided Canada near Prescott in 1838 and were transported to Tasmania—Daniel Heustis, William Gates, and Stephen Wright—wrote memoirs on returning from exile. The British colonel who tried and failed to capture Bill Johnston in 1838, Sir Richard Bonnycastle, gave the British colonial view of the 1838 troubles in *Canada as it was, is, and may be*, published in 1852.

Most Canadians and Americans captured after the Prescott raid faced court martial at Fort Henry in Kingston, Ontario. The trial scene in *Trial's Pawn* closely follows court transcripts of the 1839 trial of

Daniel Heustis and eleven other Americans. That chapter also introduces Colonel Allan Macdonell. Daniel Heustis wrote that Macdonell was a fair but profane man. Conversations between Ryan and Macdonell include unfamiliar slang (cant). The *1811 Dictionary of the Vulgar Tongue* explains the terms. You can find a free copy online.

I owe a debt of gratitude to the Thousand Islands Museum in Clayton, New York. I first *discovered* Bill Johnston while researching a college assignment in 1974. I wrote the museum asking for information on Johnston. The then curator, Stephen FitzGerald, promptly answered my request by sending a photocopy of Wraith's entire series on Johnston. I visited the museum many times since for additional material on Johnston and his family.

I also owe a debt to the wonderful people at the Mississippi Mills Public Library in Almonte, Ontario, for bringing in the rare books I requested through interlibrary loan.

This novel first took shape as a short story in the summer of 2007. Three friends who read it—Chris O'Brien, Jill McCubbin, and the late Peter Vanderlee—urged me to turn the story into a novel. I did. Thanks.

I also want to thank several friends: volunteer readers Patricia Bradley-White, George Hill, Amelia Ah You, and Arnie Francis for proofreading and suggestions; editorial advisor Jean Brathwaite for guidance in the early stage of the novel; Algonquin elder and author Jane Chartrand for ensuring that the *Indian Summer* chapter was properly respectful of the Algonquin people; and long-time Bill Johnston researcher James Eagan of Canandaigua, New York, for sharing his advice and knowledge.

Rebellion's Casualty

A thunderous boom rippled the water under Ryan's birchbark canoe. The raven perched on the canoe's bow leapt into the air.

Ryan jerked his gaze up at Fort Henry. The dun-colored edifice straddled the promontory above Kingston like a basking beast of prey in the hazy autumn sun. One of its massive cannon exhaled smoke into the cold air. After that single flexing of muscle, the fort seemed to slumber.

"I wonder what that was about, eh Zak?" he said to the bird, as it returned to roost.

He continued paddling down the Cataraqui River towards the causeway and bridge that marked the harbor's start. Three pairs of black draught horses towing field cannon and a troop of blue-uniformed men hustled across. Ryan knew Kingston was Upper Canada's army and navy stronghold, and dismissed the artillery movement as the ordinary state of affairs.

As he passed under the bridge, fishermen and pedestrians interrupted their business to scrutinize his passage. His buckskin garb, belted tomahawk, and the raven perched totem-like on the canoe symbolized the frontier. By then, November 1837, settlement had gentrified the area. Few town inhabitants knew the wilderness as Ryan had lived it. Not yet an anachronism, he was a curiosity.

His slim craft rose and fell on the wake of steamships plying the wide harbor. From the water, Ryan studied the bustling town. Boxy stores and warehouses of quarried limestone crowded the harbor and made canyons of the streets. In the slips and quays, longshoremen moved goods on and off schooners and steamers. Carriages and wagons clattered over the cobbled streets, their horses exhaling steam. Wood smoke rose from chimneys and steamboat boilers. The sharp aromas of horse dung, ashes, and unwashed humanity permeated the air. After six months away from white men's towns, he'd forgotten about the drone and stink of civilization.

Approaching the western edge of Kingston, he spotted what he came to find—a shipbuilder. The Marine Railway Company's boat works dominated a wide pier jutting two hundred feet into Lake Ontario. A brick workshop hugged the water's edge. Black smoke poured from its four-storey chimney and blew sideways over the lake. The metallic racket of a forge and the rasp of saws spewed from open doors and windows. A partially reconstructed sidewheeler rested on iron rails in a dry dock.

"Can I help you?" A slim, dark-haired man in his forties with a slight limp approached. "This is private property."

Ryan sized up the older man. At about five-foot-eight, he was Ryan's height but thinner. Sawdust clung to his boots and wood shavings poked from his pant cuffs. "Good day to ye. I'm searching for the proprietor."

"I'm Luke Sheay, the chief shipbuilder. You talk to me."

Ryan straightened his back to hide his slight shoulder stoop, stretched to his full height and looked Sheay in the eye. "Well sir, I just arrived in town and I'd be grateful for some work."

Ryan watched Sheay look him over. He was suddenly conscious of his dangling red curls and beard shadow on his chin. After so long away from mirrors, he'd simply forgotten his appearance. He tugged wrinkles from his buckskin coat. Sheay's gaze came to rest on Zak perched on his shoulder. The big raven cocked his head and returned the stare with one dark eye.

"If you're wanting to join the circus, you've come to the wrong place."

"Pardon my appearance, sir. I've been living rough for many months. But I assure ye, I'm no clown when it comes to boat building."

Sheay smiled. "You have experience, then?"

"Since I was big enough to hold a plane and mallet, I helped my father and grandfather build dories and other small craft."

"We ain't building dories, lad. We refit the biggest steamers sailing the lake."

"Yes, sir. I see ye have a most modern enterprise." He swept his hand towards the dry dock. "But I also see ye fix ship's tenders, and repair cabins and decks. I'm experienced in all manner of carpentry, and also a fair quick learner. And I need the job, sir."

"Are you educated?"

"Oh, yes, sir. I can read and write, and I'm handy with my numbers."

Sheay furrowed his brow. "Where'd you get your schooling?"

"I attended a church-run school back in Ireland and my parents made me take extra lessons from hedgerow teachers."

"How old are you?"

"Almost twenty, sir."

Sheay paused and slipped his hands into his pockets. "I have a spot for an apprentice. It don't pay much—"

"I'll take it, sir. I nary mind starting at the bottom."

"What's your name?"

"Ryan Lone Pine." In response to Sheay's raised eyebrows, he added, "I lived with an Algonquin family. They gave me a new name."

"What does your family think of your Indian name?"

"I'm alone."

Sheay waited for further explanation. Ryan stayed mute.

Sheay shrugged his shoulders. "Come see me tomorrow at dawn. What of that bird of yours?"

"Zak'll be no trouble, Mr. Sheay."

Sheay pursed his lips in doubt but didn't push the point. "Do you need a place to stay?"

"I do, sir."

"A farmer near here has a cabin for rent." He pointed west. "Look for a dock with a whitewashed boathouse. That's the place."

Both men turned at the sound of heavy boots clomping down Ontario Street. A troop of twenty redcoats, led by a tall corporal, marched two abreast past the shipyard.

"All these soldiers and such marching about," Ryan began, "is it normal here?"

"No. There's more since the rebellion."

"What rebellion, sir?"

"I guess news don't travel fast in the bush. Four days ago some fools in Lower Canada attacked a British force near Montreal. The British eventually drove the traitors into the United States. Upper Canada has its own set of fools and the fort commandant worries trouble might break out here too."

"What set them off, sir?"

"Many believe our colonial governments are corrupt and ignore people's rights. I agree our affairs could be better run, but I won't countenance armed conflict."

"'Tis none of my business."

"It may be. If the government calls up the militia, you'd have to report for training."

"I hope it nary comes to that."

*****

That afternoon, Ryan moved into a shore-side log cabin. From his canoe, he unloaded farming and woodworking tools, a musket, kitchen goods, clothing, and two well-worn books—all the worldly goods of a former family of six.

He arrived at work the next day with the southeastern sky painted in stripes of red. To fit in, he'd shed his buckskins and moccasins for linen work pants, a long-sleeved cotton shirt, a woolen great coat, and worn leather boots.

Sheay met him by the workshop's main door. "Are you up for a day of hard labor?"

"Yes, sir. I toiled on our farm since I was a boy. Work is no stranger."

"Good. I'm assigning you to that steamer in the dry dock. Your job is to do whatever the master carpenters ask. Mostly you'll be toting planks and shaping wood with a plane or draw knife." He pointed to Zak on Ryan's shoulder. "Some men think black birds are bad luck. Better not take him close to that ship."

"Yes, sir." Ryan pushed Zak gently off his shoulder and swept his hand in a wide arc, a signal the bird knew well. He flew to the workshop roof.

Sheay nodded his satisfaction. "Come. I'll introduce you."

Ryan spent the morning ripping up a section of worn oak decking with a crowbar. Through the strain and sweat, he whistled Irish folk tunes. His memories drifted to past years working in the fields with his father and brothers, and the joy of a physical job done well.

When Sheay called the lunch break, Ryan headed to the pier end. Zak followed him fifty feet above. From his lunch sack, Ryan pulled a bread crust and flung it out over the water. Zak folded his wings into a steep dive, dropped, and caught the crust before it hit the water. The raven gobbled it down. Ryan heaved another crust in a different direction. Again Zak caught it and ate it.

Among the lunching men, all eyes were on the bird. Zak enjoyed an audience.

Ryan threw a third crust. The raven caught it with ease, but this time he carried it a hundred feet up, hovered, and dropped it. Zak then rolled over and spiraled headfirst towards the lake. Two yards above the surface, he caught the crust and swept upwards on outstretched wings, powered by his own momentum. Several men clapped.

Sitting, Ryan dangled his legs over the pier to eat his cheese and bread. Zak settled beside him.

Sheay sidled over. "Will he catch for other people?"

"Yes, sir. Catch-food is his favorite game."

Sheay tossed a chunk of leftover bun. Zak leapt from his perch, skimmed over the water, and grabbed the food inches from the lake.

Sheay smiled. "You know. I think that bird's going to fit in just fine."

*****

As the days passed, the carpenters gradually assigned Ryan work that required greater skill. Besides grunt work, he repaired small boats, railings, and cabin interiors. At day's end, he swept away the accumulated sawdust and wood shavings.

His fourth day on the job, Sheay invited Ryan to join him at a local tavern after work.

"I'd like that, sir." Back in Ireland, no adults had ever invited him to socialize.

That night, while Zak snoozed in the rented cabin's porch rafters Ryan joined Sheay and other work mates at a local tavern. Hoots of laughter and snide comments about being too young to drink greeted Ryan when he announced he abstained from alcohol and tobacco, and drank tea sweetened with maple syrup. He accepted the good-natured jests as the price of company and conversation.

Sheay's prediction about rebellious fools in Upper Canada soon proved true. In early December, Ryan sat in an inn after work as his boss read from a newspaper to a rapt bar audience about rebels attacking Toronto, lead by its former mayor, William Lyon Mackenzie. Men cheered when Sheay relayed how the militia routed the ill-prepared renegades.

Mackenzie escaped to America and promised a renewed fight. Kingston roiled in the wake of this second rebellion. Ryan daily stepped aside as marching troops of militia or gun carriages drawn by teams of sweating draught horses forced residents off streets and onto sidewalks.

What Ryan feared the most happened—the local militia commandant called a general muster. By law, he had to report for militia training.

*****

On an unseasonably warm December morning, Ryan planed the keel of a dory outside on the pier, enjoying the fresh air and the blade's rhythmic rasp as he shaved wood.

An unkempt and overweight hunter ambled along the waterfront. His jowls shook as his teeth mangled a plug of chewing tobacco. Men with his rough deportment always used to set Ryan's mother exclaiming, "There goes some poor soul on an errand for the devil." Ryan kept one eye on his work and one on the hunter's progress.

The stranger entered the shipyard, spotted Zak on the shop roof, and raised his gun.

"No!" Ryan screamed. He grabbed on oar, hurled it spear-like, and struck the big man on the leg. The hunter lurched sideways and yelped in pain. His gun discharged into the air, its blast reverberating along the pier.

The factory's cacophony of sawing and hammering ceased.

The sneering hunter, his narrow eyes pits of hatred, pulled a knife from a belt sheath and limped towards Ryan. Curious men gathered by the shop's windows and doorways.

"Leave him alone, Tiny," Sheay called. "He's half your size."

In Ireland, Ryan had often battled gangs of Irish-baiting, English schoolboys. He'd never backed down, whatever the odds. True to form, he stepped forward to meet the armed giant. Unconsciously, he rose on the balls of his feet, stretching his frame to meet the taller man.

Unbeknownst to Tiny, Ryan had an ally. Zak leapt from the shop roof and swept silently in from behind. "Zrok!"

The raven knocked Tiny's wide-brimmed hat over his face.

In that moment of Tiny's temporary blindness, Ryan charged, head down and eyes closed. He rammed his assailant's torso below his rib cage. Tiny's two hundred and fifty pounds smacked the stone pier. Ryan's workmates winced at the thud and painful expulsion of air.

Ryan pounced like a terrier on a mastiff. He knocked the blade aside and pinned Tiny's arms at the biceps with his knees. He pummeled the prostrate hunter's gin-blossom nose, ignoring Sheay's calls to stop. Blood spattered Ryan's hands and shirt cuffs. His nostrils twitched at its coppery aroma.

Sheay hauled Ryan off before self-defense became manslaughter. Tiny rolled onto his knees and labored to his feet. Blood dripped from his battered nose, mingled with tobacco juice leaking from his mouth, and dribbled through his grizzled chin whiskers to add new stains on his filthy coat.

Sheay handed Tiny his empty musket. "Leave this place."

He yanked the weapon from Sheay's hands. "Hey, hothead," Tiny snarled at Ryan. "I'll get ya for this."

"What ye will get is more of the same."

Tiny spat at his feet. A viscous gob of snot, blood, and chewing tobacco ran in multi-colored tendrils off Ryan's right boot. Ryan tensed to pounce on Tiny again, but a shout from behind changed his mind.

"Luke! Ryan! In my office, now," yelled John Counter, the shipyard owner.

In his late thirties, Counter had dark hair, thick sideburns and eyebrows, a pointy nose, thin lips, and unblinking dark eyes. "Is this how you repay me?" Counter sputtered. "I gave you a job without references and you descend to fisticuffs within the first month."

"I couldn't let him shoot my bird...sir." Ryan struggled to remember his manners. His blood still pulsed with adrenaline and Counter's condescending tone added to Ryan's edginess.

"That is what hunters do, boy. They shoot things."

"How'd ye feel if he shot yer dog? My bird's the same to me...sir."

Counter shrugged off the blunt reply. "Luke, give me one reason I should continue to employ this young tough."

"Be fair, Mr. Counter. Tiny is a troublemaker, as you know. The fight was self-defense. Besides, Ryan's a hard worker."

Counter examined Ryan with one eyebrow cocked. Unflinching, Ryan held the shorter man's gaze.

"You have a nasty temper, boy. You hit him long after you had a need to. Now, go back to work."

Stepping outside, Sheay grabbed Ryan's arm and yanked him to a halt. "That was bloody reckless. Tiny probably has eighty pounds on you and he's a lot tougher than he looked today."

"I'm nary one to stand down to a bully, sir, nor am I afraid of poor odds in a fight. I was raised in disadvantage and taught to face adversity."

Sheay grimaced. "That's a fool's philosophy. Smart men sidestep trouble, not meet it head on."

Zak settled onto his human's shoulder and folded his wings. With a finger, Ryan rubbed the side of the raven's beak. The bird tilted his head and clucked softly.

"That bird's your guardian angel, lad. Without him, you'd be dead. Tiny's wicked in a knife fight."

"Ye seem to know that lout well."

"He's the reason I've had my limp these twenty years. He shot me during militia training. He convinced our colonel it was a mistake. I know it was spite because I married the woman he thought was his. Be careful. He's a vengeful man with a long memory."

*****

Ryan never tired of the rebellion news that poured into Kingston and churned through the central market and taverns. In Buffalo, New York, Mackenzie began recruiting an army of American sympathizers and refuges from the Canadian rebellion—the Patriots they called themselves. In mid-December, the Patriots fortified Navy Island in the Niagara River upstream from the great falls. Mackenzie declared the Canadian island the seat of a new provisional government.

Patriot cannon bombarded the Canadian shore from the island. In response, a band of British soldiers crossed the icy river one night in late December and raided the Patriot's supply ship, the *Caroline*. They killed one American, fired the ship, and set it adrift. In the Kingston taverns, men cheered news of the *Caroline*'s destruction.

The British attack on an American ship in a U.S. port did more to boost Mackenzie's support than any of his fiery speeches. While President Martin Van Buren shrugged off the incursion, angry Americans sent money and ammunition to Mackenzie. U.S. citizens soon outnumbered Canadians in the Patriot army. Ryan saw the raid for what it was—a rash military act that overnight changed Mackenzie's bungled revolt into an undeclared border war.

*****

Days before Christmas, Kingston soldiers arrested an Irish-American tradesman, allegedly for spying. The charge incited heated anti-American rhetoric in town. When asked his opinion one evening by a coworker, Ryan naively gave it.

"I've seen no facts in the newspaper supporting the accusations agin him. His only crime seems to be he's American."

His work mates quieted. Men at neighboring tables leaned closer.

"Careful!" Sheay put down his ale tankard. "You can't be seen taking sides with the enemy."

"Are we at war with America?"

"No, but we need to be careful these days."

"Are we not governed by the rule of law, and innocent until proven guilty?" Ryan stabbed the table top with his index finger, oblivious to the obloquy he risked.

"Don't get so fired up."

"Tis guilt by association. My family fled Ireland to leave behind such shitty doings."

"Maybe you should step outside and cool off," Sheay warned.

Ryan drained his tea cup. "Maybe I should."

At home, he put on a pot of tea and reread a thin book he'd brought from Ireland, a tattered first-edition copy of *Common Sense* by Thomas Paine. In it, the author reasoned why the American colonies should throw off British rule. Paine's words once spurred Ryan's grandfather to join the ill-fated Irish rebellion of 1798.

As he read the familiar pages, Ryan realized Canadian politics differed little from colonial America's. A corrupt and elite group of Englishmen—dubbed the Family Compact—ruled Upper Canada for its own benefit, much like back in Ireland. Ryan knew the majority of his work mates supported the government. He couldn't.

From that night on, Ryan avoided the public houses, preferring to hike the early winter woods and riversides accompanied by Zak, or to read in his cabin by lamplight. He bought a novel, *The Pirate*, by Sir Walter Scott. For the first time in his life, he had the means to purchase a book merely for the sake of entertainment.

*****

Midday on New Years Eve, with the sky blue and the temperature unseasonably above freezing, Ryan strolled into town to buy vegetables and a chicken for supper. At regular intervals, cannon blasts ripped the air as artillery squadrons exercised Fort Henry's big guns. He spotted armed steamers in the harbor loaded with troops preparing to depart, probably to Montreal and Toronto. The St. Lawrence River and Lake Ontario, normally frozen in December, remained ice free.

In Kingston's market, he maneuvered around waiting carriages and wandered past stalls crammed with farm produce, clothing, and hand-made goods. The scents of tobacco, horses, and cooking thickened the air. He examined the wares and jostled past other shoppers. On Ryan's shoulder, Zak's head rose above his human's. When haggling, vendors addressed the raven, not the man.

While Ryan picked through piles of potatoes, Tiny and two men stepped from the throng of shoppers and surrounded him. Each wore a white cloth tied around his hat—the citizen militia's simple insignia.

"Look lads," began Tiny. "There's the little Irish hothead."

Ryan held his ground, his eyes on Tiny.

"He's a Patriot sympathizer if ever I saw one."

"The government need not concern itself with me," Ryan replied calmly. On his shoulder, Zak kept one black eye fixed on Tiny.

"Our young Victoria, not yet six months on the throne," Tiny ranted to the onlookers, "shouldn't have ta suffer disloyalty from Irish scum of his ilk."

Ryan's face flushed. His right hand crept to the carving knife he now wore on his belt. Shoppers cleared a space around the four men. A young army corporal and private on patrol joined their front ranks.

Zak launched into the air and circled overhead. "Zaak!"

Tiny unsheathed his knife. He flicked his gaze from Ryan to Zak and back.

Ryan's eyes narrowed. He bent his knees in preparation for a frontal assault.

The two redcoats stepped forward. "You three!" The corporal motioned to Tiny's gang. "On your way."

"But Andrew, we were just making conversation."

"Private Campbell, when you wear militia colors, you will address me by rank. Understand?" Shorter than Tiny, Andrew carried enough muscle and authority to have his way.

"Yes...*corporal!*" Tiny scowled at Ryan and departed.

"Thank ye for yer assistance," Ryan said, as he gathered his purchases to leave.

"Hold on there." He stepped in front of Ryan. About thirty, he had pale skin and piercing blue eyes under a mop of dark hair. "You must come with us. My colonel might have questions."

"You nary questioned those three louts. Friends of yers are they?"

"I know Tiny. I do not know you."

Ryan stared the man in the eye. "Why do ye care what that fat drunk says?"

"No one attends militia training more than he. If he says you are disloyal, you must come with me."

"'Tis not fair, damn ye." He threw his hands up in frustration. "I've done nothing wrong."

"Quite right. It is unjust." The voice, with a trace of Scotland in the accent, came from a lanky young man, several inches taller than Ryan. Attired as a gentleman, he had unruly reddish-brown hair, a high forehead, and large nose.

"This is none of your business, Mr. Macdonald," Andrew said impatiently.

"Corporal, justice is the business of every free man. Just because this town has gone mad, does not relieve this man of his rights. What grounds have you for his arrest? Surely not the ravings of those three departed drunkards."

"He might be a Patriot sympathizer, sir."

"Nonsense!" he barked at the corporal. Speaking to Ryan, he said, "John Alexander Macdonald at your service. Have you engaged the services of an attorney in Kingston?"

The concept awed Ryan. In Ireland, only rich men had lawyers. "I have not, sir."

"I would be honored to be your legal counsel, if you agree to it."

Ryan bit his lip and fidgeted.

"Do not concern yourself with fees. Unless I defend you in court or conduct some legal business, I charge nothing. What do you say?"

"I say yes, sir."

"Corporal, this man is my client. Will you force me to take legal suit on his behalf, which I am sure will annoy your superiors, or will you now release him?"

"My superiors will surely be annoyed if I am slack in my duties. I must take him in."

"No need for that." A new voice came to Ryan's defense—a female one. The shoppers stepped aside for the speaker. The tallest woman Ryan had ever seen, she stood a head above people in the market. Her auburn hair flowed from under a fur hat to the shoulders of a fashionable winter jacket that flattered her large but perfectly proportioned figure. Ryan guessed her age at thirty-five. She had at least eight inches on him. He rose on the balls of his feet as she approached.

"Mrs. Burleigh!"

"How nice of you to remember me, corporal. I believe you attended our carriage last night when my husband and I arrived to dine with Lieutenant-Colonel Bonnycastle—your commanding officer."

Andrew nodded, which is difficult with one's head tilted upwards.

"We had a splendid evening. Do you know, John, "she said to Macdonald, "the colonel wants to start an art society and an institution of higher learning here?"

"I was not aware, Mrs. Burleigh, but it comes as no surprise."

She shifted her downward gaze back to Andrew. "Your colonel is a fair man. I am certain your abuse of this man's rights would find ill favor."

The corporal's shoulders sagged. "I need his name and place of employment. That much I have a right to."

"My name is Ryan Lone Pine. I'm a carpenter at the Marine Railway Company." At their quizzical looks, he added, "Ryan is the name my father gave me. My Algonquin family named me Lone Pine."

"Do you have a proper Irish surname?" Andrew asked.

"Not any more."

Andrew sighed, motioned to the private, and continued on patrol. The wall of spectators dissolved as people continued shopping. Zak landed on Ryan's shoulder and cocked a nervous eye at the giant woman.

"John, kindly introduce us."

"By all means. Ryan, this is Ada Burleigh. Her husband Cyrus is a client and friend."

"Pleased to meet ye, Mrs. Burleigh. Thank ye for speaking in my defense."

"You are welcome. Please call me Ada. Both of you."

Her green eyes darted from Ryan to Macdonald and back. "You two boys have such handsome curls."

Ryan noticed Macdonald's Adam's apple slide up and down as he gulped.

"Thank ye…Ada. Tis grand to be complimented by such a lady."

She examined Ryan from toe to head. When her eyes reached his face, he held her gaze, noticing flecks of gold in her irises. Her ample lips parted in a half smile. Zak shuffled on Ryan's shoulder.

"Croc! Rrok!"

"I believe I make your bird nervous," Ada said.

"I expect ye have that effect on most males."

She laughed huskily. "I don't seem to make you nervous."

"Not in a crowded market, ye don't."

She laughed again. "You have a fast wit for one so young." She waved to a young companion. "Come here, Kate, and meet these two fine young men.

Ryan forgot the alluring giantess as Kate approached. A foot shorter than Ada, her cat-like gait spoke of strength and confidence. About eighteen, she had tawny hair, warm brown eyes, and high cheekbones. She wore a fashionable but not expensive woolen coat and hat.

"Gentlemen, this is my cousin Kate Randolph. Kate this is John Macdonald, our attorney and friend. And this glib charmer is Ryan Lone Pine."

"Pleased to meet you both." To Macdonald Kate added, "It was kind of you to intercede against those soldiers."

"Only seeing to my civic duty, Miss Randolph."

Ryan's heartbeat quickened as Kate's focus shifted from Macdonald to him.

"My cousin is correct, you do have lovely curls." Kate raised her hand, as if to reach for Ryan's hair, but tucked it inside her muff instead.

"I rather like his blue eyes and freckles too," Ada whispered in her ear.

Kate blushed and changed the subject. "You seem blessed to have two eminent people come to your defense."

"Lady Fortune smiled on me thrice this day; once for each defender and a third time for introducing me to you."

Kate laughed, a musical cascade that sent goosebumps up Ryan's spine.

"So, do ye live in Kingston?" Ryan asked nonchalantly.

Kate raised her eyebrows and shrugged. "I am visiting from New York State. Alas, I return tomorrow."

Ryan and Kate smiled awkwardly, at a loss for words, until Ada broke the silence. "Well, we must be going. I enjoyed our meeting."

"Thank ye. I did too," Ryan replied to Ada with an added smile to Kate.

"My best to Cyrus," Macdonald called.

The young men's eyes followed the women's progress across the market square. Kate quickly disappeared among the shoppers. Ada's head bobbed above the sea of hats.

Macdonald broke their reverie. "What was that wistful tune?"

"Pardon?"

"When Ada first approached, you hummed a tune."

"Did I? I can't recall that."

"No matter. My favorite tavern is near. May I buy you ale?"

"I avoid spirits, but I wouldn't say nay to a cup of tea, if 'tis all the same to ye, sir."

"Certainly. Please, call me John. Being called sir makes me feel old."

"Ye do seem a mite young for a lawyer." Ryan replied as they nudged past shoppers.

"I am nearly twenty-three. Young, yes, but I trained with the best, I assure you."

"That soldier knew yer name and backed off. Tis all I expect in a jet."

"A jet?" Macdonald asked, holding the inn door for Ryan.

"Yes. A jet. A son of prattlement. A split cause. Back home, 'tis all cant for lawyer."

"How curious!"

They relaxed near the hearth in the Steamboat Hotel, a two-story stone inn and public house facing the market. Layers of tobacco and wood smoke hung motionless in the half-filled common room. The ceiling showed hand-hewn oak beams. A liberal layer of sawdust covered the pine floor to absorb mud, spilt ale, and spit.

Macdonald badgered the proprietor, Thomas Bamford, into letting Zak stay. "Come now Thomas, you let men enter accompanied by dogs, do you not?"

"Yes, but that's no dog."

"He is as fine a companion as any dog and deserves the same consideration."

"Well, seeing you're a good customer, I'll consent to it. But if the bird messes on the furniture, have the lad clean it up."

Macdonald ordered tea sweetened with maple syrup for his guest and a whiskey for himself. They nibbled biscuits spread with strawberry preserve. Ryan fed crusts to Zak.

Macdonald tossed back a third of his whiskey. "I assume, apropos the way you were short with the corporal in the matter of your family name, that some tragedy befell you?"

Ryan placed his tea cup in its saucer, his back ridged in the stuffed chair. "Yes, John."

"And I conclude by your current stiff demeanor that you do not wish to discuss details?"

"Correct."

"Enough on that subject then."

After an uncomfortable pause, Ryan quipped, "What of yer family, then?"

"Oh, not much to tell," Macdonald began modestly. He went on to recall misty memories of his early years in Glasgow and the uneventful crossing to Canada as a child. He described moving from one pioneer town to the next while his father failed repeatedly to succeed in business. Lastly, he spoke of his six years studying law and of his growing practice.

Perched on a chair back, Zak regally perused each new patron with his jet eyes. Few had seen this majestic species up close. Two feet long from his thick beak to his wide-spreading tail, his glossy black feathers flashed hints of metallic blue. Several customers timidly fed the raven bits of bread or tiny slices of mutton.

Ryan leaned to pour more tea. His shirt collar opened, exposing a leather thong and the curved edge of an ornament.

"That's an Indian artifact on your neck! May I see it, please?"

Ryan pulled the talisman over his head and handed it to Macdonald. On the thong hung a disk of tanned moose hide on a willow frame, with porcupine quills sewn in the shape of a windblown pine.

"My Algonquin grandmother gave me this as a parting gift."

"The workmanship is superb. Is the pine symbol connected to your odd name?"

"'Tis."

"Will you see them again?" Macdonald asked.

"I doubt I can find them. Farmers and loggers are driving the whole tribe from their lands."

"It is a terrible shame that we did not provide for the original inhabitants in our haste to colonize this land."

"English justice doesn't fall evenly on all subjects."

"True. England is the mother of democracy but she can be terribly neglectful. The rebellion would not have started if our leaders governed fairly."

Macdonald placed his elbows on the chair's arms, clasped his hands, and focused on a point above Ryan's head. "Someday soon, this country will run its own affairs in a democratic manner and all men shall be free to reach their highest potential. We can achieve freedom without taking up arms. Mackenzie is a great reformer and true populist, but too impatient."

"'Tis a grand vision. Maybe ye should run for political office."

"I may someday," Macdonald replied. He signaled for the bill.

Outside in the winter sun's miserly warmth, Macdonald said, "Be careful what you say. The rebellion has warped common sense."

"So I've witnessed."

"You do not want Bonnycastle to take an interest in you."

"Is he trouble?"

"He can be." Macdonald buttoned his coat. "Richard Bonnycastle is a brevet major in the Royal Engineers, a lieutenant-colonel in the militia, and the current fort commandant. He has great qualities—a visionary in many respects—but he will throw you in jail as soon as look at you if he thinks you are disloyal."

"I'd best avoid the man."

"Should you need my help, please ask. My law office is at 169 Wellington Street, two blocks from here. I live on Rideau Street. Ask anyone for directions."

"Thank ye, John."

*****

Next morning at the shipyard, Sheay intercepted him on the pier.

"Ryan, I have bad news."

He read his boss' grim expression. "I'm sacked, am I?"

"Yes. Tiny told Counter you avoid militia training. To the boss, that's a sin."

"I'm sure another shipyard will have me if bloody Counter won't."

"I'm afraid not. He put the word out. I'm sorry."

Ryan kicked a stray board into the dry dock and strode away. All day, he hiked the bits of remaining forest and along bleak country roads. Zak rode on his shoulder, cooing occasionally. By night fall, he had a new plan.

The next day, he petitioned the Steamboat Hotel's proprietor for a job.

"You're Macdonald's friend, aren't you?" In his forties and inch shorter than Ryan, Thomas Bamford was bald, bearded, and going to fat.

"Yes, sir. More importantly, I work hard and don't drink."

Bamford grasped the advantage of a bar employee who wouldn't guzzle his profits. "You can start today, but the bird stays outside."

"Zak'll stay outside, if 'tis what ye want. But keeping him inside may be good for yer business. He received much attention when we were here with Mr. Macdonald."

Bamford chewed his lower lip and examined the floor in thought. "I believe it is worth a try. I'll fix him a perch near the door where everyone can see him."

"Thank ye. Zak'll enjoy that."

*****

Six days a week, Ryan served customers and cleaned the bar and tavern. Most nights he came home after midnight with a sleepy raven on his shoulder. Ryan's nose, formerly accustomed to the acrid scents of sawdust and forged iron, welcomed the savory aromas of tobacco and ale. He ate well. Chatter filled the air and men left newspapers behind. He eavesdropped on conversations and read all the latest rebellion news.

With the military on full alert and the headlines warning of doom, Ryan believed Kingston's anxiety level had reached its peak. Yet, one name, Bill Johnston, seemed to double it. In early January, newspapers reported he joined Mackenzie on Navy Island.

To anyone who grew up on the St. Lawrence River's shores and islands, Johnston—smuggler and War of 1812 privateer—was a living legend. It was said that no man knew the Thousand Islands better than he. For a generation, local parents had raised children on apocryphal tales of Pirate Bill, a pistol-packing bogeyman who stalked into people's rooms while they slept. Mothers warned naughty boys he would come for them unless they behaved.

Now Pirate Bill had joined the Patriots.

*****

Alone in the hotel's common room in mid-January, Ryan whistled an Irish folk melody while he wiped the bar in preparation for lunch. After three weeks on the job, he had put on weight and kept a growing money stash in a sock at the cabin.

The tavern door banged shut. "Croc! Rrok!" Zak warned.

Tiny and his two thug companions sauntered to the bar, leaving trails in Ryan's newly raked sawdust. Sober and smiling, Tiny ordered ale.

Ryan's eyes narrowed. An adrenaline rush tingled his fingertips. He rose on the balls of his feet. "I'll see yer money afore ye see any drink."

Tiny drew a blade from his belt. "I want that ale now."

Two feet of wooden bar top separated the three burly men from Ryan. His eyes flicked down to a bread knife lying on a shelf below the bar. Judging by Tiny's tobacco-stained, I-dare-you grin, the thug guessed Ryan had a weapon at hand. Ryan knew if he grabbed the knife, Tiny could claim self-defense in a fight.

"If I don't see my ale soon, I'll come and help myself."

"The hell ye will," Ryan hissed.

The four men flinched at the metallic click of a pistol hammer being cocked. Framed by the kitchen door, Bamford aimed a flintlock at Tiny's ample chest. "There's no service for you. Out!"

Tiny sheathed his knife. "I know lots of places a man can drink in this town without having to wait on some Patriot hothead."

"I'm not a Patriot!"

"Then, why do ya never report to the militia?" Tiny doffed his hat to Bamford in mock respect and exited with his two friends.

"Is that true?" Bamford asked. "You have avoided militia duty?"

"Tis true."

"I am going out this Sunday afternoon. Come with me. The training is not rigorous."

"I am sorry, but I cannot."

"Why?"

"I'll nary bear arms for England. I can't salute British officers and call them sir." Ryan slapped the bar with his hand.

Bamford cocked his head. "Why are you so angry with the British?"

"Under the British, we Irish suffered hundreds of years of being servants in our own house." Ryan's voice rose as he spoke. "They kept us poor and ignorant so the English might rule and prosper. My grandfather couldn't attend school because the Penal laws forbade it. My father had to pay a huge tithe to the Anglican Church each year, though it was nary our religion. I could talk for hours on the subject."

Bamford chewed his lower lip, composing his words. "This is a new land with new opportunities. You must leave the old troubles in the Old World."

"I cannot."

"You have a future in Kingston and good prospects at this establishment, but those blessings have a price. You must help defend the colony."

"I cannot."

"Then I can't employ you any longer. I'm sorry."

*****

Outside the inn, fat flakes of falling snow announced winter's late arrival. With Zak on his shoulder, Ryan hurried to Macdonald's law office.

Inside, he found the young lawyer reading documents at an oak desk. Light pine boards covered the floor and ceiling. Maroon wallpaper gave a somber feel to the room. Several stuffed chairs filled the corners. The air held the sharp scent of lamp oil.

"Ryan, what is wrong?"

"Bamford sacked me because I won't attend militia training. Tis the second time that fat snitch Tiny has done me in."

"No one in this town will hire you if you maintain your recalcitrant attitude to militia duty. Every able male must serve. I do. I was in Toronto fighting against Mackenzie's rebels in December. Tiny may inform Bonnycastle. He could jail you."

Ryan's jaw tightened. His right foot tapped a staccato beat on the pine floor. Zak shuffled nervously on his shoulder and cooed softly.

Elbows on the desk, Macdonald clasped his hands together. "The future is more important than the present, Ryan, because it lasts longer. I always wanted to be a lawyer, marry a good woman, and have children. What do you want?"

"To become a shipbuilder or a farmer, maybe both. A wife and wee ones, too."

"Then, as your attorney and friend, I urge you to swallow your pride and attend militia training."

"I will not!" Ryan shouted.

Macdonald gaped, nonplussed at Ryan's intransigence.

"I want to be left alone. If not here, then Kingston be damned."

"Where will you go?"

"If this country won't let me live in peace, I'll canoe to America."

"It is too late to cross. I saw ice forming along the shore this morning."

"I'll go as far as I can and winter in the islands, if I must. The Algonquins taught me how to live off the land."

Macdonald rose, his fingertips touching the desk. "That is utter folly. You have not experienced a Canadian winter. The coldest day in Ireland is balmy by comparison."

"If I freeze, 'twill be as a free man. Good-bye to ye, John."

Winter's Pupil

John Counter inspected the work shed the next morning and urged each smithy and carpenter to work doubly hard before freeze-up closed the dry dock. He paused to peer out the window at the snow squall raging across the lake.

"Luke! Come see what that intemperate boy is up to now."

A hundred feet from shore, partially obscured by horizontal streamers of driven snow, a lone canoeist fought the elements. The man repeatedly drove his paddle into the turbulent water, with scant progress. Luke Sheay could not identify the heavily dressed occupant, but the raven perched on the bow named him.

"He's leaving town, I guess."

"In this weather, I wager he will not survive the morning."

"Well, sir, you would lose that bet," said Luke, turning on Counter.

"Luke! Why do you always defend that rebellious boy?"

"He's a hothead, I'll grant you that. But, the same determination he's using to fight forward in that storm, he put into his work."

"He is a scofflaw. I cannot abide that."

"If we didn't have this wretched rebellion, I've no doubt he'd be a stalwart citizen."

"I have no doubt he will end up in jail or dangling from a gibbet."

*****

Ryan fought a persistent headwind east into the Thousand Islands. Every stroke of his paddle rewarded him with mere inches. Snow and ice pellets whipped his face. He wrestled with the cruel tempest, a malevolent beast that tried to shove the canoe broadside to the waves. If he lost the struggle for a second, the canoe might flip and plunge him into the fatally frigid lake.

The water turned slushy gray as it tried to freeze. Only the roiled surface prevented ice formation. Cold spray froze on the gunwales. Zak, who usually stared ahead, faced his human, his back into the wind. He tilted his feathered head sideways as if asking why.

The storm forced Ryan to stay close to the limited shelter near the shore. He slipped past Fort Henry into the lee of Cedar Island. In the relative calm, he cast a glance up the long slope to the fort. The fat digits of cannon poked black and threatening into the swirling white.

With anger-driven muscles, Ryan paddled deeper into the islands. His shoulders already aching, he sought pockets of less turbulent water behind isles and headlands. He knew he must change course south at some point to reach America, but the fierce wind's angle prevented that. With the sunlight fading in late afternoon, he canoed across the channel to Howe Island and camped in a sheltered bay at the island's western end. He'd traveled only eight miles in nine hours. His shoulders leaden, he could barely drag his canoe from the water. Under a lean-to of spruce boughs, he spent a cold night wrapped in woolen blankets as snow deepened beyond his crude shelter. Zak slept in the spruce trees above.

In the windless morning, Ryan awoke to find an inch of ice clinging to the beach rocks. He had to chop a channel to launch the canoe. On the river, the open water shrunk around him. Table-sized disks of frozen slush calmly drifted in the current, collided with others, and fused. Glassy new ice formed on the open water and crackled as he paddled through it. The sharp edges threatened to slowly shred his birchbark canoe. Ryan knew only hours remained until the whole river froze solid and trapped him in its intractable grasp.

Paddling around Howe Island, Ryan spotted a log shanty on the island's south shore. Landing to investigate, he found the door open and crunchy autumn leaves littering the floor. Gaps showed in the cabin's chinking and not a stick of firewood or furniture remained in the cold interior. Ryan had the experience and tools to fix the defects and cut wood, but not much time. The previous day's storm had given way to a northern cold front. The plunging temperature showed no sign of abating.

"Zak, I guess this be home."

"Crickity! Croc!"

Ryan marched into the forest with an axe in hand and a canvas satchel on his belt. He'd learned the best place to find dry firewood in the wilderness is on trees. Wood on the ground absorbs moisture, but dead branches on the lower trunk are cured and dry. First he carried armloads of dead branches into the cabin for kindling. Next, he cut down a dead but still sound maple and reduced it to a pile of split cordwood using a crosscut saw and splitting maul. Into his satchel, he put tinder components: shreds of white birch and cedar bark, clumps of lichen, and a chunk of tinder fungus he found growing on a birch.

In the cabin's stone hearth, he set a slice of tinder fungus smoldering with sparks from his flint and steel, and fed the tiny flames bits of kindling. Soon he had a good fire roaring and set water to boil for tea. He tied cedar boughs to a pole and swept the floor, putting the dried leaves on his growing fire.

Next, he stalked around the cabin's interior searching for outside light showing through the log gaps. He jammed long strips of cedar bark into each hole to reduce drafts. Clay and moss would be better, but bark was the only available material in the snowy landscape.

That night, Zak helped him celebrated his twentieth birthday, January 21, 1838, with a meal of rabbit stew.

"We didn't make it to America, Zakkie boy, but we are safe and free."

"Zaak!"

Sitting on a rocky point the next day, Ryan gazed southeast. He had a clear view of Wolfe Island's eastern tip to the right, the western end of Grindstone Island to the left, and the much smaller Hickory Island in the middle. A faint blue ridge in the distance marked the American shore. It did not tug at him as he expected.

When the ice firmed up, he could build a sleigh and drag his belongings across the ice to that far shore. After the tumult of Kingston, the winter solitude of his cabin consoled him. America could wait until spring.

*****

Each day Ryan trod the snowy land cutting firewood, hunting, setting snares, and building traps like the Algonquins had shown him. The pelts of muskrat, mink, otter, and beaver would become the currency of his domain, something to trade for supplies, as well as the source of winter mittens, hats, and boots. He hummed old tunes his mother had taught him while he worked. Zak responded to the dulcet tones with whistles and clucks.

Isolated as both were from their own species, the man and bird learned each other's language. Ryan chatted constantly to Zak in simple sentences, the way one does with a toddler. When Ryan said, "Let's go home," the bird flew towards the cabin. Or, if he said, "let's go find some deer," the bird soared above the trees searching. In nature, ravens work in pairs or flocks to find food and watch for enemies. Flying ahead, Zak spotted game long before his human and communicated those discoveries. With the extensive vocal range of his species, the raven's calls varied subtly when he sighted a deer, a moose, or a wolf. Over time, Ryan learned the meaning of Zak's calls.

At the end of a hunt one day, Ryan said, "Zakkie boy, let's go home."

"Ko 'ome!" the raven mimicked.

"Yer speaking English!"

From that day on Zak occasionally answered Ryan with a parroted word or two.

On a sunny and cold mid-February morning, with the ice safely solid, Ryan set off to trade furs. He plodded through the soft drifts of the leafless winter forest of Howe Island. He admired a winter world reduced to four colors: the intense blue of the cold sky, the dazzling white of powder snow, the warm greens of conifer needles, and the gray tones of tree trunks.

Out on the river ice, the reflected warmth in the sun caressed his cheeks. He smiled at the sight of thousands of flashing snow crystals beneath his feet.

"Zak, I bet 'tis what diamonds look like."

"Zaak," responded the raven from thirty feet overhead.

Ryan neared a north-shore hamlet and crossed a short stretch of thick snow to the rough road that ran between the cluster of log-and-frame buildings. He pushed open the door of a pioneer general store. Zak flew to the roof to wait.

Ryan shrugged off his pelt-laden pack and waited for his eyes to adjust from winter's dazzle to the store's interior gloom, its air scented by an odiferous blend of tea, tobacco, wood smoke and ripening potatoes. A short, rotund shopkeeper eyed him from behind a counter. In the man's furrowed brow, Ryan recognized distrust. He blamed it on his Algonquin garb.

"Gidday. I have furs to trade for supplies."

The man flipped through the furs Ryan pulled from his pack.

"Good enough quality," he said with a curt nod. "Whadda yah want in trade?"

"I need snowshoes, a brick of tea, a pound of salt, and a big sack of flour."

The man pointed to a corner. "Pick yer snowshoes there."

Ryan sorted through a half dozen snowshoe sets and picked a pair with a symmetrical frame and tightly stretched hide. He spotted several collapsible, brass telescopes on a shelf. That would be handy for spotting game, he thought.

"I'll take this, too," he said back at the counter. "Either that or I keep a few furs. They're all top quality. Fair's fair."

The proprietor scowled but conceded with a nod. "Do yah live around here?"

"Yes, sir. On Howe."

"By yerself?"

"Yes," Ryan replied hesitantly. The man seemed to be prying.

"Yah in the militia?"

Ryan packed his trade goods, picked up the snowshoes, and departed without a word.

*****

A week later, outside events disrupted Ryan's peaceful world. As Ryan scanned the frozen river with his new telescope, he saw the usually vacant Hickory Island swarming with armed men. Over the day, they built shanties, constructed log breastworks, and mounted cannon.

"Zak, I believe we have a Patriot invasion coming."

"Zaak."

A convoy of sleighs ferried an army from the American shore. By nightfall Ryan estimated the rebel force at two hundred. Shivering with cold and anticipation, he spent the night gazing at the distant twinkle of scores of lanterns. Before morning the lights dwindled and vanished.

An hour before sunrise, several companies of militia and a cavalry troop marched past Ryan's island towards Hickory Island. At their head rode an officer. Ryan guessed him to be Lieutenant-Colonel Bonnycastle. Telescope to his eye, Ryan chuckled as militiamen, eager for a fight, smashed the abandoned Patriot shanties in frustration.

With the military excitement behind him, Ryan set off the next day to trade furs. At the north-shore hamlet, he followed fresh sleigh runner tracks to the general store. Zak flew to the roof. Ryan leaned his snowshoes against the wall and stepped into the gloom. To the blend of smells he recalled from his last visit, someone had added stale human sweat.

Two men stepped from the shadows. Each held a bayonet-tipped musket and wore the scarlet tunic of the British infantry under gray greatcoats. Ryan recognized Andrew, the corporal who tried to arrest him two months earlier in the Kingston market. "What is it now? Are ye still taking cues from Tiny?"

Andrew glanced over Ryan's shoulder. Ryan read the corporal's expression and jumped sideways. It saved him from a sucker punch to the head.

"Private Campbell! Stand down," Andrew ordered. "If I bring this man to the colonel in pieces, he'll have my stripes."

"Ah-h, Andrew—I mean corporal—I wasn't going ta hurt him much. Just take the wind from his sails."

"I'll let the wind out of ye afore that ever happens," replied Ryan, reaching for his tomahawk.

"Halt!" Andrew brought his bayonet tip within an inch of Ryan's chest.

Ryan raised his empty hands in the air.

"You are under arrest on the order of Lieutenant-Colonel Bonnycastle," Andrew said as he pulled the tomahawk from Ryan's belt. "Come with us."

"What am I arrested for?"

"That is not my concern. The colonel will tell you in due time."

"Can I grab my gear?" Ryan pointed to his pack.

Tiny shoved him towards the door empty handed. "Outside, hothead."

Ryan marched at bayonet point to a waiting sleigh pulled by a pair of black Percherons. The driver set the horses plodding off towards Kingston with Ryan seated beside the young private facing Andrew and Tiny. Zak followed at a discreet distance.

"Why'd ye bring him for?" Ryan pointed to his tormentor.

"He volunteered."

"Out for sport, is he?"

Andrew glanced at Tiny, who studied Ryan with half closed eyes. "He likes action. He came with us to Hickory Island."

"Too bad your Patriot friends ran away," Tiny blurted through clenched teeth. "I wanted ta skewer a few American bastards."

"They're no friends of mine." Ryan turned to Andrew. "Why does he hate Americans?"

"They killed his father at Crysler's farm in 1813."

"'Tis no reason to hate a nation. 'Twas war."

Tiny leaned forward. Ryan grimaced at the stale tobacco and beer on his winter fogged breath. "If yar pa died from the malice or stupidity of others, how'd ya feel about them?"

A memory leapt unbeckoned into Ryan's mind from the place he kept it hidden. His father—the last of his family still alive—lay fighting cholera with all the dignity his weathered fifty-something body allowed him. They had arrived at Grosse Île near Quebec City, where British health inspectors forced all steerage passengers, mostly Irish immigrants, to disembark from the ship for quarantine. They allowed the healthy first-class passengers, mostly minor English gentry, to sail on to Montreal. In brutal irony, Grosse Île harbored cesspools of disease to inflict the healthy. Typhus took Ryan's older brother Thomas and sister Annie days before their father gasped his last. Ryan huddled near the three graves in the shelter of a cedar tree in all manner of foul weather. He shunned the filthy barracks. After fifteen days, the inspectors sent him away alone.

Tiny caught the disturbance on his face.

"I hit close ta the mark, eh." He laughed, setting his double chin jiggling. "Who kilt yar pa, eh, hothead? Who do ya hate?"

Ryan looked away and stared at the passing winter landscape.

*****

Hours later the sleigh entered Fort Henry and stopped inside the iron-studded, wooden west gate. Soldiers in blue artillery uniforms shoveled snow from the cobbled upper parade square and brushed off the great cannon lining the advanced battery's perimeter.

Tiny and the two soldiers marched Ryan down a ramp between rising stone walls into the dry ditch surrounding the main fort, across an equipoise bridge, and through another set of gates. The corporal called a halt on the fort's lower parade square.

"Wait here until the colonel is ready," Andrew ordered.

The private and Tiny kept guard while the corporal reported in.

Ryan inspected the fort. While the exterior view presented modest-looking walls atop steep slopes, the fort's inner construction surprised him with its elegance and ingenuity. He faced a two-tiered set of stone barracks. A portico of seventeen flowing stone arches—reminiscent of woodcuts he'd seen of Italian colonnades—provided access to the second-story barracks. He admired the painted wooden doors and the sparkling glass windows of the officers' quarters to his left. He counted eighteen massive cannon on the ramparts.

The corporal returned. "The colonel will see you in the duty room. Private, you are dismissed."

With the fat militiaman behind him, Ryan followed the corporal around the corner into a frugally furnished office with a vaulted brick ceiling. Ryan looked out a window to his left to where Tiny waited. To his right he glimpsed a slice of the dry ditch through a gun slit. A fire in a red-brick hearth kept the narrow room reasonably warm.

In the only chair, Bonnycastle posed resplendent in his red officer's uniform, medals on his chest, a sword at his side, and a swagger stick on the table. A clean-shaven, dark-haired man in his mid-forties, he had large eyes, a bulbous nose, and full lips. He fingered a stack of reports on his plain pine desk.

Bypassing any pleasantries, he commenced his interrogation. "You live on the south-facing side of Howe Island. Correct?"

"Yes." All the manners Ryan's mother drilled into him as a boy evaporated before a British uniform.

"Kindly address me as colonel." Bonnycastle glowered and pressed his ample lips together. To Ryan, he seemed a peremptory martinet, not the visionary Macdonald had described.

"Wouldn't brevet major be more accurate?"

Bonnycastle's ears reddened, but he did not acknowledge the slight. "From your vantage point, you have a good view of the river to the American side. Correct?"

"Yes."

The colonel tightened his lips again and stared at his prisoner, waiting. Ryan returned an unblinking, deadpan visage.

"Seen any activity lately?"

"There are always people on the river." Ryan shrugged.

"Do not be evasive. Have you seen any military activity?"

"Only a few redcoats and lots of militia marching about."

The colonel silently read the top sheet of paper. "I have a report you bought a telescope to spy for the Patriots."

Ryan swore under his breath at the nosey shopkeeper. "The 'scope is to find game. I spy for none and keep to myself."

"Why do you live out there alone?"

"Because that big-mouth lout standing outside yer door," he jerked his thumb sideways, "got me sacked twice, and I had no money to live in town and damned few prospects."

Bonnycastle studied a report in the center of his desk. "Are you referring to the incident in the market on New Year's Eve?"

"Yes. That and another occasion he caused me grief."

The colonel glanced out the window at Tiny. "While he may be disreputable, I can count on his loyalty. I cannot say the same for you."

"The government need not concern itself with me."

"Maybe so, but I cannot help feeling you are guilty of something."

"I'm guilty only of being poor and Irish."

"Do not play the downtrodden Irish with me," Bonnycastle barked. He rose and stared at Ryan with predatory intensity. "I completed this fort using Irish labor. I have nothing but respect for a loyal Irishman."

Ryan, unbowed by the choleric outburst, shifted his weight to his toes and lifted his heels an inch off the floor to be eye-to-eye with the colonel. "Tis so? How many of those loyal Irish did ye invite home for supper?"

Bonnycastle's jaw tightened. "You are guilty of not reporting for militia training."

Ryan shrugged. "Can I talk to my attorney?"

"You have an attorney?"

"Yes. John Macdonald."

"It is in the report, colonel," the corporal said softly.

Bonnycastle dropped his eyes to the report. "Yes. I see." Looking up, he continued, "If I find a shred of evidence you are disloyal, no attorney will keep you from jail."

"The government need not concern itself with me."

"So you have said." The colonel examined another report. Ryan's attention drifted to the crackling fire while he waited for the officer's next question.

"Do you know Bill Johnston?"

"Nary met the man."

"Avoid him or you will answer to me." Bonnycastle addressed the corporal. "Escort our *loyal* friend back."

Andrew shoved Ryan out the door. With Tiny at his rear, they hurried him up the ramp and out the fort's east gate.

"That is as far as we go. On your way."

"No sleigh home? I'm to be sent out into the cold to freeze, am I?"

"Colonel's orders. You are on your own."

"Do ya regret tangling with me yet," Tiny asked, a leer on his grizzled face.

"I regret not killing ye when I could."

Andrew handed back his tomahawk. "Keep that in your belt."

Tiny spat a wad of masticated tobacco at Ryan's feet. "Have a nice cold walk, hothead."

*****

With no money on hand for an inn and no blankets or shelter, Ryan started the twelve-mile walk home. He had no choice.

Ryan knew he had to avoid a strength-draining hike in the road's deep snow. He headed down slope from the fort to the frozen river. Since he had no snowshoes, the wind-packed snow on the ice offered a better route. From a tree on the nearby cliffs, Zak spotted his human and flew to his shoulder.

When the sun set, any modest winter warmth vanished. The already sub-freezing temperature dropped. Snow squeaked under his boots, a warning note snow makes only on the most frigid nights.

A full moon rose behind a veil of thin clouds and illuminated his way with a shadowless, even light. His solitary world became hundreds of shades of gray. The wind gusts sped up. The squeaking snow rose in pitch. His Algonquin garb kept him from freezing to death quickly, but the layers of hides over woolen underwear could not keep anyone warm on such an arctic night.

Macdonald's warning held true. He never imagined cold this harsh. Ice boomed on the river. A great tree on an island split open with a crack like musket fire. Ryan's fingers and toes burned despite their fur coverings. The bits of his face not shrouded in a scarf seared with fire when blasts of cold jabbed past the parka hood.

Zak suffered too. If on his own, the raven would roost in sheltered stands of spruce or cedar. But he stayed with his human. Ryan sensed Zak's discomfort, opened the parka, and tucked the raven inside. The big bird snuggled against his human, totally enclosed for the first time since inside his egg.

The wind found tiny holes in his clothes, holes Ryan didn't know existed. His legs chilled, making each step an effort as cold muscles stiffened. Numbness replaced the burning in his hands and feet. His body struggled forward without any conscious guidance from his heat-deprived mind. He plodded on, his thoughts drifting.

The moon shining behind the thin clouds reminded Ryan of home, the way the candlelight shone through the thin bed sheets his mother hung to dry near the hearth—sheets often in need of mending but always kept clean.

He stumbled and dropped to his knees. He desperately wanted to nap, only for a minute, a quick rest. Zak squirmed under the coat. Ryan struggled up and shuffled stiffly east.

Other old memories flared in his addled brain.

His mother stood in their poor house, laughing at something his father said, while Ryan and his three siblings giggled. Poverty did not grind them down. They found joy in simple pleasures and truths. His parents believed in justice for all, God, honest labor, and educating their children.

Ryan stumbled again and dropped to one knee. Ahead he recognized the dark, looming silhouette of Howe Island's western end. Its shape reminded him of an overturned rowboat.

A vision of Grandfather Ryan, his namesake, joined the family parade. He planed the oak keel of a dory, as he told his grandson how he must remove the thinnest shaving on each stroke. He explained the job demanded persistence and patience, the way water erodes stone, and the same way the Irish would eventually wear down and throw out the English.

As Ryan lurched drunkard-like into the bay by his shanty, the clouds parted. Unshielded moonlight bathed the snowy land in a white dawn. His elongated moon shadow preceded him into the cold cabin. He perched Zak on a chair back. In the hearth, not a single hot coal remained. Survival depended on starting a fire. He had wood at hand, but no easy way to make flame.

With mitten-clad hands, he smacked his flint bar against a steel rod, hoping for a spark. The flint flew from his hands. He tried again but the steel rod slipped from his grasp. Wearing mittens, he couldn't hold the flint and steel securely. Seeing no choice, he removed them, exposing his fingers to dangerously cold air. He clasped the flint and steel in numb fists and clumsily struck them together repeatedly to create sparks.

A lucky spark fell into the tinder fungus. He piled on dry grass and blew into the smoldering bundle until a tiny flame licked at the fuel. He used a fork jammed between his unresponsive fingers to lift kindling slivers and twigs onto the feeble flame. He warmed his stiff hands in its rising heat and winced in pain as his fingers thawed. In an hour, with a roaring fire in the hearth, he dropped onto his rough mattress, unconscious in an instant.

*****

"Zaak!"

Ryan jolted awake. A beam of orange sunlight lit the cabin's rear wall. The one window faced due south into the winter sunrise.

"Need to go out, do ye, Zak?"

He rolled off his straw-stuffed mattress and pushed himself to his feet. The weight of his body on his hands sent a bolt of pain up his left arm.

"Tis odd. I don't remember hurting myself."

"Zaak!"

He fumbled with the door latch and let Zak out to hunt for food. The night's extreme cold had vanished and the day seemed almost warm. He examined his left hand by the open door.

"Jesus Christ!"

Frostbite blisters marred three fingers. On his smallest finger, dark purple flesh extended from the top knuckle to the tip.

Ryan had witnessed enough farm injuries growing up to recognize dead flesh. He also knew gangrene would feast on his dead cells and, if untreated, would mean a lingering, painful death.

He needed a doctor but refused to go near the suspicious Canadian colonists again for any reason. He stepped outside, telescope in hand, and tossed a bread crust to Zak.

"Can we walk across the ice to America, Zak?"

"Kalk! Kross!"

He searched south for the faint blue ridge. Nothing! A gray wall obscured the far shore. The foggy mass shifted north. Soon Hickory Island lay behind its veil. Ryan stared as Grindstone Island and Wolfe Island faded from view. Streamers of gray stretched across the blue sky. The sun reddened.

"Tis a blizzard coming, Zak. There'll be no traveling this day."

The raven sensed the storm and flew to a dense cedar grove behind the shanty. Ryan knew time was limited. He quickly carried in three armloads of firewood. He filled a water bucket from a hole cut in the ice. With the first flakes of snow pelting him on a rising south wind, he clipped branches from scrubby willows growing along the river.

Inside he hung two pots of water over the fire to boil. He peeled willow bark and tossed strips into one pot to make a mild painkiller. He would need it.

The cabin groaned when the storm front hit. A white whirlwind obscured the world three feet beyond the window. A big snow dump meant he could not cross the ice without his lost snowshoes when the storm passed. No chance remained to reach a doctor.

Ryan held his hand at eye level. The little blisters would heal, but not the finger tip. "Tis such a little thing. I'll hardly miss ye when yer gone."

In the corner of his shanty used for a kitchen, Ryan clinically assessed each of his late family's cutting utensils for their weight and sharpness. He selected his mother's old cleaver. With a whetstone, he worked the iron until it neared the sharpness of a straight razor. He laid it on glowing hearth coals. After dipping a metal cup into the willow tea, he set it aside to cool.

With lye soap and hot water, he scrubbed the surface of his butcher's block—a two-foot-high, debarked oak stump—until he sanitized every nick and slice in the wood. At the window he sipped his bitter medicinal tea and watched snow form drifts in the lee of rocks and trees. He wished for maple syrup.

With the cup drained, he refilled it and set it aside. He stripped to his waist and used his undershirt to grasp the hot cleaver handle. Its sharp edge glowed a faint red. He knelt beside the chopping block and clenched his left hand into a fist with the little finger extended. He laid the erect digit flat on the stump, with his fist resting against the side.

Ryan paused to think through his next move. A quick chop guaranteed the least pain, but he doubted his accuracy—he might cut off too little or too much. He had to sever the finger at the second knuckle for a clean cut. An open bone-end would heal slowly and invite infection.

A minor shiver began at his spine's base and rippled up his back. A rush of sweat from his brow flowed in rivulets over his face and stung his eyes. Tremors began in his gut and spread up his torso and across his shoulders. In seconds, perspiration coated his chest and spine and soaked the waist of his trousers. He placed the cleaver on the hearth.

"'Tis fear. Nary else," he muttered to himself. Inhaling deeply, he paced in circles. "Get a grip, lad."

He flopped down next to the hearth and let its warmth bathe his chills. Slowly the sweat and shakes subsided.

"Let's finish this."

He seized the cleaver, knelt, and placed his left fist beside the block, digit extended as before. He touched the blade's furthest end to the wood past his target digit. White smoke rose in a brief puff from the glowing metal's radiant heat.

"Good. That heat will stem the blood flow."

With the blade's contact point providing stability, he slowly lowered the hot blade until it hovered less than an inch above the second knuckle's outside edge. He checked his aim, filled his lungs, and leaned down with all his weight. Searing flesh hissed. Rent bone and cartilage crunched and snapped.

A howl startled Zak from his slumber in the grove.

*****

Only days after amputating his fingertip, Ryan began constructing snowshoes to replace the ones lost when arrested. He searched for hours to find a tamarack because the Algonquian word for that tree, *akemantak*, means 'wood used for snowshoes.' As he struggled to bend it in a teardrop shape and weave strips of deer hide, he wished he'd spent a winter living and learning from the Algonquins instead of one summer.

Mobile again, he hunted and trapped on his wintry island haven avoiding any contact with other humans for two months.

In early April, spring arrived in the Thousand Islands. For several days, sunny blue skies melted the ground snow. The river ice spoke in booms and gurgles while it softened and shifted. With the St. Lawrence River swollen with melt water, the ice lurched apart and departed downstream in a grinding roar. Sheets of ice, some the size of Ryan's shanty, piled up on the rocky upstream ends of islands and lay melting for weeks afterward. As the frost quit the ground, musky scents rose into the spring air.

"Zak. I believe the earth is exhaling after sleeping all winter."

"Zaak!"

For weeks, he and Zak hunted by canoe in the bays along Howe Island. The raven flew ahead and cawed if the next bay contained migrating ducks or geese. With Zak scouting, Ryan soon had more fowl than he could use. He also had a stock of pelts built up over the winter.

He scanned southeast with his telescope. The border was an imaginary line somewhere in the river. The U.S. shore lay eight miles away.

"Zakkie boy, 'tis time to explore America."

Spring's Refugee

On a shimmering late-April morning, Ryan risked the open-water crossing to New York State. With his birchbark canoe sitting low in the water with its load of furs and fowl, he paddled two miles across open river in gentle swells and light wind to Wolfe Island's sheltering shore, then four miles east in its lee. From there, his muscular arms and shoulders propelled him across a mile of increasingly choppy water to Hickory Island.

He circumnavigated the former Patriot stronghold, scrutinizing the remnants of shanties and log defenses between the leafless trees. Perched on the bow, Zak tilted his head back and forth to examine the strange human structures.

Leaving Hickory, Ryan crossed the invisible border on his way to Grindstone Island. He followed that island's calmer southern margin until abreast of Clayton and scanned the village from offshore. It straddled a wide peninsula, with deep bays to the west and east. A road hugged the shoreline. Wood-sided warehouses and two-storey shops lined the riverside. Jetties and wharfs bustled with gangs of men unloading freight, processing fish, and building boats. Houses, inns, and stores occupied every inch of the road's far side. Beyond the waterfront, Ryan spied church steeples and the cedar-shingled roofs of more houses.

"I wonder Zak, if we'll be more welcome here than in Kingston."

At the public wharf, he began unloading his trade goods. He calculated that the sight of a redheaded young man in Indian garb with a tame raven would draw curious shoppers. Zak sat atop a wharf piling observing the milling humanity.

"Gidday ladies and gentlemen. If any of ye needs fresh ducks or geese, I've plenty to sell. I also have excellent pelts, proper cured and stretched."

He found eager buyers for his furs and fowl. Soon sold out, he explored the town with American coins heavy in his pockets. Clayton's business area and market buzzed and clattered with enterprise. People talked and strolled with a jaunty confidence. He explored the town with Zak on his shoulder. To his surprise, smiling strangers passed a polite greeting.

Unlike the quarried stone architecture of Kingston, Clayton's founders built with wood. The freshly painted clapboard homes sported bright trim colors rarely seen in Upper Canada.

"I guess Zak, this is how free people live."

"Zaak!"

He rented a room with a river view at a Water Street inn. Sitting on the veranda in the warm glow of a spring evening, he and Zak ate a meal of grilled perch, mashed potatoes, bread, and boiled beans. Town folk strolled by leaving trails of scented pipe tobacco, some going home for supper and others on their way to the taverns.

A man in his fifties—barrel-chested, strongly built, about six feet tall—caught his attention. Ryan noted his large nose, wide chin, gray hair at his temples, and the copper complexion of a man often outdoors. Hatless, he wore woolen work clothes in shades of brown. He had the thick-necked, square-jawed visage of a thug, but everyone the stranger passed greeted him warmly. Ryan overheard someone call him Bill. The stranger drew near on the wooden sidewalk. Ryan spoke on a hunch.

"Sir, would ye be Bill Johnston?"

The big man stopped and glowered with feral, blue-gray eyes. Zak hopped off the veranda railing and shuffled across the table closer to his human.

"Who wants to know?" The voice spoke, baritone and menacing.

"Ryan, a son of Ireland, who gets trouble from the British every time the name Bill Johnston appears in the newspaper."

The man tilted his head and laughed, the menace gone. "Bill Johnston I am. Troubling the British be my calling. I am sorry if they caught you in their net. They do tend to punish the innocent as often as the guilty." He paused to examine Ryan and Zak. "Be you the lad staying in Old Tim's cabin on Howe Island?"

"I'm not sure, sir. Twas empty and I had want of shelter."

"Be it the one-room cabin on the south shore nigh the end of a circular bay?"

"Yes, sir."

"That was Tim's, a trapper and fisherman. He passed two years or so ago. Don't be surprised. Nothing happens on these shores or islands that I miss."

"Would ye care for a cup of tea?"

Bill nodded and sat where he could face the street. "Be you new to these parts?"

"Tis my first visit to America. I arrived in the Canadian colonies a year ago."

"Did you come across alone?"

Ryan stiffened and handed Zak a piece of toast. "No." He studied Bill's face, hoping he understood the response meant he didn't care to talk about it.

Bill shrugged. "That wound on your finger looks fresh. An accident was it?"

"If ye call sending a man to freeze to death an accident, then aye, 'twas an accident."

Bill cocked his eyebrow—a wordless request for more details. Ryan told him the story of his arrest and cold struggle home.

"Bonnycastle's doing, is it? I never met the man. My informants in Kingston tell me he wants to meet me badly."

"So does every magistrate in Upper Canada, according to the papers."

"In that regard, nothing has changed in twenty-five years." He paused for a sip of tea. "You know lad, you should come over to this side. A man of your enterprise and courage can do far better in this republic than under those corrupt despots."

"The idea has merit. I must leave Howe soon. The farmers are cutting all the forest."

"You sound sad."

"'Tis a beautiful thing those great forests of beech, maple, and hickory. The sunlight slanting down through the upper branches reminds me of the high windows in a cathedral I visited in Dublin. 'Tis a place of peace and grandeur. I don't know why they must destroy it all, sir."

"Most farmers feel the forest must be removed to prosper. Many, I truly believe, fear its darkness and mystery."

"Fear it! It draws me like the open arms of my mother."

Bill nodded in agreement. "I will probably see you before you depart." He rose to leave. "Until then, I bid you good evening, lad."

"A good evening to ye, sir."

*****

Over tea the next morning in the dining room of his modest Clayton home, Bill Johnston contemplated his house guest, Daniel Heustis. If Bill hadn't witnessed Heustis give his all for the Patriot cause, they would never have become friends, for in every other way, they were so different.

While he clothed his bulky body in cotton and homespun garments in basic earth tones, Heustis stylishly attired his well-muscled form in a knee-length, blue frock coat over a tan vest and trousers. Two inches shorter and twenty-five years younger than himself, Heustis had a full face and prominent chin framed by long, wavy, brown hair. He had dark, brooding eyes and the resolute expression of a man who is a fervent follower of religion or some great cause.

Bill envied Heustis' advanced formal education in contrast to his meager four years of schooling. Heustis was a staunch Presbyterian, while Bill had avoided church from the age of eight.

"Daniel, care for a stroll?" Bill began. "Let's go find that young lad I told you about."

"Indeed! An after-breakfast constitutional would be most gratifying."

After a leisurely stroll into the center of town, Bill spotted Ryan finishing his breakfast on the veranda of the same inn. His raven perched on the railing, waiting for food scraps. The raven spotted Bill and cawed a warning. Ryan looked up.

"Mind if we join you?" Bill said.

"I'd be grateful for the company," the young man said, rising to his feet. "Would ye care for tea?"

"Not for me," Bill answered. "We just had several cups." He looked at Heustis, who simply shook his head.

"Ryan, this be my friend Daniel Dunbar Heustis. He be a captain in the Patriot army up from Watertown for a visit."

"Pleased to meet ye," Ryan said, standing to shake the man's hand.

"You know who the Patriots are, I presume?" Heustis asked.

"Yes, sir. So far, thanks to the Patriots I was hounded from Kingston, hauled before Bonnycastle, nearly froze to death, and," he held up his left hand, "lost half a finger."

Heustis puffed out his cheeks and blew slowly between puckered lips.

"What can I do for ye two?"

"I just wanted Captain Heustis to meet you," Bill replied.

A moment of silence passed while that statement's mendacity hung in the air. Ryan waved the men to seats and changed the subject. "Can ye explain to me what happened on Hickory Island this winter? I saw an army build up and then vanish."

Heustis rolled his eyes. "I'll let Bill explain."

"Were it not for a drunken dandy," Bill began, "we would have taken Canada."

"Who's the dandy ye speak of?"

Bill leaned forward, his eyes on Ryan. "His name is Rensselaer Van Rensselaer. He be the idiot grandnephew of a bloody incompetent American general. His uncle attacked Canada nigh Niagara in 1812 and managed to lose badly to a lesser force. On the strength of that failure, William Lyon Mackenzie made the younger Van Rensselaer the Patriot army commander, a man with no military experience. Mackenzie be a great man, but he cannot separate leaders from laggards."

"Start at the beginning, Bill," Heustis suggested.

"After we quit Navy Island in January, I sat Mackenzie and that damned Van Rensselaer down and explained an attack plan me and General Donald McLeod devised. McLeod will be in town soon. You can meet him."

Ryan shrugged.

"With three hundred men, McLeod would attack Canada nigh Windsor and I would take an army to capture Gananoque. Both were diversions from the main assault on Kingston. We armed five hundred discontented farmers in the Midland District to attack the fort once it emptied in response to our two invasions. I had a man in the fort to spike the cannon and blow the magazines. It was a bold and winning strategy, ruined by Van Rensselaer." He threw up his hands and slumped back in his chair.

"I saw yer army. What went wrong?" Ryan asked.

"What went wrong? That drunkard Van Rensselaer took charge of *my* army. So, while the farmers waited in taverns and inns for word to attack, Van Rensselaer paraded around Clayton and Hickory Island with his fancy uniform, a cutlass in one hand, and a bottle of brandy in the other. He insisted we wait until February twenty-second because it be George Washington's birthday." Bill put his meaty hands together and began cracking finger joints. The pops punctuated his diatribe. "Being a poltroon at heart, Van Rensselaer wanted a reason to delay. We were ready for the raid two days earlier. I wanted to attack then. He said no."

"The wait took a toll on our men," Heustis began in the dry tone of a schoolmaster. "Our Hickory Island shanties provided poor shelter and the cold was dreadful. Many men tired of waiting and went home.

The same thing happened in January on Navy Island. Van Rensselaer dithered. Men saw him dither and lost enthusiasm for the fight."

"By the twenty-second," Bill continued, "word made it to Bonnycastle. He put guards on all the inns to keep the farmers pinned, arrested fifty of them, and he led a large force to Hickory. We retreated from the island. Daniel and I were the last two to leave."

Bill paused and took a deep breath to calm himself. "When be you heading back?"

"When the wind and chop calm."

"Have a safe voyage." Bill and Heustis rose to leave. "See you next time."

"Yes, sir. And nice to meet ye, Captain Heustis."

*****

A week later, with all his possessions and a sack of ducks in his canoe, Ryan set out again for Clayton. He bid his isolated cabin farewell and paddled off to rejoin humanity.

He retraced his first journey to Clayton—across to Wolfe Island, then east along the island's north shore, and on to Hickory Island's south side. As he neared the old Patriot stronghold, a steamer flying British navy colors emerged around a headland and bore straight at him. He instantly comprehended its mission.

Ryan swung southeast, hoping to cross the invisible border before the ship could overtake him. He refused to surrender to Bonnycastle again without a fight. He leaned into each stroke and pulled back with his whole body. One man paddling could not propel a canoe any faster.

At first, Ryan kept the steamer at a distance as he crossed a shoal between two small islands too shallow for the ship's draught. His goal was the border somewhere just ahead. The British sidewheeler bore down on him. A voice commanded him to stop.

"Bugger off," Ryan shouted into the wind.

A carronade boomed behind him. A geyser of water rose to tree height in the river twenty feet past his bow. Ryan rested his paddle and let the boat drift on its momentum.

The vessel—its name, *Bull Frog*, emblazoned on the paddlewheel covers—slowed and stopped two yards away. His canoe bobbed in its wake. A naval officer and two armed marines leaned on the port rail next to a stout man in civilian clothes.

"*Damnú ort!*" Ryan cursed in Gaelic when he recognized Tiny smiling from the deck.

"I am Lieutenant George Leary of the Royal Navy," the officer roared. "You are under arrest on the orders of Lieutenant-Colonel Bonnycastle for associating with Bill Johnston."

"Why'd ye bring that fat bastard?" He pointed to Tiny.

"I require positive identification. He claims to know you. Come aboard!"

"I'm in American territory. Ye have no authority here."

Leary pointed a musket in Ryan's direction. "This gives me my authority. Come aboard, now!"

At the sight of the weapon, Zak leapt from the bow and pounded the air until he doubled the height of the steamer's mast. He circled and watched.

Ryan ignored the weapon. He had withstood months of frustration, injustice, and demolished dreams under the British. This illegal arrest, on the day he was finally free of British rule, sent hot blood rushing to his face. His lips curled in a snarl.

"I'll see ye in hell first."

"You will come aboard. Mark my words." Leary aimed and fired.

The musket ball tore a hole in the canoe's hull between Ryan's feet. Water spurted in.

"Croc! Rrok!" Zak called from above.

"Damn ye!" Ryan pulled a cooking pot from a canvas bag and started bailing as he tried to block the hole with his other hand. He believed he might save the canoe if he could keep ahead of the gushing water and plug the hole.

"Bail, hothead." Tiny hollered. He spit chewing tobacco juice into Ryan's boat, tainting the water welling around Ryan's ankles.

Leary sniggered briefly at Ryan's efforts to bail. Then, bored of the spectacle, he said, "You will come aboard or drown."

Tiny accepted a proffered musket from Leary and aimed towards the canoe's bow. At the sight of the big man pointing a gun towards his human, Zak began a steep dive.

Grinning like a child at Christmas, Tiny fired a musket ball through the hull eight feet ahead of Ryan. Water poured in through the second hole.

A moment too late, Zak knocked Tiny's hat off from behind. Tiny grabbed another loaded musket from a marine. "I'll kill that demon bird."

Zak dropped below the main deck and glided around the stern to the starboard side to put the entire craft between him and the fat human. Tiny lowered the musket. His red visage of rage softened to mirth when he returned to Ryan's struggle in the river. The canoe, now beyond saving, steadily filled. Ryan kept bailing.

"I heard the Irish do not float," Leary remarked.

"Yes, sir. It must be true, judging by the number sleeping in the Atlantic."

Once again, Tiny's belligerent voice pried loose ineffable memories. For a moment, Ryan swayed again on the pitching deck of a two-masted sailing ship, five days out of Dublin. His youngest brother, Seamus, slipped beneath the ocean in a sailcloth shroud as the skipper read the Bible. The previous night, a fierce storm rocking the vessel had knocked loose a great iron skillet hanging in the steerage common area below decks. It caved in his thin child's skull. Then two days later, Ryan's grieving mother miscarried. He sobbed at her side while life bled from her. As the captain read a Bible verse, Ryan's mother and her premature daughter slipped beneath the leaden waves while Ryan's remaining family consoled each other. He overheard one crewman say the sea floor held enough Irish to populate a sizeable town.

Ryan shook off the nightmare and reached for his tomahawk. The Algonquins had taught him how to throw the weapon and bury the blade in a target. Killing Tiny meant Ryan's certain death but that no longer mattered. All he wanted at that moment was to fling the weapon at his repugnant, laughing face.

A deep boom resonated across the river. A metallic bang exploded overhead. A hole appeared in the steamer's smokestack.

"Rrok! Cric! Croc!" Zak had spotted people coming.

Leary scanned the river to the east with a telescope. "Over near Grindstone...a rowboat of some kind," he barked.

A louder boom echoed off the islands. The railing Tiny leaned on erupted, flinging a spike-like oak splinter into his arm. He stared dumbfounded at the wooden barb protruding through his sleeve and the venous blood dripping from his cuff.

"It's carrying a dozen men," Leary continued. "One of Johnston's boats."

"Load the bloody carronade," Tiny yelped. "Blast the traitor to hell."

"We cannot engage him in American waters. Hard to starboard and full speed, helmsman," Leary yelled.

As the vessel bore away, Tiny bawled on the deck. "What about my arm? Damn it, I need a doctor. Someone help me."

*****

With twelve men at her oars, a narrow boat raced across the water faster than some steamboats at full throttle. Bill Johnston crouched low, loading and firing a long-barreled rifle swivel-mounted on the bow. He shot twice more at the fleeing *Bull Frog*.

Guided by Zak flying in circles, Bill found Ryan treading water. The canoe gone, the lad clung to the floating canvas sack of ducks, smiling.

"I didn't expect to find you grinning after all that," Bill said.

"Tis because I saw a bully get his due."

Bill and a younger man hauled him aboard. Zak settled on the bow gun. Ryan had only his Algonquin clothes, the tomahawk on his belt, and the talisman on his neck. The river had claimed the last mementos of his Irish family and his former life.

"Thank ye kindly, Bill. How did ye know 'twas I in trouble?"

"We didn't at first. Hugh Scanlon there," he said, pointing at the shaggy-haired man in his late twenties who helped haul Ryan aboard, "spied the British ship lurking nigh Hickory. We decided to run her from American waters. When I saw your bird, I knew it be you."

"I am grateful," he said to Bill with a nod to Scanlon. "I nary want to see that ship again."

"Never fear lad. We take care of our own."

"Yer own! Am I a smuggler or a Patriot?"

"Hopefully, both!"

The twelve oarsmen bent to their work and headed towards Clayton. Scanlon's blue shirt rippled on his muscled frame as he rowed. All the boatmen wore shirts that matched the boat's river-blue paint.

"Tis clever camouflage," Ryan pointed at Scanlon's shirt.

"Aye, this garb makes us tougher to see."

"And 'tis quite a craft. I've not gone this fast over water by oar."

"This be a gig," explained Bill, "a larger version of boats we used in the war to attack British shipping. It be narrow to go fast. The cedar wood makes it light. Back in the war, when the British chased us, we could maneuver through channels too narrow for them to follow or portage the boat across an island to safety. This bow gun here," he patted the weapon," comes from those days. It can hurl a one-inch ball a mile."

"People in Kingston call ye a traitor for fighting for the Americans in that war."

"I might have fought for the British had they not arrested me on false charges and stolen all my property. My parents were Loyalists. They fled America when the revolution ended and settled in Bath, nigh Kingston. I was born along the way."

"So, ye pioneered, then?"

"Damn right. I helped build that colony. We and our neighbors prospered despite the government nepotism and corruption."

"Someone said you kept a shop in Kingston." Ryan settled lower into the boat to avoid the chill wind on his wet garments.

"Not until later. I left the farm at sixteen and apprenticed to a blacksmith for six years. It was a great experience. Many men came in just to talk politics. I do believe my republican roots began then. When I wasn't at the smithy, I hunted in the islands with a few Mohawks I befriended as a lad. When I quit the smithy, I went into business for myself. I bought me boats for moving…ah…goods."

"Goods?" Ryan cocked an eyebrow.

"I started smuggling tea. The British tax tea so highly that I can sell it at half the official cost and still make hefty profits. I've been told that three-quarters of tea drunk in Upper Canada be smuggled in.

"Besides the smuggling, I had me a farm, a store, a wife, and a young family. If not for the war or if the British had not gone so hard against me, things might be different. Like I've said, the British punish the innocent as often as the guilty. In my case, I punished them back in the war."

"I'd like to hear some of yer war stories."

"Later! These lads have heard all my tales once too often."

"That's fer sure," said Scanlon, winking.

"I hear a familiar tongue," Ryan began. "Where ye from?"

"I've lived in Kingston for decades." He paused to inhale as he rowed. "I came with my family from Cork as a lad. Bill tells me yer over here a year now."

"I just survived my first winter."

"Gets cold, don't she?"

Ryan grunted. "She sure does."

The crew chatter ceased. Ryan relaxed to the comforting click-clunk rhythm of oarlocks and the sough of water on oar blades.

*****

In Clayton, they landed at Bill's private wharf. While his men stowed the gig in the warehouse, Bill escorted his wet guest to his modest house on the opposite side of Water Street. His family gathered on the covered porch at his arrival.

Ryan eyed the knot of well-attired strangers, their clothes so clean, he caught the scent of soap. Bill's four sons—Jim, Napoleon, John, and Decatur—ranged in age from thirty to sixteen. They had the height of their father, with similar dark hair and gray eyes. Each wore dark cotton trousers held up by suspenders. Jim sported a white cotton shirt with blue stripes under a dark buttonless vest, in contrast with the other sons' conservative cotton shirts in pale hues of green or blue.

Bill's full-figured, brown-eyed wife, Ann, stood in front, wearing a neck-to-ankle yellow cotton dress and matching bonnet over her gray hair.

"Pardon my sorry state, ma'am."

Ryan knew he looked like a bedraggled savage, with his hair and thin beard long and scraggly, while dressed cap-a-pie in wet Algonquin buckskins far from sweet smelling.

"No need to apologize. My boys have arrived home from the river looking worse than you," she replied.

A silhouette darkened the hallway behind Ann. A giantess stooped under the doorframe and stepped into the sunlight.

"This is my niece, Ada," Ann added.

Ryan's gaze alighted first on her low-cut mauve blouse, and then quickly rose to safer territory. He noticed the faint lines around her green eyes. He admired the ridges of her cheekbones and the auburn hair that framed her oval face.

She smiled. "We have met."

"How be that possible?" Bill asked.

"Remember I told you I interceded for a boy in the Kingston market. Well, this is that charming young man."

"Nice to meet ye again."

"Such a small world," Bill added. "But then, you must have met my daughter too?"

"I met a lass named Kate Randolph."

"I lied about my real name," spoke a voice from behind Bill's sons. The brothers parted for their sister. She wore a floor-length, white skirt with a blue hem, and high-collared, white blouse that flattered her petit figure far better than the winter coat she wore in Kingston. "In Canada I use my mother's maiden name to avoid trouble from the British."

"Lady Fortune has blessed me again," Ryan replied, smiling. She acknowledged his compliment with a slight nod of her head.

"Decatur, fetch a set of your clothes for this boy," Ann said to her youngest son. "And Kate, please prepare him a bath."

Stepping closer, Kate ran her fingertips up Ryan's cheek and through his curls. "It will take more than a bath, Mother. That hair and fuzz also require attention."

Ryan's pulse accelerated at the gentle caress. A hint of rose water wafted from her hand. For a moment, only Kate existed on that porch with him. His eyes locked on her lips. Ryan had never kissed a woman and decided Kate would be his first, but not just then.

"Come inside, lad," said Bill, breaking Kate's spell on Ryan.

On entering, he beheld polished furniture, carpets, a carved walnut wall clock, curtains on windows, and shelves full of books. After so long living in the bush, he had some adjusting to do.

*****

With her barber equipment laid on a side table near the window, Kate paced the room, marveling at the vicissitudes of fate. She recalled the primal thrill she felt meeting Ryan in Kingston and the sadness of a parting she believed then was forever. And now he was in her house.

Ryan edged into the room and stood smiling at her. She found him more attractive in the clean cotton trousers and buttoned shirt than his smelly buckskins. He had rolled up the sleeves, showing tanned and sinewy forearms.

"Come sit in this chair. I need the light from the window."

"Yes ma'am," he said in teasing tone.

She was aware as she lathered his cheeks that his eyes never left her face. The ends of his fingers twitched nervously.

"Do not worry. I do this often for my father and brothers."

"I'm not worrying."

"Are you certain? You seem twitchy."

"Yer scissors and razor are no matter. Tis being close to such a beautiful lass that has me twitching."

Kate laughed. Ryan smiled at the sound.

"That must be some of that legendary Irish blarney."

"Blarney's another word for inflating the truth. For true, yer the best-looking woman I've seen in the New World."

"Really! I think you lived too long alone in the wilderness. Now, hold still or you will be missing an ear as well as a finger."

Ryan sat still, though she felt his eyes follow her every move.

"What was that tune you hummed earlier?" Kate asked.

"Pardon?"

"When Ada approached you earlier on the porch, you hummed a wistful tune."

"Did I? I don't recall it." Ryan shrugged.

"Don't move while I have a razor on your throat."

Ryan stilled himself and said nothing until Kate began cutting his red curls.

"What's today's date, Kate?"

"Why?"

"I want to take note of my first day free from the British."

"May 5, 1838. Welcome to America, Mr. Pine."

*****

That night at dinner Ryan and Bill traded stories about how circumstance drove them from Canada. Ryan told them his problems started when he questioned the arrest of an American in Kingston, and then escalated when he refused to train with the militia.

"That be remarkable," Bill began. "My history has much in common. When the war started, I joined the militia, but refused to continue when an officer berated me for a minor infraction."

He ran the fingers of his left hand through his thick hair while he collected his memories. "I think my greatest crime was one of compassion. In the winter of 1812, the war trapped American civilians in Kingston. The British refused to let them go home, so I bailed several out and smuggled them home.

"I remember one businessman in particular. Seba Murphy was his name. He set out on foot to cross the ice one frigid night in December and suffered terrible frostbite. British guards caught him and dragged him to the Kingston jail. I bailed him out and brought in a doctor. Sadly, he lost both feet to gangrene. My support for Americans like Seba and my disinterest in the war so angered the British commandant that he sent soldiers to arrest me in 1813 on a charge of spying."

He picked up his dinner knife and shook it in Ryan's direction. "I swear, to that moment I was a loyal subject. But that night, when a boyhood friend in a scarlet uniform came to arrest me, everything changed. No jail can hold me, and I escaped that night. The British confiscated my house and store in Kingston, and four hundred acres of good farmland in Bath. They also jailed two of my brothers out of spite." He slammed the knife on the table.

Bill's family knew his stories by heart. Ryan noticed them nod at dramatic moments.

"But I paid them back." He leaned back in his chair. "You know that fancy canal up there, the Rideau. I built that. Not directly. Me and other privateer commanders near closed the St. Lawrence to British supply boats in that war. They spent a king's ransom to build that backdoor to Kingston in case they had to face me again."

"Another war seems underway," Ryan remarked.

"That be so. A different war. Not a war of nations, but one of ideals."

"That was how my grandfather Ryan viewed the Irish rebellion of 1798. He said 'twas not ridding ourselves of the English that mattered, but setting our own course as a people."

"Was he a rebel?"

"Yes. His fought in County Wexford until the Irish defeat at Vinegar Hill."

"The British massacred hundreds of captives after that battle. Your grandfather survived?"

"Yes, he…ah…he escaped," he answered, compulsively rubbing his half finger with his right thumb and forefinger.

"Lucky for him. Where be he now?"

"He died a month afore we departed Ireland."

"My grandfather also hailed from Ireland," Bill continued, "and I am named after him like you be named after yours. He was a man of spirit, fight, and generosity. He died at one hundred and four. Too bad he didn't live to see this latest struggle."

"Is the struggle still going? Tis been quiet since Hickory Island."

"The Patriot movement is taking a new form. Right now, a secret society called the Hunters has pledged to liberate Canada. Remember Daniel Heustis?"

"Aye."

"He helped start a Hunters lodge in Watertown. Most members be Americans who wish Canadians to have the same liberties they do. Might you join us?"

"What do ye have planned?"

"There is a new enterprise afoot. Until then, there is rum and tea to move across the river, if you be willing."

"I am. At least the British will have a reason to hound me for once."

"To start, Kate will show you our hideouts around Grindstone Island."

Ryan raised his eyebrows.

Bill waved his hand to sweep aside Ryan's doubts. "Her boating skills match any man on this shore and she has a vixen's cunning. Besides, you will draw less suspicion with her than with me or one of my boys."

"That plan sits well with me, sir." Ryan smiled at Kate.

Kate ignored his silly grin and changed the subject. "I am curious. How did you obtain the name Lone Pine?"

"How did you find Zak?" Bill asked.

"What was it like living with Indians?" Ada added, with a shudder.

"Tis a long story, if told right."

"We have tea and dessert to come," Ann interjected," and plenty of time."

"Do ye have maple syrup?"

"Yes. Where did you develop that sweet tooth?"

"Tis part of the story."

Ryan composed his thoughts and recited the tale of his previous summer.

Indian Summer

After two months in the New World, in a land of mostly stumps—some so fresh they still oozed sap—the sight of one massive pine's soaring spire told Ryan the frontier lay near. He drove his paddle into the turbid water and steered his canoe towards the grandfather tree standing alone on the river bank. His gaze moved up from its six-foot-wide base to its crown a hundred feet above. Breezes wheezed and sighed through its upper branches.

Since leaving Montreal in May 1837, he'd seen acre-sized rafts of thick pine logs float down the St. Lawrence and Ottawa Rivers, but no living giant, until that moment coming around the river bend.

As instructed by a land agent in Bytown, he journeyed up the Mississippi River, a tributary of the Ottawa River. A hundred yards upstream from the lone pine, the pioneer hamlet of Pakenham Mills hugged the plain between denuded hills. His land grant lay some distance beyond.

He put two dressed duck carcasses—part of yesterday's successful hunt—in a canvas sack and entered the young village. It boasted a general store, post office, gristmill, inns, a school, log and frame homes, and several churches on the hillside. Horse-and-wagon traffic rattled across a wooden bridge above the dam. Men directed logs through a timber slide. The pungent aroma of newly cut pine wafted his way from the sawmill.

He stepped inside the first inn and let his eyes adjust to the dusky light in the common eating room. A stout, older man, with curly white hair, thick gray sideburns, and a ruddy face, fussed over his accounts at a corner table. He wore a pale cotton shirt, pressed linen trousers, and a silk vest that had seen better days.

"Pardon me, sir. Are ye the proprietor?"

He glanced up from his books. "Aye, William MacFarlane. How can I help you, lad?"

Ryan smiled at the warm Scots accent. "Would ye be willing to trade a loaf of bread and some directions for a brace of ducks?"

"It seems you're selling them a bit cheaply. How 'bout I add a meal to the deal?"

"That's generous, sir. I'm grateful," he said, extending his hand. "I'm Ryan. Pleased to meet ye."

"Isabella," MacFarlane called to the kitchen. "My dear, we have ducks for the larder and a guest for luncheon." MacFarlane's wife, a stocky woman of fifty with a wide smile, gathered up the ducks and soon served plates of fried eggs and buttered bread.

"Where do you want to go?"

Ryan, whose youthful appetite always raged, wordlessly pulled a paper from a pocket as he chewed.

MacFarlane examined the grant's lot and concession number. "I've hunted bear up there. I can tell you right now, the location is not prime. All the best farms went ten years ago. This one's up where the rock starts. You might find patches of good land, but not the whole lot."

"Sir, we lived on five acres in Ireland. Any more is a blessing."

Isabella set down a tea tray and china cups and returned to the kitchen.

"Would you care for some tea, lad?"

"I've nary had tea, sir. At home, only the English could afford it."

"Welcome to Upper Canada. The old rules and limitations are gone."

"All of them, sir?"

MacFarlane smiled at the lad's skepticism. "Aye, not all. But we have room to move and grow in this new country."

Ryan's face puckered from the tea's bitterness.

"Try adding a bit of that syrup,' MacFarlane suggested, pointing to a ceramic jar.

Ryan stirred in a teaspoon of the golden liquid and sipped the tea. His eyebrows shot up. "What manner of stuff is this?"

"It's made by boiling sap from maple trees. Something we learned from the Indians. There'll probably be some maples on your lot. Mind you don't cut them all."

"For this heavenly taste, I'll cut nary a one."

After tea, they stepped into the brilliant sunshine. Both men pulled their hat brims down to shade their faces. Ryan looked downstream at the big pine.

"Why was that big pine left standing when all its kin were felled?"

"There's a bit of a curve in it. Not good for lumber. And it's on land that's no good for farming."

Ryan nodded. The explanation seemed reasonable. "Can ye tell me the best way to get to my land?"

"Well, you could take the roads, but they're muddy this spring. I'd advise against that if you have a boat."

"I came by canoe."

"Then your best route is by water. Go upriver and turn into the first navigable creek on the right. Head upstream until you pass the last farm. Look around for the surveyor stakes that mark your lot, or ask someone."

Ryan looked towards the river. "Why do they call this the Mississippi? At first, I thought I was at the top end of that big American river, until I saw 'twas flowing the wrong way."

MacFarlane shrugged. "The name is a regular subject of speculation. Some say it comes from local Indian words meaning mosquito river. I don't know." He continued. "The creek you want can be hard to see under the overhanging trees but look for an Indian camp."

"Indians!"

"It's a family of Algonquins, a youth and his grandparents. They're peaceful."

"What are Indians like?"

"They keep to themselves. Though I admit I've not tried making friends."

"Well, 'tis time I departed. I bid ye thanks for yer kindness and advice."

"Drop by when you come to town. I'm always happy to trade for fowl or fish."

*****

Ryan portaged his canoe around the village dam and headed upriver. In less than an hour, he came abreast of the Algonquin camp. One conical dwelling made of long poles wrapped in animal skins stood in the shade. A buckskin-clad old man and a youth filleted fish, while an old woman in a mismatched outfit of woolen clothing placed them on a wooden rack to dry.

Ryan waved a greeting. Immobile, their eyes watched him glide past and up the creek.

Fresh evidence of pioneer land clearing—stumps and felled trees—littered the creek banks and adjoining farm fields. The farms along the creek were newer than most he'd seen. Land clearing was still under way. It takes years for a farm family to remove a hundred acres of trees with axe and saw. Stands of great leafy trees and conifers remained.

One such forest grove spanned the narrow creek. For a few seconds, Ryan paddled through a forest tunnel. Massive trunks rose around him. The canopy's interlacing foliage blocked most sunlight and few plants grew on the forest floor.

He emerged from the false evening gloom into the searing sunlight. Along the rocky bank to his right lay the wilting boughs of a felled old hemlock. The trunk was newly hauled away, probably for lumber. Ryan could see a tangle of bare sticks within the smooth, short, dark green hemlock needles. From its midst came a faint squawking.

Ryan beached his canoe and traced the noise to a raven chick in the scattered remains of a stick nest. Dark gray down covered its frail body. Its wings sprouted new flight feathers, more pearly shaft than actual feather. Of its parents and siblings, he found no sign.

The bird opened its mouth, showing an expanse of pink palate, and let out a weak squawk, "Zik!"

Ryan had enough experience with chickens and farm geese to recognize a cry of hunger. He held the raven next to his chest with one hand, while he flipped over rocks along the creek shore. Under one lay a fat white grub. He squished it between his fingers and placed it in the chick's mouth. Gone. Swallowed in an instant.

"Zik!"

Under another rock, he found an earthworm. He chopped it into pieces and placed them in the bird's mouth. Gone one by one.

"Zik!"

Freshwater mussels lay half buried between rocks on the sandy creek bottom. He broke one open with a rock and placed the slimy contents in the bird's pink maw. Gone.

"Zik!"

After another mussel and two grasshoppers, the chick showed its contentment by pooping in Ryan's hand and falling asleep.

He nestled the sleeping bird into a crude nest of hemlock foliage in the canoe's bow and headed upstream. He passed the last farm and found a brushed-out surveyor's path. Following this artificial line, he located his lot and began exploring.

Round hills and ridges of granite covered the west half. The remainder was flat land bisected by the creek. For the first time in the New World, he hiked through an undisturbed forest. He admired each tree for more than its majesty: as a carpenter, he respected the uses and value of wood.

He estimated he had at least forty acres suitable for farming once cleared, plus plenty of intact woodlands for a lasting source of lumber, firewood, and beauty.

In a grove of black ash, butternut, and basswood, where a long series of gurgling rapids ended in a deep pool, he cleared the low brush and weeds with an axe and a sickle to make his camp. He scraped aside old leaves, twigs, and humus to expose the sandy soil below for a fire pit.

His camp ready, Ryan sat on a flat rock by the rapids mesmerized by the sinuous bands of tumbling water. The comforting gurgle and cool dampness filled the grove. Wild berries grew along the creek amidst wildflowers of countless hues. In the water swam fat catfish and darting fishes he had no names for yet. Every male nesting bird called from its territory in a pleasing din of squawks, chirps, and melodies. An earthy smell of organic life filled the grove.

"Zak, 'tis a magical place."

In the growing dark, he ate Isabella's bread and fed the raven chopped mussels. He chatted to Zak as a man keeps company with a dog.

"I guess we're stuck with each other now, eh bird?"

"Zaak," he replied, the weakness gone from his voice.

"Ye will need a name. What'll it be?"

"Zaak! Zaak!"

"'Tis settled then. Zak it is."

"Zaak!"

Lying on his back, Ryan watched, through the narrow opening in the branches above, the evening's last light play across the sky. The lowest cloud wisps were already below the last shafts of sunset, just bluish-black smudges against the robin's-egg-blue sky. Higher, small cloud slivers still glowed brilliant orange. While he watched, the orange began to fade, first to crimson and then red. Along the cloud edges furthest from the sun, blue-black shadows appeared and expanded. Finally, shadow devoured the last faded red tinges of color. The sun was set. The sky darkened.

Ryan looked around him in the last light of dusk, at the creek, the great dark trees, and the abundant wildflowers. He listened to the creek tumbling over rocks and the musical murmurs of songbirds going to roost. He inhaled the fresh, scented air. "God has blessed this place. Too bad ye did not get to see it, father." He prayed for the souls of his family.

That night, as in other nights, Ryan slept under his overturned canoe, protected from any rain but at the mercy of mosquitoes. Zak also nestled under the canoe on a pile of moss that Ryan gathered for him.

*****

He awoke when the robins began to sing. He stripped and bathed in the creek as the sun rose. He ate wild strawberries and bread for breakfast and set out to explore his land.

The next afternoon, Ryan packed for a trip to Pakenham Mills. He wanted a sack of flour, some seed potatoes, and advice on constructing a log cabin. He took surplus tools to use for barter in case he couldn't shoot enough ducks to trade.

By the last downstream portage, the coming darkness made it impractical to continue. He'd departed his camp too late. At the river junction, he steered his canoe on a whim to the Algonquin camp and pulled up next to a large Indian canoe. He eased towards the campfire carrying a plump goose he'd shot that afternoon.

The old native man hefted his tomahawk. The youth moved to stand between the old woman and the stranger. Ryan guessed the Algonquins had no experience with friendly visits from white men.

"Gidday. My name is Ryan. Ye have a nice fire, and I have this fat goose." He held up his goose, pointed to himself and to the fire, and then swept his hand in their direction. If they didn't speak English, he thought they'd understand his offer to share food.

The youth and old man conversed in Algonquian. With a hint of shyness, the young Algonquin approached and held out his hand. Ryan almost shook the outstretched palm before remembering he was outside of his culture. He passed over the goose.

"Grandfather welcome you to our home. Sit, please, by fire."

"Thank Grandfather for his kindness," Ryan said, sitting on a log away from the smoke.

The old woman brought him a battered metal cup containing tea of steeped herbs. It tasted bitter. He wished he had some maple syrup. He smiled and sipped.

The Algonquin family readied the camp for night and prepared food. Instead of slowly plucking the feathers before roasting the goose, the old woman skinned it. She then sliced its dark flesh into strips, tossed them in an old iron skillet, and fried them in the goose's own fat. In the coals, she roasted a root that reminded Ryan of potatoes. He later learned they were cattail tubers.

They sat around the flaming logs and ate in silence. Ryan passed bits of goose to Zak. The bird seemed relaxed in the strange company.

"Zaak!"

The youth smiled at the sound. "You not have bird first time we see you."

"I found him in a fallen tree."

"What name you give him?"

"I call him Zak, from the sound he makes."

The youth repeated the story to his grandfather, who spoke back.

"Grandfather says it wise to let things take their true names, if they can."

"What's yer name?"

"Nika Wabizi."

Ryan tried to repeat it but stumbled on the syllables.

The youth grinned. "It mean white goose."

"Do ye mind if I call ye Nick?"

"You give me nickname?"

Ryan gagged on his tea at the Algonquin lad's English pun. Nick and Ryan laughed The grandparents grinned at the happy youngsters.

"Nick is good white man name. I thank you."

"Are ye the only one speaking English?"

He nodded. "I also speak the French man's language."

"Where did ye learn yer languages?"

"We camped for years at mouth of Kitchi Sibi."

Ryan knew he meant the junction of the Ottawa and St. Lawrence Rivers.

"There, some church men tried make boys civilized. They taught us their god and ways of working for money and ways of living in crowded places. I learned speak white men languages, but I not like civilized."

"Where are yer parents?"

Nick translated the question for his grandparents before answering. "Mohawks killed my father when trapping at the big lake to the south," he said dispassionately. "Mother died of white man sickness at place with church men."

The old man asked a question.

"Grandfather want know where your parents are."

"Dead, but not killed by Mohawks, though diseases played a part."

The boy studied him, waiting for more.

Over the next two hours, with fireflies twinkling in the blackness beyond the campfire and breeding toads humming in the reeds along the river, Ryan told the Algonquins of his life in the Old World. With his eyes fixed on the sparking fire, he told them of Ireland, of land taken centuries earlier by the English and leased to the Irish. He told them of tiny farms too small to support a family, of enforced poverty, bloody rebellions, and self-serving English magistrates. Of his lost family, he said little.

As Ryan spoke, Nick translated for his grandparents. Grandfather sighed at points in the story. Grandmother stared into the campfire, reliving sad days of her own.

A haunting bird call pelted from the dark forest nearby. "What makes that loud sound? The one that goes ko-ko-koo-hoo?" Ryan asked.

Nick laughed. "It is owl bird speaking its name. In our language, it called *Kokokòho*."

All night long Kokokòho repeated its name making sure Ryan never forgot his first word of Algonquian.

*****

They finished the goose at breakfast and Ryan prepared to leave for Pakenham Mills. Nick and Grandfather came to the shore.

"Grandfather has question."

"Ask me."

"Grandfather ask why you come take our land like English take yours?"

The old Algonquin could not have wounded him more if he'd hit him with his tomahawk. Ryan's shoulders sagged. His mouth gaped. His paddle fell from his limp hand. He lurched backwards into the river, recoiling step by step from the terrible truth in that question.

With water up to his chest, he looked away to hide the tremors twisting his face. The burden of his wet clothes and the tragic history of two peoples weighed him down. For a moment, the vision of submerging forever appealed to him. A voice reached out to him, "Croc! Rrok!"

Ryan filled his lungs and exhaled slowly to calm his beating heart. He fought the tugging river mud to shore, picked up his feathered friend, and sequestered to a waterside rock. Through the morning and long past midday, he poked the wet sand with a sharp stick. He tried to rationalize ways to farm and ignore the Algonquins, but he could not abandon his ideals. He considered paying them, but rejected the plan as mere compensation for theft. Zak sat on his shoulder, cooing.

His stick poking faded to occasional jabs in the sand. The young raven's growing hunger finally broke the spell.

"Zaak!"

Ryan tossed his stick in the water and approached the campfire. Without a word, Grandmother placed a wooden bowl of beans from her riverside garden and chopped fish in his hands. He fed Zak and then himself.

Nick approached and crouched beside him while the sun fell away from the river valley. "You can ignore Grandfather. If you do not farm, another white man come. Nothing changes"

"I cannot," Ryan replied. From a pocket, he pulled his land grant paper. With a sigh, he tossed it in the flames. "'Tis the end of that."

The boy, now nearly a man, and the young man, recently a boy, stared at sparks rising from the fire while the grandparents prepared the camp for night.

"Nick, can I stay with yer family? Can I learn yer ways?"

His eyebrows shot up. "I like idea. Wait. I ask Grandfather."

Grandfather joined Nick and Ryan by the fire. Nick spoke for the old man.

"Grandfather say he show you how be one of us if you teach me how be one of you."

"What can I teach you?"

"Grandfather say I must learn how live once forests and moose gone. Can you show me how use tools to shape wood?"

"Carpentry! Yes."

Nick and Grandfather conversed.

"I learned talk English but I can read only little," said the boy. "Can you help me read and write more?"

"I can try."

"Can you tell me how make big numbers from small numbers, and small numbers from big numbers?

"Addition and subtraction. Yes."

The boy spoke with Grandfather. The old man nodded to Ryan to seal the deal.

*****

Ryan's first hunting lesson came the next morning. Ten minutes into the bush, Grandfather halted and scolded Ryan in rapid Algonquian. The man's jowls and long gray hair shook in anger.

Nick translated. "Grandfather say good name for you is Thunderfoot. He say you must hope all animals are deaf or you go hungry."

"I wasn't making that much noise."

"Three times you step on stick and tell forest some big thing comes. You make little stumble two times. That noise not natural. Any game hearing it knows hunter comes."

Grandfather barked again.

"Grandfather say you must learn walk like fox, not duck."

"I don't walk like a duck."

"You do. Like most white people, you move legs forward in—I can't remember English word, when two things go in same direction?"

"Tandem? Parallel?"

"Yes, parallel. I show you."

Exaggerating all his movements to make a point, Nick paced back and forth with his feet splayed out. He pushed off with his heel at each step, his legs wide apart, and his shoulders hunched forward. Grandfather smirked.

"See, when you step, feet move parallel with toes turned like duck foot. Fox walk this way." Nick straightened his back. He lifted his feet using the muscles of his upper legs with his toes pointed forward. "With fox, each paw go in front of other paw. Learn fox walk. Is better way."

Ryan tried to copy him.

"Place each foot in front. No put heel down first like white men do. Put outside edge of foot on ground first and roll to inside."

For the rest of the hunt, Ryan practiced fox walking. It seemed unnatural, but he adapted. Grandfather did not bellow at him again that day, though he did give him several stern looks.

*****

The second week, the two young men traveled up the creek to fetch the rest of Ryan's belongings. At his old camp, they rested on rocks by the gurgling rapids, wordless in the grove's numinous majesty.

"Good spirits live here," Nick said. "I see why you happy in this place."

"'Tis all yers now."

"Nothing is ours now."

The passing days fell into a pattern. In the mornings, Grandfather and Nick showed Ryan how to track, hunt, and set traps for fish and mammals. Grandmother taught him how to skin animals, to cure pelts, and how to turn hides into boots, gloves, and clothing.

Zak became Ryan's second shadow. By midsummer, he'd grown into a handsome creature with strong wings and a majestic beak. Grandmother said Zak had a special spirit.

In the afternoons, Nick became the student. Ryan started by teaching English numbers and measurements—knowledge a carpenter needs. Lacking a chalkboard, he used wet sand and a stick to show basic addition and subtraction. For math and reading, he drew on lessons from his best teachers in Ireland.

He taught Nick multiplication and division, and drilled him whenever possible, even when they stalked game in the mornings with Grandfather.

"See those three does in the meadow," said Ryan. "If each doe has two fawns and then each fawn grows up to be a doe, and if all does from both generations have two more, how many deer are there?"

"If wolves not eat any," Nick began, "there be twenty-seven. But after I shoot that fat one, most we have is eighteen. I think eighteen is enough."

For carpentry, he passed on lessons from his father and grandfather. Ryan showed Nick how to make boards from a log and smooth them with a plane; how to shape wood with an adze, drawknife, and spoke shave; and, how to join lumber with wooden dowels and dovetail joints. He demonstrated how to set the iron blade in the plane's wooden form so that it cut shavings as thin as a hair, and how to sharpen tool edges with a file and whetstone.

Reading lessons included words written in wet sand with a stick. Once Nick learned several dozen nouns and common verbs, Ryan let him read his one novel, *Gulliver's Travels* by Jonathan Swift. Ryan worried his friend might not comprehend satire and take the tales literally. Nick surprised him. He found the stories of tiny men, giants, flying islands, and talking horses hilarious. He suggested Swift was surely inflicted with strange visions to have written such a book.

The more Nick read, the better his spoken English became.

By summer's end, Nick had built a modest post-and-beam shanty and its furniture, and could read every passage in *Gulliver's Travels*. Ryan could stalk and shoot a buck, butcher it himself, cure the hide, and turn it into a comfortable jacket.

*****

One afternoon in late summer while Grandfather checked his trap line, Nick and Ryan reposed on a ridge of exposed rock on pillows of sage gray reindeer lichen. Herbal scents rose from the sun-baked rock. Whiffs of pine and spruce wafted up from the dark woods below. Zak perched nearby, snoozing.

"To hunt well," Nick began, "it is not necessary you make no noise. Our world is never silent. The noise you make must not stand out from the noise that is always around you. Listen. Tell me what you hear."

Ryan closed his eyes and concentrated. "I hear the maple leaves fluttering in the breeze. There's a squeaking sound of a tree rubbing another in the wind. There's rustling of old leaves that may be a chipmunk foraging on the forest floor. I hear the buzz of a thousand insects and the calls of dozens of birds."

"Send your ears further downhill. Block out other sounds and tell me what remains."

He sifted through all the noises around him, trying to shut them out. Finally, one sound remained. "I hear something like chiseling wood."

"Yes. A beaver is cutting a tree by the marsh. Go grab him by the tail."

"Are ye crazy? Tis impossible."

"Is possible for an Algonquin. Maybe impossible for an Irish."

Ryan rose. "Ye dare me now, do ye?"

Nick nodded. "Remember those sounds you heard and be part of them."

Ryan stepped into the dark forest and paused. He examined the ground ahead and mapped a route that had the least undergrowth. He fox-walked forward. His eyes fixed ahead, Ryan read the ground's rough contours through his moccasin soles.

When the wind rose and the leaves fluttered briskly, he stepped faster. As the breeze faded, he stopped, and then took short steps with varying pauses between each; that way, his sounds had no pattern. If the chipmunk rustled the old leaves, he shuffled through the leaf debris. Soon, he could see the beaver a hundred yards away engrossed in gnawing a young maple.

Ryan memorized the pattern in its chewing sounds: scrap, scrap, scrap, scrap, pause, and repeat. He crouched to hide his silhouette, moved four short steps in time with the beaver's bites, and paused behind a tree.

The beaver shifted around the maple to chew the other side. It now faced Ryan, who held himself rock still behind a pine trunk and waited. The chiseling sound paused when the beaver shifted sides. Once more, the big rodent faced away. Ryan slipped to within ten yards and paused to slow his beating heart.

He heard a faint rustling to the left. A wolf entered the grassland bordering the marsh. The beaver spotted the predator and dove into the water with a smack of its fat tail. Ryan charged from the forest screaming and flung a rock at the startled canine.

On the hilltop, Ryan found Nick lying on his back on the thick cushion of lichen, trying to breathe through peels of laughter.

"I almost had him. Tis not fair to laugh."

Nick snorted and rolled over on his side, holding his belly.

"I would have grabbed his tail in another minute if not for the wolf."

Nick wheezed, "Only a crazy white man tries to grab a beaver by the tail."

Nick pounded a fist into the lichen in unbridled hilarity. Ryan's shocked expression gave away to a smile. He pulled the stopper from his canteen and poured the contents over the boy's head. Nick sat bolt upright, sputtering.

"I did that for yer own good. Ye were about to pass out."

"If you did grab his tail, what you do with forty pounds of mad beaver," Nick asked.

Ryan hooted at the he vision Nick's question created and flopped down beside him. They laughed and howled until Grandfather returned and scolded them for making too much noise.

*****

In mid-September, MacFarlane rowed upriver from Pakenham Mills in the morning mist hunting migrating geese. Passing the Indian camp as dawn's effulgence flooded the river valley, he spotted Ryan skinning a muskrat. The young Indian boy crouched beside him shaping an axe handle with a drawing knife. Sturdy new wooden tables and chairs littered the Indian camp.

"What manner of topsy-turvy is this?" MacFarlane called out from off shore.

"Mr. MacFarlane! Welcome. Come ashore, please." Ryan calmed the uneasy grandparents with a few words in Algonquian.

"Let me introduce ye to my friend. Mr. MacFarlane, this is Nick. Nick, this is Mr. MacFarlane."

Nick held out his hand. "Pleased to meet you, sir. Welcome to our home."

Startled by the formal greeting from a native, MacFarlane shook the boy's hand and uttered a limp, "Thank you."

"So good to see ye, sir. Such a summer I've had."

"Aren't you supposed to be farming?"

"Take a seat, sir. Have some Indian tea. I have a story to tell."

MacFarlane listened to Ryan's reasons for giving up farming and frowned. "It makes no sense to me, lad. Someone will farm that land. Wouldn't it be better to stay and have an Indian-friendly farmer in the area?"

"I cannot be party to the theft of their country. What we're doing here is worse than the English stealing Ireland. There are millions of Irish. Someday we'll take our country back. But settlers already outnumber the Algonquin."

"What are your plans, then?"

"Nick and his family are leaving soon for their winter camp. I plan to journey down the Rideau helping with harvests and search for carpentry work when I reach Kingston. Do ye know the best route?"

"My advice is to canoe this river as far as Ferguson Falls. Farmers pass that hamlet on their way to market. They can take your canoe to Perth. From there, you can paddle down the Tay River to the Rideau system. It leads straight to Kingston."

"Thank ye. I'll do as ye advise."

After a cup of herbal tea, MacFarlane said good-bye and sculled away downstream, but not before he paid Nick a shilling for a pine table. Buoyed by his first sale, Nick showed the coin to everyone in the camp several times.

*****

That evening around the fire, Grandfather told Ryan to choose a proper name.

"What is wrong with my name?" he asked in Algonquian.

"It means nothing. It is only noise. It does not speak of you."

"What do you suggest?"

"You must take your own name, like Zak and Kokokòho. Look inside you."

Ryan stared at the embers and let his mind wander through a tableau of images from the past months. Visions of soaring eagles, powerful bears, clever wolves, majestic bucks, mighty rivers, earth-shuddering thunderstorms, and all manner of beauty in fish and fowl came to mind. One image appeared three times, and he twice rejected it. When the image persisted, he asked for advice.

"When I first paddled to the white man's village downriver, I saw one big pine alone agin the sky. A vision of that tree haunts me. Should that be my name?"

Grandfather said no. To Ryan's surprise, Grandmother jumped into the conversation. The old couple argued for some minutes at a pace that Ryan could not follow. Grandfather ultimately shrugged his shoulders in resignation.

"If the tree keeps entering your thoughts," Grandmother began, "you must not ignore it. My husband does not think tree names are good people names, but he knows I am closer to the spirits and he now agrees."

"I guess my new name is Lone Pine. How is that said in your language?"

"We have no easy words for that."

"Should I pick another name?"

"No," Grandfather replied. "Speak the name in your own language. I see no reason to say it in our words."

"You must now think of yourself as Lone Pine," Grandmother explained. "The spirits know you by that name. You can use your old name with the settlers because the importance of names is lost to the white man."

"I will use part of my old name and my new name, to honor both my families."

*****

Summer school ended one chilly morning in October. For days maple trees had shed red leaves into the river, and a fuzzy layer of hoarfrost coated the wilted reeds and grasses at dawn. Nick and Grandfather dismantled the family tent and readied their canoe for travel.

Nick explained they had a winter camp near the Mississippi River's headwaters where they could still find moose. No one spoke a word on the subject, but Ryan knew the Algonquins expected him to go his own way soon.

The two canoes abandoned the camp with Zak flying overhead. For two days, Ryan journeyed with his friends. On the third morning, they parted at Ferguson Falls.

Ryan gave Nick several woodworking tools—an axe, saw, drawknife, plane, file, and a whetstone. He kissed Grandmother on the forehead, much to her embarrassment, and gave her one of his mother's sturdy iron pots. He handed Grandfather a hunting knife that had belonged to his late father, in a leather sheath made by his grandfather. When Ryan explained the knife's history, the old man nodded in the manner Ryan now knew to be a sign of respect and gratitude.

Nick gave Ryan moose hide winter boots lined with muskrat fur. Grandfather handed him a new tomahawk. Grandmother hung a talisman around his neck, a round disk of tanned moose hide with porcupine quills sewn in the shape of a windblown pine. She said it would bring him luck.

Tears dribbled down Ryan's face as he said farewells to the grandparents in Algonquian. Lastly, he put his hands on his friend's shoulders. "I'll miss ye Nika Wabizi. Ye have taught me so much."

"I have learned much from you too, Lone Pine."

"It saddens me to think I may nary see ye again."

"Grandmother had a vision where our paths do cross. She is sure it will happen but she says it is many years away."

"Is she right?"

"She is sometimes wrong but her visions are always right." Nick grinned. "We will meet again."

They paddled away without a look back. Ryan fought tears as he lost his second family.

Smuggler's Apprentice

Ryan awoke in a proper bed for the first morning since he sailed from Ireland. He snuggled beneath the covers and sniffed the air-dried scent lingering on the clean pillowcase. Then remembering he promised to spend a day on the river with Bill's comely daughter, he abandoned the bed's comforts for a quick breakfast of porridge sweetened with wild strawberries and maple syrup.

He pulled his boots on under the porch covering and crossed to the Johnston wharf. He tossed fish bits into the air for Zak until Kate arrived carrying a wicker picnic basket.

"Are you ready, Mr. Pine?"

"I am, Miss Johnston."

They grinned at their faux formality as they slid Kate's river skiff into the water. Ryan set the oars in the oarlocks and rowed facing Kate in the stern. She lounged elegantly against the wicker backrest, with her full skirt pulled an inch above her ankles. Zak scanned the river ahead from his bow perch.

"Which way do we go?" Ryan asked.

"See those two islets straight ahead? Pass by the upstream end of the west-most one."

The clinker-built skiff—narrow and pointed at both ends—sliced through the glassy water, its v-shaped wake the sole surface disturbance on that windless May morning. Ryan soon eased into the physical rhythm of rowing, an exercise that frees the mind to wonder. He admired the natural scenery…and his passenger. When Kate glanced away, his eyes traced the curve of her neck, caressed the thinness of her waist, and rested on the tantalizing glimpse of her bare ankles.

In ten minutes, he had rowed the half-mile distance to a teardrop-shaped island. A hill of broken rock topped with scruffy trees rose thirty feet from the river.

"This is Governors Island. You can land a boat at the low end. It serves as lookout point and a temporary drop-off for goods or people. It is easily watched from the second floor of our house."

Ryan smiled at her officious tone.

"Now, go over to Grindstone Island," she said, pointing, "the big one ahead, and go upstream following its shore."

"Yes, ma'am," he said, smiling.

Twenty minutes later, the skiff coasted into the shallows of Grindstone Island, a steep-sided, hilly island of dense forest.

"To visit all our hideouts and depots around this island, we will be out all day. If you need me to row for awhile, I trust you will be man enough to ask."

"Only if we're far enough away none can see us." He laughed. "Tis not hard work. Besides, I've nary rowed a craft so swift and easy as this."

"Father bought this skiff from a builder near Cape Vincent reputed to make the lightest and fastest boats."

The narrow boat sliced the clear water, startling fish at its approach.

"I love it out here," she said. "I have explored every nook and cranny of these islands from Kingston to Alexandria Bay."

"Sounds like ye were a tomboy."

She laughed. "Yes. I wore trousers until mother forbade it two years ago. I row whenever I can." She held up her palms. "I still have the calluses to prove it."

Ryan pursed his lips in exaggerated mock disapproval.

"Do you believe me less a lady?"

"I like ye the way ye are," he replied with too much enthusiasm. Feeling himself blush, he changed the subject. "Do ye help Bill smuggle?"

"No. My brothers help with that. Since I was sixteen, I have spied for Father."

"By yerself?"

"Yes, in my canoe or skiff. My job is to tell him if the British are on patrol and what other smugglers are up to."

"Why does Bill care about other smugglers?"

"If I tell you, you must keep it a secret. Only a few people know."

"Surely. I'm not known for my loose lips."

"Until recently, Father worked for the Revenue Service. He reported on smugglers coming over from the Canadian side."

"So, yer saying Bill spied on Canadian smugglers coming into America at the same time he smuggled goods to Canada."

"Exactly. The Revenue Service knew he smuggled, and they turned a blind eye to it since he moves most of his goods one way."

"Bill's not working for them now?"

"No. He stopped when Mr. Mackenzie appointed him Patriot navy commodore. Father did not want to embarrass his friends in the service."

They neared a dense stand of rushes growing from the water at the island's head.

"Change your course a tad to starboard—that is your left—and head to that small island off the tip of Grindstone," Kate said. She pointed to a tree-covered, granite island about seven hundred feet long and twenty feet high at its peak.

"That is Whiskey Island," she said. Ryan rowed closer. "It gives a clear view for ten miles upriver on both sides of Wolfe Island."

She pointed to a rock face. "See that cliff with the overhanging pines. That is where Father and Hugh spotted the British steamer chasing you."

They crossed the short gap back to Grindstone and followed the north shore twenty yards out. For several minutes, Kate silently focused on the passing island.

"This island is perfect for smugglers or anyone living outside the law. The border is a short distance from the north shore. You can see patrol ships coming from miles away and pick an opening to cross."

Zak flew up from the bow.

"What is he doing?"

"Exercising his wings."

Zak soared above the island's forest canopy. Trees rose from the river in tiers, often with three or four distinct layers. Near the water grew willows, ash, and birch. Next up the slope, hundred-foot oaks with dark, polished leaves rose above the island's cliffs. Massive red and white pines capped the cliff tops. Their great height reminded him of Ada.

"What brings yer cousin Ada from Upper Canada?"

"Mother invited her. With Father now involved with the Patriots, I believe she needs the support."

"Her and your mother seem close."

"Yes. Ada came to live with my parents as a girl. She escaped Canada with Mother and Jim in 1813. She lived with my parents until she married. That was before I was born." Kate paused and tilted her head. "Why the interest in Ada?"

"Just curious."

"Men are always curious about my cousin."

"Are men also curious about ye?'

"Are you?"

Ryan smiled and looked her in the eye. He expected her to blush and turn away. Instead, she held his gaze with unblinking intensity.

"I suppose I am."
"You suppose! When you are sure, let me know."
"Aren't ye curious about me?"
"No," she answered with teasing smile.

*****

An hour later their skiff rounded a headland.
"This is Thurso Bay," she said. "Turn in here and follow close to the lee shore." She pointed at the cliff base. "Look above the waterline below those cedars and wild grape vines, see it?"
He peered into the foliage shadows. "I see nary a thing."
"Row closer. Slowly."
He rowed to within an oar's length of the rock wall and let their craft drift. "I see it now. A flat ledge of rock."
"You can pull several boats out there and a whole fleet passing by will not notice you," she explained. "During the war, Father sometimes attacked the British bateaux and Durham boats from this bay. He could move unseen," she pointed north, "through that long string of Canadian islands and surprise them. If a British gunship chased him, he portaged from the head of this bay across the island."
"I know now why the British go crazy when they hear his name."
"I wish he was not so infamous."
"Are ye worried?"
She sighed. "Let us return to the channel and continue downstream. Stay between Grindstone and all the islands on our port side. Most of those are in British territory."
Three miles further they passed the mouth of a narrow bay.
"This is Delaney Bay. It cleaves Grindstone nearly in two. At the far end is a short portage to the south side."
"Are ye going to show me the portage point?"
"We have no time for that today. Keep heading east for now."
"Yes, boss," he teased.
She stuck out her tongue.

*****

At the eastern end of Grindstone Island, Kate pointed to a lone island. "That is Fort Wallace, one of Father's special hideouts."
"Want me to row over?"

68

"Not now. We do not land there by day. It is too easy to be seen. Keep following this shore until it bends south. I know a nice spot where we can stop for lunch."

They picnicked on a sloping field of wildflowers and long grass. Kate led them to a cluster of flat rocks beneath an ancient oak tree. They had a panoramic view of Wells Island—large, steep, and forest covered—a mile east across the blue St. Lawrence. Zak landed on a branch above.

"Kach! Kood!"

"Did he speak English?"

"Yes. He wants someone to play the catch-food game with him. He's a natural mimic and smart enough to know how to ask for food."

"Amazing," she said, reaching into her picnic basket for bread crusts.

"Have ye involved yerself in the Patriot troubles?"

"No. Not directly." She unpacked the lunch, handed Ryan an egg sandwich, and tossed another bread crust. Zak swooped and caught the crust in midair.

"Ye say 'not directly.' Is there a meaning in those words?"

"One day when the Patriots held Hickory Island, I had to guard a prisoner."

"For true? Did ye tie him up and hold a pistol on him?"

"No. No. He was a nice man from Gananoque. Father thought he was a spy and put him in our sitting room with a guard outside. Mother and I served him tea and chatted. He was so taken with our company that he seemed sad to be released."

"I understand his disappointment," he replied with exaggerated sincerity.

Kate ignored his remark and studied Zak on his perch.

"What do you admire most about your bird?"

"'Tis his freedom. He can live his life unbound by politics or history."

"He is free to leave anytime. Why does he stay when no tether holds him?"

"Zak stays because I raised him, feed him, and protect him."

She shifted her eyes to Ryan. "I feel in some way he is a replacement for your lost family." She lay on her back in the grass. "Someone to watch over you."

"I nary mentioned my family. How'd ye know?"

"It is easy to read the empty places in your sentences."

He sighed and lay beside her propped up on one elbow. Her eyes closed, she wore a faint smile. This close, he observed the length of her eyelashes and the little dimple in her chin. He thought her lips—with the fuller lower lip and the pronounced central groove in the upper lip—perfect. He couldn't shift his eyes from her warm, pink mouth.

"If you try to kiss me, I will smack you," she said, without opening her eyes.

"What!"

She jerked up and grabbed his chin. "It is too soon to be taking liberties, Mr. Pine."

She rose and brushed grass from her dress.

"Let us continue."

She packed the picnic dishes while Ryan slipped the skiff into the water.

"Are you tired yet? I can row well, you know."

"In Ireland, I hoed fields all day since I was a boy," he answered. "I cut firewood all last winter. I'm used to this type of work."

"How much rowing have you done?"

"Not much lately. I paddle often."

"As I suspected. You have no rowing muscles. Canoeing is not the same. You will hardly be able to lift an arm tomorrow."

"I doubt that very much."

"As you wish. I will take the oars eventually. Like your bird, I need exercise too."

*****

Ryan kept close to the big island's shore, rowing in and out of reedy bays.

"It seems to me," he began, "thinking over what I've learned of Bill so far, he takes many risks in his war on the British."

Kate stared at the passing hills of Grindstone. "He does. Even when he is not fighting the British, smuggling comes with risks. There is no law in these islands and every man is armed."

"Still, ye and yer family seem well provided for."

"We are prosperous now, but not always. My parents lost everything when they fled Canada. Most of my life, I can remember being short of money for clothes and good furniture. Much of our food came from fishing and hunting. In the last years, since Father opened his warehouse and store, we have done well."

"Now Bill's organizing armies and raids for the Patriots. I'd expect a man his age to settle down."

Kate hooted. "Not my father. At least not yet. He is a living legend in these islands, and he revels in that role. He relishes leading a crew on a smuggling trip. I believe he would rather perish at the end of a rope than die of boredom."

"I hope it nary comes to that. The rope business I mean."

"I doubt it. He fights hard and moves fast. He is difficult to capture and says no jail can keep him unless he decides to stay. I do worry he may go too far, though."

*****

In a half hour they cleared the southeastern end of Grindstone Island. Kate directed Ryan to land the skiff at a rocky beach on the east side of an island in sight of Clayton.

"This is Abel's Island. Father uses it to store goods."

With Zak on his shoulder, Ryan followed Kate along a narrow path through thick second-growth forest. They emerged into a clearing dominated by two wooden shanties made of rough-cut pine boards. Several gigs and skiffs of various lengths lay on their sides near stacks of oars and unmarked barrels. A well-muscled man of Ryan's height rose from a log stump seat by a cooking fire.

"Welcome Miss Catherine. Hello Ryan."

"Scanlon! Why are ye here?"

"It's my home when the weather's warm. I guard the place fer Bill. Come on over to the fire. I've coffee brewed."

Scanlon poured coffee into three metal cups and, knowing Ryan's tastes, added maple syrup to one. Zak perched on a shanty roof waiting for someone to toss food.

"Careful now. Them cups are hot."

They sat on stumps next to a cook fire and blew on the hot liquid.

"Thank you Hugh. This is delightful. I adore camp coffee. Ryan could use a rest. Poor boy has been rowing me around like a queen all day."

"That's ye fer sure Miss Catherine, the Queen of the Thousand Islands."

"Yer the only royalty I'd ever row for."

"Such a lovely afternoon for coffee in the woods with two gentlemen."

Scanlon passed a tin of biscuits and at Ryan's bidding tossed one in the air for Zak to catch. "So Ryan," he began, "did ye e'er hear the story of when I supped with the departing gov'ner of Upper Canada?"

"Who's that?"

"He means Sir Francis Bond Head. Until recently he was the lieutenant-governor of Upper Canada."

"That's him. The very man that let the Family Compact drive people into rebellion."

"How'd ye come to be having a meal with that bug?"

"Well, I'll tell ye." Scanlon chewed on a biscuit for a minute, ordering the details in his head. "In March I was staying at Luther Gibson's hotel in Watertown. In walks Judge Jonas Jones, one of the biggest swells in the Family Compact. He's alone except fer an odd servant fellow. The hotel's full of Canadian refugees and American Patriots. The judge acted like a fox cornered by hounds. None lifted a finger to harm him, but he was given the benefit of many harsh opinions on the state of Canadian politics."

"Where's Bond Head in all this?"

"Be patient. I'm getting to that part. More coffee, Miss Catherine?"

"Yes please, Hugh."

He poured her another cup.

"When talking to the judge, I notice his servant slink off. After he'd been gone a bit, I went searching fer him. I found him sitting in a wheelbarrow in the stable looking all glum. I come up close and recognize him. Jeez, if it ain't Sir Francis himself, the man who led the militia against Mackenzie's men in Toronto. So, we start chatting. I tell him he'll come to no harm at our hands, though I dearly wanted to kick his arse. Pardon my language, Miss Catherine."

"Do not worry Hugh. Please carry on. I love this story."

"So, Sir Francis the jerk tells me he's called back to England. He's afraid to travel in Canada because people hate him. So he decides to go in disguise to New York. The judge insists on being his guard. I tell him that he badly bungled things in Upper Canada, and would ye believe it, he half agrees with me. So, I invite him to dinner and introduce him to the lads."

"How'd they take it?"

"Ryan, we ain't the murderers and scoundrels the Family Compact colors us as. We're fighters in a noble cause. In a convivial mood that day, we bought Judge Jones and Sir Francis the best meal the hotel offered, and sent them off with three rousing cheers."

"Is that story true?"

"It is," Kate answered.

"What did Bill say when ye told him the story?"

"He said I should have handed Sir Francis over to Mackenzie. He had a five-hundred-pound reward on his head."

"Tis a lot of money."

"For sure, but I doubt Mackenzie ever had five pence to spare. Besides, our action was the nobler."

After an hour trading stories and badinage over coffee, Kate put down her cup. "Evening nears gentlemen. Mother will be angry if we are late for supper."

The three young people and the raven returned to the skiff. To Ryan's surprise, Zak perched on Kate's shoulder for the walk to the beach.

"Zak's nary ridden on any other but me. It seems ye can charm more than men."

"Like any male, he gravitates to the source of good meals."

"Are we that easy to manipulate?"

"You are. Now sit in the stern. It is my turn to row. I insist."

Zak landed on his usual bow perch. Ryan took the unfamiliar seat in the stern. He tried to take Kate's turn at rowing casually but his face reddened when Scanlon couldn't resist a parting dig at Ryan.

"Hey, look who's queen of the islands now."

*****

Bill sent Ryan out with a smuggling crew under Scanlon's command the next day. They set out from the wharf at first light in a blue gig designed for six men to row in pairs, one oar per man. Everyone wore blue shirts. As usual, Zak rode on the bow or flew overhead.

Ryan's shoulders, biceps, and triceps ached as if someone had attempted to twist his arms off. He tried to keep the discomfort to himself but he couldn't hide it from Scanlon.

"Ryan, lad. Did ye fall out of a tree? Yer face looks mighty pained at times."

The crew sniggered at Scanlon's teasing.

"Tis nothing. Just pulled a wee muscle this morning."

The crew propelled the boat around the upstream end of Grindstone Island to Thurso Bay on the north side. From there they crossed into Canadian waters and hopped through a chain of islands. At each island, Scanlon landed the gig and climbed to a high point to scan the river with a telescope. When assured of clear passage to the next island, he let them row on. Bill insisted on such precautions during daylight runs, Scanlon explained.

They landed in a bay on the St. Lawrence's north shore and met several silent farmers. With the crew's help, they moved the contraband bales of tea onto wagons and covered them with straw. Scanlon pocketed a roll of pound notes and they headed home.

Late in a warm evening two days later, Ryan joined a smuggling crew dressed in dark clothing. Their captain was Bill's eldest son, Jim. In appearance, he was a younger, thinner version of his father. Twenty-nine, unmarried, and quiet by nature, he kept his own counsel. When he did speak, he had an odd falsetto voice in contrast to his father's baritone. Old friends called him Squealin' Jim.

Jim directed the gig past the downstream end of Grindstone Island, across to the west end of Wells Island, and up along its north side. With a moon sliver faintly illuminating the dark river, Jim ordered everyone to rest oars. The boat drifted towards a gap between two rocky islands.

"That channel ahead is Fiddler's Elbow." Jim directed the comment to Ryan. "It's part of the shipping route on the Canadian side."

Ryan peered at the Stygian channel between gray island silhouettes.

"And that near island to starboard is Depot Island, one of our hideouts. Ten men with rifles or one cannon can control the channel's approach from there."

"A most strategic position!"

"It is. Father did lots of scouting and spying in the war. He used that island often. I'm sure he'll tell you some stories."

"I'd enjoy that."

Their gig entered Fiddler's Elbow, a narrow channel framed by sheer granite cliffs. The river rushed through it like water down the narrow end of a funnel. The river roiled up from the rocky bottom. Powerful eddies peeled off from jutting points on Ash and Wallace Islands. Jim wrestled the tiller to keep the gig in mid-channel.

Out of the channel they continued northeast. In places, steep islands loomed so close together that their trees formed a dark canyon with a ribbon of starry night sky above. Jim steered them into a deep bay on the Canadian shore crowded with willows and rushes. Again they met silent men with hay wagons and exchanged tea for money.

On the return journey, Ryan hummed a quiet tune. The biting insects—persistent tormentors in the otherwise perfect spring—

couldn't find them out on the river. Owl hoots from Kokokòho and the repetitive calls of whip-poor-wills cut the still night air. Ryan reveled in the team exertion propelling the six-man boat. The harmony of human muscle power in each sweep of oars and the whoosh of rushing water at the bow relaxed his mind and banished bad memories.

Not a bad life, he thought.

Back in Clayton in the growing dawn light, Jim paid Ryan his share of profits from the last two smuggling runs. He ate a quick breakfast of eggs and toast at the Johnston home and hurried to the Water Street shops. He intended to buy new clothes and shed the Johnston hand-me-downs. He found cotton shirts and trousers more practical for everyday summer garb than buckskins. He chose neutral colors to better blend in with the forest and rocky shores.

Once again, Ryan began to taste prosperity.

*****

The next day, surprising everyone, Ryan moved out. He tried to explain his decision to Kate and her mother.

"I've an income now and feel I should pay my way and stand on my own. I'm renting a room in Bill's warehouse and I've fixed up a shanty on Abel's Island, where I'll spend some nights with Scanlon."

"Are you not comfortable with us?" Ann asked.

"Too comfortable. I fear 'tis making me soft. Ever since my summer with the Algonquins, I prefer the feel of a hard bed and the chill of a morning's bath in a river. It'll just be for the summer."

"You can sleep in the yard and throw yourself in the harbor each day if you want," Ann replied. "At least here you have good meals."

"Yes. Your cooking is the finest, and if ye don't mind, I'll stop by regular for yer heavenly fare. I just prefer the owls hooting at night over the clatter of a town and the brawling of drunks."

"Suit yourself. Bring your clothes for a proper wash. No use smelling like you live in the woods."

"Listen to Mother. Do not grow too woodsy or you really will be Lone Pine," Kate added with a smile.

Pirate's Helper

On Ryan's second morning staying on Abel's Island, Bill Johnston stalked into the camp and woke him and Scanlon. As they dressed, he paced in darkness thinly diluted by a gray hint of dawn. Two flintlock pistols and a dirk hung on his wide leather belt.

"You two, come with me. I have in mind to show you something."

"Gee, Bill. We ne'er heard ye arrive," Scanlon murmured through the strands of brown hair flopped over his face.

Ryan eyed Bill. Until then, Ryan viewed the pistol-packing bogeyman stories of Bill as apocryphal, mere beer-inspired tavern embellishments. Tugging on his boots, he wondered if the legend reflected the real man or the man lived up to the legend.

Not daring to complain about missing breakfast, Ryan trotted behind his impatient captain to the shore where ten rough-looking strangers waited beside a long gig painted yellow and red. Obviously not a smuggling craft, Ryan thought. Scanlon nodded greetings to several men as he tied back his hair. Bill introduced Ryan and addressed the crew.

"Each of us has a distinct history," Bill pontificated, "with one thing in common." He hooked his thumbs into his weapons belt and marched back and forth, crunching gravel on the stony beach. "We be all refugees from Canada, driven out for one unjust reason or another. Each of us looks to the day we can even the score. That chance be coming soon."

Zak squirmed on Ryan's shoulder. Bill had never appeared so menacing.

"Ryan, do you know the way to our hideout at Fiddler's Elbow?"

"Yes, sir."

"Good. Then, take the tiller. I will row. I need me some exercise."

"Why's he on the tiller?" asked a short, heavyset man named John Farrow. "By rights, it's my turn. I've been longest with this crew."

"Shut it, Farrow. I will tell you when it be your turn."

As the first robins tuned up their voices for the dawn chorus, the twelve-oared gig pushed off and picked up speed. The boat seated six pairs of men each pulling one long oar. It flew across the glassy water so fast that when Zak raised his wings on the bow, the wind launched him into the air. Ryan grinned at the boat's speed and grace while he guided the team of synchronized muscles through the Thousand Islands' morning magnificence.

In the effulgent glow of a fresh sunrise, they fought the jerky currents near Fiddler's Elbow and pulled into a sheltered cove on the upstream end of Depot Island. They carried the gig across a cobbled beach to a hidden boat ramp in the trees. The crew climbed to the island's rocky spine and waited under cover of pines, oaks, and maples.

A dark smudge appeared on the western horizon—the telltale smoke from a steamer's stacks. Bill trained his long glass on the approaching ship.

"That be what we came to see. Take a good look lads when she passes."

Soon a sleek sidewheeler passed so close that Ryan could see the color of sailors' eyes.

"That be the newest steamer on the lake, the *Sir Robert Peel*," Bill bellowed over the steamer's chugging engines and sloshing paddlewheels. "She be one hundred and sixty feet long and thirty across the beam. She runs regular from Niagara to Prescott, usually taking this channel on the downstream leg and the south channel on the upstream leg."

"Did we come to gawk at a ship?" Robert Smith muttered. A balding man in his twenties, he matched Bill in height and girth.

Bill scowled at Smith. "Yesterday that ship dropped off a dozen Patriot prisoners at Kingston. More fodder for the dungeons of Fort Henry. One was John Montgomery. Does that mean anything to you?"

Smith shrugged.

"He ran an inn north of Toronto. Mackenzie's force gathered there last December for their assault. Montgomery didn't lift a finger to help Mackenzie, except to serve him dinner, but the British burned his inn and sentenced him to hang. He be a victim like all of us, a brother."

"Are you figuring to bust him from the fort?" Smith retorted.

"Don't be mad! We cannot attack the fort but we can take revenge. That ship stands for everything we be against. And you know Hugh," he said, turning to Scanlon, "it be part owned by your old friend Judge Jones."

"I had dinner with him once, but we didn't part friends. I can guarantee ye that," said Scanlon as the ship disappeared up the channel.

"Back to the boat, men," Bill ordered.

Ryan noticed several kegs and long objects wrapped in canvas hidden beneath an overhang of rock.

"Bill, what do ye have there?"

"Some munitions. I have stock piles in a dozen hideouts in these islands."

Ryan asked no further questions.

Back on Abel's Island, Bill pulled Ryan aside. "The lads be staying here today. Come home for lunch. You always enjoy Ann's cooking. Besides, there is someone I have in mind for you to meet." Bill motioned two crewmen to carry a gig with two sets of oars to the river.

"Sure Bill. I welcome some food. By the way, where'd ye buy that colorful gig?"

"A shipwright nigh Cape Vincent builds most of my boats. I decided a colorful gig or two would be good for pleasure travel and legitimate commerce."

Bill's bulky muscles and Ryan's youthful vigor propelled the rowboat to Clayton against a wind and light chop. Zak glided ahead, using the headwind for lift. The clear sky of morning had given way to hazy gray and the air smelled of rain coming.

"Bill, I meant to ask ye a question."

"Go ahead."

"I saw a book in yer library I'm curious about. The author is Bonnycastle."

"You mean the history of Spanish America?"

"Yes. Is that the same Bonnycastle?"

"Indeed. He published it twenty years ago."

"Why do ye have it?"

"Writers always give clues to themselves. It be best to know your enemy."

"Sounds sensible."

After a minute of silence, Bill asked, "Did I ever tell you how I captured British plans for an attack on Sackets Harbor?"

"No Bill, but I'd love to hear it."

"It was in late summer of 1814 on Lake Ontario. I was hiding nigh Presqu'ile behind a tree by the main road between Kingston and Toronto used by British military dispatch riders every day. When the westbound rider came close, I jumped out, pistols in hand. I confiscated his weapons and satchel, shot his mount, and sent him home on foot. Then I waited. An hour later, a dispatch rider came from the east. I stopped him, took his dispatches, and sent him home."

"Back in Sackets, we discovered the satchel held plans for another attack on the fleet there. Commodore Isaac Chauncey—he was the

American naval commander—said that having those plans forced the British to cancel the attack."

"Were ye promoted or rewarded?"

"No. I was a spy and privateer. I was Chauncey's secret agent. Other men got glory. I got satisfaction."

*****

At Bill's wharf, a stranger in his late fifties fished in the warehouse's shade.

"Donald," Bill called out. "I have someone you should meet."

The man rested his wooden pole on the warehouse wall and came over. He was Ryan's height, with thinning gray-hair, tanned face, and darting brown eyes.

"Ryan, this be Donald McLeod. He be one of Mackenzie's generals, one of the few with military training, and one of a handful I trust with my life. Donald, this be Ryan."

They shook hands. "Bill told me all about you," McLeod said with a trace of a Scottish accent. Heavily built, he dressed like a shopkeeper—neither poor nor fancy. "You could be a real asset to our cause."

Ryan hesitated. He shifted his eyes to where Zak sat on the warehouse roof. He embraced a smuggler's life but remained undecided about his role with the Patriots.

"I appreciate the compliment, sir."

"Let's not jump ahead of ourselves Donald. He's not a Patriot or Hunter, yet."

"Well. That can be readily amended."

"To lunch! We can talk then."

Ryan forgot his unease as Kate pulled him aside on the porch. "Welcome, Mr. Pine. So nice to have you home after only two days." Kate ran a single finger through the curls above his left ear.

"Kate," Ann called from the house. "Stop pestering the lad and let him come to the table. We're all waiting." They exchanged smiles and joined the family in the dinning room for a meal of fresh bread, grilled fish, asparagus shoots, and strawberry pie. Ryan nodded to Bill's sons and smiled at Ann and Ada.

"Everyone knows General McLeod," Bill began. "I invited him to bring us the latest news on the Hunters Lodge."

McLeod swept his gaze around the table, meeting each person's eyes. Conversation stopped. The sound of cutlery scraping plates dimmed to a level quieter than the parlor clock's gentle ticking.

"We have hundreds of Canadian refugees living in America, most in this state. Many Americans have sided with them, angered over the *Caroline*. That's a British atrocity men pledge to avenge. The monsters who could plan, and the savages who could perpetrate a deed so dreadfully horrible and so terribly appalling ought, in all conscience, to be served in the same manner." He paused. "Ann, this is excellent fish."

"Thank Decatur and Kate. They caught it this morning."

"Ah, yes, but the chef prepared it to perfection."

"Let's say it was a family effort."

"Quite right. Where was I?"

"Ye mentioned the *Caroline* and angry Americans," Ryan replied.

"Yes. The lodge formed to harness that burgeoning anger and organize an army of liberation. The idea is spreading through the border towns like fire in dry grass. Legions of brave men have flocked to our banner. New lodges form weekly in towns as distant as Wisconsin and Maine. The Watertown lodge has over one thousand members alone." He paused to let that number sink in.

"Really, that many?" Decatur asked.

"Yes, lad. My lodge in Lockport also has a thousand."

McLeod glanced across the table to Ryan. "If you desire to join the Watertown lodge, Bill can sponsor you."

Ryan glanced at Bill. The slight raise of his shoulders signaled he could decline the offer without repercussions.

"I must think on that, sir."

"By all means. It is a monumental commitment," McLeod said, sitting back in his chair. He drummed his fingers on the table while he thought over his next words. "Bill tells me your grandfather fought the English in the last Irish rebellion."

"Yes, sir."

"So then, your family has a history of sacrifice in the name of freedom?"

"I suppose, sir."

"The Irish and Canadians both have a right to experience the joys of liberty."

"Well sir, from my time in Canada, I can see Canadians deserve better government but they have far more freedom than any Irishman in Ireland."

McLeod's brow furrowed.

"You should talk to Hugh," Bill began. "He be a Hunter."

"For true?"

"Yes. So be all the men you rowed with this morning."

Ryan focused on the sons. "Are any of ye lads Hunters?"

"Not me," said Jim. "I've no interest in politics."

"Napoleon and I," John began, glancing at his older brother, "are trying to establish business careers. The lodge may provide excellent contacts, but the organization borders on illegal. We decided not to risk it."

"I wanted to join," Decatur said, "but Father says I'm too young."

"You see, Ryan," Bill said, "everyone be free to make their own decision," he glanced at Decatur, "once they be of age."

"Are women's opinions allowed?" Ada's question silenced the table. She stared down at the general beside her. He seemed to shrink under her gaze.

"Yes, dear," Ann replied, smiling. "I doubt we could stop you, if we tried."

"I was born not far from here and I've lived on both sides of the border. I agree the Canadian colonies are not well run, but day-to-day life is bearable." She held Ryan captive for a moment with her gold-flecked eyes. "Let the Canadians manage their own affairs and eschew war as long as the British respect American borders and sovereignty."

"My husband already knows my opinion," Ann said. "I'll not say more."

Only Kate had not spoken. All eyes at the table shifted her way, waiting.

"It is not my place to tell men what risks they should or should not take. I doubt you would take my counsel, if I did." She rose from the table. "I believe the tea is ready." At the kitchen door, she paused. "We have no more maple syrup, Ryan. Will honey do?"

"Yes. Thank ye." Turning to McLeod, Ryan said. "As I said, I must think on yer offer, general. For now, I'll help Bill if he needs me."

"By all means!"

*****

Ten days later, Ryan tossed bits of fish in the air for Zak from the Johnston wharf, as he often did. The raven did barrel rolls and steep dives as he chattered and squawked.

Though the end of May, Ryan wore a coat. A chill blew from the east and clouds touched the hills of Grindstone Island. He hummed a tune to himself while he played with Zak. Smuggling suited him—the right mix of physical activity and adventure. And he had money. The account Ann kept for him already totaled more than any sum his father ever amassed. Ryan spent as much time with Kate as her household choirs and his duties allowed. They strolled along Water Street looking in shop windows or meandered along the town's quiet residential streets admiring gardens.

"Life is fine, eh Zak?"

"Kach! Kood!"

At Zak's request, Ryan tossed a fish head in the air.

"Rrok! Cric! Croc!"

Ryan looked over his shoulder as the wharf boards creaked under heavy footsteps. "Gidday, Bill. It's gotten a wee bit wet."

Bill tossed a piece of fish high. Zak swooped, caught it, and swallowed.

"But a fine day for an enterprise, don't you think?"

Ryan recognized the word *enterprise* as a code. "Today?"

"Tonight. After dark."

"What can ye tell me?"

"Keep it to yourself." He paused and looked over his broad shoulder. "Remember that steamer I showed you?"

"The *Peel*?"

"Yes. We plan to take her for the Hunters."

"You mean steal her?"

"I prefer commandeer."

Ryan gazed upstream, rubbing his half finger. Smuggling had been an easy choice—the penalties were minor, if caught. But you could hang for stealing a ship.

"Sounds like piracy."

"In the last war, we captured British ships and they did the same to us."

"Are we at war?"

"I am. I have been since 1813. Aren't you? Remember why you ran from Kingston. Don't forget being cast from the fort to freeze to death."

"Can I think about it?"

Bill nodded. "If you have a mind to join us, be at Abel's Island at dusk. If not, say nothing and sleep in the warehouse tonight."

The last sentence held a hint of menace. "Yes, sir."

"Good. Maybe I'll see you tonight."

*****

Ryan spent the day fishing with Zak for company. He reflected on his grandfather and his reasons for joining the 1798 Irish rebellion. The old man had spoken of his pride in taking up a just cause with no guarantee of success.

Ryan built a fire on Whiskey Island and cooked a lunch of pickerel for himself and the raven. "You know Zak. When I was a boy, my grandfather said 'ye must stand up to the bully even if ye can't win. If not, the bully will ne'er change his ways and ne'er leave ye alone.' What do ye think of that?"

"Croc! Rrok!"

He rowed back to Clayton in the early evening with a string of fish for Ann. The family ate supper in silence, without Bill. Everyone had sensed trouble from the patriarch's furrowed brow before he departed —but only Ryan knew the brash plan. After dessert, he called Kate outside to the covered porch.

"I have some business with Bill tonight. Can ye keep an eye on Zak for me? He'll likely perch in the veranda rafters."

"Of course." She caressed his cheek with her right hand. "I do not know what Father is up to, but I do know you can stay out of it. He will not hold it against you."

"I know." He shrugged. "But if my friends be in danger, I should be there."

She sighed. "Be careful."

*****

In the late spring twilight, Ryan rowed downstream with the current to Abel's Island. Light rain fell and beaded on his woolen coat. At the shanty camp, armed men talked and drank rum around a bonfire. He recognized Hugh Scanlon, Donald McLeod, Samuel Frey, William Anderson, John Farrow, Robert Smith, Chester and Seth Warner, and others from the earlier trip to view the *Peel*.

In his shanty room, he removed his manufactured clothes and slipped into his Algonquin buckskins. He clipped his tomahawk to his belt, set a wide-brimmed slouch hat on his head, and joined the men at the bonfire.

"Ryan. Glad to see you," Bill hollered. Two pistols and a long-bladed bowie knife hung on his belt. He wore hunting clothes and paced while he talked.

"Men, we be bound for victory. Listen closely. I don't intend to explain this twice."

All chatter ceased.

"Tonight the *Sir Robert Peel* passes up the American Narrows on her regular run to Lake Ontario. She always docks at McDonald's wharf on Well's Island to load wood for her boilers. This time the crew and passengers be in for a surprise. General!"

Sitting by the fire, McLeod picked up the story. "Our plan is to take the *Peel* and use her to capture the big steamer *Great Britain* tomorrow. We'll then use the two steamers to carry troops in our next glorious attack on the British."

"Just the twenty-two of us?" asked Scanlon?

"That be plenty. General McLeod has a pledge of a hundred and fifty armed men to help hold her and sail with us. They shall start arriving by boat soon."

"What of the passengers and crew?" Ryan called from the shadows.

"We will put everyone off at the wharf. Hurt no one unless they draw a weapon. Our fight be not with them." He surveyed the men. "Be there more questions?"

"When do we head out?" Frey said.

"An hour. Prepare yourselves."

Unlike Ryan, the others showed no misgivings. They painted their faces with streaks of color, attached feathers to their hats, and laughed like children at a party.

"Ryan," Scanlon began, "you lived with some Indians. How do we look?"

"Pitiful. Ye look more like clowns than Indians."

Scanlon laughed. "I can see the headlines now: *Sir Robert Peel attacked by clowns*."

McLeod led a lanky stranger over to Ryan. "Have you met Lyman Leach yet?" He pointed to the slim man about forty beside him.

"No, general."

"He's a solid Patriot. He was with us at Hickory Island."

"I brought a company of men from Syracuse for that affair," Leach said.

"I hear 'twas difficult there."

"It was frustrating waiting in the cold for days, yes."

"Now ye are here with us."

"It seems a worthwhile enterprise, if the Hunters are to prevail."

"Worth going to prison for?"

"Worth hanging for." Seeing Ryan's concern, he added, "Don't fret. We'll have fun."

On Bill's orders, they extinguished the bonfire, and a gallimaufry of oddly costumed men boarded two red and yellow gigs. Ryan wondered why they chose the colored gigs for a raid—everyone on the river knew their owner.

They rowed downstream through the American Narrows to Well's Island eastern end. They tied up to trees in the island's shadow and waited. No one spoke. Their silence seemed to amplify the sound of breathing and raindrops plunking into the river.

Minutes after midnight, the *Peel* steamed past the raiders. Ryan admired the steamer's sleek lines and polished woodwork gleaming in the lantern light. The two gigs slipped into the steamer's wake, staying in the shadows beyond her lights. The chug-chug of her steam engines hid their oarlocks' creak.

*****

Captain John Armstrong, in the *Sir Robert Peel*'s pilothouse, moved his helmsman aside and guided his pride and joy to McDonald's wharf. A gray-haired veteran of years in the islands, Armstrong had the self-assurance and arrogance of a man who knew his business better than most. He edged the big steamer towards the dock's downstream side. Mere feet away, Armstrong reversed the paddlewheels for a second and then halted them. The steamer came to a standstill. Two sailors leapt to the dock and secured the ship with thick hawsers. Two other sailors lowered and secured the gang plank. Armstrong ordered the engines shut down and sent most of his crew to their bunks. He then departed to meet the chief woodcutter, James McDonald, on the wharf.

"Evening Jim. Hope you kept the fuel dry in this rain."

"Tis not rain you should worry about tonight, captain."

"Is that so?"

"There's been strange men in long boats lurking around this island."

"If some brigands mean trouble, let them come. I have sixty sturdy male passengers and twenty crew. If they have no more than one hundred and fifty, I am ready."

"Suit yourself, captain, but I'll have my payment in advance tonight, if you please."

"I'll have the purser bring it out shortly. Please commence the loading. I have my schedule to keep."

The head woodcutter signaled two of his men to load the firewood. Armstrong ordered six of his crew to do the same.

As instructed, the steamer's purser opened the locked cabinet in the captain's cabin to count out payment for the woodsman. Besides hundreds of pounds in ship's funds, the shelves held six thousand pounds in transit to pay British troops in Toronto.

The purser noted the payment in a ledger and locked the cabinet. He went ashore to pay the woodcutter, and then retired, expecting a peaceful slumber.

*****

Bill landed his boats at Ripley's wharf, five hundred yards downstream. He called the men together by the light of a single lantern.

"Work your way through these woods and regroup nigh the *Peel* at the clearing edge. Put out the lantern. Be quiet and don't lag."

The pitch-dark forest concealed the narrow trail to McDonald's wharf. Without light, each man forged his own trail. The dark forest filled with muffled curses from sightless raiders stumbling over wind-toppled trees and slipping on the rain-slicked granite rocks. Ryan keyed his ears to the river's gurgle where it sluiced past shoreline rocks. By keeping that aural guide close to his left, he stayed on track in the confounding tangle.

An easy ten-minute walk in daylight became an hour of painful slogging through swamps and tangled brush. Ryan arrived at the clearing wet, sweaty, and bruised. Bill, McLeod, and Scanlon waited beneath a spruce tree on the edge of an acre-sized clearing near the wharf. Anderson, Frey, the Warner brothers, and five others arrived several minutes apart, exhausted and wet, their playfulness gone along with some of their feathers and silly war paint.

"I think the rest be lost in the dark," whispered Scanlon. "Are we going to wait or go searching?"

"Neither," Bill growled. "We have thirteen and that be my lucky number."

"How many men on that steamer, sir?" asked Ryan.

"No matter. We're armed and have surprise on our side. Follow me. Stay quiet. When I give the signal, make enough noise to wake the devil."

*****

Captain Armstrong toured the main deck. Fifty passengers held third-class tickets, which did not buy cabin space. They snoozed outside on chairs and benches sheltered from the drizzle by the upper deck's overhang and the canvas awning near the stern.

On this trip, Armstrong proudly carried several of Upper Canada's prominent citizens among the first-class passengers. He paid each a personal visit.

He exchanged small talk with Ella Sampson, wife of Kingston's mayor, and her daughter. Next, he joined a celebration in the stateroom shared by Colonel Richard Bullock and James Holditch, a prominent businessman. In his mid-forties, Bullock served as adjutant general of the Upper Canada militia and advisor to the lieutenant governor of Upper Canada. Among his party guests was Colonel Richard Fraser. In his early fifties, Fraser held the patronage job of collector of customs in Brockville and commanded a militia regiment. Captain Armstrong joined the group, drank two toasts—one to Bullock and Fraser, both decorated War of 1812 veterans, and one to the steamer's safe passage—and bid the men goodnight.

Lastly Armstrong inspected the mooring lines and the wood loading. Seeing that several hours remained until the men filled the hold, he went to his cabin to nap.

The chatter in Bullock's cabin soon faded to snores from the somnolent effects of late-night drinking on middle-aged men. Only the eight men carrying wood remained awake.

*****

A pace behind Bill, Ryan steadied his breathing the way Nick's grandfather taught him when stalking moose. Their footsteps made no sound on the sodden ground. When they passed the woodcutter's shanty, Bill raised his arm and brought it down. "Now!"

The men erupted in war whoops and rushed downhill towards the steamer. The eight wood-loaders dropped their burdens and scattered into the night forest.

Bill led his men up the unguarded gangplank. On the main deck, he directed four men to take over the engine room and remove sailors from the lower decks. He posted Ryan and Anderson to guard the gangplank. With six others, the pirate captain roused sleeping third-class passengers from benches and chairs and ordered them off the steamer.

In seconds the raid sounded like a brawl. Grouchy deck passengers cursed loudly and often while the pirates hustled them towards the gangplank.

The affray awoke most cabin passengers and crew. Captain Armstrong ran from his cabin straight into the Warner brothers. They shoved the protesting captain down the gangplank to the growing mob of angry passengers on the rainy dock. Armstrong glowered at the two armed strangers blocking his return. Anderson spit on the gangplank. Ryan adjusted his hat brim to shield his face from view.

With the crew and third-class passengers driven off, the raiders attacked the cabins on both decks. Doors crashed open, men hollered, and women screamed.

*****

The purser awoke with Samuel Frey's bayonet inches from his throat. He rolled off the bed with a thump and scurried half-dressed from his cabin. Laughing and whooping, Frey chased him until he fled the steamer.

Mrs. Sampson arose at the sound of yelling passengers and glanced out her curtained windows. She spied armed men running on deck. "Get dressed dear. We have trouble afoot." She and her daughter fastened their final buttons as someone pounded on the cabin door.

"Open now or I will break it in," called a baritone voice.

Mrs. Sampson composed herself, opened the door, and faced Bill leaning with both hands on the doorframe. She placed her fingertips on his damp arm and said, "I am Mrs. James Sampson. What do you want?"

"You must leave this steamer, ma'am. It be now a prize of war."

"Surely you will give us a moment to collect our coats and baggage."

"Yes, but please don't tarry," Bill replied courteously and then moved to the next cabin.

She did not tarry. In her rush to reach the wharf, Mrs. Sampson dropped a silk apron on the deck.

Scanlon, the Warner brothers, and two others smashed into Colonel Bullock's party cabin. They pushed in the splintered door and prodded the drowsy occupants with muskets. Dulled by too much champagne, the men had slept through the melee. Holditch reached in the dark for his coat and grabbed Colonel Fraser's military jacket by mistake.

"Look lads, a British officer," cried Chester Warner. His brother Seth punched the diminutive Holditch in the nose.

"Please," Holditch wheezed. "It's not my coat. I'm a businessman."

"Then whose is it?" Seth Warner stared at the other occupants.

"The coat is mine, you bloody brigand," answered Colonel Fraser in his thick Scottish accent, rising to fight.

Seth Warner drove the butt of his musket into the officer's gut. Colonel Fraser buckled but stayed on his feet, too proud to drop to his knees. The raiders hustled the passengers out. On emerging from the cabin, Colonel Bullock snapped from his stupor at the sight of Frey swearing obscenities and chasing two women dressed in nightclothes.

"You bastards."

Colonel Bullock grabbed a long piece of cordwood dropped earlier by a fleeing crewman. He smashed Scanlon on the arm and knocked him to the deck. Then with bare fists, he began wailing at the raiders with some assistance from the recovered Colonel Fraser. Their anger and gallantry proved no match for a gang of alert, younger men. After a quick scuffle, the only effort to confront any *Peel* pirate ended with bloody noses and split knuckles. Anderson escorted them to the wharf.

*****

Twenty minutes after the raid started, Bill surveyed the knot of angry passengers and crew. Like Bill, other insouciant raiders stood by the railing in plain view in the lamplight. Ryan resented their naive recklessness and stayed in the shadows.

A *Peel* crewman stepped forward in the crowd. "The devil seize the likes of ye."

"Remember the *Caroline*, Pat" replied Anderson, who recognized the speaker.

"Is it Caroline O'Toole ye mean? If so, it ain't the likes of thee she'd be lookin' fer."

Anderson laughed. "Come aboard and take away your kit."

"Do ye think I'll go aboard and see myself kilt by heathen like thee."

"Cast off the lines." Bill's stentorian baritone echoed down the river as he departed for the wheelhouse.

The current tugged the steamer away from the dock. Ryan picked up a silk apron lying on the deck and shoved it in a pocket, then joined Bill in the pilothouse. He found him cursing while he tried to guide the drifting steamer.

"We succeeded, sir. Why do ye fret?"

"We have failed, lad. We have failed. We won the battle but lost the campaign. Find McLeod and bring him here."

Ryan located McLeod in a forward cabin drinking brandy with Frey and Anderson. "General! Commodore Johnston wants to see ye in the pilothouse."

McLeod tipped back his brandy and hurried from the stateroom with Ryan two steps behind.

*****

"What is it, Bill?" McLeod asked, entering the wheelhouse.

"What happened to the promised men?" Bill stared out at the water trying to steer the steamer away from the rocky shore. Without the paddlewheels turning to provide momentum, the rudder did not respond. The steamer had no more self-direction than a twig on the tide.

"I'm not sure. I talked to Abbey. I thought we had an understanding."

"An understanding!" Bill turned and roared at McLeod. "Did you obtain a pledge from the Cleveland committee or not?"

McLeod gulped. "I thought you had a pledge from Abbey or Heustis."

"Damn you to Hell, Donald. You said Patriots were coming from Cleveland. Abbey and Heustis be Watertown Hunters."

Bill grabbed McLeod's lapels. Ryan saw sweat on McLeod's forehead glisten in the lamplight.

"Remember the plan? I take the *Peel*," Bill began, inches from McLeod's ashen face. "And you secure reinforcements and engineers. Taking this steamer was your bloody idea in the first place. Now we have the goddamned *Peel* but not enough men to capture the *Great Britain*. And no man among us has the skills to start and operate the cursed engines."

"Can't we send a boat to fetch some crewmen to run the engines?" Ryan suggested.

"Good idea. I wish I had thought of that earlier but it be too late. That mob will overpower anyone we send. We lack the men to hold this steamer and make a stand against them on the wharf."

Bill paused and gazed upon the water ahead.

"McLeod! Tell Frey and Anderson to drop the anchor and then bring everyone aft on the main deck." The general scurried out. "This be not the last you hear from me about this," Bill shouted at his retreating back.

"What do ye mean to do now?"

"If we cannot use her, no one can." At a questioning expression from Ryan, Bill elaborated. "I mean to loot her and burn her."

"Loot her if ye must, but ye can't destroy a steamer as fine as this. Tis a sin."

Bill's eyes narrowed to slits. "Never lecture me on sin," he bellowed. He moved towards the door. To his surprise, Ryan stepped in his way.

"I won't let ye burn her," he hollered, rising on the balls of his feet.

Bill put his hands together and cracked his knuckles. "Step aside. I don't care to hurt you, but I will have my way."

"No!" Ryan charged head down and eyes closed.

Bill stepped aside and pushed lightly downwards on Ryan's head as he passed, putting him off balance. Ryan skidded on his belly across the wooden floor into the pilothouse wall. He rolled over. A gash bled on his forehead.

"Where did you learn to fight? Always keep your eyes open when you attack a man."

Enraged, Ryan sprung to his feet and charged again, eyes open. Bill shifted his weight to his right foot in a fake. As Bill expected, Ryan instinctively altered his direction to intercept where he thought his target would be. Bill hopped to his left foot and knocked Ryan's feet out from under him with a leg sweep. Ryan slammed head first into the paneled wall.

The steamer jerked when the anchor caught the river's rocky bottom.

McLeod entered the pilothouse. "The men await." He pointed to Ryan dazed and bleeding on the floor. "What happened to him?"

"He slipped when the steamer lurched. Help him up."

*****

The assembled men quieted at Bill's approach. Leaning on the rail, he spoke to the dark water. "We were let down again. Our reinforcements have not come. Our plans now must change." Turning to face his men, he continued, "Pillage this steamer from end to end, top to bottom, and bring anything of value to me."

The river echoed at the gleeful whoops of plundering men. Some of their lost compatriots rowed over in Bill's two gigs and joined the melee.

At Bill's feet, men unloaded linen and silk garments, jewelry, and plates and candlesticks of silver. Into his pockets, Bill stuffed three hundred pounds from Colonel Fraser, sixteen hundred pounds belonging to Holditch, plus the fortune Scanlon found in the captain's cabinet.

His head pounding with migraine intensity, Ryan shuffled to the deck and added the silk apron to the booty pile.

"Have you searched every stateroom and storage locker?" he asked, when the men reassembled. Everyone nodded.

"Put everything of value in the boats."

The looting complete, Bill stepped towards the nearest cabin, torch in hand.

"Don't do it," Ryan whispered.

The other raiders fell silent, their eyes on Bill. He paused, glanced at Ryan, and shook his head.

"Remember the *Caroline* men. She sank five months ago to this day. The British knighted the officer who burned her." With that, he tossed the torch onto the cabin's bedding. "I will warrant they don't knight us."

Laughing at Bill's joke, Smith strutted along the deck smashing lanterns with an axe. Flaming oil spread across the deck. The Warner brothers each dipped cushions in the flames and tossed them onto beds in other cabins. The raiders retreated to the gigs and pulled away.

With eyes that couldn't clearly focus, Ryan witnessed the fire spread along the steamer, scorching the polished wood and peeling her paint. The river, islands, shore, and low-hanging clouds soon reflected its bloody light. Smoke hung in the damp night air. The crackle and roar of raging fire soon obscured all others night sounds.

Bill studied the conflagration until certain of the steamer's destruction, and then ordered the men to Abel's Island.

*****

At McDonald's wharf, the ejected passengers, some in tears, huddled in the rain, unable to take they eyes from the distant burning steamer. The fire consumed the anchor lines and set the blazing steamer adrift. She crunched to a halt on a rocky knoll. The *Peel* burned to the hull and capsized as the smoke stacks toppled. The flames died in a cloud of smoke with a roar like a gust from a gale. Her boilers and engines pitched into deep water. One scorched paddlewheel broke the surface to mark her resting place.

Not everyone on Well's Island stayed to gawk. Long before Bill tossed the fateful torch, two crewmen departed for Kingston in a rowboat under the purser's command. Simultaneously, Captain

Armstrong hurried by lamplight to Ripley's wharf and hired a boatman to row him to Upper Canada. Heading downstream in the shadow of Well's Island, Captain Armstrong passed the *Peel* unseen by its rampaging captors. He witnessed fire light up his steamer. He could do nothing, except seek revenge. He landed hours later on the Canadian shore and hiked twenty-five miles to Brockville. He woke the chief magistrate and gave his story. Simultaneously in Kingston, the purser reported events to Bonnycastle at the fort.

At dawn the steamer *Oneida* pulled up to McDonald's wharf to load fuel wood. Though downstream bound, the *Oneida*'s captain shepherded the steamer's passengers and crew upstream to Kingston. There they added exaggerated personal accounts—some claimed fifty men boarded the ship—to the news raging across the colony.

*****

In his shanty room on Abel's Island, Ryan cleaned his head wounds with rum. His mood penitential, he accepted the alcohol's sting as partial punishment for his role in the *Peel* raid.

Most men drank rum toasts over a breakfast of eggs and grilled beef. Lyman Leach and two other raiders, missing since midnight, arrived in a stolen boat and prodded others for their stories. Each storyteller's role in the raid seemed to expand with the telling. Bill sipped tea by himself.

Shortly before noon, Bill assigned the booty and large sums of money to his most trusted men for safekeeping and told everyone to go home. The drowsy raiders drifted away, basking in their particular version of glory.

Ryan and Bill stayed on Abel's Island until the last raider shoved off. Neither spoke a word about their fight. They rowed to Clayton in silence. Ryan replayed the night's events. He had wreaked a measure of revenge on the British and Kingston elite, but it gave him no joy. The *Peel*'s destruction did nothing to assuage his anger over his treatment in Kingston. At the wharf, he went straight to the warehouse, stripped off his buckskins, and tossed for hours before sleep came.

*****

At dinner that evening, Ada, Kate, and her brothers retold stories they'd overheard in the Clayton market and along the wharfs.

"Ten men are under arrest already, including Hugh," Kate said.

"Damn it. Hugh had that fat packet of pounds with him," Bill replied.

"The constables recovered money, silver and other valuables," Decatur added.

"I saw a list of men wanted for arrest. Your name is on it, Father," John said. "No one has the courage to come here yet, but that may soon change."

"The town's in a funereal mood," Jim said as he stared at his father. "The people idolize you but balk at obvious piracy."

"The British authorities in Canada are livid and demand action," Napoleon offered. "The attack has embarrassed the governor. I expect he'll do something soon."

Kate looked her father in the eye. "I believe it best if you decamp to the islands." She raised an eyebrow at Ryan. "Both of you."

"Kate is correct, you must hide." From Ann, everyone knew her suggestion was an order.

"Before I go, I have a present for you, Kate," Bill said.

He pulled a folded fabric of embroidered silk the color of tarnished brass from one of his greatcoat pockets. Ryan recognized the apron he recovered on the *Peel*. "This belonged to Mrs. Sampson. She dropped it in her haste."

"Thank you Father. I will cherish it always."

Ada cleared her throat. Eight heads turned her way. "What happened between you two?" Her eyes flashed from Bill to Ryan and back.

"Nothing. Why?" Bill replied, running his right hand through his hair.

"You two have not exchanged a word or glance."

Ryan sipped tea and stared at the parlor clock. Bill toyed with a bowl of strawberries.

"Ada has a point." Kate glanced at Ryan's forehead wound. "Tell me what happened."

He couldn't lie to her, nor tell the whole truth. She loved her father too much. "Bill and I had…words. I was agin burning the steamer. He had his way. Tis all."

"Too bad he didn't listen," Jim said. "Burning her was damned stupid."

Bill glared at his eldest son. Jim remained silently defiant, arms crossed.

"I'll have no fights in this family," Ann barked. "Bill, you best be on your way until matters and tempers cool."

Bill rose. "I will go to Fort Wallace this night." He paused. "You coming?"

"I see no other choice." Ryan rose. "I'll pack my kit and meet you on the wharf."

*****

His belongings stowed in a canvas sack, Ryan starred at the starry sky on the Johnston wharf, his foot tapping rapidly on the boards. At the sound of the wharf creaking, he turned expecting Bill.

"You seem tense," Ada said. A yard away, she clasped a shawl around her broad shoulders.

"Jim is right. Burning that steamer was stupid, and I had a part in it."

"What will you do now?"

He paused, trying to coalesce liquid thoughts. "Maybe I should go away."

She stepped closer and ran a hand through his hair and caressed his scalp with her fingertips. "We would all miss you…especially Kate."

"Thoughts of leaving her make my heart ache."

Ryan enjoyed the feel of Ada's fingers in his hair and inched closer. Her shawl slipped off her left shoulder. His nose was inches from the shadowy cleft at her low neckline. He looked up, away from the alluring mounds, to her full lips. He found no safe harbor there and tilted his head to catch her lowered eyes.

"You cannot leave and disappoint me."

"Disappoint ye in what manner?"

"I expect to be in Kate's bridle party at your wedding."

"Oh!"

*****

Bill and Ryan set out in a twin-oared skiff past familiar islands. In a night illuminated by a rising half moon, the air heavy with the perfume of fruit-tree blossoms, they rowed for hours without talking. Zak roosted on the bow.

Shortly after the shadow of Grindstone Island's eastern end slipped astern, Bill guided their boat straight at the north face of a rocky island. At no more than ten feet away, he ordered Ryan to ship oars. He complied, swinging the oars inside the gunwales. Bill did the same. The boat's momentum carried them forward.

Instead of crashing into solidity, shadow swallowed the boat moments before it ground to a halt on an invisible gravel beach. Bill lit a lantern to illuminate a long narrow cave formed by the overhanging roof of two sides of a large fissure. The hideout included rough-hewn wooden tables and chairs, benches that doubled as bunks, barrels of rum, bricks of tea, a stack of rifles, and a store of firewood.

"Welcome to Fort Wallace, your home for now. Be a good lad and start a fire. Keep it small. We can't have a lot of smoke showing."

He said nothing and did as asked. Over the fire, he made tea and warmed the biscuits Ann had packed.

Bill sipped tea on a wooden bench. "I gather you be angry at me, lad, because I walloped you."

"I hold no grudge that ye bested me in a fair fight."

"Then, it be the steamer, right?"

Ryan nodded.

"That ship was a symbol of the Family Compact, the people that provoked the rebellion and the same people that drove you from Kingston. Burning her was our way of showing those bastards they be not immune from justice."

"She was such a fine craft."

"It was just a pile of boards. They can build another."

Ryan sighed. "I guess I should be grateful ye didn't kill me."

"Don't be daft. You be my friend. Besides," he paused for a sip of tea, "I am not the killer people make me out to be."

"A belt full of pistols and knives says otherwise."

"That be it exactly. I use the threat of harm to have my way. I will tell you a secret, if you promise not to repeat it."

"Aye, I promise."

"Outside of war, I have killed none. I would kill in defense of my person, family, or friends, if I must, but I am not a murderer. Never have been."

"But ye are a rebel and pirate."

"Guilty as charged."

*****

The next morning Ryan explored the oblong island. Wide and sparsely treed, it sloped several hundred feet from the high granite walls on the west end to the low east end. Drooping pine boughs obscured the cave entrance. Vines and brushy foliage sheltered the roof gap. He picked a shady nook where he could remain hidden and watched Zak hunt for food.

Bill crawled into the shade beside him. "Did I ever tell you about the first real battle I was in?"

"No, but I'd love to hear it."

"When I smuggled my family from Canada in 1813, we first settled in Sackets Harbor, the main American naval base on Lake Ontario. In late May most of our warships were nigh Niagara attacking a British fort. The British picked that time to attack Sackets. We were unprepared and helpless, but they anchored offshore and twiddled their thumbs for a day. That gave us a chance to prepare.

"The fighting was fierce with continuous cannon fire and musket volleys from both sides. We were outnumbered. The town seemed ready to fall when they retreated and sailed away. Jim, a boy then, remembers grapeshot hanging from posts and stumps, and of filling his pockets with musket balls. I still recall the blood, the dead, and the wounded. Human flesh has no resistance to cannon, muskets, and bayonets."

*****

In the gloaming hours next evening, several *Peel* pirates arrived in a stolen boat.

"Can we hide here, Bill? The law's after us," asked John Farrow. "We brought some bread and flour."

"Yes, but remember we be in a state of war and I be in command."

Ryan helped unload the boat and passed around mugs of tea. The newcomers had barely settled when a woman's voice called from outside the cave.

"Hello." A canoe glided into the cave's lamplight, with Kate at the bow and Scanlon at the stern.

"We brought more food Father, including a side of bacon."

"And some rum, too," Scanlon added.

"Hugh, I thought you were in jail."

"I was Bill. They granted bail on a promise I'd return for trial."

"When be the trial?"

"Earlier today," he laughed.

"Have you news of the others?"

"Nine are still in confinement. Most everyone else involved that night are wanted men. The only name not on that list is yers." Scanlon gestured to Ryan. "None recognized ye."

"The British set a reward of five thousand dollars for your capture, Father," Kate said.

"No matter. They cannot find me in these islands. And if they get lucky, I will escape. I have me many good men now and more shall come. We will plan and train over the summer and launch new campaigns in the fall." Bill, pleased with his optimism and vision, smiled at Kate, Ryan, and Hugh.

Kate smiled back. By nature, she would stand by her father on whatever path he chose.

Ryan and Scanlon glanced at each other and then at their feet.

"What? Be you not up to new enterprise?"

Ryan spoke first. "I believe in yer cause. But I doubt ye can win." He ignored Bill's frown. "If ye were in command, thousands would follow, but ye are cursed with bad leaders, drunkards, cowards, and men who talk better than they fight. Look at yer history. Even when ye had superior forces and ample provisions, every campaign failed."

Bill shrugged off the pessimism.

"What of you, Hugh? What be your story?"

"Ah, Bill! A court can find ten witnesses that put me on that steamer with a musket in me hand. I should leave. Ryan has a point. I was with ye on Hickory Island and the *Peel* raid. T'others let us down each time."

"Where will you go, Hugh?" Kate asked.

"There's a trail across the Adirondacks to Lake Champlain. From there I'll head to New York City."

"And you, Ryan?"

She stepped forward and held his right hand in both of hers. His pulse quicken. He locked his eyes on her, trying to memorize every detail of her soft face.

"I'll help Scanlon get to Lake Champlain. Then I'll decide whether to return or head west to the frontier. This big land holds many opportunities."

"Does that mean we may not hear from you again?"

Ryan pulled her close and planted a quick kiss on her lips. It was not the first kiss he envisioned. Still, he knew he'd run out of opportunities.

Kate raised her right hand to strike him; instead, she twirled a finger in his red curls.

"Ye'll hear from me again, Kate. Trust me on that."

"Ahem!" Bill pulled a roll of pound notes from his pocket and handed it to Hugh. "That ought to keep you two for awhile. It be worth close to three hundred dollars."

"Thank ye, Bill. All the best. I'll look for ye in the newspapers."

"Write if you have a chance, Hugh," said Kate.

"Yes, Miss Catherine. We'll leave yer canoe at Alex Bay."

Ryan looked at Kate, trying to think of something else to say. Scanlon tugged his sleeve. "Time to go. We should be far from here by sunrise."

Ryan grabbed his bag of belongings, shook Bill's hand, winked at Kate, and climbed into the canoe's front seat. With Zak on the bow, he and Scanlon paddled into the night.

"I hope he comes back," Bill said. "I think he would make a fine son-in-law."

"A good son-in-law, yes. A good husband, maybe not," Kate replied. "Like that bird of his, he is half wild and not happy when confined."

The Firm's New Partner

Six days after leaving Fort Wallace, Ryan and Scanlon strolled through the village of Westport on the southern arm of Lake Champlain. Tired and scruffy from a tough hike through mountainous terrain, they pulled up chairs on the veranda of a small inn. Zak perched on the railing.

"I'm dying for ale. What do ye want to drink?" Scanlon asked. "I'm buying."

"The usual, thanks."

Scanlon waved over the proprietor. The lanky, elderly man scowled at the raven but kept his thoughts to himself as Scanlon ordered a tankard of ale, a cup of tea with maple syrup, and a double order of fried eggs with ham and buttered bread for each of them.

"See that canal boat down there?" Scanlon pointed to the harbor. "That's my ride to New York."

"Do ye still think the big city suits ye?"

"I do. A man can easily get lost in the crowds, and opportunities abound if ye have a wit of intelligence." Scanlon leaned towards Ryan. "And, I'm 28, time to find a wife and start a family. What's yer next move?"

"As we hiked, I imagined myself going to Texas, or exploring the uncharted Canadian west, or heading to California. Every idea 'twas exciting but seemed wrong."

"Wrong how?"

"I came to understand each plan 'twas an excuse to run away. Deep in my soul, I know I can't abandon Bill in a period of such turmoil."

"Does the charming Miss Catherine have anything to do with it?" Scanlon asked, grinning.

Ryan blushed and nodded his head. "That quick kiss at Fort Wallace has tugged at me like a hound on a leash."

"I can't say I blame ye."

The proprietor arrived with their beverages and meals. Neither hungry man spoke again until their plates were clear. Zak received generous portions of egg and bread crusts from both men.

"What's my best choice for going back without retracing our steps?" Ryan asked.

"Go by water to Montreal and then up the St. Lawrence to Clayton," Scanlon said, unfolding his wad of money. He gave half the bills to Ryan. "Here, take this."

Ryan counted out ten pounds and gave the remainder back to Scanlon. "Ye keep that. Ye'll need it in New York. In a few days I'll be back working for Bill."

"Aye, thank ye. I'm going to miss ye lad," Scanlon said, pushing back his plate. "Maybe fate will guide our paths to cross again some day."

"'Tis the second time a departing friend has said that."

*****

Five days later, Zak perched on the veranda railing at a waterfront inn in Ogdensburg, New York, waiting for food scraps and peering at passersby. Ryan fed the last orts of his breakfast eggs to the raven and poured a cup of tea. Beside his empty plate lay a folded newspaper and a third-class ticket on the *Oswego*, departing in an hour up the St. Lawrence to Kingston with a stop in Clayton.

Without reading the paper, Ryan guessed that Bill Johnston dominated the headlines. In table conversation at the inn and chatter on the street, he kept hearing Bill's name and reference to a proclamation.

"It seems ye and me are heading back into trouble, Zak."

"Cric! Croc!"

Ryan flipped open the newspaper and frowned in mild disapproval while he read the letter reprinted on the front page.

To all whom it may concern

I, William Johnston, a natural born citizen of Upper Canada, certify that I hold a commission in the Patriot service of Upper Canada, as commander-in-chief of the naval forces and flotilla. I commanded the expedition that captured and destroyed the steamer Sir Robert Peel. The men under my command in that expedition were nearly all natural-born English subjects; the exceptions were volunteers.

My headquarters is on an island in the St. Lawrence River without the jurisdiction of the United States, at a place named by me Fort Wallace. I am well acquainted with the boundary line, and know which of the islands do and do not belong to the United States. In the selection of the island, I wished to be positive and not locate within the jurisdiction of the United States, and had reference to the decision of the Commissioners under the sixth article of the Treaty of Ghent, done at Utica in the State of New York, 13th June, 1822. I know the number of the island, and by that decision, it is British territory.

> *I act under orders. The object of my movement is the independence of the Canadas. I am not at war with the commerce or property of the people of the United States.*
>
> *Signed this tenth day of June in the year of Our Lord, one thousand, eight hundred and thirty eight.*
>
> *William Johnston*

Ryan refolded the paper and, with Zak on his shoulder, headed to the wharf at the confluence of the St. Lawrence and Oswegatchie Rivers. His buckskin garb and raven drew stares. People stepped aside to let him pass.

Across this narrow portion of the St. Lawrence River, Ryan spotted the Union Jack fluttering at the Prescott wharf. Downstream on the Canadian side, a stone windmill loomed by the shore, its sails turning in the light breeze.

*****

On its way upriver that afternoon, the *Oswego* chugged past the *Peel*'s grave. Silent passengers lined the starboard rail to peer at the charred paddlewheel visible above the water. Ryan lingered on the port side, focusing on the river ahead. A few miles upstream, the captain docked the sidewheeler at a wharf on the St. Lawrence's south shore to load firewood.

"Hey. Isn't that Johnston?" yelled a roly-poly young man several positions along the ship's rail from Ryan.

A dark blue gig with six oarsmen crossed the channel close to Wells Island. With his telescope, Ryan confirmed Bill at the tiller. The gig disappeared behind an island.

On the steamer, women clutched their husbands. Mothers grabbed their children. The *Oswego*'s captain scanned the river and whispered to his first mate.

"Captain," called the young man who spoke earlier. "I know Mr. Johnston. Let me take a boat over and inquire to his intentions."

"No. Too dangerous. That man's a pirate."

"Begging yer pardon, captain," Ryan began, "I'm also acquainted with him. I'm sure the two of us will have no trouble. We can keep him occupied until ye load yer wood."

The captain conversed with the mate. "I've reconsidered. We'll lower you a boat."

Ryan, Zak, and the young stranger prepared to set out in a dory. A well-dressed man hurried over.

"Wait, please. I must speak with you."

"Speak then," Ryan replied.

"I'm Alvin Hunt, editor of *Jeffersonian*...the Watertown newspaper."

"What can we do for ye?"

"When you return, tell me everything Johnston says. My readers devour news of him."

"Why don't you come with us?" suggested Ryan's boat mate.

Hunt stepped back. "No, thank you. I prefer to remain here."

The two young men exchanged smirks and sculled towards the island where they'd last seen Bill's gig. "I should introduce myself. I'm Charlie Hawes from Clayton."

"Pleased to meet ye, Charlie. I'm Ryan, also from Clayton. How do ye know Bill?"

"I attended school with John and Kate. Naturally, I met Mr. Johnston once or twice."

The way he spoke Kate's name annoyed Ryan. "How well do ye know his daughter?"

"We were in the same school grade. We played together as children. Sometimes we rowed out to the islands for picnics. Have you met her?"

"Once or twice."

"Isn't she the prettiest woman in the county?"

"I've not yet met all the women in the county," Ryan snapped.

Bill's gig emerged from hiding and headed their way propelled by six men Ryan didn't recognize. Ryan and Hawes shipped their oars and waited for the gig to pull alongside. Bill examined the two young men with an expression Ryan interpreted as concealed surprise.

"Zaak!" Zak flew over and landed on the gunwales near Bill.

"It seems your bird knows him, too," Hawes began. "Hello, Mr. Johnston. I'm Charlie Hawes, a friend of Kate."

"I remember you. Your father and I used to fish together."

"I believe you have met Ryan. I didn't catch his last name."

"That's 'cause I didn't tell ye."

Hawes ignored the edge in Ryan's voice and continued. "We came to inquire as to your intentions regarding our ship. Passengers were alarmed at your appearance out in the open with the law after you."

"That be all you want?" Bill asked, looking at Ryan.

"Yes, sir. Tis all."

"A newspaper fellow wants to know every word you say," added Hawes.

"That be so, Charlie? Well, you can tell him this.

"One thing you may be rest assured of, I will never be taken alive. I be a fair mark to shoot at, but I be not a man to dangle in the air. Whoever comes after me must bring his own coffin, as I have no leisure for cabinetmaking. I have two other boats, well manned and armed, within signal view. I be sitting on the *Sir Robert Peel*'s colors and mean to continue sitting on them 'til they rot. Steamers on the river need have no fear of me. I have no intention of molesting them. I be now fully avenged for the *Caroline*.

"Can you remember that?"

"Yes, Mr. Johnston, every word."

"Then I bid you both adieu. I might see you soon."

Ryan knew Bill meant the last words for him.

"*Allons-y!*" At Bill's barked French, his crew dipped their oars in unison and sped away.

Hawes kept his mouth shut on the return trip to the steamer, and sought out the newspaper editor without a glance at Ryan.

When the *Oswego* docked in Clayton, Ryan and Hawes left the wharf moments apart. Ryan crossed Water Street and knocked on Bill Johnston's front door. He looked back and smirked at Hawes, who had taken the same route. Kate answered the door. Ryan put his hands on her slim hips and kissed her lips lightly. Her eyes registered surprise, but she did not resist.

"Why, Mr. Pine! I do believe you missed me."

"Pardon my boldness. I was overcome at the sight of ye."

Her gaze shifted from Ryan's face to a distance over his shoulder. She lifted her hand and waved. "Hello, Charlie."

Hawes raised his arm in a flaccid wave and forced a smile. Ryan grinned.

"You seem happy. Come in. Mother has tea ready. I'll bring something out for Zak. Will you stay a day or two?"

"I should join Bill, but I doubt he'd begrudge me a day."

"Have you ever driven a carriage?"

"I've driven farm wagons since I was eight."

"Good enough. A friend of John's has a cabriolet we can borrow. What would you and Zak say to a ride in the country with me tomorrow?"

"I say yes, for sure. How about ye, Zak?"

"Crik, crik!"

*****

The next morning, John delivered a black cabriolet pulled by a sturdy bay gelding.

Ryan stepped off the porch with Kate. "Tis a fine rig," he said.

"It's the finest two-wheeled carriage in Clayton," John replied. "And very cozy," he added with a smile.

Kate climbed onto the bench seat and slipped a wicker picnic basket into the storage space behind her. Ryan circled the carriage and stopped by the horse's head. Holding the bridle, he stroked the gelding's neck below the ears.

"Tis a fine big animal. He must be sixteen hands."

"Yes, and he's calm and trained for a carriage. Do you want the hood up or down?"

Ryan raised his eyebrows at Kate. "Down please, John," she replied.

The men folded the carriage top's accordion-like pleats. Ryan climbed aboard.

"You make a lovely couple," said John.

Kate wore a pale yellow, neck-to-ankle summer dress with gauzy sleeves, a matching sun bonnet, and slippers. Ryan showed off his new short-sleeved yellow shirt tucked into blue cotton trousers over leather work boots.

"Thank yer friend for us, John."

"Thank you, brother."

"My pleasure. Have fun you two."

Zak glided from the porch railing and alighted on the gelding's rump. The horse, clearly not fond of ravens, reared up in the harness.

"Zaak!" Zak leapt skywards.

"Better follow us, Zakkie boy, or ride on the carriage."

"Critiky! Croc!"

With Ryan at the reins, they headed south on James St. and into the Arcadian countryside at a trot. The gelding's shod hooves beat rhythmically on the sun-baked dirt road. A mist of dust rose in the carriage's wake and drifted east in a faint breeze. Farm fields, thick with hay, young wheat, and corn, promised a bumper crop.

Kate craned her head to inspect each farmhouse that came into view: typically one-and-a-half-storey clapboard structures with a covered porch and modest displays of fretwork. Ryan examined passing pioneer barns constructed of massive logs from the long-depleted virgin forests. Some farms included a second-generation barn —a post-and-beam structure with pine siding.

After several hours pointing out special houses and barns to each other, they arrived at the village of Depauville straddling the Chaumont River. Ryan guided the carriage into the shade of towering willows by a patch of grassy shoreline. He unhitched the horse and tethered him on a long lead to a tree to rest and graze. Kate spread a quilt on the ground close to the languid river and unpacked a lunch of breaded fish fillets, buttered bread, pickles, strawberries, and spring water flavored with mint leaves.

"It is so nice to avoid my daily house chores." Kate lay back on one arm and stared above where Zak waited for handouts. "Ada kindly offered to take my place."

"Big-hearted," he replied.

"Big everything," she quipped.

Ryan blushed and looked away. Kate's peels of laughter filled their picnic grove.

"You dirty-minded boy," she managed to say between giggles.

"Kach! Kood!"

Zak landed between them, saving his human from further embarrassment.

"Looks like your bird is tired of waiting for his lunch."

"Did ye bring crusts?"

She handed him a canvas bag. "Take this."

Ryan tossed bread crusts to the raven by the riverbank while Kate laid out their lunch. On his return to the quilt, she passed him a mug of mint water. He sipped the cool drink and gazed into her eyes over the cup.

"Did ye see any farms that caught yer fancy?"

"One or two, why?"

"Have ye ever thought about farming, or are ye a town girl at heart?"

"I adore the countryside. I would be happy on a farm...under the right conditions."

Smiling, she stared into his blue eyes.

"'Tis good to know." He smiled back.

Ryan leaned forward, his lips puckered. He examined Kate's eyes, wondering if she welcomed such a liberty. She tilted her chin upwards to meet his lips and slid her fingers through his curls as their mint-tinged mouths touched. Unlike previous kisses—the mere peck on the lips that Ryan expected—Kate jerked him close so their breasts pressed together. The force threw them off balance and they tumbled to the ground. Ryan landed on his back, with an arm across Kate's shoulders. He rolled them over until Kate lay beneath him on the fragrant grass. Kate held him by his curls and kissed with more passion than he'd ever experienced.

*****

Next morning, with the concealment of night lifting, Ryan rowed into the hidden cleft in the wall of Fort Wallace, once again entering Bill's renegade world. Six French Canadians, refugees from the Lower Canada rebellion, also occupied the cave.

"Glad to see you without that silly lad tagging along," Bill called.

"Glad I am to be rid of him."

"Zaak!"

"It be good to have Zak back, too. Sit and have tea. What news do you bring?"

Ryan held out the newspaper he'd carried from Ogdensburg. "Who wrote that proclamation for ye?"

"I did."

"Well, Bill, ye be smart but nary educated enough to write those words."

"You be right, I confess. A lawyer friend of mine in Watertown, name of Bagley, wrote it for me." He paused for a sip of tea. "Have you other news?"

"Kate tells me British crews are snooping around in skiffs. I bet 'tis not tea they are looking for."

"Anything else?"

"The British are pressing the President to support them in ridding these islands of pirates. Half the local populace support him and t'other half don't."

"Van Buren has little support in the northern counties. There be hundreds of homes where I can count on a warm reception."

"What enterprise are ye up to now?"

"I have five hundred new rifles and a supply of cartridges we must move. Instead of having everything in two or three places, smaller arsenals in many locations be better in case the British find some hideouts."

"Why so many rifles?"

"They belong to the Hunters. Sooner or later they shall stop talking and start fighting. I will deliver them when the time comes."

"Do ye want my help?"

"If you be up to it, yes. I could use me a trusted hand."

"I guess I'm yer man."

"Good. I can show you a few more hideouts."

The next morning before sunrise, they departed Fort Wallace. Ryan wore a light cotton shirt because the day promised to be a scorcher. Bill, wearing his usual modest homespun gray pants and bulky cotton shirt, carried two pistols and a dirk in his belt. Fifty rifles and a fishing pole lay beneath the gig's seats.

They rowed east across a mile of open water to the shadowy shelter of Wells Island, and then followed its west and south shores as the sun rose a steamy orange to the east. Zak flew ahead, gliding in the light breeze.

"How come ye didn't bring t'others from the cave, Bill?"

"I've never entrusted all my secrets with anyone outside of my family, except Hugh. Now that he be gone, I count on you to take his place."

"For sure, Bill."

As the sun rose over the islands, they passed the *Peel*. Without a word spoken, they both stopped rowing and let the gig's momentum and the current take them past the charred hulk.

"I don't expect there will be much wreckage to see next year. When the ice goes out in the spring, it will push her off the shoal into deeper water."

They rowed in the bright daylight as the summer heat intensified. They began to sweat in the humid air. Most people took no notice of two men in a plain-looking gig. A few farmers and fisherman did recognize Bill and waved. He acknowledged each greeting. He refused to play the role of fugitive, yet.

Near midday, they paused beside a round island near Alexandria Bay —little more than a large granite rock topped with scrawny pines and cedars. Its sheer sides rose fifteen feet above deep water. Staying an oar's length offshore, they circled the island to a wedge-shaped notch in its eastern end.

"That be Devil's Oven Island. That notch leads to a narrow cave. I don't keep weapons here anymore because it be in plain sight of town and too well known by the locals. I sometimes camp inside, making sure to arrive and leave in the dark. It has no place to hide a boat, but you can pull a canoe inside."

They crossed the narrow shipping channel and slipped in behind a chain of smaller islands that protected a reedy bay on the south side of Wells Island. They circled a heart-shaped island opposite Alexandria Bay until them came to a cleft in the rock.

"This be Hemlock Island. The cavern beyond that crack goes in eighty feet. In the war, we had fifty men inside at times. I never use it for a main hideout now—too well known it be—but I sometimes stay overnight or in bad weather."

From Hemlock Island, they rowed north between Well's Island and Hill Island. At two secluded coves along the American side of Lake of Bays, Bill hid two dozen rifles in narrow clefts in the granite. Leaving the bay, they sculled into a narrow channel.

"Just ahead," said Bill as they fought against a churning current," the islands be just thirty-five feet apart. I have often swum this channel, going from America to Canada in a few strokes. During the war, the British maps showed these two islands as one. The channel did not exist for them. We used this passage to hide boats, and we swung across on ropes hanging from trees."

Exiting the channel, they journeyed through a massive archipelago in Canadian waters. Bill paused often to point out a supply depot, hiding place, or escape route. They camped that night on Depot Island.

"How did ye ever find all those caves and hidden routes?" Ryan asked over tea by their campfire.

"Most we learned from the Mohawks. Some I found myself."

"Ye should call these islands the Thousand Hiding Places Islands."

"How about the You Can't Find Me Islands?" Bill retorted with a baritone guffaw.

*****

After a breakfast of porridge mixed with handfuls of wild blueberries Ryan picked on the island's rocky knolls, Bill said, "There be too many rifles hidden on this island. Load half in the gig."

"Do ye prefer rifles over muskets?"

"Both have their purposes. A rifle has longer range and better accuracy but the tight fitting ball makes it slower to load. The musket be smooth bored and less accurate, but a trained soldier can load and fire it three times faster. In battle, the musket be for close range fighting and the rifle be for snipers. Let me show you."

He pulled a paper-wrapped cartridge from a wooden box. He tore off the cartridge end with his teeth and tipped some black powder into the rifle's frizzen pan. Next he poured the remaining powder into the barrel and dropped in the ball. It lodged an inch down, and Bill forced it to the barrel's end with the ramrod.

"That was faster than usual because the gun be new and the barrel be clean."

He pulled back the hammer and handed Ryan the weapon. "Here. Try it"

"Where's my target?"

"See that skinny birch tree on that next island. That be at least a hundred yards. Hit it."

"Are ye sure. I wager Boone couldn't hit that tree with my old musket."

"Daniel Boone was a great marksman, mostly because he used a rifle. Now shoot."

Ryan aimed, held his breath, and squeezed the trigger.

"Zaak!"

The gunpowder smoke cleared, revealing a gaping wound in the birch.

"Bloody hell!"

"You be lucky to hit a man at a hundred yards with a musket, but you can hit the same man at one hundred and fifty with a rifle."

Ryan handed the weapon to Bill, but he waved it away. "Keep that. It replaces the musket you lost when your canoe sank. Now reload it. We have work to do."

For three days, they distributed arms and ammunition throughout the maze of islands from Hill Island upstream to Wolfe Island. On the last evening, they dropped off a dozen rifles at Whiskey Island and then slipped over to Governors Island across from Clayton. They climbed to the high, stony end.

"Put your scope on the warehouse. Be there a green pennant flying?"

Ryan extended the telescope and placed it against one open eye. "Aye. What does it mean?"

"It means it may be safe to go home tonight."

Bill waved an oar. Ryan scanned the Johnston house across the water. Lantern light flickered for an instant from a tiny, second-floor window.

"I think someone acknowledged yer signal."

"That be either Kate or Ada. They take turns watching for me from those two owl's-eye windows in the attic. They'll send someone to confirm if it be safe."

Twenty minutes later, Jim Johnston pulled up to the island in a gig.

"Nice to see you, son." Bill slapped Jim on the right shoulder. "Be it safe to visit?"

"Yes, Father."

"Be there news?"

"There's much to tell," Jim said in his odd falsetto voice. "Samuel Frey was arrested in Ohio for the *Peel* raid. He was released soon after for lack of witnesses."

"I wish him well. What else?"

"The American authorities chartered the *Telegraph* to help the British hunt for you."

Bill shrugged. "Where be the ship now?"

"She passed by this morning. I expect she's in Ogdensburg. No one in Clayton this evening has the will or the courage to come after you."

"Good. What else?"

"This morning, a state grand jury issued indictments against you, Van Rensselaer, and Mackenzie for offenses under the Neutrality Act for the Hickory Island occupation."

"So, they have another reason to arrest me. Anything else?"

"President Van Buren repeated his belief in neutrality. He supports the British in all efforts to capture you."

"Van Buren can kiss my arse. The coward."

Jim turned and spit in agreement. "Also, forty Patriots raided Short Hills near Niagara in early June. Most were captured."

"Fools. You cannot attack a country with forty men. Anything else?"

"One sensitive matter," Jim said in a clandestine tone. "It is news from our man in Kingston."

"Go ahead, Jim. We can trust Ryan."

"He said that Bonnycastle's adjutant found your hideout and weapons at Depot Island."

Bill showed no emotion. "We moved most armaments off that island last week. What else?"

Jim continued. "Yesterday, Bonnycastle headed downriver in a steamer. Officially, he is inspecting forts and naval stations along the river. Under cover of darkness, a company of militia slipped into the hold. The ship has a band playing on deck, and officers are strolling around like they're holidaying."

"Tis a curious manner to behave," said Ryan.

"It be Bonnycastle trying to lure me into a trap. Jim, where be it now?"

"At Prescott. It's expected to head this way tomorrow."

"It be time to give Bonnycastle a bit of a scare."

"What do ye have in mind?"

"Sometimes the fox bites the hound."

*****

The next night, Ryan and Bill lay atop a thirty-foot granite cliff on Ash Island overlooking the roiling waters of Fiddler's Elbow. Two anchored nautical mines of Bill's design—watertight black powder kegs with flintlock detonators suspended from floats—bobbed in mid-channel.

"How much damage will those do?" Ryan whispered.

"Enough to send her to the bottom, but not so fast most can't get off." He looked at Ryan. "You be worried for Bonnycastle?"

"Ha! Nary a chance of that, but there are others onboard. What of them?"

"This be war. If Bonnycastle captures me, I'd hang as fast as he could find a rope, and the other men on that ship would help him tie the hangman's knot."

Bonnycastle's steamer entered Fiddler's Elbow and chugged cautiously upstream in the dangerous passage. In the eerie light of a moon nearing full, brightly clad British officers chatted on the foredeck. Ryan's half finger throbbed as the ship's course drew it closer to calamity.

A mere dozen yards before the first mine, an officer spied a suspicious-looking object in the water and shouted a warning. The helmsman swerved the ship in the narrow channel with such skill that he avoided both mines and the deadly stone palisades. The sidewheeler belched black smoke and sped from sight.

"We didn't sink it, but I wager we rattled Bonnycastle. I take satisfaction in that. Let's retrieve those kegs and go."

Rowing to Fort Wallace, Bill said, "Did I ever tell you how I tried to blow up the biggest warship on Lake Ontario during the War of 1812."

"No, Bill, but I'd love to hear it."

"It was September of 1814. The lake war was stalemated. Both sides were building warships, hoping for naval superiority. The Brits had built the *St. Lawrence*, then the mightiest craft under sail on the Great Lakes. She carried one hundred and twelve cannon. I hear she was larger than Lord Nelson's flagship."

"Really, Bill?"

"Truly. The Americans had nothing to match her. I convinced Commodore Chauncey to risk a mission to sink her before her launch. He agreed. Five of us crossed to Kingston one night in two boats and snuck into Navy Bay in the shadow of the fort. One of our boats had a copper cylinder filled with black powder and topped with a detonator. The plan was to attach it to the ship's hull and light a slow fuse."

"Did ye succeed?"

"Sadly, the *St. Lawrence* sailed earlier that day."

"What happened to that big ship?"

"The war ended that winter, and she retired without ever striking a blow. The British stripped off the guns and let the great ship rot."

*****

Hiding in the brush of Fort Wallace next morning, they monitored Bonnycastle's efforts to find them. His steamer cruised methodically from island to island. Officers swept each island with telescopes. The formerly sequestered militiamen now filled the decks, muskets in hand.

In turn, Ryan examined the steamer's every detail through his telescope. On pure reflex, he growled.

"What do you see?" Bill asked.

"Remember that fat militia bastard I told you about. He's on that ship looking for us."

Twice the sidewheeler cruised within a hundred yards of their island, but did not stop to investigate. From the water, Fort Wallace Island presented bare rock, thin shrubbery, and wind-gnarled trees to the viewer—seemingly too small and barren for a proper hideout.

Bonnycastle directed the search from the upper deck. Ryan gasped as Bill cocked his rifle and aimed at the colonel. Ryan knew the few men at Fort Wallace could not fight off the colonel's force if gunfire gave away their position. And there would be no escape.

Bill followed Bonnycastle with his gun sights and whispered, "Pow!" Lowering the rifle, he asked, "Did you believe I intended to shoot?"

"I admit I had such a thought."

"There be satisfaction in having an enemy in your sights, knowing they be at your mercy. Try it."

On the ship's second pass, Ryan played Bill's game. Locking his new rifle's sights on Tiny, he waited until the steamer sailed in close. "Bang! *D'anam don diabhal!*"

"Was that Gaelic?"

"Aye. I just sent his soul to the devil."

"Satisfying, be it not?"

"Aye."

Later, with the sun setting behind the Canadian shore, Ryan slipped into the cave for the evening meal. Bill had a gig ready.

"Where are we going?"

"I be staying. These French lads will take you to Clayton."

"Why? Don't ye need me?"

"My family requires an income. Jim cannot do it alone. He could use your help. My other boys be interested in legitimate enterprises these days and balk at working for the family firm. I need me a new partner I can count on."

"If 'tis what ye want, I'll do it."

"Good lad. I will drop by from time to time. Make sure Kate and Ada keep watch in the evenings."

"Checking up on Kate is not hard work."

Bill laughed. "I can always count on you for special assignments."

*****

The following days fell into the idyllic routine Ryan recalled well from the weeks before the *Peel* raid. Two or three nights a week, he guided shiploads of tea to the usual rendezvous points in Canada. Between smuggling runs, he made minor repairs to boats and equipment at the Johnston wharf.

Fallout from the *Peel* raid and Bill's shadowy presence in the islands made June an exciting month. The trial for the captured *Peel* raiders began in Watertown. William Anderson stood in the docket first, charged with robbery and arson. The prosecution called a long list of witnesses, including the *Peel*'s captain and purser.

Every day, Kate and Ada sifted through chatter in the market and on the wharfs, searching for facts about the trial and other events. At the midday meal, Ryan and the family ate in excited silence while the two women related details.

Ryan set aside the late afternoons for walks with Kate. Some days, they strolled along Water Street looking at ships tied up at the wharfs. Other times, they crossed the new bridge over French Creek to view farms on the far side. In the country, beyond the view of town gossips, they held hands and kissed in the shade of trees. At such intimate moments, Zak kept guard and squawked if anyone approached.

Returning from a stroll on Water Street in the last week of June, they spied Ada hurrying to the Johnston wharf.

"Ada! What's wrong?" Kate asked.

"I saw a signal from your father on the island."

"Do not fret, cousin. We will take a little row out that way and have a look."

Ryan grabbed two sets of oars and chose a gig with double oarlocks. He and Kate rowed in a wide circuit to approach Governors Island from the back side, unseen by anyone in Clayton. From a distance, Kate descried the unmistakable bulky silhouette of her father sitting on a rock. Limp clothes clung to his chest and legs. Zak flew ahead and greeted him first.

"Father, did you swim here?"

"Yes. Why the surprise?"

"You are fifty-six. Men your age do not swim three thousand feet of open water."

"I don't care what other men do."

"Have ye no boat, Bill?"

"No. My crew dropped me off on the far side of Grindstone two days ago. I needed me some exercise, so I hiked over to John Farrow's place. His boat be under repair, so I decided to swim. The water be warm enough."

"Are ye coming home?"

"Yes. For a night or two. Then we must be off."

"Some new enterprise?"

He smiled and nodded. "A party."

"What party, Father, and where?"

"We be having a Fourth of July celebration at Fort Wallace. I've invited sympathetic local notables. I expect all my family to attend."

"Are you mad, Father? Won't that give away the secret location?"

"I figure it be a matter of days before one side or the other finds it. I already removed the armaments and most provisions. So, I be holding a party to rub Bonnycastle's face in it."

"Might a patrol invade yer celebration, Bill?"

"Not much chance. On my suggestion, a couple of farmers nigh Brockville shall report tomorrow that I was seen in the area with five men and a load of rifles. That should keep Bonnycastle's boys busy long enough. And the American patrols will do their patriotic duty and stay home on the Fourth to celebrate."

"It does sound like fun, Father."

"It will be. So, what news have you?"

"Your lawyer friend Bernard Bagley defended William Anderson for free on arson charges for burning the *Peel*."

"How'd the trial go?"

"A jury acquitted Anderson yesterday despite all the eyewitness accounts."

Bill clapped his hands. "I love Jefferson County juries. What of the others?"

"The state postponed further trials, expecting a similar outcome. Sadly, they are keeping the other accused in jail."

"They won't be there long, I wager."

"Let us head home and find you some dry clothes, Father."

At dinner that night, John told his father about a new bilateral agreement. Setting aside old rivalries, British and American commanders had agreed that either country could hunt for Bill anywhere in the Thousand Islands, regardless of borders.

"Is Bonnycastle behind it?"

"No," John began. "Captain Williams Sandom made the deal with our military. He's taken as much interest in you as Bonnycastle."

"I saw something like that coming," Bill said. "That be why I've redistributed our munitions and why I must abandon Fort Wallace."

"Who is Sandom," Ryan asked.

"He be the Brit naval commander around here. He be about my age and a top navy man. It be nice to know I got their respect."

"It's a dark time for America," Jim began, "when British gunboats can patrol American waters searching for Americans."

"Many are angry about it," Decatur added.

"Ada and I heard the two nations have five steamers and five hundred men assigned to find you, Father."

"It must be costing those Brits a fortune," Ada replied.

"It be so," said Bill, smiling.

*****

On the Fourth of July morning, the Johnston family shipped in tubs of salad, jars of pickles, baskets of fresh buns, buckets of strawberries, barrels of ale, crates of rum, and other provisions to Fort Wallace. Bill's crew set up cooking pits and barbeque spits for a pickerel lunch and a venison supper, and built a bar next to the shore shaded by a canvas awning.

The guests arrived near midday. Bill's sons guided flotillas of rowboats to the island. Men wore dark coats, light trousers and shirts, and colored cravats. The wives that chose to attend dressed for a garden party, with cool cotton and pastel silks the most common fabrics. To fend off the sun, male guests wore top hats and ladies donned bonnets or carried parasols.

Ryan, Bill, and the Johnston sons wore new work clothes: high-quality, dark linen pants and long-sleeved, loose white cotton shirts. Napoleon and John, both young men in their twenties and keen to establish business connections, also wore silk vests. They stayed close to the merchants, traders, and professionals among the guests, listening to conversations on the state of local business, the current recession, and the British impediments to free trade along the river.

Ann Johnston commanded her husband's crew like a general in battle. Ryan spotted her white bonnet bobbing through the throng all day, as she made sure her helpers correctly stored, prepared, and served food. The scent of wood smoke and seared meat stirred everyone's appetite.

Kate, in a white summer dress with a pinched waist and high ruffled collar, greeted each new boatload of guests and directed them to the food and drink. The silk apron her father looted from the *Peel* flattered her narrow hips.

Ada, youthful and high-spirited, held court above a knot of male admirers. She wore a sleeveless, flowing peach-colored dress in the latest fashion, low cut across her back and chest. She out-debated any man on political topics without hurting anyone's feelings. The men cheered when she said President Van Buren was sinning against the republic's founders by allowing British ships to search for her uncle in American waters. Several admirers said they regretted a woman could not hold public office, since Ada was a natural politician.

Ryan tended bar. He kept tankards topped with foaming ale and ceramic cups brimming with rum for the endless toasts. Kate tossed a bun into the air to start the catch-food game. Zak played with anyone he could engage, and many did.

Bill picked his guest list with politics in mind: town, state and national politicians, bureaucrats, prominent businessmen, old friends from the Revenue Service, and men to whom Bill owed favors.

Jim Johnston stayed away from intoxicating beverages and made it his duty to ensure that no tipsy guests tumbled off the island's steeper edges. Decatur, too young to drink, took charge of the thirty guest boats, mooring or stowing each properly.

From the moment the first boatload of guests arrived, Bill remained the event's cynosure. Friends and admirers clustered around. He retold old war stories. He recounted the story of how and why he fled Canada in 1813 after the British falsely accused him of treason and confiscated all his wealth without due process.

To a hushed audience at lunch, he gave a minute-by-minute description of the *Sir Robert Peel*'s final hours. He boasted no one could capture him alive unless he chose to surrender. He swore his fight with the British and preparations for the liberation of Canada would continue. Of that, he gave no details.

With cicadas humming in the late afternoon heat, mint tea became a popular beverage while men fought off the soporific effects of ale and rum. Languid revelers napped in the limited shade or the once-secret cave, resting for the evening ahead.

*****

In the festive lull, Ada ducked under the canvas roof and sidled up to the oak-plank bar in Ryan's beverage cantina. Zak, by then overfed, snoozed on a nearby branch.

"I'd like some lemonade, please, if possible."

"I have some chilling in the river." Ryan grabbed a clean mug and turned to fill it from a ceramic jug.

Ada sighed softly when Ryan bent to fetch the container and his trousers tightened across his muscular buttocks. He turned, caught her watching him, and smiled. She made no attempt to look away.

He added a mint leaf to the drink. "Here ye go, Mrs. Burleigh."

"You call me *missus* again and I'll geld you."

His eyes widened. "Sorry, Ada. I was speaking like I was taught."

Ada leaned forward and looked him in the eye. Ryan held her gaze. She could see him examining her face. She had to assume he liked what he saw because he didn't turn away or look embarrassed.

She noticed his eyes flit downward, drawn by the clear cleavage view her loose blouse allowed. She expected it. Ada believed men could no more avoid a quick peek than they could halt a sunrise. She measured a gentleman by how soon he averted his eyes. Ryan quickly pulled his attention back to her face.

"I find nothing wrong with your manners. I prefer people use my first name or my maiden name, Randolph. I rarely use my married name unless I am with my husband."

Before Ryan could form another question, Ada cut him off. "No further questions regarding my husband. Let's talk about you. Do you love my cousin?"

"That's put bluntly."

"It is my way. Don't evade the question. Do you love Kate?"

"I'm not sure how love feels. I have strong feelings for her. I enjoy our time together."

"*Enjoy* is such a feeble word. You might use it to describe an afternoon fishing."

"Tis not the same. I might give up fishing, but not Kate."

"If you plan a future with her, settle down. She worries you may be too wild. Show her you are solid and reliable. She is the most eligible young woman in Clayton. She won't stay single forever."

"I'll think on yer advice. Do ye care for anything else?"

She laughed in a lusty fashion and rose to go. "What I want is not available."

*****

Ada sauntered away, her dress swishing on her full hips. So much different in appearance than Kate, Ryan mused, but equally exciting.

"I guess there be different kinds of beauty, eh, Zak."

"Critiky! Croc!"

Kate ducked into the cool shade of Ryan's bar.

"What did Ada want?"

"Lemonade," he replied deadpan.

"I heard that tune again as I walked in here."

"What tune?

"The melody you hum every time Ada comes near you."

"I nary do that."

"Yes, you do. I guess I don't blame you. She is certainly a formidable woman." She glanced over her shoulder where Ada had settled in the shade with two dapper businessmen. "Men follow her like lost puppies, though she is married. I will never have such appeal."

"Do ye desire a puppy? I can get ye one."

She lunged towards Ryan, leaning one elbow on the bar, and grabbed his hair. "Sure. Maybe an Irish setter that comes when he is called."

"Keep guard, Zak."

"Zaak!"

Ryan bent forward, caressed her lips briefly with his own, and pulled back. Her eyes narrowed and brow furrowed in the universal expression that asks why stop. He bent forward, kissing her firmly and long.

"Rrok! Cric! Croc!"

They recognized Zak's warning and pulled apart. Kate exhaled and fanned her face.

"Have you any lemonade. I am feeling flushed."

*****

At sunset, the partygoers found their second wind, ate a second meal, and descended on Ryan's bar. Community leaders and merchant princes, now loquacious and merry as grigs, raised more toasts, too often lapsing into the maudlin logorrhea of the soused.

With a moon sliver rising above the river and the northwest sky still glowing a faint orange from the vanished sun, a state assemblyman made the evening's most memorable and well-spoken toast.

"On this propitious occasion, I propose that, from this day forward, our great host shall be called Admiral Sir William Johnston, Knight of the Thousand Islands. If the British can knight a colonel for burning the *Caroline*, we can knight Admiral Johnston for burning the *Peel*."

The speaker then presented Bill with a flag bearing his new title. The toast and flag stimulated the longest and loudest string of cheers that day. It also unleashed another stampede to Ryan's bar.

After dark, Jim and John set off fireworks that lit up the water between Grindstone and Wells Islands. Bill handed out loaded rifles to the revelers and, with a simple countdown—three, two, one, fire—led them in a musket volley aimed at the Canadian shore. Tired and sober, Ryan thanked God none of the armed drunks shot each other. Zak huddled on Ryan's shoulder seeking safety from the bright lights and booming noise.

The musket salute marked the finale. Its fading echo acted like a signal. Partygoers prepared to depart. Sir William shook hands with each guest. The Johnston women made sure every boat had a lamp blazing in the bow and the most sober person on the tiller. Well after midnight the Johnston family rowed home, except Decatur. While Ryan and the crew relaxed around the ebbing fire eating leftovers, Bill gave his youngest son a new pistol and toasted his seventeenth birthday with watered-down rum.

The next afternoon, Bill's sons removed the cups, cutlery, and anything else of non-military value. Ryan and Bill's crew moved the military paraphernalia to other hideouts within an hour's row of Fort Wallace. They emptied the cavern except for two cracked barrels and Bill's new flag.

"Are ye not taking yer flag?"

"No. That be a present for Bonnycastle, so he knows I was knighted before him."

Bill sent his French Canadian crew with the last load of rifles to a hideout on Wells Island. With Ryan and *Peel* raiders Robert Smith and William Robbins, Bill led the somber evacuation of Fort Wallace in late afternoon.

"Tis hard to leave this place, Bill. Tis a symbol of yer cause."

"Fort Wallace will continue to exist in spirit wherever I make my camp."

Rowing away from the cavern, Ryan watched the big man at the tiller, his eyes focused on some distant place.

Queen's Suitor

For five days after abandoning Fort Wallace, Ryan, Bill, and the remaining crew camped at a tea depot a hundred yards into the woods near the end of Delaney Bay on Grindstone Island's east side. They could no longer safely cross open water by day. The British and American patrols doubled when word of Bill's party spread. Military steamers and schooners plied all the main channels. Armed soldiers in skiffs navigated the backwaters and poked into secluded coves.

Ryan and Zak hunted the forest by day for the group's supper. Bill disappeared for hours by himself to, as he said, "ponder me next move." Smith and Robbins idled away the day, drinking and sleeping.

On the sixth day, Bill roused the crew after breakfast.

"I need me some exercise. Leave your gear. We will be back in two or three days."

"Where are we going?" Ryan asked.

"To see John Farrow."

"Isn't he wanted for the *Peel* raid?"

"Since Anderson's acquittal, arresting him be low priority. No one be searching for anyone but me now."

Bill led them southwest across the big island. They scaled granite ridges, skirted swamps, and tromped through dark forests. By midday, they came to a bay directly across from Clayton. Further along the shore, a well used trail led to a clearing. Less than half an acre in size, it held a cabin and a barn.

"This be Farrow's place. We will stay here a night or two."

Farrow stepped from his cabin and leaned his stubby bulk on a porch post.

"Good day to you, Bill."

"Hello, John."

"I hear you had a big party I wasn't asked to."

"I invited people I may need favors from. I don't have to buy me your loyalty, do I?"

"No, Bill."

"Then you won't mind if we stay. We will sleep in the hayloft, so we won't be a bother to your wife or kids."

"Help yourself."

"Any chance of food, then?"

"Come inside. We have beans on the boil and fresh bread."

After eating, Ryan and Bill hiked to a pebble beach with a view of Clayton. Zak hopped along the shore searching for morsels to eat.

Ryan scanned Clayton with his telescope. "I guess we can't go home. There's no green pennant flying."

"No matter. Did you know I have family here on Grindstone?"

"No, sir. Who'd that be?"

"My cousin Samuel. He can be difficult, but his wife Jane be nice and she cooks near as well as Ann."

"Do ye visit them much?"

"Sometimes. Samuel disapproves of my ways. I have tried to bring him into smuggling—he could use the money—but he refuses. He be a firm believer in the law, even if it means he cannot clothe his kids." Bill started walking. "Let's pay them a visit."

They followed a shore-side trail to a rough-looking farm. Corn and potatoes grew on five acres of cleared land. A simple cabin snuggled by the forest edge. Bill knocked on the plank door. A man in his forties answered. Shorter and lighter in build than Bill, he bore an unmistakable family resemblance.

"Hello, cousin."

Samuel frowned at Bill and at the two flintlock pistols in his belt. "Whatta you want?"

"I came for a little visit."

"You're hoping for a meal is more like it."

"We already ate, but I take that as an invitation to tea. By the way, this lad be Ryan."

"Pleased to meet ye, Mr. Johnston." He held out his hand. Samuel ignored it.

"You ain't bringing that bird inside with you?"

"No, sir. He'll stay outside."

"Who's that, Sam?" called a woman from inside.

"It's my pirate cousin and one of his bandits come for tea."

"Well, let them in. And mind your manners."

The door entered into the kitchen. It reminded Ryan of his home in Ireland, poor and basic, but clean and tidy, with a scent of baking pies in the air.

A pale-haired woman in her thirties gave Bill a quick hug.

"There's been so much news of you these last weeks." She held his hands lightly and gazed up into his smiling face.

"Hello, Jane," Bill said with open affection. "This here be Ryan."

"Welcome, young man. Please have a seat."

"Thank ye, ma'am."

They faced Samuel across a long, homemade maple table. Samuel stared Bill in the eye. Ryan had to give him credit; he certainly showed no fear of his infamous cousin.

"Why don't you turn yourself in and save everyone a load of trouble?"

"The summer be too fine a season to spend in jail."

"You'd be better off surrendering to the local magistrate. If the British get you, you'll dangle for sure."

"It be my business and decision, not yours."

Samuel grunted. "You're a disgrace to the family. Why can't you abide the law like the rest of us?"

Bill put his big hands together and cracked several knuckles. "There be a fat reward for my capture. If you be so damned law-abiding, turn me in."

"There'll be none of that," Jane interjected. "Family sticks together. Right, Sam?" After a long pause that made Ryan squirm, Samuel nodded in agreement.

Ryan stayed mute, except for the occasional 'please' and 'thank ye' while Jane served tea. Bill switched the discussion to economics and local politics, something he and Samuel wouldn't lock horns over.

When they rose to depart in mid-afternoon, Jane asked, "We can find room for you if you want to stay."

"Thanks, but I have exhausted Sam's hospitality. I should rejoin my men at Farrow's."

Bill hiked back to Farrow's, scowling and wordless. That night, he assigned Smith, Robbins, and Ryan each to three-hour guard shifts.

"Why? It ain't something we do normal," Robbins commented.

"Because Farrow be a wanted man. You never know when some sheriff might drop in and discover us by mistake."

Ryan recognized the lie. The others didn't.

*****

On third watch, Ryan witnessed the black night dissolve to gray through an open hayloft hatch. The robins hadn't started singing yet when Farrow's two leashed mutts sprang to their feet in the yard and growled. A stick snapped in the woods.

"Bill! Lads! We have visitors."

"Rrok! Cric! Croc!" Zak launched from the barn roof and began calling as the dogs howled. "Rrok! Cric! Croc!"

From a dead sleep, Bill snapped awake, leapt from his blanket in the hay, pistols in hand, and peered into the dawn gloom.

"British! Down the ladders, quick."

They hurried to the barn's lower stalls and peered out a door. A British officer and fifty men in the Royal Navy's blue uniform formed a line at the clearing's north side.

Ryan recognized their leader as the man who sunk his canoe that May. "I know that officer."

"It be Lieutenant Leary, one of Bonnycastle's assassins," Bill said.

"Why is he waiting?" asked Ryan.

"Because he ain't alone, I bet. It be a trap. Follow me, lads."

Bill sprinted out the barn and towards the deep forest thirty yards away as fifty American soldiers entered the clearing's south end. Both forces fired at once. The rolling roar of a hundred muskets startled the still sleeping birds from the trees, set dogs baying for miles, and woke half the population of Clayton.

Something tugged Ryan's pant leg and stung like a dozen hornets. He kept running. Robbins cursed and clutched his arm. Bill crashed through the thick underbrush that always grows at the edge of clearings and led his crew into the dark woods. Another volley of gun fire thundered from behind. Musket balls thudded into trees around them.

On a trail only he could see, Bill headed in a northeast direction over the rocky ridges of Grindstone Island. Little dawn light penetrated the primal forest, and they soon lost their pursuers. After an hour of traveling at a trot, Bill called a rest by a brook. Zak settled on a rock next to Ryan.

"Thanks for the warning, old friend," he whispered to the raven.

"Kriend!" Zak replied.

"Rest," Bill ordered. "Have water. Anyone hurt?"

"My arm's hit."

"Let me look. I dressed lots of wounds in the war." Bill pulled off Robbins' shirt. "That be not a killer. The ball went through and missed the bone. I will sling it for now and doctor it up better at our camp. Anyone else hurt?"

Ryan lifted a flap of torn pant to reveal a shallow gash in his flesh. "I have a flesh wound, but 'tis not bleeding much."

Bill examined the damage. "Clean that with rum at the camp. It will heal fine."

His ministrations complete, Bill paced back and forth, scowling and cursing. Ryan spoke the question they'd all been thinking. "How did the British and Americans know where we were?"

"Ain't an accident that both forces found us at the same moment," Robbins added.

"You don't suppose Farrow snitched?" Smith suggested.

"Not him. He'd never soil his own nest."

"Then who, Bill?"

He didn't answer. Ryan had his suspicions, but kept quiet.

After an hour's rest, Bill led them at a light pace to the tea depot they'd departed the day before. The hungry men descended on the stock of food and rum. Bill dressed Robbins' wound and made a proper cloth sling. Ryan cleaned his own wound, but kept it unbandaged. The gash had already clotted. The air would do it good.

He fell asleep on a bed of moss. Zak snoozed on a branch above. The other men soon napped too, except Bill. He crouched on a rock, staring at his feet and stirring up the old leaves with a stick.

Ryan awoke a little after midday to find Bill packing a sack with provisions and ammunition. "Are ye leaving?" he whispered.

"Yes. Tell everyone to go home."

"What will ye do?"

"I have in mind to check on Farrow to see if he was hurt in the raid and then have me a word with my cousin. After that, I will shift downriver and off Grindstone. Tell Kate to bring supplies in two days. Look for me near the cave at Hemlock Island."

"I'll be glad to help her with the rowing."

"No. Only Kate and Ada for now. The British have spies watching us. Each time Kate departs to meet me, you or the boys head off in boats a little in advance. Divert attention."

"Ye've nary taken such precautions afore."

"Bonnycastle has committed every resource at his disposal to catch me. He has succeeded at every task he's taken on in life until now. I be the one flaw in a perfect career. He be relentless. I be safest alone."

"If 'tis what ye want, I'll do it."

"Good lad. Move all my boats off Abel's before someone confiscates them. Put them in the warehouse. They won't dare raid Clayton. Also ship some tea across. We need the income." He slung his sack over a shoulder and headed west.

When the men awoke, Ryan relayed Bill's orders. Without debate or question, they packed and crossed to Grindstone's south side near

Abel's Island. Robert Smith, fit and youthful, swam the four-hundred-foot gap to the island and rowed back in a gig to get them. At the shanty, Ryan bathed and put on clean clothes. He directed Smith and Robbins to take a gig each to Clayton, while he led in a skiff.

"Ah, Zak," he spoke as he rowed. "It'll be grand to be back smuggling and taking walks with Kate."

"Critiky! Croc!"

*****

Ryan arrived at the Johnston home in mid-afternoon to find a small British naval steamer, the *Bull Frog*, anchored in the bay off French Creek. Armed men in blue uniforms patrolled its decks. A line of Clayton residents along Water Street stared sullenly at the British gunboat. Ryan overheard "bloody British" muttered by laborers and merchants alike.

Over afternoon tea on the front porch with the Johnston family, Ryan recounted his adventures with Bill since the party a week before. "The last I saw him, he headed over to see if Farrow was well and then moved on to his cousin's place. That's all I know."

"I went to Farrow's today," Jim explained. "He and his family are unharmed. The bloody British shot his watchdogs for doing their job."

"Why did my husband visit his cousin a second time?"

Ann's astute question quieted the ensemble and made Ryan uncomfortable. He couldn't bring himself to accuse Samuel of treachery.

"Never mind," she said. "Your silence is telling. Jim, row me over tomorrow."

"Yes, Mother."

"Who's commanding the *Bull Frog*?" Ryan asked.

"Lieutenant Leary," Decatur answered.

"He's the one that sank my canoe and raided us at Farrow's."

"After he departed Grindstone Island, he headed straight to Fort Wallace," Kate said, her forehead furrowed. "He knew exactly where it was and expected to discover Father there."

"That reminds me. Bill wants you to bring supplies to Hemlock Island in two days."

"Can you and Zak will come with me?"

"Bill says I'm to leave ahead of you in a different direction to distract the Brit spies watching this family."

"I will leave tomorrow then and stay overnight with mother's cousin in Alexandria Bay. Hemlock is a long journey."

"What about me?" asked Ada.

"Bill said you can go with Kate."

"Then I will. I'd love a little jaunt."

"We must drive the damn British from our waters," said the usually quiet Napoleon.

"How are you going to do it?" asked Decatur.

"John and I have a plan. Wait and watch."

"This family has much to do tomorrow," Ann said. "Anyone for rhubarb pie?"

*****

The next morning, Ryan and Zak rowed to Whiskey Island to spend the morning fishing. Lieutenant Leary on the *Bull Frog* kept his telescope on Ryan until his skiff disappeared behind the western tip of Grindstone Island.

Ann and Jim departed for Samuel's farm in a second skiff, also watched from the *Bull Frog*. Jim carried two pistols in a canvas sack. Ann brought a carpetbag stuffed with clothing her children had outgrown.

Ada and Kate sashayed to the wharf in long white dresses, carrying a picnic basket between them. With great flourish they launched a skiff themselves and headed downstream. Ada rowed. Kate lounged in the stern sheltered by a pink parasol. Under cover of darkness that morning, Decatur and Napoleon had concealed supplies for their father beneath a canvas cover on the floor of her boat. As usual, Kate had her rifle and flintlock pistol tucked away.

Jim and Ann landed across the channel at Aunt Jane's Bay. Jim put both pistols in his belt and led the way up the tree-shaded cart track to Samuel Johnston's farm. Jane stepped outside, wiping her hands on her apron. "If you want my husband, he's gone."

"Where? What happened?"

"Bill came back yesterday. Sam saw him striding across the yard and bolted into the forest. I haven't seen him since. I'm not sure if I care."

"Did my husband talk to you?"

"Yes. He mentioned the raid at Farrow's. He said he suspects Sam passed information to the American patrol, and they coordinated an attack with the British. He might be right. Sam was gone for a spell after Bill's earlier visit. Bill promised he wouldn't kill Sam, but he was unclear what he intended."

"How are you holding up, Jane?"

"You know how it is. You must be strong for the children."

Ann put her bag on the porch. "I expect your youngsters are growing fast. Here are some boys' and girls' clothes I'm sure yours can use."

"Thank you. They will be put to good use."

"You and the children are welcome. Come by for a few days. Your eldest should be big enough to row across now."

Jane understood the welcome didn't extend to her husband, and she accepted it. "Thank you, Ann. I'm comforted knowing you are over there."

"Jim and I must go now. I have lunch to prepare, and the store requires looking after."

"Good-bye. And God bless you."

*****

In mid-morning, Bernard Bagley, a prominent Watertown lawyer, arrived by carriage at the Johnston wharf. Two days earlier, John had agreed to help him to serve legal papers on a Grindstone Island resident. In his mid-forties, and tall and lean in stature, Bagley was a Patriot supporter with a reputation as a feisty and hot-tempered republican.

"Good day, Mr. Bagley. Nice day for a trip on the water."

"Indeed. The weather is a blessing this week."

"This way to the skiff, sir. Mind yourself stepping into the boat."

Bagley questioned the handgun in John's belt. "What is that for?"

"It never hurts to have a weapon. The islands are full of pirates," John replied without a hint of irony. "Would you care to see that British ship up close? It is a minor detour."

"Yes. By all means. Let me say, I am not happy with it being here."

"Me neither, sir."

John rowed into the natural harbor formed by the mouth of French Creek where the *Bull Frog* lay. Thin ribbons of black smoke rose from the idling ship's stacks. From the foredeck, Lieutenant Leary inspected the approaching rowboat. It contained a large man, who fit Bill Johnston's physical description, with a pistol in his belt and the clear intention to come within shooting range of his ship.

"Helmsman," he yelled. "Ahead slow. Intercept that rowboat off the bow."

"Aye, lieutenant."

John had his back to the *Bull Frog* as he rowed. He heard the churn of water when the paddlewheels started to turn. He caught the expression on Bagley's face when the steamer's course became obvious.

"It is coming our way. What in the name of God are they up to?"

Lieutenant Leary hollered over the rail. "Stop where you are. You are under arrest."

The gunboat bore down on them with a wave of water rolling out from its bow. The helmsman reversed the paddlewheels and brought the ship to a halt. John and Bagley gripped their boat's gunwales while the steamer's wake rocked them.

"Who the hell are you to interfere with Americans going about their lawful business?" Bagley demanded.

"I am Lieutenant George Leary of the Royal Navy. I am authorized by agreement with your government to arrest anyone aiding Bill Johnston or his ruffians. Come aboard now or I'll make it hard on you."

Red-faced, Bagley clambered aboard the British vessel. John followed quietly. The firebrand lawyer was unlikely to truckle before the officer—in fact, John counted on it.

"What are your names?"

"My name is Bernard Bagley, attorney to many prominent men in Jefferson County. Your British bosses will hear from me, trust me on that."

Nonplused, the officer turned to John. "And your name?"

"John Johnston."

"Any relation to Bill Johnston?"

"Yes. He's my father."

"I'll have that pistol," Leary commanded.

Two armed sailors pointed their bayonets at John. He slipped the handgun from his belt and handed it grip-first to Leary.

"Guard. Take him below."

"The sins of the father do not fall on the sons," Bagley barked. "Even your despotic British laws recognize that. You have no case."

Leary held up his hand. The guard halted.

"Why did you approach my ship?" Leary asked John.

"Just a little sightseeing on our way to Grindstone Island."

"What is your business there?"

"My firm's affairs are none of your concern," Bagley barked, stepping closer to the shorter Leary. "John is in my employ. Now, unless you have a question pertaining to your proper duties, we will take our leave."

Leary had to stand down. Diplomacy limited his powers, despite the agreement with American authorities.

"Very well," he said, returning the pistol.

As they rowed away, Bagley bellowed, "We threw you bloody British out before, and we will do it again. You have my word."

Bagley kept his vow. That afternoon, he ranted to politicians, clergymen, merchants, and anyone of influence. By evening, the tale had taken on the proportions of an international incident. From Sackets Harbor to Ogdensburg, it spread faster than a salacious rumor. The story reached Ada and Kate in Alexandria Bay. They laughed like lunatics and drank toasts with sherry to John and Napoleon's clever gambit.

Within days, New York Governor William Marcy, tired of trying to calm delegations of angry visitors to Albany, moved to stop the problem at its source. The district military commander told the British to keep their warships out of U.S. waters.

*****

Though politics now divided the forces hunting for Bill, no place in the islands provided refuge. Both countries continued to search for him. He carried a sheet of canvas for shelter, a frying pan, some fishing line, and weapons. He avoided daytime boat travel because his hunters traveled by water. He camped in the secluded hills and dense forests of Grindstone, Wells and Hill Islands.

He hunted and fished, but relied on his family for some sustenance and all his ammunition. He most wanted information. Once a week, his children or Ada delivered supplies and news. They met at different locations and only for an hour or two. At each parting, Bill gave a general location of where to find him next time.

*****

On a sunny July morning, Ryan worked outside the Johnston's warehouse, shaping a new oar with a draw knife and sipping mint-flavored spring water. Overhead, Zak soared on thermal updrafts rising from the hot roads and roofs of Clayton.

"Rrok! Cric! Croc!" Zak called.

Ada approached with two canvas-wrapped bundles.

"What have ye there, Ada?"

"Clothes and dry goods for Jane. Can you row me over there?"

"I'll get a boat ready."

With his back to Zak on the bow, he rowed facing Ada. Casual and confident, she wore a light cotton dress that showed as much bare skin as Clayton society would accept. Her auburn hair glistened in the summer light and fluttered in the light breeze. Their eyes met. For a moment, Ryan imagined Kate the way she might appear in fifteen years or so—beauty accented by maturity, and personality fortified by experience.

Ryan caught Ada studying him. Her eyes admired his muscles as they moved and flexed under his thin cotton shirt. Her gaze swept over his red hair and locked on his blue eyes. She smiled, making no effort to hide her attraction.

"What are ye thinking, Ada? You resemble a cat that's seen a mouse."

"Are you saying I appear predatory?"

"No, Ada. You look…er…hungry. Like someone laid supper in front of ye."

Ada laughed with a lustiness Ryan had never experienced from a woman. "If I was ten years younger, I'd be dining on you and you'd beg to be another meal."

He lost his timing and jammed one oar into the water during the oars' forward motion through the air. The miscue sent the skiff downstream and jarred his right shoulder.

"Zaak!" Zak launched into the air.

Ryan swallowed at the tightness in his throat. "What is it ye be trying to tell me?"

"I'm sorry. Our conversation is as off-course as this boat." She titled her head back in laughter, exposing the ivory curve of her long neck. With tears in her eyes she continued. "Let's change the subject. When do you plan to show my cousin you are serious?"

"I am serious about her." Ryan had regained his rowing rhythm. "I told ye before."

"Really? Most women her age, if not already married or engaged, imagine husbands and children. What do you imagine?"

He paused to think. "I imagine being a shipbuilder or a farmer, maybe both, and a family, too, someday."

"Someday is what men say when they prefer to keep a woman on a tether. I want to see your commitment."

"I am committed."

"No. You are committed to Bill and his intrigues, but not to Kate. You cannot be true to both."

"I'll think on yer advice, agin."

*****

British and American commanders suspected the Johnston family knew Bill's whereabouts and paid agents to watch them. Throughout the summer, Lieutenant-Colonel Bonnycastle's spies regularly reported Kate rowing alone or with an older female companion. Young Kate became Bonnycastle's main suspect.

One early August morning, Kate set forth alone from Alexandria Bay with a load of supplies for her father. She had rowed from Clayton the day before and stayed with friends overnight. The silhouettes of Alexandria Bay's clapboard homes and shore-side warehouses, dark against the lavender dawn sky, guided her path through the narrow harbor to the river.

She crossed the shipping channel to the backside of Hemlock Island. With that island between her and the village, Kate then guided the boat close to Wells Island's shore to find cover from its forest and cattail stands in the predawn sepia light.

She rowed through the narrow gap between the downstream end of Wells Island and Mary Island, shipped her oars, and let her skiff drift. The border lay ahead in the middle of a wide bay. Hill Island, a half mile away, was British territory. She wished her father would stay on American islands: he wouldn't hang if captured.

The bay had no islands to obscure her passage. With sunrise a half hour away, light illuminated the river. The thin veil of mist on the water gave no cover. She scanned the bay for other boats. Any carelessness could lead the British to her father.

Seeing no other craft, Kate dipped the oars and started to row. Her skiff sliced the glassy river. Water gurgled on the bow. She worked her athletic muscles to their limit. The oarlocks made a rapid clink-clunk in the morning quiet. Within minutes, the rhythm of her labored breathing matched the oarlock's cadence: a deep inhale when she pulled the blades from the water and swung the oars forward in the air, and a sharp exhale—almost a grunt— when she pulled the blades back through the water.

The sun cleared the horizon. Kate, perspiring from effort in the cool dawn air, steered her skiff into Hill Island's leafy shade. She waited ten minutes and scanned for other boats. Seeing none, she began rowing slowly, keeping the shore close to her port side. She didn't know exactly where her father hid. He'd find her.

She rounded the southeastern tip of Hill Island into a cove. A pebble splashed into the water next to her seat. She steered the skiff towards the shore and ground on a strip of sand. Her father emerged from the brush and pulled the boat half way out with one great tug.

"Fine morning to be on the water, Kate."

"Yes, Father. It was a pleasant voyage."

Together, they concealed the skiff behind a stand of young willows.

"I brought you clean clothes, more cartridges, three loaves of bread, some strawberry jam, a watermelon, a fresh tea brick, and ten pounds of beef jerky. Will that do? You seem thin."

"That be plenty. A little thinning be healthy at my age. Keeps me fast and fit."

"Are you certain?"

"Yes. You have brought too much. Help me eat that watermelon."

"I would love to."

Bill cut slices off the melon with his bowie knife. Kate leaned on a mossy rock to rest. Her arms ached.

"So, what news do you bring?"

"We are well. Ryan and Jim are keeping the tea business going. My other brothers take turns minding the store. Ada has a cold, but is on the mend. Mother sends her love."

"That Ryan be a blessing, don't you think?"

"I suppose so."

"Is there more?"

"Some rebellion news."

"Tell me."

"Those fifty farmers Bonnycastle arrested in February as part of your plot on Kingston are all free men."

"Good news. How'd that happen?"

"Most never went to trial because of insufficient evidence. Eight who did were defended by the lawyer I met in Kingston last December, John Macdonald, and received acquittals."

"He sounds like a fine lawyer. What else?"

"Remember the Patriot raid at Short Hills?"

He nodded.

"The British hanged their leader a week ago. The other prisoners were sentenced to transport for life in Van Dieman's Land."

"Their leader be the lucky one. I hear that penal colony be a living Hell."

"I also learned that Daniel Heustis planned to raid the local jail to release the prisoners, but the British shipped them to Kingston before he could organize his men."

"Good of Daniel to try. What else?"

"Mr. Montgomery and eleven other Patriot prisoners are free."

"Free! Are the British going soft?"

"They tunneled from Fort Henry at night during a storm and escaped across the river two days ago."

"They escaped? From the impregnable Fort Henry? Ha! I will have to talk to Montgomery some day and hear the details. That be a miracle. Any more news?"

"No. That is all."

"Except for that poor fellow's hanging, you brought some very fine news."

Kate and her father ate watermelon and chatted about life on the river for another hour.

"Father, do you really need to move about so often. Surely you could stay at one of your interior camps on Wells Island and avoid the patrols."

"It be not the British or Americans I worry about. I think Bonnycastle might enlist the Mohawks to find me. They be loyal British allies and the only scouts I truly respect. I must keep moving and hide my trail."

"Yes, that sounds best, Father."

Kate departed as the day's full heat began to bear down. She rowed at an easy, but steady pace. Stealth and speed were less important now, or so she thought.

As she rounded the tip of Hill Island on her return journey to Alexandria Bay, a British army captain and a naval ensign in a rowboat spotted her. Since rowers face the stern, Kate didn't notice the other boat until too late.

"Halt," called the captain. "You are under arrest, Miss Johnston."

She shifted in her seat to face them. "I am surprised you recognize me."

"We've been shown a flattering sketch of your likeness, miss."

"How charming. British officers are so well mannered."

"Thank you, miss. Now to the matter of your arrest. Kindly tie you boat to the stern and come aboard."

"Do you arrest people simply for being in Canadian waters?"

"Lieutenant-Colonel Bonnycastle ordered your arrest for aiding a known fugitive."

"If you mean my father, I have not seen him for weeks. He is in Rochester."

"Nevertheless, miss, we have our orders."

"Yes. I suppose you do. Please tie my bow line to your stern."

The captain nodded to the ensign. Sweating in his heavy blue uniform, the ensign retrieved the rope's end from Kate's boat and tied it to a cleat on the stern of his craft.

"May I fetch my parasol? The sun is going to be frightfully hot today."

"Yes, by all means."

Kate turned her back to the officers. She had no parasol. She had stowed her father's dirty clothes—which the British must not find beneath the canvas at her feet—next to her rifle and pistol. She slipped the handgun into the fold of her dress between her knees. She faced the officers, cocked the rifle's hammer, and sighted on the captain's chest.

"Sorry, captain. Our plans have changed. We are heading to Alexandria Bay."

"Miss Johnston. You are making matters much worse for yourself. Put that weapon down this instant."

"Captain, I am a crack shot. And, I am my father's daughter. I will shoot if I must."

"You have only one shot, young lady," began the ensign. "We both have pistols close at hand."

"Shut up, you fool," the captain bellowed.

"I have a pistol between my knees if I have to shoot the second one of you. Now, drop your weapons into the river. You first, ensign. Pick it up slowly by the muzzle. I will shoot at any sign of treachery."

Red-faced and sweating, he did as Kate commanded. The heavy handgun made a satisfying plop. The captain dropped his weapon overboard next.

"Thank you, gentlemen. I am pleased I did not have to kill such handsome young men on this perfect summer day. Now, if you would please start rowing. I am expected in Alexandria Bay."

The two angry and perspiring officers pulled at their oars towards the American shore, towing Kate. She lounged in her skiff with her weapons at the ready. When their boats came abreast of Hemlock Island, the captain begged a favor.

"Miss Johnston, please release us. We shall not survive the humiliation if all Alexandria Bay sees our predicament."

"You are safe now in American waters," the ensign added. "You have our word that we'll depart peacefully."

"As you wish, gentlemen."

The officers stopped rowing, untied her skiff, and pointed their craft home.

"Good day, miss."

"Good day to you, captain. All my best to Lieutenant-Colonel Bonnycastle."

*****

The next day, when Kate related her adventure to her family over supper in Clayton, the table erupted in laughter and applause.

"You do this family proud," said Jim.

"The British will think twice before they interfere with the Queen of the Thousand Islands again," John added.

Ryan said little. He recalled stories his grandfather had recited about Gráinne Mhaol, a legendary Irish pirate queen. In his boyhood, he imagined traveling back to the sixteenth century to join her crew. He never dreamed he'd be eating supper with her in real life.

*****

Between Kate's supply runs to her father and Ryan's nighttime smuggling sojourns into Canada, plus all their other duties, they had managed little more than an occasional stroll around town together. That night after supper, Kate winked at Ryan and slipped out onto the porch ahead of him.

"How have you been, stranger?" she said, pulling him into the porch roof's shadow.

He slipped his hands behind her waist, pulled her close and kissed her forehead.

"'Tis grand to see ye if only for a wee time."

"I have an idea. Let us go picnicking tomorrow on Whiskey Island."

"'Tis a fine idea. When?"

"After breakfast. Once my chores are done."

"I'll hardy sleep a wink tonight thinking 'bout it."

The next morning, Kate joined Ryan and Zak on the wharf. She wore an ankle-length cotton day dress, white with a floral pattern of rose petals. It hugged her waist and flowed over her hips. The neckline cut low above her breasts, a change from her usual high-necked garments.

"Tis a flattering dress ye have on."

"Thank you. I bought it last week. It had puffed sleeves, which I can't abide in the summer. I cut them off. They interfere with my rowing."

Her short sleeves revealed the clearly detailed biceps and triceps of a rower.

"Mother disapproves. She tells me it is terribly unfashionable for a woman to show she is not a frail flower."

"Tis one reason I like ye."

"What are the other reasons?"

Ryan laughed. "What do ye have in that picnic basket?"

"A bush lunch of hard-boiled eggs, cold chicken sandwiches, sliced cucumber, and rhubarb cake. There is a jug with lemonade. I wrapped it in several layers of wet towels to keep it cool."

"Sounds grand! Yer boat awaits, Miss Johnston."

"Lead on, Mr. Pine."

"Come, Zak."

"Zaak!"

The summer heat and humidity had already passed the comfort level, and the day's peak lay hours away. Ryan wore a sleeveless shirt of light, unbleached cotton over pale brown cotton trousers. His bare feet braced on the skiff's ribs as he flexed and relaxed with each stroke. Sweat soon trickled from under his straw hat and darkened his shirt collar. On the bow, Zak panted in the still air. Kate opened a frilly pink parasol and shaded her unadorned head.

"Perhaps I should have worn a bonnet today like a sensible woman."

"Bonnets are for old ladies. I admire yer loose hair."

She dangled a long-fingered hand in the river and patted her face. "There are some lovely shady nooks on the north side of Whiskey."

"We'll be there in an hour, if the sun don't kill me."

She gazed away, her expression somber.

"Is something bothering ye?"

"I was wondering when you planned to tell me what happened to your family."

Ryan's half finger throbbed. Collecting himself, he replied, "I suppose it is a story ye should know." He paused. "Six of us departed Ireland. I arrived in Montreal alone. Do you want details?"

"If it is not too painful, yes."

He sighed and started talking. By the time they reached Whiskey Island, he had recounted every detail of the sad tale.

"Thank you for confiding in me. It is better not to have secrets between us."

"It does lighten my load."

"Do you mind if I share your story with my family?"

"I don't mind as long as I don't have to hear it told."

Kate directed Ryan to land the skiff on a narrow gravel beach. Together they hauled it from the water and into concealing shade. Zak flew to a nearby oak.

"Why are we hiding yer boat?"

"A moored boat is an invitation for others to stop for a visit. I do not desire the company of others today."

Ryan waded into the shallows and crouched to wet his hair and face.

"Such heat! If I was alone, I'd be in for a swim."

"Do not let me stop you."

"I can't be stripping down in front of a lady."

"My brothers often swim in their undergarments with me present."

"Well, they're yer family. Besides, I wear no undergarments in summer."

Kate blushed. "I do declare, Mr. Pine, you can be such a savage," she said with a demure nod.

Ryan hooted at the naughtiness in her tone.

"Kindly bring that jug from the boat. I am flushed and wish a cool drink."

He fetched the jug, the wicker basket, and a canvas sheet to spread in the shade. He passed a cup of cold lemonade to Kate and poured one for himself.

"Want to know one of my secrets?" she asked.

"Yes, please."

"Do not tell my parents this, but when I was younger, I often came here and swam without a stitch on. It is so liberating."

"Tis a might dangerous for a young lass."

"I stayed near my pistol. Father taught all his children to shoot as soon as we had the strength to hold our weapon with a steady hand." She opened the picnic basket. "Care for a sandwich or egg after your hard journey?"

"Perhaps an egg."

She passed him an egg on a tiny plate and plucked a sandwich wedge from the basket.

"Zaak!"

She tossed a crust to the raven. "He takes after you—always ready to eat."

A gust of wind sent a hot blast of summer air into their shady refuge.

"If we do not swim Ryan, I fear we will bake."

"What do ye propose?"

"You disrobe where we landed the skiff. I will use that rocky nook to my left. We cannot see each other from those positions. When we swim out, only our heads will show. Thus, modesty is preserved."

"Tis so! What would yer mother say?"

"She'd be scandalized," she said, laughing. "Off you go. I will meet you out there." She pointed to the river.

Ryan stripped off his garments, nearly tripping as he yanked off his pants. He waded to a depth where the cool water came to his chest and waited for Kate to appear. He spotted her head bobbing his way, her tawny haired tied up. They each breast-stroked towards the other. Ten feet apart, she ordered him to halt.

"Stop there! The water is not murky enough to conceal us if we get closer."

In fact, the water was clear. A distorted outline of her pale body tantalized him. An idea jumped into his thoughts, and it showed on his face.

"Why are you grinning?"

Ryan pushed with his outstretched arms, palms upwards, and propelled himself underwater. Water blurred his sight but did not conceal her slender legs, the flare of her hips curving inward to her waist, and her breasts, the size and shape of halved peaches. The water tugged at his stiffening penis as he surfaced. He expected Kate to be angry at his voyeuristic prank.

She smiled when he surfaced. "My turn." She propelled herself underwater.

Ryan, embarrassed by his growing tumescence, pushed with his arms to spin away from her view. When Kate surfaced, it was not behind him as he expected. She popped up five feet in front, treading water, her bun now dissolved into tendrils of wet hair. This close, her naked body glowed pink in the water, its shape distorted by ripples generated by her swaying arms.

"This is exciting, is it not?" She laughed when he blushed. "Actually, I am flattered that Mr. Pine so quickly grew a new limb."

His mouth dropped in shock. Did she take lessons from Ada, he wondered. Kate dissolved in a peel of laughter so violent she had trouble staying afloat. Her laughter salved his nerves.

"Careful! I'll have to come there and rescue ye."

"You have to catch me first."

She dove porpoise fashion, gracing Ryan with a flash view of her smooth bottom. It only served to stiffen his erection. He took two strokes towards her but halted with a gasp. The force of moving water bent his manhood in a direction it was not designed to go.

Kate crawled twenty yards away and looked back. "Too much of a gentleman to chase a naked woman, are you?"

"'Tis that exactly," Ryan lied.

"Rrok! Cric! Croc!"

"Zak sees someone."

"Let us dress and eat. I have worked up an appetite now."

After devouring the picnic basket contents, they napped in the shade until the day's heat began to wane. When Ryan's eyes fluttered open, Kate's face hovered inches away.

"What are ye doing?"

"Watching you sleep. Thankfully you do not snore, but you drool a tad."

"If 'tis the worst of my faults, I've nary to be ashamed of."

Her smile faded to a more solemn expression. "Are you disappointed that I am not so…endowed as Ada?"

He arched his neck and planted his lips on hers. She held his kiss. He raised an arm and pulled her closer. She pressed her pelvic area against his briefly, and then she pushed away and rose.

"We must leave now…while I have most of my virtue intact."

"Must we?"

"Yes." She sighed. It is for the best."

Secret Society's Novitiate

All summer, Bill Johnston frustrated the multinational forces allied against him. By moving daily and changing islands, by traveling off trail, and by camping well away from open water, he evaded capture.

By the end of August, the game of cat and mouse turned in Bill's favor. The British and American navies reduced the number of ships and men searching for him to a token force. The cost to keep a fleet and army in each country constantly on the prowl proved too high. Canadian and American authorities still wanted Bill, but fewer people actively looked for him.

Psychological pressure lifted, too. Jim Johnston learned that Bonnycastle indeed did ask the Mohawks for help, but they turned Bonnycastle down. They had too much respect for the big, white pirate. The chiefs said that hunting Bill Johnston in the islands was like following a bear into his cave. The bear usually wins.

*****

In early September, Ada espied someone on Governors Island signaling for a boat. She grabbed a wide-brimmed summer hat and crossed Water Street to the family wharf.

"Rrok! Cric! Croc!"

Ryan watched Ada stride over.

"Ryan! I think Bill's waiting on Governors Island."

"I'll go over and look."

"I'm coming with you. I've been up in that attic too long."

Into the water, Ryan slipped a twenty-foot river skiff with two sets of oars. He set a pair in the forward oarlocks and pushed off. Ada steered the skiff by tugging on ropes attached through two pulleys to the tiller. The sun retained summer's warmth. A light wind from the north pushed choppy waves towards them.

Ada wore a pale blue cotton dress. As usual, she exposed bare arms, shoulders, and good portion of her upper chest. She smiled at Ryan as he rowed. He smiled back, enjoying the attention. They traveled in friendly silence until half way across the channel.

"Tell me how ye ended up living with Bill and Ann years back."

"There is not much to tell." She shifted her gaze to the far shore. "My family moved from this state to a farm near Kingston when I was a girl. Good farmland was less expensive there. A falling tree killed my father. That forced my poor mother to take care of the family. Ann and Bill offered to lighten her load by taking me in. I was nine."

"Why did ye flee during the war instead of going home to yer mother?"

"Ann needed my help. She'd just lost her first daughter and she had two boys to care for. Also, I loved my life with the Johnstons. They helped me live with my infirmity."

"Why, were ye ill?"

"No, I was a freak!"

Ryan's eyes widened as the sound of Ada's harsh self-criticism.

"My height was a curse. I towered over other children. No one my age would play with me. They snickered and teased."

"'Twas better at Bill's, then?"

"Yes and no. Bill and Ann better perceived the torment I suffered and always advised me to ignore the taunts and to concentrate on being a well-rounded person. I buried myself in schooling and household activities. I became a good seamstress of necessity. No store-bought clothes fit me. I also drifted towards reclusiveness."

"I cannot picture ye like that."

She sighed. "You have no idea what it is like to be so visibly different. By ten, I was taller than most women. By twelve, I surpassed most men. I was built like a young tree: skinny, long and no curves."

"Now yer a fine looking lady who dines with colonels and high society."

She smiled. "My husband and marriage changed me."

Their boat approached Grindstone Island. Ada swung the tiller to point their skiff towards the backside of Governor's Island, where Bill would be hiding.

"How'd ye meet yer husband?"

"I visited my family for Christmas in 1818. While there, I met Cyrus. He was the first man to treat me like a normal woman. His shorter size did not bother him. When he asked for my hand, I accepted without hesitation. I was seventeen. Being the wife of a successful man changed my social status. Having children gave me a sense of purpose. In time, I learned to use my height and my improved figure to advantage."

"Rrok! Cric! Croc!" Zak rose on air-thumping wings.

Ada looked over Ryan's shoulder. "There's Bill. Over by that big rock."

Zak reached Bill first and landed on his shoulder. Bill passed the raven a fish head he had saved for that moment.

"I see yer dry. How'd ye come over?"

"Farrow brought me. He fixed his boat."

"You look thin. Are you well?"

"No worry, Ada. I be fit as a fiddle," Bill said. He climbed into the skiff and grabbed the second set of oars. "Lots of hiking and swimming. I have the build of a man twenty years my junior. But the nights be cool and I desire me some of Ann's cooking."

With the extra power of Bill's hardened muscles on his big frame, the skiff sped across the water to Clayton.

"Do ye think 'tis safe going home?"

"Safe enough. There be far fewer boats looking for me. Besides, Heustis told Farrow he wants to see me. I be heading to meet some Hunters in Watertown tomorrow. You should come."

Ryan had no more interest in the Hunters' intrigues then than the day McLeod tried to recruit him, but a request from Bill carried weight. "Sure, Bill, if ye need me to."

"Idiot," Ada mumbled.

Bill Johnston climbed from the skiff onto his wharf in Clayton in the early afternoon. Instead of crossing the dusty road to his house, he strolled down Water Street's wooden sidewalk for three blocks on the river side and back towards his house on the opposite side followed by Ryan and Ada. On show, he greeted all he met by name. People smiled and men shook his hand. A murmur began on Water Street that rose to a swell and swept through the business district and up residential streets: Bill is back.

From the store and warehouse, his sons and Kate joined his parade. Bill strode up his home's walkway, mounted the porch steps, and slipped into Ann's arms. When the family stepped inside, Ada grabbed Ryan's wrist and hauled him aside on the porch.

"Listen to me. If you want a future with Kate, stay away from the Hunters. She does not plan on taking a pirate or rebel for a husband."

"Yer wrong! She's half pirate herself, and the best soldier in her father's army."

"No! She never wanted to be a rebel's daughter. All this summer, she's worried he might die any day. Her actions and efforts come from love and loyalty. She is tough, but does not court danger. She craves a safe harbor."

Ryan had no response. Ada's view of Kate differed much from his. He shrugged.

"Answer me this question. When are you the most happy? Is it when you are leading your own life and courting Kate, or when you are involved in Bill's lawless intrigues?"

"Tis not a fair question. I owe my life and good fortunes to Bill."

"Ada! Ryan! Where are you?" Kate called in a sing-song voice from inside. She stepped onto the porch. "Mother has apple pie and peach ice cream." Kate's expression changed. "What is wrong?"

"Ada's telling me to stay away from the Hunters. Bill wants me at a Hunter meeting. What do I do?"

Kate's brown eyes searched his face. "Remember when we discussed what you admire about Zak?"

"Yes. I said 'tis his life unbound by politics or history."

"Are you not risking a life more deeply entwined in politics and history if you get involved with the Hunters?"

Ryan leaned on the wall and weighed the truth of her words. "Maybe I must pay a debt to history before I can be free of it."

"Do what you think best." She tugged his hand. "Now come inside for pie."

Ryan followed her and avoided Ada's glare.

*****

At midday, their coach arrived in Watertown, the political and economic center of Jefferson County. Cleaved in two by the steep Black River gorge, the town's waterfalls powered mills and factories. Ryan and Bill crossed to an inn on the town's public square. Daniel Heustis waited for them.

"Bill! Ryan! Good of you to come," he said. He rose to greet them and signaled the innkeeper for a pot of tea. "Please be seated. If you are hungry, they make a proper cottage pie, with mutton instead of diced beef."

"Good. I cannot eat enough since I came in from hiding."

"Same for me, please," Ryan said.

The innkeeper arrived with the tea and left with their meal order.

"So, Daniel. Why did you send for us?"

Heustis poured each man a cup of tea before he answered, smiling. "Always straight to the point, Bill."

"Well Daniel, I didn't come this far to discuss the weather."

Heustis stirred a lump of sugar into his tea, took a sip, sighed, and continued. "The Hunter leaders are having a convention in Cleveland soon."

"So what?"

Looking down, Heustis aligned his cutlery into meticulous order as he spoke. "Cleveland is the headquarters for the western region. Since the convention is in that city, those of us in the east worry the top positions may go to western delegates." He looked up. "We want you to attend."

"Will you be there?"

"No. I am fully engaged raising money and organizing for the fall."

"Organizing for what?" Ryan asked.

"We expect to launch a major enterprise in November." He sounded like a man announcing some minor social event—not a war—but Ryan noticed his dark eyes widen.

"Why wait that long, Daniel?"

"It is simple economics, Bill. Many of our men are farmers. They will not leave the land until the harvest is in."

"That makes sense. Any specific points you have in mind for me to make at the convention?"

"You must be elected to the executive," Heustis replied.

"How do I do that?"

Heustis leaned back and smiled. "Insist on it, Bill. They will not refuse you. No one in Cleveland will have your level of real experience."

Bill raised an eyebrow and nodded.

"Ryan," Heustis began, "I believe you know where our weapons are hidden in the islands?"

"Yes...sir," he replied between sips.

"Soon enough, we will need to gather them up."

"Yes, sir. I'll do it."

"My superiors insist that the man gathering the weapons be a Hunter."

"Ye can trust me."

"I believe you, and Bill vouches for you, but there is too much at stake. Bill will have to recruit Hunters to help him."

"I'm Bill's partner. I always help him."

"I am sorry, Ryan."

"There be a recruitment meeting this afternoon," Bill began. "I can sponsor you. You be near a Hunter anyway."

Ryan looked from Bill's encouraging smile to the earnest stare of Heustis. He wondered whether his grandfather faced such pressure to join the Irish rebels in 1798.

*****

From the inn, Heustis, Bill and Ryan crossed the town square and knocked on a large mansion's ornate door. Donald McLeod answered. He shrank back a half step at his first sight of Bill since the failed *Peel* raid.

"Hello, Donald," Bill said with exaggerated politeness. "You remember Ryan from our little *bungled* enterprise. He wants to join the lodge. Is that possible?"

McLeod's Adam's apple bobbed as he swallowed. "By all means, Bill. Have him wait in the front parlor until called for the oath, if that suits you." He pointed to a side room that held three young men.

"It suits me if he be first."

McLeod quickly nodded. "Give me a minute to prepare the others, and then bring him in."

"Turn around," Bill asked Ryan. "I must blindfold you. It be required for the initiation."

Ryan hesitated.

"By accepting the blindfold, you show that you be ready to trust the men who are about to become your brothers."

"I trust ye, Bill."

Bill tied the blindfold. He removed the hunting knife Ryan carried in a belt sheath and placed it in his pocket. Bill steered the blindfolded young man by the shoulders down the hall and through a door. Bill marched him ten steps and then commanded him to kneel. Ryan complied. He kept his spine straight and his unbound arms at his sides.

Ryan used the listening skills he developed with the Algonquin to learn what the room held. No one spoke, but he could hear dozens of men breathing. The scent of horse and cattle sweat on clothes suggested many came from farms. The swish of fabric rubbing fabric meant men crowded together. He learned the room had at least two windows on opposite sides from the faint sounds of horse hooves and carriage wheels outside. The stillness and heat meant the windows were closed. The astringent scent of old ashes told him the room had a hearth not in use on this warm night. The faint aroma of tea meant Bill was close by, his homespun linen coat impregnated by long contact with tea bales.

Footsteps approached. Paper rustled as someone unfolded a document.

"Are you the man they call Ryan Lone Pine?" asked an unfamiliar voice.

"I am."

"You have come before us today seeking admittance into our society, have you not?"

"I have."

"Once you are admitted to our brotherhood, you are bound to be true to these vows for life. You may back out now and no harm shall befall you. Do you wish to leave or go forward?"

Ryan sighed. "Proceed."

"Repeat the following oath of admittance after me. I solemnly swear in the presence of Almighty God and the assembled Hunters…"

"I solemnly swear in the presence of Almighty God and the assembled Hunters," Ryan repeated.

The voice continued. "… to do my utmost to promote and defend republican institutions and ideals throughout the world…"

Ryan recited the words.

"… and especially to devote myself to the propagation and protection of these institutions in North America."

Ryan repeated the sentence.

"I pledge my life, my property, and my sacred honor to this society," the voice continued.

Ryan parroted the words.

"I bind myself to its interests, and I promise, until death, that I shall help to destroy by any means that my superiors may think proper…"

He repeated the words flawlessly.

"…every power and authority of royal origin upon this continent; and never to rest until all tyrants of Britain cease to have any dominion or footing in North America."

He spoke the words.

"I further swear to obey the orders delivered to me by my superiors, and never to disclose any such order, except to a brother Hunter of the same degree or higher. So help me God."

He recited the last words. The voice spoke again. "Brother Ryan, you have taken the first step into this society. We have four degrees of membership. You must start at the lowest degree, the snowshoe. I will now read the vow for that degree. Just listen."

The speaker noisily unfolded another piece of paper.

"I swear in the presence of Almighty God and this lodge of Hunters that I shall not reveal, write, print, stain, stamp, scratch, or engrave upon anything the secret sign of the snowshoe degree to anyone, not even other members.

"I swear that I shall not reveal any secrets of this society which may come to my knowledge through members of higher rank.

"I swear that I shall give timely notice to another brother if I know of any evil, plot or design that has been carried on against him or this society.

"I swear that I shall render all assistance in my power, without injuring myself or my family, to any member who shall at any time make the sign of distress to me.

"I swear that I shall attend every meeting of my lodge if I can do so without injury to myself or my family.

"Do you so swear as you shall answer to God?"

"I so swear," Ryan answered.

"Ryan Lone Pine, you are now welcomed as a Hunter of the snowshoe degree."

Bill stepped forward and removed the blindfold. A long bowie knife rested on a table at Ryan's eye level with the blade pointing forward.

"The dagger symbolizes the manner of your death should you reveal our secrets or betray this society in any manner." The speaker was a man of average build in his late forties dressed in rural garb.

"I am Colonel Dorephus Abbey," he said. "Welcome to our brotherhood."

"May I stand now, sir?"

"Please do."

Forty men applauded. The Hunter flag clung to the wall above the hearth. In its center, an eagle, symbolizing America, carried aloft a lion, emblematic of Britain. The Hunter motto read: Liberty or Death.

"Brother Ryan. We have additional members to bring into the fold tonight. Please accompany Captain Heustis. He will instruct you in the secrets of the snowshoe rank."

Heustis led Ryan from the meeting room into a side parlor.

"What I am going to show you now, you must retain for life. Understand?"

"Yes, captain."

"You must keep them secret. Do you so aver?"

"I do."

"There are five signs, tricks, and secrets all snowshoes learn. First, shake my hand."

When their right hands connected, Heustis gave Ryan's right cuff a brief tug with the thumb and finger of his left hand. Then, he clasped his right hand with both of his in a hearty handshake.

"That is the Hunter handshake. If both parties are Hunters, both tug the cuff of the other. If you mistakenly make this sign with a non-Hunter, that person will dismiss it simply as an over-friendly action. Try it."

They shook hands. Ryan did as shown.

"Excellent. Next, I will show you how to signal to other lodge members that you are a Hunter. Spread the fingers of both hands widely, and then lay the left hand palm over the back of your right, so that your four fingers line up, like this. Pretend you are stretching stiff fingers."

He copied Heustis.

"Close! Hold your hands in that position for brief moment and then drop your hands in a relaxed fashion to your sides. It is both actions, the hands together and then relaxing, which comprise the complete secret sign."

"Yes, sir."

"Show me the whole thing. Make it brief and discreet, but do not be sloppy with the positioning."

Ryan demonstrated the technique.

"Good. Now, here is another secret sign you can make if the hand sign is too obvious or inconvenient. Watch me."

Heustis raised his right hand and pushed the top of his right ear forward a fraction of an inch with his index finger, as if he was brushing off an insect.

"Try that."

He did as directed.

"Close. Keep the palm facing forward and do not push the ear that much. Try again."

Ryan complied.

"Excellent. If someone makes either sign to you, return the sign, and then confirm him as a Hunter using the handshake."

"Yes, sir."

"Next. If someone asks if you are a Hunter, you never answer the first inquiry with a yes or no. Instead you say the name of the day following the day the question is asked."

"So, if 'tis Wednesday and ye ask if I'm a Hunter, I must answer Thursday?"

"Correct! If the person seems puzzled by the answer, you know he is not a Hunter, and if he repeats the question, you answer no. Understand?"

"I do."

"One last thing. Agents of both governments try to infiltrate us by pretending to be members. We have devised a simple way to trap a person posing as a Hunter."

"How's that?"

"Devise some innocent way to convince the person to draw or describe the shape of a snowshoe. If the person complies, he is obviously a fake. Hunters take a vow never to make that sign. If this happens, alert your superiors immediately. Do you understand?"

"Yes sir. I trust, by making snowshoe tracks in the winter, I don't violate my oath."

Heustis smiled. "I am sure that will be fine."

*****

Back in the meeting room, Ryan studied the features and demeanor of each man. One knot of men in a shadowy corner across the room caught his attention. He could not hear them speak, but their gestures and postures suggested a conspiratorial conversation. A short, dark man in his thirties, dressed in garb that suggested a merchant, commanded the most attention.

"Bill. Who's that dark man in that group over there?"

"William Estes. He be a Hunter organizer and money raiser from Cape Vincent. He seems to have influence, but other than that, I know nothing about him."

The meeting concluded in early evening. Bill and McLeod treated Ryan to dinner at Luther Gibson's hotel.

"I presume you grasp the importance of your oath and monumental commitment to liberty tonight, Ryan," McLeod asked.

"Don't start blathering Donald," Bill growled.

Ryan changed the subject.

"General. Bill tells me ye led the Patriot attack near Detroit last winter."

"Yes. The effort was valiant, but a waste of resources and men once Van Rensselaer faltered at Hickory Island."

"One of our problems is the lack of officers with army experience," Bill said. "McLeod was a sergeant in the British army. Most of our leaders have no military experience."

"Were ye in the army long, general?"

"I joined the British navy in 1803 at twenty-four and switched to the army after five years. I fought Napoleon at Waterloo and the Americans in Canada from 1812 to 1814."

"Donald and me be allies now, but were on different sides in that war."

"I led men at Queenston Heights," McLeod explained, "and helped defeat an army commanded by Van Rensselaer's uncle. I fought other America armies at Lundy's Lane and Crysler's farm."

"In fact, Donald and I probably shot at each other at Crysler's."

Ryan noticed Bill and McLeod warm to each other as they traded stories. He tried to encourage it. "Really! How's that, Bill?"

"I was one of seven thousand Americans under General James Wilkinson. We headed downriver in November of 1813 in hundreds of Durham boats to attack Montreal. The British regulars and militia dogged us along the shore and in boats from our rear. General Wilkinson, drunk as usual, ordered us to land and confront them. Donald was on the British front-lines, I believe."

"You are correct."

"We engaged them for hours and eventually lost though we had superior numbers."

"Were the British better fighters? I keep hearing they won agin bigger forces."

"If truth be told, we were not," McLeod answered. "The American regulars rivaled the best soldiers I've fought. Better than the French, I can assure you. When we beat them—and we didn't always—luck was often on our side or poor organization plagued them."

"Now ye are fighting agin the British."

"Yes. After I demobilized and settled in Prescott, I witnessed how poorly the Family Compact managed the colony. I published a newspaper advocating reform. Last year, a despicable Tory mob wrecked my presses and forced me and my family into exile. Now I am fighting back."

"We all be fighting back, Donald," Bill began, "together."

The two old warriors shook hands.

Ryan smiled. "I believe I'll have some tea."

*****

The next morning, Bill and Ryan returned to Clayton by coach, arriving for lunch. Ryan dug into a steaming bowl of squash soup and then a plateful of roast chicken, string beans, and mashed potatoes with gravy. As he mopped up gravy dregs with bread, he realized silence had supplanted the usual family chatter. He sensed a quiet anger emanating from the head of the table. Bill ran his gaze around the table. Only Ada and Ryan did not avert their eyes. Kate excused herself and retreated to the kitchen.

"So, Ada. Am I right to believe there's been some family talk behind my back?"

"Yes. We had discussions, but no agreement."

"What have you to tell me?" This he addressed to the table.

"Well, Father," Napoleon began, "we prefer matters to return to the time before you took up with the Patriots and Hunters. We don't want to be the children of an accused pirate and wanted man."

Bill slammed an open hand on the table. "What would you have me do?"

John replied, "We want you to turn yourself in and then ask for clemency based on your war record. Several prominent men assure me you'd serve a short sentence, maybe a matter of months."

"Do it for the family," Decatur explained. "You are a legend on the river, but that may be our downfall. John, Napoleon, and I find businessmen reluctant to take us on as apprentices or partners."

Bill drummed the fingers of his right hand on the table. "Does everyone agree?"

Ada nodded her agreement. Ann shrugged.

"No," Jim replied. "I want you to stay away from them Hunters and burn no more steamers, but I don't counsel jail. If you turn yourself in, you have no control over what happens. You might rot for years. Avoid new trouble and let the old troubles fade away. No one's been killed yet. Until that happens, everything is forgivable."

"Jim, I believe that's the most you've ever said at one time," his mother remarked.

"Thank you, son," Bill added. "That was a well argued. What be your opinion, Ryan?"

"'Tis a family matter."

"I be asking your advice," he barked.

"I side with Jim on this. Jail is no place for an outdoors man like yerself."

Bill stared out the window at the river and ran his fingers through his hair. Everyone else looked at their plates with their hands in their laps. To Ryan, they appeared like people saying grace, except for the half-eaten meals.

"I think I will have second helpings," Bill said, ending the nervous quiet. "John, pass the chicken and potatoes. Ryan, you're still hungry, eh?"

"Surely, Bill."

"Let's attend to the meal at hand. Kate! You can come back now. Bring more gravy if you have it."

Bill caught the questioning expression from Ann. "I will take your opinions to heart. I promised to attend the Hunter convention, and I mean to keep my word. After that, we will see. And I promise to burn no more steamers," he added with a wink to Jim.

"While I be away, you and Ryan keep the tea flowing north."

*****

In the feeble gray light of an overcast mid-September dawn, Ryan and his smuggling crew arrived at Clayton after another tea run to Canada. Up early, Ada saw an opportunity to steal a few minutes alone with Ryan.

She pulled a housecoat over the silk chemise she had slept in. A mug of hot coffee in hand, she tiptoed out the door and crossed the street in her slippers, holding the housecoat closed against the morning chill with her other hand. She counted on the early hour to ensure her improper attire would go unnoticed.

Once the men stowed the gig in the warehouse, Ryan paid them and waved good-bye as they trudged home for breakfast. He too counted on the early hour for privacy. Sweaty and grimy from his labors, he stripped naked and slipped into the cold river to bathe. He slathered his chest and arms with soap, swam briefly to rinse, and climbed the wooden ladder onto the wharf.

"Rrok! Cric! Croc!"

Ada rounded the side of the warehouse. He had no nearby towel or garment to cover himself. For a second, he considered running into the warehouse or jumping into the river. No, he thought, she's the one who caused this awkward moment. He decided to stand his ground and watch her reaction.

She halted twenty feet from his nude form, seemingly transfixed as he stood dripping. On a body devoid of fat and hairless except for his head and groin, every sculpted muscle of his legs, abdomen, chest, and arms shimmered with wetness.

"I brought you hot coffee." She held out the cup, an invitation to come closer.

Ryan surprised himself. Standing unclothed felt naughty, and he liked it. For a moment his natural reaction worried him—might it alarm or disgust her. If it bothers her, he thought, she can turn and leave.

Padding barefoot across the wharf, he stopped a yard from Ada and accepted the mug from her outstretched hand. He eyed her over the mug while he sipped its steamy contents.

"Ye put honey in it. Thank ye," he said in a near whisper.

"You are welcome." Her hands now empty, she dropped them to her sides. The unclasped housecoat parted, revealing most of the chemise's frontal area. Ada made no attempt to close the coat and wore nothing beneath the chemise.

She intended for him to have a good look, and he didn't disappoint. The hemline ended six inches above her knees. The silk garment curved in at her waist and flared over full hips. The décolletage barely concealed her nipples standing out proudly from breasts the size of a halved melon.

Why do I always think of fruit, Ryan wondered.

Ada's legs began to tremble. She half closed her eyes. A slow grin lit up her face.

Ryan instantly recognized the danger he faced. Despite his fondness for the flirtation and titillation, he had to bring the seduction to an end for Kate's sake.

"When ye came from the house, was Kate awake yet?"

Her name hit Ada like a bucket of cold water. She pulled her housecoat closed, and sighed.

"I'm sure she's stirring by now. I'd better return."

"Thanks for the coffee and the…er…company."

"My pleasure."

Captain's Aide

Summer waned. The morning mists obscured the islands as the river ceded its warmth to the chill air. Long lines of geese passed southbound high over the river. Most days remained warm and the biting insects had vanished.

As Ryan carried out his daily duties in the shop or on the river, Ada's advice about Kate haunted his thoughts. The mention of marriage had forced open a door he couldn't shut. He remembered his loving home life in Ireland, and began to entertain the prospect of starting a family of his own. He hung around Clayton shipbuilders, observing the men at work and talking to foremen. A job was available, they told him, for a man with his experience.

One afternoon in the last week of September, Ryan leaned on a workbench in the Johnston warehouse as he fitted a new leather bushing to an oar. Most oarlocks on locally built skiffs consisted of vertical metal pins, usually brass, attached to the gunwales. Oar-makers drilled a hole in the oar's shaft and these holes fit over the metal pins. To protect the wooden oars and gunwales from wear and to eliminate annoying squeaks, Ryan always form-fitted a leather bushing.

Ryan first softened the tanned calf hide with oil to make it easy to bend and then cut the leather into shape. Next, he lined the oar hole with leather and wrapped hide around the oar shaft where it contacted the gunwales. As he nailed the last hide strip in place with brass tacks, Zak called from the roof outside. Bill entered the workshop.

"You have a nice touch there, lad."

"Thank ye. Tis rewarding work."

"I had an interesting seven days at the convention."

"Did ye." Ryan didn't want to discuss the Hunters.

"Yes. Imagine one hundred and sixty hotheads arguing and cursing each other for a week."

"Is Captain Heustis happy with the results?"

"No. Most top spots went to western lodge members. Lucius Bierce, a lawyer from Akron with no real military experience, was made the senior general. There were better choices. They affirmed me as admiral. Donald McLeod be now Secretary of War. That be good."

Ryan focused on the leather bushing and didn't comment.

"There be a new enterprise planned."

"'Tis so?"

"Yes. They suggest twin attacks on Upper Canada nigh Windsor and Gananoque in late November, but it be only talk. Bierce claims the Hunters have twenty-five thousand men ready to bear arms to liberate Canada. We may have that many members, but I doubt a tenth of them will fight."

"Sounds familiar."

"Yes! Bad leaders and big talkers."

"What do we do now?"

"We wait."

"Suits me."

That afternoon, Kate and Ryan followed the French Creek shore to the edge of town and onto the bridge that crossed the creek at the narrows. Zak rode the gusts blowing in from the west. Ryan stopped at midpoint and stared at the wind-churned water.

"You are quiet today. Are you in a mood to be alone, Mr. Pine?"

"No. I'd nary avoid yer company, Kate. I have much on my mind."

"Is it the Hunters?"

"Yes, and more. I've been listening to yer brothers. Maybe 'tis not only the Hunters I best leave behind, but smuggling too. If I did, I'd be letting down yer father doubly."

"You must live your life, not my father's."

"A man I worked for in Kingston said to leave the old troubles in the Old World. 'Tis hard. The British have given me cause here and back home to hate them. That I share with the Hunters."

She pulled his face around with her fingertips. "Are you considering a path that leads away from old hatreds?"

"Yes, I am."

"Well, that is good news." She kissed his cheek.

*****

In October, Heustis sent word from Sackets Harbor to collect the hidden weapons and ammunition in the islands. Ryan did not hesitate. The job did not commit him further than he'd already agreed.

Over the next ten days, Bill supervised the operation, but, at his sons' insistence, stayed home. While the chill of October accelerated the changing leaf color and frosts were common at night, Ryan and Bill's crew of French Canadian refugees visited each depot and delivered the munitions to the shanties on Abel's Island. Bill arranged for sloops and large gigs to ship them on to the Hunter arsenal at Sackets Harbor.

With the weapons shipped out, Ryan enjoyed a quiet afternoon fishing on the wharf with Zak for company. A weak sun behind translucent clouds barely warmed the fall air.

The wharf boards creaked under the weight of a visitor.

"Zaak!" Zak flew up from his perch on a wharf piling and landed on Bill's shoulder.

"That was a job well done," he said.

"'Twas a pleasure to be on the water."

"I had word from Heustis."

Ryan didn't respond.

"Something be up. We must go to Watertown."

Ryan stayed quiet.

"Are you not up to this?"

"To tell ye the truth, Bill, I'm torn. I'm tending towards the direction yer boys are headed, but I made a vow to the Hunters."

"What do you have most in mind to do?"

"I want to build boats and maybe buy a farm."

"Maybe a wife and family too?"

"Yes. I'm starting to think along those lines."

"I'm losing faith in the Hunters myself. I believe my boys have a point about avoiding more trouble. Still, we owe it to the brave men who died for the Patriot cause to attend this meeting in Watertown. There be a fellow named Birge we must meet."

"If yer going, then I'll accompany ye."

"Good lad."

*****

Two days later, Ryan put Zak in Kate's care while he and Bill caught the morning coach leaving Clayton. They arrived in Watertown in early afternoon, with Ryan's hungry stomach growling. Bill marched past any source of food to the Hunters' mansion.

Twenty men lounged in chairs or clustered in groups, talking and smoking, including the mysterious William Estes. Ryan's gaze settled not on him, but on a pair of men next to the blazing hearth. One heavyset man in his forties stood out—he easily matched Ada's height and exceeded Bill's girth. The other, a six-foot, dark-haired man in his thirties, displayed a confidence and manner that he'd seen only in aristocrats.

Dorephus Abbey approached.

"Welcome Bill. It is always a privilege to have you attend. Hello to you too, Ryan."

"Gidday, Colonel Abbey."

"Dorephus, be Heustis here?"

"No. He is in Sackets Harbor tending to the arsenal and preparations."

"What preparations?"

"General Birge will explain."

"Who be this fellow and how'd he become a general?"

"John Ward Birge leads the Hunters in Onondaga County. He is organizing the next attack."

"Be he a politician?"

"No. A dentist."

"Who made him a bloody general?" Bill's tone verged on shouting.

Abbey stepped back. "Ah! He did."

"Does he have any bloody military experience?"

"Ah! Not that I am aware."

"So why be you all following this man into battle—in case you need your fucking teeth fixed?"

Abbey reversed another step as the room went silent. The two men Ryan observed earlier came their way. The heavyset man locked his eyes on Bill and towered inches from him. Bill returned a withering glare and cracked his knuckles.

"Ryan, this be Martin Woodruff, sheriff of Onondaga County and a colonel in the state militia. He helped organize the enterprise on Hickory Island. He be one of few in this room with military experience. That must count for something." Bill's words were complimentary, but his tone derisive.

"What do you want?" Woodruff snarled.

Bill unbuttoned his coat to expose a dirk in his belt. "I came in my capacity as admiral of the Patriot and Hunter navy to observe."

In the battle of bravado, Bill won. The big sheriff's fists clenched in frustration and his shoulders sagged in resignation. The second man stepped forward.

"Gentlemen. We are all comrades in the same righteous cause. Please stand down." He spoke with an uncommon accent.

The two antagonists stepped apart. Bill drew his coat closed.

"Allow me to introduce myself. Nils Gustaf Ulric von Schoultz at your service, Mr. Johnston."

"Where do you hail from?"

"I have a modest salt works near Salina in Onondaga County. Prior to that, I lived in several countries in Europe, principally Poland, Sweden, and Finland."

"He has military training," Abbey said in an appeasing tone," and fought with the Poles against the Russians."

"How do you come to be taking orders from Birge?"

"I originally contacted General Bierce in Cleveland and offered to raise a company of Polish exiles, if required. But, General Birge had more immediate need of my services. I must say, I am overjoyed to have you allied with our enterprise. Your exploits are legendary."

"I have not decided to be part of this enterprise yet."

"What impediment do you face?"

"Birge has no authority from the central executive to mount a campaign. In fact, his unilateral action will interfere with Bierce's plans." Bill frowned at Abbey. "Why be this lodge straying from the fold?"

"We are not the only lodge. It's all the eastern lodges. Bierce has not kept us informed of his plans. We've had no instructions from General McLeod. Our men are anxious to attack before winter."

"Has anyone told Bierce of your plans?"

"Not that I know of."

"You bloody fools. If I didn't known better, I'd swear Van Rensselaer was in charge here."

"That is not fair," Woodruff began. "Birge is a much better leader."

"In what way?"

Woodruff paused, momentarily at a loss for words. "Well! He is not a drunkard."

"A sober incompetent be more pernicious than a drunken one because he be not obviously incompetent."

Bill's gaze swept across the three men. "Ask yourselves this: if you follow this man to Canada, how great are your chances of dangling at the end of a rope."

No one answered. Everyone in the room stared at the floor, except von Schoultz. He watched Bill, analyzing his expressions.

"What time is the bloody meeting, Dorephus?"

"Seven."

"We will be back. Come Ryan. Let's eat."

At an inn on the square, Bill ordered a big bowl of beef stew and a tankard of ale—a rare beverage for him. Ryan ordered lamb stew and tea.

"I'm confused, Bill. How can a man make himself general and everyone follows?"

"The Hunters have talked too long. There be a head of steam building up and men are eager for a fight."

"Is that dentist going to be a good leader?"

"I doubt it, Ryan. Except for the foreign fellow, I don't see a real leader among them."

"Von Schoultz does stand apart, that's for certain."

"Yes, but, be he a good leader or just looks good compared to the rest?"

Ryan shrugged. "What are ye going to say at the meeting?"

"Probably too much," he said, grinning. "Keep this hidden in your belt." He slid a pistol across the table.

"Are ye expecting trouble?"

"I be sure of trouble and I need you to watch my back."

*****

Two hours later, they re-entered the mansion. A hush fell over the seventy-five men in the meeting room—the earlier argument now known to all. Only von Schoultz greeted them.

"Welcome back Admiral Johnston. Did you sup well?"

"No complaints. Where be Birge?"

"He will join us momentarily. He is conferring with his officers."

"Have ye any rank, sir?" Ryan asked.

"Not yet," he said, extending his hand. "Nils von Schoultz. We were not introduced at our last meeting."

"Ryan Lone Pine. Pleased to meet ye." He gripped the extended hand. Von Schoultz had long limbs and bright eyes. His grip, neither strong nor weak, gave nothing away.

"I recognize the unusual name. You are the young man who gathered arms for us."

"I helped in that regard, yes."

"You are clearly of Irish lineage."

"Yes, sir."

"You may know, I was part of a vain attempt to liberate Poland from the Russians. The Poles and the Irish have much in common, you know. Both have fought for generations to drive an oppressor from their lands."

"I didn't know that about the Poles, sir."

"I have pledges from five hundred Polish exiles to help in our crusade to liberate Canada. This fight draws all men who love liberty and justice. I expect our numbers will include Irishmen too."

"I couldn't say, sir."

"I sincerely hope you will be with us when our operation commences."

The entrance of John Ward Birge into the meeting room saved Ryan from answering.

A man of medium build and height in his early thirties, he shook hands with Estes and strode to the central area near the hearth. When the applause and huzzahs subsided, Birge spoke.

"Gentlemen! Patriots! Hunters! Welcome. We assembled here tonight because we believe in liberty for all Christian men of intelligence and free thought. We are here because we have the courage, the means, and the commitment to carry the banner of Lady Liberty to the lands of men less fortunate than ourselves.

"Soon, our forces will rise up, gather their arms, and liberate Canada from British tyranny.

"Among us tonight are our senior officers. Each officer's duty in the coming days is to imbue the men with fire, courage, and the glorious task ahead. Each man must know he will be part of a fighting force of at least twenty-thousand men, a force unequal in size since the last border war twenty-five years ago.

"Tell each man they shall receive ten American dollars monthly in wages while in our service. Each man who crosses into Canada to fight will receive eighty dollars and one hundred and sixty acres of good Canadian farmland.

"Each man will be part of an army of liberation and will be welcomed with open arms in Canada. Three-quarters of their militia troops will throw down their arms in solidarity. Nine-tenths of the Canadian colonists will rise up to support us. I have talked with many a poor downtrodden Canadian. I know this to be true. The British forces will wilt like tender shoots at a hard frost.

"We are on the verge of greatness. We can change the course of affairs on this continent. Soon, the spirit of '76 that created this great country will sweep across the St. Lawrence and liberate our brothers in

Canada the same way others liberated Texas two years ago. I pledge before God that we shall not fail. Who is with me?"

The room erupted in applause and cheers. Swept up by the hortatory message, Ryan joined the applause. Only Bill was unmoved by Birge's rhetoric. When the hubbub began to fade, he brought the room to silence.

"Excuse me, *general*. I have questions."

The people standing nearest to Bill stepped away. Woodruff edged closer to Birge.

"Who is speaking, please?

"Admiral William Johnston, the only person in this room with authority from General Bierce to plan a campaign of war."

Birge was not intimidated. "I have little time for questions, so please be brief."

"I have several, so don't be in such a rush. First, who gave you the authority to plan an invasion under the Hunter banner?"

"We did. We do not need the western lodges to give us legitimacy."

A murmur of agreement swirled through the room.

"Where do you plan to attack?"

Birge hesitated to answer.

"If you plan to use any form of water transport in the Thousand Islands, you will have to tell me. If not, I will stop you."

"You will stop twenty thousand men!"

"I doubt you will have that many. Even if you do, I will stop them. I stopped the British in 1813 and 1814."

Birge glanced at Abbey and Woodruff. They nodded. "We plan to take Prescott and Fort Wellington."

"Then you must rethink your plan."

"Pardon me!"

"The people around Prescott be the most loyal citizens in Upper Canada. They be the sons of Loyalists and refugees from the American Revolution. They will not rise up to support you. More likely, they will rush to shoot you. You'd be better off attacking Gananoque. The Midland farmers may come over to your side."

"Are you done with your questions?"

"No. Who be the fool that promised to give each man one-hundred and sixty acres?"

"That would be me."

"Logically, the land you promise must first be confiscated from Canadians. When word spreads in Canada, not a single man will join you if they know you plan to steal their land or a neighbor's land."

"Really, Admiral Johnston, this has gone on too long."

"Talk with Bierce and the people in Cleveland. They may be able to help your operation, perhaps create a diversion."

"We will take your opinions into consideration."

Bill glanced at Woodruff, Abbey, von Schoultz, and back at Birge. "I expect you and your senior officers will concede that a better plan is possible."

"The plan will succeed. The operation is underway. I see no reason to change anything."

"You bloody fool. You be sending men to their death. I have commanded men in war. There be no higher responsibility than planning to bring as many back alive as possible."

"Is that all, *admiral?*"

"One more question."

"Yes?"

"Do you plan to be at the head of your men when you land in Canada?"

"By all means!"

"I very much doubt it."

With the speed of a cat, Bill reached inside his coat and drew out a flintlock pistol, cocked the hammer, and leveled the barrel at Birge twenty feet ahead. Ryan opened his coat to expose his pistol's grip and pivoted to face the throng of men behind Bill.

The dentist general stumbled back, his hands in front of his face. Woodruff hovered in petrified surprise. Von Schoultz stepped in front of Birge and glowered at Bill.

"Not to worry gentlemen. I do not intend to shoot anyone—today." He eased the hammer forward and slipped the pistol into his coat. "That man be a braggart and a coward. You follow him to your doom. Good evening!"

Ryan followed Bill out.

Walking to the coach to Clayton the next morning, Bill said, "I will have nothing more to do with that bunch of fools. I be finished with the Hunters."

Ryan did not respond. Bill knew him well enough now to read the silence.

"You have another opinion?"

164

"Did ye see the way Mr. von Schoultz jumped in front of yer pistol? If he was the leader ..." he paused. "Yesterday I wanted with all my heart that ye'd walk away from the Hunters. Now, I don't know."

*****

A week later, Ryan rejoined the Johnstons for an evening meal. The supper table confabulation covered the usual topics: the family businesses, the Johnston sons' budding careers, and local politics. It wasn't until Kate and Ada cleared the dessert dishes that Bill asked the question on everyone's mind.

"So, Ryan. How was your week in Sackets Harbor?"

Ryan placed his tea cup on its china saucer, ignoring Kate's sigh and avoiding Ada's frown. "'Twas eventful, Bill. General Birge appointed Mr. von Schoultz colonel and second-in-command."

"Well, that be a modest improvement. Who be the other officers?"

"Mr. Woodruff and Mr. Abbey are colonels. A fellow named Daniel George is paymaster."

"Heustis should be a senior officer too. He has experience. What part will you play in the invasion?"

"I am aide to Captain Heustis. He's commanding the men and supplies in Sackets Harbor."

"You didn't answer my question."

"I've told Captain Heustis that I'll help him all I can, but won't cross into Canada."

"Well, that shows some sense at least," Ada said.

"When does the enterprise begin?" Bill asked.

"On November 8, Colonel Woodruff will bring a force from Oswego. They'll board the big steamer *United States* in disguise. When she docks at Sackets Harbor, Captain Heustis and I will board with another company. Later, we'll meet two schooners. In command of Colonel von Schoultz, the three ships will sail to Prescott. I'll stay on board the steamer."

"Where be Birge?"

"Already in Ogdensburg."

"How many men have you?"

"We have one thousand ready now, with five hundred more coming, Poles from New York."

"And arms?"

"We have rifles for all. We have eight cannon, from three-pounders to an eighteen-pounder, and a supply of powder and balls."

"That be a large force for certain, but a far cry from the twenty thousand Birge promised. A thousand men cannot prevail for long if the people do not rise up in support. The British can assemble regulars and militia in greater numbers. There be no chance of success if they attack Prescott."

"Tis not my decision. All officers know your opinion, but General Birge and General Estes are set on Prescott. By capturing Prescott, they can cut traffic between Kingston and Montreal, and secure a foothold in Canada."

"So Estes be a general now, too. Not surprising. Self-appointed, I expect."

"Yes. I distrust him, but he doesn't meddle in daily affairs."

"Do the officers take precautions against spies?"

"What spies?"

"You always have spies when the army be publicly recruited. If all your men know the plan, you can be sure the authorities on both sides also know it."

"I'll pass that information to Captain Heustis when I return tomorrow."

Bill looked across the table.

"Jim. Any word from our man in Kingston on this?"

"No. We can't reach him. Bonnycastle is suspicious and has guards follow him wherever he goes."

"Then let's stay away from him. No use having him hanged. Ryan, keep your eyes and ears open for any man who asks a lot of questions and finds excuses to be nigh the officers."

"I will. Thank ye."

Bill smiled like someone about to tell a ribald joke, and then said, "I'll meet you in Ogdensburg. I'll go in one of my boats."

Everyone at the table straightened in their chairs.

"This is news, Bill," Ann remarked.

"Well, if Ryan and Heustis insist on being damn fools, I should be there to assist in their salvation, if necessary. By going there, I can keep out of the way of all parties."

John sighed at the illogic of his father's last statement. "We expect you at least to stay in American waters and away from the British."

"Yes, John. I promise."

*****

The next morning, Ryan waited on Water Street for the coach to Sackets Harbor with Zak on his shoulder. He wore laborer's clothes. His Algonquin medallion rubbed his chest inside his shirt. A canvas sack next to his feet held his tomahawk, telescope, and other clothes. Against the November chill, he wore a heavy woolen coat lined with warm, white flannel Ann had made for him.

The air hovered near the freezing mark. A light snow started an hour earlier and had already begun to accumulate on wooden fences and conifer boughs. It clung to the wisps of remaining spider webs like strings of tiny pearls. The road and rock walls retained enough warmth to melt the snow as it touched. Ryan could hear a faint swish as thousands of snowflakes hit autumn leaves lining the street gutters.

The bird spotted Kate and flew over to greet her. She carried a package.

"I brought you some roast pork sandwiches for lunch." She slipped the paper-wrapped food into one of Ryan's large coat pockets.

"Thank ye. The food here is far superior to what we eat in Sackets Harbor."

"What does Zak do when you are busy playing soldier?"

"Zak keeps me company while I carry out the duties Captain Heustis gives me, and he plays the catch-food game with other men."

"I wish you were not going back, but I understand why. You are an idealist and crusader like Father. He cannot be comfortable in a life without risks."

"I'm not so much like Bill. I know I can be happy in a quiet life. I intend to settle soon. I have to get past this business with the Hunters first."

"You have spoken similar words before."

"Once I reach Ogdensburg and unload the men, I'll take the next ship back."

"There is always one more thing with you."

"This time, I mean it."

"I hope that is true, Mr. Pine."

Colonel's Recruit

Ryan hurried to the Union Hotel, the Hunter's headquarters on the Sackets Harbor waterfront. Being November 8, Ryan assumed news had arrived about the successful hijacking of the steamer in Oswego. Leaving Zak outside, he entered the three-story stone building. On the second floor, he tapped twice on Captain Heustis' door.

"Ye wanted to see me, sir?"

"Yes Ryan, the *United States* is delayed due to repairs until Sunday."

"Is that a problem?"

"If the men become restless, they may go home. I observed that tendency last winter on Hickory Island."

"What can I do?"

"We must keep them busy. Increase the frequency of drills. Have young Vaughan help you. And set up a shooting competition outside of town. I'll supply a bottle of good bourbon for the winner."

"Yes, sir."

"Any more thoughts on possible spies?"

"Several men ask lots of questions. I can't narrow it down."

"Keep trying."

"Yes, captain."

"That is all for now."

*****

Over the next three days, Ryan discovered first hand the shallow devotion to the Hunter cause. Young men, lured to Sackets Harbor by a promise of adventure, lost interest when forced to wait. Drills and contests did not stem the outgoing tide. He urged men to be patient. Hunter Vaughan, a teenage volunteer eager for battle, berated his friends and acquaintances—men he had recruited weeks before—for losing faith. Despite Ryan's patriotic monologues and Vaughan's vitriolic insults, four hundred men departed.

On Saturday, two chartered schooners, the *Charlotte of Oswego* and the *Charlotte of Toronto*, set sail from Oswego, New York, under command of Nils von Schoultz. They carried purchased provisions and munitions, troops, and cannon stolen from state arsenals with the help of Hunter supporters.

That same day across the river in Kingston, two spies informed Captain Williams Sandom that a Hunter army was on the move, the likely target being Prescott. Sandom had faced sixty enemy engagements in forty years of military service. Experienced in war and command, he knew his duty. He readied every steamer at his disposal for battle.

*****

Early Sunday morning, November 11, the passenger steamer *United States* fired up its boilers and made ready to depart. As the captain, thirty-year-old James Van Cleve, prepared to cast off, a long column of passengers in civilian clothes—mostly young men with no baggage—boarded the ship. Martin Woodruff, Dorephus Abbey, and Daniel George milled about among the new passengers.

Hours later the *United States* docked in Sackets Harbor. Ryan and other Hunters lounged nonchalantly on the wharf in the afternoon sun as the crew lowered the gangplank. Colonel Woodruff descended and sought out Captain Heustis.

"Good day, colonel," Heustis said.

"Good day to you, captain. How many men have you?"

"Besides myself, I have twenty-nine. Have you the five hundred Polanders from New York?"

"Only six have come."

"What is your strength altogether, colonel?"

"Only one hundred and sixty."

"So few! Our scheme will fail, I fear. We shall be defeated."

"I know it," Woodruff said. "But I can't back out now and neither can you. I'd prefer to be shot. We must go and do our best."

"I will go," Heustis conceded. "I would rather die than be branded a coward. Whatever might be the issue, we ought to meet it as men fighting in a good cause."

Ryan overheard the grim conversation. For several seconds, he hovered on the wharf, debating his next move. Zak cooed on his shoulder.

Captain Heustis stared at Ryan from the main deck with an expression that asked "are you going to desert me too?" Ryan boarded the ship.

*****

Near Cape Vincent, Heustis nudged Ryan and pointed to two anchored schooners. "Those are ours. They carry all our provisions and more men."

Daniel George passed by and winked. They followed. George mounted the steps to the upper deck and entered the wheelhouse.

"Excuse me, captain. I am Daniel George. I run a shipping business in Oswego."

"Yes, Mr. George. How can I help you?"

"Those two schooners over there in the bay are mine. I must sail them to Ogdensburg, but the wind is not favorable. May I employ you to tow them to that port?"

"Certainly. Our fee for that service is fifty dollars per ship."

"Agreed. I expect a receipt."

Soon, with a schooner lashed to each side, the *United States* set off. Ryan counted scores of wooden boxes and barrels on the schooner decks, but no men.

The *United States* stopped at the wharf in Clayton. Eight more Hunters boarded. Ryan swept his gaze over the throng of passengers and friends that always assembled when a steamer arrived. No Kate. He gazed past the wharf to the two round windows in the Johnston house where Ada and Kate used to watch the river. Did they see him? He waved at the house. In that single motion of his hand, he again committed himself to continue the voyage.

*****

Minutes after leaving Clayton, the two schooners revealed their true nature. On the *Charlotte of Toronto*, von Schoultz emerged from the hold with a sword scabbard visible beneath his long cloak. Hundreds of other men emerged from doors and hatches on both schooners. They pried open the crates lashed to the decks and armed themselves with rifles. The army sailing to Prescott now numbered four hundred. While far less than Ryan expected, the improved odds gave him some cause for optimism.

Von Schoultz crossed to the *United States* and approached the group of Hunter officers standing near Ryan.

"Colonel," Woodruff began, "I believe you know everyone here, with the exception of this fine officer." He pointed to Heustis. "May I present Captain Daniel Heustis. He commands the Sackets Harbor company."

"Pleased to meet you, captain." They shook hands. "I have read many a complimentary report on you."

"It is a pleasure to meet you colonel. Let me introduce my aide, Ryan Lone Pine."

"I have had the pleasure of meeting this young man previously. I am gratified to see you with us on this expedition, Ryan."

"Thank ye, sir."

"I have not met this handsome bird of yours" He nodded at Zak perched on Ryan's right shoulder. "*Corvus corax* is said to be the smartest bird on the planet. It is famous in myth and legend."

"Critiky! Croc!"

"You know, some ornithologists say the raven makes at least thirty distinct sounds, enough, I believe, for a simple language."

"I know Zak has lots to say, sir."

"Did you know that arctic explorers, John Franklin for one, observed ravens active in the long arctic night where few other birds survive."

"No sir. I've nary seen Zak fly at night."

"It is true. They can, if they so choose."

"Say hello, Zak."

"Kello!"

"Exceptional mimics, as well." Von Schoultz smiled. "Let us adjourn to a private place. I wish to review our plans."

Ryan followed the officers to a cabin on the main deck. Woodruff posted two armed guards.

"Gentlemen," von Schoultz began, "General Birge gave instructions to dock at Ogdensburg before crossing the river to attack Prescott. He expects to have five hundred men ready there to join us. I do not believe this is prudent. Evidence abounds that men may desert given an opportunity. We should attack Prescott at the first opportunity and send a ship to obtain additional forces from Ogdensburg. Are there any objections?"

There were none.

"Under cover of night, I propose we cut the schooners loose from this steamer and sail to Prescott. We will dock at the main wharf at Prescott, unload our men, and form into three columns. Our principal objective is to capture Fort Wellington to the east. I will lead one column through the town center. Colonel Woodruff, you will take men around the north side, and Colonel Abbey, you will lead a column along the town's waterfront. We will unite at the approach to Fort

Wellington. I expect little resistance. After we take the fort, we will secure the town and set up our cannon to control the river."

"And then what do you expect?" Heustis asked.

"Once we have shown our strength, I firmly believe the Canadians will flock to our banner and other Hunters will cross the river to join us."

"Where is the best place to cut loose from the steamer?" von Schoultz asked. "Anyone have a suggestion?" All the officers shrugged.

Only Ryan knew the river well. "May I speak, colonel?"

"By all means."

"Once ye are abreast of Morristown, you are beyond the islands. There are few obstacles and the water is deep."

"That suggestion makes sense," Heustis began. "This steamer is scheduled to stop in Morristown. We should disengage before that event."

"That is a sound plan. Thank you, Ryan. Colonel Woodruff, the *Charlotte of Oswego* is your command. I will command the *Charlotte of Toronto*. Make sure our men are off this steamer by nightfall."

*****

After supper, Colonel Abbey ordered all men off the *United States* to the schooners. In the ranks of raiders milling by the rails, Ryan spotted a familiar face.

"Lyman," he called.

Lyman Leach recognized his fellow *Peel* raider and came over followed by another man. "Ryan, good to see you again."

"Where did you board?"

"I came up from Oswego with this fellow," he said, pointing to his companion. "This is William Gates from Lyme." Gates, in his mid-twenties, equaled Ryan in height but carried more bulk.

"Nice to meet ye."

"You too. Are you joining us on the schooner?" Gates asked.

"No. My orders are to stay with the steamer," he lied.

"Perhaps, we'll see you tomorrow," Lyman said.

A harried looking Colonel Abbey interrupted them. "Where's Colonel von Schoultz?"

"I saw him earlier on the fore deck," Ryan answered. Curious, he tagged along as Abbey scurried off. They found von Schoultz readying to leave the steamer.

"Sir," Abbey began," half the men refuse to leave the steamer and board the schooners, despite the threat of being shot for desertion."

The colonel scowled. "That is the curse of a volunteer army. We lack sufficient discipline and order. You stay aboard and attempt to rally the men to join us."

On deck, Ryan watched the schooners untie from the *United States*, raise their sails and disappear silently into the dark. Zak slept on his shoulder. The chugging steamer's engines and slosh of churning paddlewheels rumbled across the dark water.

Shortly after 2 a.m., as the *United States* approached Ogdensburg, the pop of several musket shots rolled across the river from Prescott. Then, a cannon boom echoed between the river banks. Ryan guessed the schooners had made Prescott. Did the landing succeed or fail? He had no way to know.

When they docked at Ogdensburg, everyone disembarked, except for a few Hunter watchmen. Ryan approached an assembly of restless men near the steamer wharf. A big man emerged into the light shed by the steamers lamps.

"Hello, lad. Glad I be to see you."

"Hello, Bill. Is there any news from the far side yet?"

"None. We will know more in the morning. I have a room at an inn. You look like you could use some sleep."

"I guess a few hours will do me some good."

*****

At dawn, Bill and Ryan hurried to the waterfront, eager for news of the schooners. Despite the cold wind and overcast sky, hundreds of Hunters and townspeople thronged the wharfs and jetties. The two Hunter schooners wallowed offshore on mud flats coughed up by the Oswegatchie River where it joined the St. Lawrence.

"To my boat, lad. Hurry!"

Ryan and Bill rowed out and tied up to the *Charlotte of Toronto*. Bill went aboard to confront von Schoultz.

"As Admiral of the Hunter navy, I be taking command. Any objections?"

"Certainly not. I welcome any assistance you can provide."

Bill paced once around the deck inspecting the rigging and the ship's position in the mud. He then climbed onto a hatchway where the crew could see him. "Listen! You still have the jib up. The wind be pushing her into the mud. Reef all the sail, now!"

Several men scrambled to do his bidding.

He pointed at two men. "You and you. Take a boat to town. Commandeer a barge or scow. Bring it out here. Go! Now!"

Three men, not two, scurried away and departed in the ship's tender. Bill instructed the remaining men. "When they return with a barge, load all the munitions you can onto it to lighten this boat. Transfer the heaviest crates first."

"What happened last night, colonel?" Ryan whispered to von Schoultz.

"Favorable winds blew us close to Prescott. Upstream from our objective, we dropped the sails and lashed our vessels together. We drifted in the moonlight towards Prescott. As we came upon the wharf, one of our men jumped ashore and attempted to make fast our ships. Alas, the current was too strong and the line broke.

"Our vessels slammed an abutment in the harbor, thankfully with no damage done. Then, a few militiamen fired on us. Frustrated in our loss of surprise, we hoisted sail for Ogdensburg. Our hired schooner captains were in unfamiliar waters and ran into the mud."

"Maybe 'twas lucky that rope broke. I saw an army in Prescott this morning through my telescope."

"If we had succeeded in landing our force, I am certain the people of Prescott would have dropped their arms and we would have prevailed. Sadly, we have lost the element of surprise. Still I am convinced most people will embrace our cause once we show that our strength is great enough to hold off the British regulars."

Within an hour, Hunters under Bill's command transferred a hefty pile of cargo to a barge and the *Charlotte of Toronto* started to float. At Bill's direction, the crew anchored the ship in deeper water. The Ogdensburg populace gave a mighty roar of approval. The barge crew crossed to the other schooner and began off-loading cannon.

"Thank you Admiral Johnston for your timely assistance."

"You be welcome, colonel. I must to see to the other ship, now. Come Ryan."

Bill and Ryan tied up to the *Charlotte of Oswego* just as another rowboat carrying Birge came along side. Ryan and Bill eavesdropped on the conversation.

Captain Heustis leaned over the rail. "Come aboard, general."

"That will not be necessary. I came to give you your orders."

"What must be done?"

"Go to the Canadian side immediately. Get the cannon ashore. I will organize reinforcements from town."

"Leading from the rear are you, general?" Bill called out.

Birge scowled. Without a word to von Schoultz or Woodruff, he ordered his men to row to shore.

On board the big schooner, Bill strode up to Woodruff. "I be in command now. Any objections?"

Woodruff shrugged. Bill circled the deck twice inspecting the ship and the mud below. He then climbed to a position where the crew could hear him.

"Attention! This ship be deeper in mud than its smaller sister. You need a tow. I will arrange it. Until then, unload any supplies you can to barges."

Ten minutes later, Ryan and Bill pulled up near the steamer wharf. Bill stayed in the boat.

"Ryan. Find some men and commandeer the *Paul Pry*. She be a wee steamer that I warrant can tow the schooner off the mud. I be going back to direct the men on the scow."

"Sure, Bill."

*****

For only the second time, Ryan disobeyed one of Bill's orders. He set off to find Birge. His inquiries led him to the stone customhouse by the harbor's edge.

"General Birge."

"Yes. Who are you?"

"I'm Captain Heustis' aide. You must do something. All these Hunters came at yer bidding."

"What do you propose, young man?"

"Take command of the *United States*, sir. Tow the big schooner off the mud or run munitions across."

Birge consulted another Hunter officer, a stranger to Ryan. "What do you think, Pierce?"

Oliver Pierce was an itinerant lecturer on grammar and phrenology, a man with enormous confidence but no military experience. "Yes. Taking the *United States* will demonstrate action."

"Then, let us be off!"

Soon, two hundred armed men swarmed onto the steamer and forced its crew to start the steam engines. Ryan, Birge, and Pierce went to the wheelhouse. Zak flew to the wheelhouse roof. Shortly after nine in the morning, the big steamer pulled away from the wharf. Ryan, now ravenous, had missed breakfast.

The *Charlotte of Toronto* was by then under sail towards the Canadian shore. A tow line from her stern pulled a heavily laden barge. With his telescope, Ryan recognized the unmistakable bulk of Bill Johnston following the barge in his boat. Clearly, he intended to cross the border in total disregard of his family's wishes, and despite the deadly consequences if captured.

"Be careful, Bill," he whispered into the air.

"General," Pierce began, "I suggest we approach the grounded schooner from the north side. We can maneuver closer that way."

"That means we must cross the border, does it not?"

Pierce glanced at the young helmsman, Solomon Foster, with a questioning look.

"Yes, general, it does," the young man said.

*****

When the *Charlotte of Toronto* crossed the river's invisible borderline, a British steamboat departed the Prescott harbor at full speed. The *Experiment* carried an eighteen-pound carronade and a three-pound cannon on a swivel mount. Her commander was Lieutenant William Fowell, a career-minded naval officer in his mid-thirties with a reputation to build.

On the *United States*, the crew's efforts to row a line across to the grounded schooner held everyone's attention. The mud bar kept the big steamer at bay and no rope onboard could reach the schooner. On Pierce's orders, Foster swung the big steamer around and headed upstream. Only then did they notice the gunboat.

"Is that British steamer heading this way?" cried Birge.

"I think she's heading towards the *Charlotte of Toronto*," Ryan answered.

"Foster," Pierce ordered. "Steer a course that puts us between that gunboat and the schooner at the windmill. I want you to block their shots."

"Yes, sir."

Foster steered the *United States* towards the British ship. As the big steamer overtook the small ship, the British gunners fired the carronade and three-pound cannon. Birge went pale. Everyone braced for the smashing impact of cannonballs, but nothing happened. They missed. On the *United States*, two hundred Hunter riflemen returned fire. Zak flew from the ship in a cloud of spent gunpowder smoke and circled high in the sky, observing the action.

Birge clutched his abdomen. "Excuse me gentlemen. I seem to have a bad bout of seasickness. I must go below. You are in command Pierce."

"How do ye get seasick when the river is a sheet of glass?" Ryan said to no one in particular once the general vacated the wheelhouse. Foster smirked. Pierce ignored the question.

Pierce had Foster keep the *United States* between the *Experiment* and the *Charlotte of Toronto* to defend it as her crew unloaded seventy men, supplies and three cannon, and then returned to the American port. Though not a naval man, Pierce seemed to know his duty. Hunter riflemen peppered the British ship with lead. Gunners on the *Experiment* fired three more broadsides before Fowell ordered his men to cease. Two cannon balls thudded into the *United States*, but merely cracked the heavy hull planking. All other shots missed the mark.

"I don't believe the Brits have their best gunners today, Mr. Foster," Pierce remarked.

"It's also that carronade," Foster explained. "The short barrel gives her less range and accuracy than cannon."

"It may be that two hundred men on our decks shooting at them keeps the gunners from taking better aim," Ryan added.

The *United States* and the *Charlotte of Toronto* tied up at the Ogdensburg wharf. The *Experiment* halted in mid-river and started firing grapeshot at the still stranded *Charlotte of Oswego*. Most discharges plunked into the mud, but a few projectiles tore the ship's rigging. Ropes and spars crashed onto the deck. Helpless, the schooner crew could only run for cover.

"Those bloody British," Pierce began. "They are firing on an American ship in our waters."

Ryan nodded and said, "Excuse me, Mr. Pierce. I have to do something Admiral Johnston asked earlier."

"Hurry back. I plan to re-cross to the windmill shortly."

With Zak on his shoulder, Ryan approached a large knot of Hunters talking on the wharf.

"Any of ye know how to run a steamer?"

A man stepped forward. "Yes."

"Admiral Johnston wants men to commandeer the *Paul Pry* and pull the big schooner off the mud. Can ye do that?"

"Yah. She's docked up the Oswegatchie. Why didn't you ask sooner?" The man didn't wait for an answer. He and four others hurried away to find the ferry steamer.

"Next, Zak, we find some food."

"Zaak!"

*****

With a meal in his belly and Zak on his shoulder, Ryan boarded the *United States* in early afternoon. In the wheelhouse, he unwrapped a supply of buttered bread and cheese for Pierce and Foster.

"Here. I figure ye'd be hungry by now."

Foster reached for a piece of bread. "Thank you. I was more worried about dying from hunger than those British cannonballs."

Pierce ignored the food offer. "Good timing. We are ready to embark. I have a company of armed men on board led by Colonel Abbey to join our brave lads at the windmill. That damn British ship has rekindled the fighting spirit in our men."

The *United States* belched black smoke from its two lofty metal stacks. The paddlewheels on either side began to churn the water and the big steamer pulled away from the wharf. Foster swung the wheel and steered the ship towards the windmill. The *Experiment* waited for them.

"Excuse me a minute, Mr. Pierce. I must talk to the men," Ryan said.

Out on the upper deck, he called to the men along the rails. "Hunters! Everyone move to the port side. Keep continuous fire on that British steamer. Make the gunners fear for their lives so they can't fire off an easy shot."

Turning to Zak, he said, "There's about to be some shooting. Best ye go aloft."

"Zaak!" The big raven launched from the wheelhouse roof and soared into the sky.

The men did what Ryan suggested. Within minutes, one hundred and twenty armed men leaned on the railings of both decks. With frizzen pans primed and hammers cocked, they waited for the *Experiment* to come within range of their long-range rifles. As one, they fired. Through the rolling thunder and smoke, bits of wood splintered on the British steamer where lead balls slammed into her. The feisty steamer stayed her course towards the *United States* and fired the carronade. The ball sailed past and splashed beyond in the river.

The men on the *United States* cheered and reloaded.

"Make sure ye don't all shoot at once," Ryan yelled. "Keep up continuous fire."

Several men nodded in acknowledgement. They organized themselves using hand signs and started firing at the *Experiment* in groups taking turns to reload. Ryan watched the shooters concentrate their fire in the area closest to the British ship's carronade and cannon. As the little steamer passed close by going in the opposite direction, her gunners let go a second broadside. The carronade missed again. The ball from the swivel-mounted cannon knocked a hole in the wooden cover over one paddlewheel, but did no real damage.

Once more the men on the *United States* roared in triumph. The big steamer, now at full speed, soon steamed beyond range of the *Experiment*.

Foster brought the *United States* to rest near the windmill. Pierce ordered the crew to drop anchor.

"Why is that ship staying away from us now, I wonder?" said Pierce to Ryan, pointing to the *Experiment* in mid-river.

"If ye look to the windmill, there are three cannon in place. Maybe that ship's skipper doesn't want to come within range of them."

"Look. Here comes the Admiral." Foster pointed to a boat pulling away from the stony shore.

Once onboard, Bill asked, "Where's Birge?"

"He's in Ogdensburg recovering from a sudden illness."

"Scared sick, be he? I be not surprised. Who be in charge now?"

"I am. Oliver Pierce at your service."

"You did a superb job crossing over with that damned little boat making such a nuisance. I have half a mind to take a party over and board her. But first, we must land your men, if that suits you."

"It does."

"We have only two boats at our disposal. Each can take six men. It will take a few hours."

"Let us start immediately, then."

"Do you have any supplies, Mr. Pierce?"

"No. Just men."

"Damn! So far, I've seen no food or medical supplies go ashore."

"That material is on the grounded schooner."

"Admiral," Foster called. "Look over towards Ogdensburg."

A small steamer approached the grounded schooner.

"That's the *Paul Pry*, I assume," said Bill.

"And there goes the *Experiment* to cause more trouble," Pierce said.

The *Paul Pry* was built for swallow water. In minutes, the little ferry pulled the big schooner off the mud. Closing in, the *Experiment* opened fire. Bits of rigging fell from the schooner. To everyone's surprise, the schooner fired back.

"What the hell was that?" Bill bellowed.

Ryan scanned the scene with his telescope. "Seems someone fired one of the field cannon lashed on the schooner's deck," he replied. "The *Experiment* is hit. I see men down. She's moving off. Our big schooner is safe now, but I doubt she's fit to sail."

"Damn! We need the supplies on that schooner."

"I shall endeavor to bring some over on our next run, Admiral," Pierce volunteered.

"Good man."

*****

For the next two hours, the *United States* disgorged its tiny army. Shallow water off Windmill Point forced the ship to anchor well out, while rowboats ferried the men. When the last load of men climbed into the boat, Ryan asked, "Are ye returning with us, Bill?"

"No. I will stay until after dark and help organize the defenses. I will meet you by the steamer wharf later."

"Take care. Don't let the British catch ye."

"Never fear. There be not a Brit born that can slap me in irons."

The *United States* lifted anchor for the return trip to Ogdensburg. The *Experiment* ignored its wounds and came about to pounce again.

"Mr. Pierce. We have a problem."

"What is it, Ryan?"

"We don't have a hundred riflemen to cover us anymore."

"Not to worry. I have another idea. Foster!"

"Yes, sir?"

"Steer for that British vessel. I mean to ram her. Keep our bow facing our foe to present the smallest target."

"Ram her, sir?"

"Yes, ram her. Our superior size will prevail."

"We may both sink, sir."

"Then sink we do."

Solomon Foster, a *United States* crew member, not a Hunter or a Patriot, followed Pierce's orders with enthusiasm. With the ship's engines roaring and her speed nearing ten knots, he kept the *United*

States on course to crash head on into the *Experiment*, a ship one-third its weight.

Fowell seemed to guess what the *United States* commander intended. He instructed his helmsman to hold steady until told otherwise. He ordered his gunners to prepare their weapons. Then he waited.

The two ships sped towards each other at a combined speed of eighteen knots. With the crew on the *United States* braced for a crushing impact, Fowell gave two brief orders, seconds apart.

"Helmsman, hard to port…gunners, fire!"

The nimble *Experiment* swerved and passed so close to the big steamer that her gunners could not miss. A ball from the carronade tore blades off the starboard paddlewheel. The ball from the swivel gun hit the wheelhouse, bursting walls and windows on its way in and out. The close blast, the crash of splintering wood, and the cacophony of exploding glass knocked everyone on the *United States* to the deck. The big ship steamed away on an odd meandering path.

Zak, flying above the battle, dropped to the damaged steamer's wheelhouse searching for his human. Perching on a window frame now devoid of glass, Zak called to Ryan's prostrate form lying among the bodies on the floor.

"Crik, crik!"

Ryan stirred. So did Pierce.

"Zaak!"

Ryan opened his eyes, rolled over, rose, slipped, and crashed to the floor, landing partly on Pierce.

"Steady there."

"Sorry, sir. Tis something slippery on the floor."

"Oh my God!"

Foster slumped in the corner, most of his head missing, sheared off by the cannonball. Ryan had slipped on brain curds. His stomach churned. He fought the rising sickness.

"It seems we have our first casualty." Pierce pushed himself casually to his feet and grabbed the steamer's wheel.

"Ryan. Please find another crewman who knows how the steer this ship. I doubt I can berth it on my own."

Ryan did as ordered, happy to leave the bloodied wheelhouse.

Later in Ogdensburg, the solemn crew removed the body of brave, young Foster wrapped in a canvas shroud.

*****

Bill rowed back in the overcast night. He found both Hunter schooners berthed in Ogdensburg. More than half of the Hunter's supplies remained onboard. In the light of the *United States'* main deck lamps, he found Ryan trying to scrub blood off his woolen coat with a rag and cold water.

"I heard about Foster."

Ryan didn't respond.

"The first time you see a comrade fall, it be hard."

"Do ye mean it gets easy?"

"No." He studied his young friend for a minute. "Where be your bird?"

"He's roosting across the bay there in a tree."

"Are you up for another crossing? I've found three men willing to join von Schoultz."

"Only three?"

"That be all. I hiked every foot of Ogdensburg, telling every young buck Hunter I found they had a duty to cross and help their brothers. Most said they will have nothing to do with it now. It be Birge's fault. The men see his cowardice and have lost faith in the man and his pretty words. We will take one last trip across and go home. What do you say?"

"Yes."

"We must leave immediately. The local military commander has arrived in town. His troops will soon seize our ships and this steamer for breaking the neutrality laws, and arrest anyone they find."

Ryan methodically poured the bucket of pinkish water into the river and draped his rag over the rail.

"Be you not well?"

"I'm fine."

"Follow me."

At Bill's boat, three recruits huddled in the damp cold. Ryan and Bill rowed off across the dark, choppy water. The squeaks of other oarlocks in the night told them they were not alone.

"Seems there's lots of traffic this night," said one recruit.

"It be this way for hours," Bill answered.

"Are the boats taking men across to join?"

"Boats take men across. Some stay. Some go over sightseeing. Some men got cold feet and return home. I think we lost the same as we gained."

"Are any of the generals over there?" asked the man.

182

"Estes went across late this afternoon, but didn't stay."

"My name is Orrin Smith, Admiral, and I mean to stay. I'm a Hunter, a Patriot, and a damn rum gunner. I'm here to kick the British arse."

"Are you the man who fired on the *Experiment* today?"

"One and the same."

"You have the honor of drawing first blood Orrin. I daresay, it won't be your last."

In mid-river, they noticed a steamer, lights blazing, coming downstream. "That will be the *Telegraph*, I suspect," Bill began. "Captain William Vaughan commands her and plans to stop more Hunters from crossing."

"I met him once," said Smith. "Tough bugger."

"I knew him well. Vaughan, I, and a few young officers commanded the crews that attacked British shipping in the last war. He was a pompous ass—always made sure he was mentioned in reports."

"Were you mentioned in those reports, too?"

"No. I was a spy and a privateer. My name was purposely kept from reports."

On the Canadian shore, someone waited beneath the windmill, lantern in hand. Bill used the faint light to guide his way. When their boat ground up on the rounded rocks, Ryan recognized Daniel Heustis holding the lantern. Nils von Schoultz stood beside him.

"What word have you, Admiral?" asked von Schoultz.

"I've three more volunteers. I be sorry, but that be the best I could do. Birge's cowardice has dowsed the fire of bravery in most recruits."

"Three? I count four."

"Ryan be with me to help row. He be coming back with me."

"No," Ryan said softly. "I'm staying...on condition."

"What!"

"I'm staying, Bill." Ryan stepped from the boat.

"Get in the bloody boat!"

"I've followed yer orders, good and bad for months. Today, I'm following my heart."

"Why do this?"

"To fight the British, like I pledged."

"Nothing you do here will help Ireland or the Irish," Bill insisted.

"'Tis for my grandfather."

"What? He be long dead."

"I did not tell you the whole story of his part in the Irish rebellion. He fought with the rebels for months. But at the Battle of Vinegar Hill, he broke and ran when he saw the British force. He regretted his cowardice the rest of his life. I fear, if I run from this fight, I too will take regret to my grave."

Bill threw the nearest oar into the bow of his boat. The wooden thunk echoed off the bank and across the dark river. "Damn you! What am I going to tell Kate?"

"Tell her I'm sorry. Ada too."

"What is your condition for joining us, Ryan?" asked von Schoultz.

"Well, colonel, I don't intend to shoot anybody. Today, I witnessed the terrible damage men can do to each other. I'll not make widows or orphans. I'll run messages and tend the wounded. But I won't fire a shot. Agreed?"

"I accept your condition. Why do you not join us too, Admiral?" von Schoultz said. "We could use a man of your great experience and leadership."

Bill's brow furrowed. "Experience? Yes, I have plenty. Every battle or fight I joined, I first made sure either I had a good chance of winning or the path of retreat was clear. You cannot withstand the force the British will muster against you. By morning, the British and Americans will cut every avenue of retreat across the river. You are a fool. Brave yes, but no less a fool. Your men are well intentioned Patriots being led to their doom."

"If I am fool for staying, are you not a coward for leaving?"

Everyone within hearing gasped. Bill's hand went to a pistol on his belt. Instead of drawing it, he exhaled in a slow, audible hiss.

"If those men did not need you so much, I'd cut you down." He spoke through clenched teeth. "I be admiral of the Hunter navy. The Americans impounded our navy. This boat is the last that can cross this night. My duties here are done."

He moved amidships and grabbed a set of oars.

"Do what you can for us over there, Bill."

"I will try, Daniel. Five hundred Hunters remain in Ogdensburg. If I can find transport and convince them to cross, I will. Take care of yourself. You are too fine a man to lose."

"Thanks, Bill. I will survive. I promise."

"Ryan. Push me off."

"Sure, Bill." He placed both hands below the bow gunwales, then lifted and shoved.

"Ryan, did I ever tell you how the British nearly captured me in the war?"

"No Bill, but I'd love to hear it."

The boat drifted slowly into the dark.

"It was the summer of 1814," Bill began. He paused to set his oars in place. "I was scouting for Commodore Chauncey in Canadian waters. A storm came up fast and smashed our gig on the rocks east of Kingston. We were uninjured, but stranded. Someone spotted us and we soon had a detachment of redcoats and Mohawks on our heels.

"My men were regulars in the navy; so they'd be treated decently as prisoners of war. I told them to surrender and claim they were looking for American deserters. I had to run. There was a good chance I'd be summarily executed if caught."

"Did they surrender?"

"Yes. Within two weeks they went home under a mutual parole of prisoners. I wish I'd had it that easy. The British and Mohawks searched for me for days. I headed north. I knew they would be combing the shore for me, so I went in the opposite direction. I stayed in the forests for over two weeks, eating roots, berries, and raw crayfish. I worked my way east and returned to the river. I stole a canoe from a farmer and paddled home. I put another crew together and was out spying for Chauncey the next day."

No longer visible in the dark, Bill's voice carried well. "Take care of yourself, Ryan. I'm sorry now I ever got you into this."

"Don't be sorry. I'll see ye again. That I promise."

Bill started rowing south. Ryan listened for any squeak from the oarlocks. There was none. Weeks earlier, he'd put new leather bushings on his oars. No patrolling ship would hear Bill's boat that night.

War's Attendant

Tuesday, November 13, 1838

In the first faint glow of dawn, Ryan climbed the windmill's seven flights of steep wooden stairs and ladders. He poked his head out the trap door in the domed roof for his first view of the hamlet of Newport. Across a narrow dirt road lay ten stone buildings—a tavern, a carriage house, several homes—and a wooden barn. To the west, a rock wall surrounded a grove of butternut trees. For now, the Hunters claimed that slice of Canada as their own.

To the west, he could make out the Union Jack flying above the earthen embankments of Fort Wellington and beyond that, the church spires of Prescott.

His raven landed on the windmill's peak. "Zaak!"

"Zak. Ye found me again. What do ye see from there?"

The raven nodded his head and shuffled his feet. "Rrok! Cric! Croc!"

Ryan looked in the direction Zak faced. Three armed British steamers glided like ghostly whales through the cold river's silver morning mist. One he recognized as the *Experiment*. With his telescope, he read the names on the two larger steamers' paddlewheel covers: *Cobourg* and *Queen Victoria*.

"Someone find Captain Heustis," he shouted to the ground. "Gunboats are coming."

The windmill stood five yards from a steep set of rock ledges that formed the riverbank. Next to the windmill, the three Hunter cannon faced the river behind a wall of piled rocks. Their biggest gun, a six-pounder, posed no serious threat to the British steamers unless they came close to shore.

"Better go aloft, Zak. Something's about the happen."

"Zaak!" The raven climbed several hundred feet in the air, and drifted in wide circles over the virgin battlefield.

*****

Captain Williams Sandom commanded the fleet from the *Queen Victoria*. To him, this was merely another engagement in defense of Britain's imperial interests. A strict old-school officer, carrying out his duty to the honor of the Royal Navy was his primary goal.

On board the *Experiment*, Lieutenant William Fowell welcomed the conflict ahead as an opportunity to prove himself in battle. At his signal, the sidewheelers formed a line and slowed to a halt.

*****

The first coordinated broadside boomed like thunder in a summer storm. Cannonballs plowed into the steep river bank, sending columns of pulverized limestone into the air and shock waves up the tower.

Ryan scurried down the stairs to the gun placements at the windmill base. The whine of a second incoming broadside from the British ships greeted his return to ground.

"Get down," Heustis yelled.

Ryan flopped onto his belly, arms over his heads, and heart pounding. Again, most balls hit the bank. One ball tore away part of the windmill's roof near where Ryan stood minutes earlier. Bits of splintered wood plopped into the shallow snow around them. He covered his ears as the Hunter cannon boomed in return. Three plumes of water rose in the river short of their target. A cloud of spent gunpowder smoke washed over him.

"Come in closer, you bloody cowards," Orrin Smith yelled at the ships.

Ryan finally had a clear view of the gunner he'd met the night before. Wiry and short, Smith had receding brown hair, reddish whiskers, a wide mouth, and wild-looking gray eyes.

"Hold your fire unless they come in range," Heustis ordered. "Conserve the powder."

The rolling boom of a third British cannonade pounded their ears. Again, men dropped to the ground. Two cannonballs tore chunks from the limestone ledges and flung them into the river. One ball tore a sail off the windmill, sending bits of fabric drifting towards Newport like windblown leaves. Another smashed into the windmill's second story. The eighteen-pound iron ball bounced off and rolled down the bank into the river. A handful of rock chips fell to the ground and the air filled with the scent of hot stone dust.

"Did ye see that?" Ryan climbed to his feet and brushed off snow.

"Those windmill walls are four feet thick and round," Heustis said. "I doubt any gun out there has sufficient force to break through. Our munitions are stored inside for that reason."

They crouched at the roar of another British broadside and the wail of descending cannonballs. They all struck inside the village. One reduced a wooden roof to kindling. The discordant splintering reminded Ryan of a tree crashing in the forest.

"The navy gunners are getting their range," Heustis remarked.

Ryan nodded in agreement. "By the way, I didn't notice any food in the windmill. Is it stored somewhere else?"

"We have several tins of biscuits. That is all. But I have worse news than that."

"What can be worse than starving?"

Heustis sighed, but ignored the remark. "Last night, four of us went to the last inhabited house in Newport to purchase a meal. When I told the woman there that we expected Canadians to flock to our banner, she shook her head. Her teenage daughter told us the people dislike their government, but will not be traitors."

"Bill did say people in these parts are loyal."

"I never disagreed with Bill on that. Generals Birge and Estes led us astray." Heustis sighed. "We are on our own, I fear."

A broadside from the British ships cut their conversation short. One ball gouged the soil nearby, spewing particles in all directions. Both men cussed and jerked away.

"Ye hurt, captain?"

"Nothing serious. You?"

"My face stings."

"Yes. You have small stone cuts."

"So do ye."

"I must talk to Colonel von Schoultz. If you need me, I'll be at his headquarters." He trotted to the tavern.

"Orrin," Ryan asked, "could ye hit those ships with a double load of powder?"

"I tried. They're beyond range. Too bad we didn't bring over the eighteen-pounder we had on the big schooner. I could have done some damage with that."

Overhead, Zak croaked a warning. "Rrok! Cric! Croc!" He repeated the call. It could mean only one thing. Ryan ran to the tavern.

"The British are coming from the west."

"Did you see them? How many?" asked von Schoultz.

"My bird saw them."

"Really, Ryan. I doubt—"

Heustis cut him off. "I know this bird, sir. If he says troops are coming, I believe him."

"Then alert our men, captain."

*****

Within half an hour, anyone could see the British regulars and militia marching from Fort Wellington. The column of advancing soldiers stretched beyond sight.

Ryan's mouth went dry. His half finger tingled. Until that moment, he'd constructed his concept of battle from tales overheard and stories read. The approaching troops affected him as the cannon fire had not. The men on the British ships were indistinct figures to the naked eye. Now, armed men marched closer every second. Soon he'd be able to make out faces and features.

He climbed to a window on the windmill's second story. The British troops swung onto the snowy November fields to Newport's north and formed a long, three-deep line, shoulder-to-shoulder facing the Hunters.

"Zaak!"

Ryan scanned the opposing force with his telescope. A few dozen men that morning wore the red uniforms of regular infantry and British officers. The majority wore the simple garb of farmers and shopkeepers. White strips of cloth tied around their arms or hatbands marked them as the inexperienced citizen militia. Facing them were young American farmers and laborers. Most fighters on both sides faced their first battle. Ryan wondered if Thomas Bamford, his former employer, was among the men about to attack.

Von Schoultz strode from the tavern, his cloak flowing behind him. Cutlass in hand, he approached the knot of Hunter officers surveying the British line.

"Colonel Woodruff. Colonel Abbey. Move the men out. Take positions closer to the enemy."

"Where, sir?" Abbey asked.

"Move them behind those rail fences and boulders." He pointed north. "Tell them to wait for my signal to fire."

"Captain Heustis. Get the marksmen in position. Tell them to fire when the enemy comes into range."

"Yes, sir."

A hundred and fifty Hunters abandoned the safety of the stone buildings and sprinted across the open field on Newport's north side to whatever flimsy cover they could find. Snipers climbed to the upper stories of houses, the tavern, and windmill.

From the British lines, a bugle hooted the command to advance. The wall of militia commenced its determined march towards the Hunters. The muffled beat of boots on partly frozen ground rolled before them. Along the Hunter defense lines, men pulled back rifle hammers and crouched to make themselves smaller targets.

A minor shiver rippled along Ryan's spine. Perspiration beads trickled down his chest and spine. A paroxysm of tremors tightened his gut and spread up his torso and across his shoulders. It was the same fear that gripped him the previous winter when he prepared to amputate his finger.

"Damn it," he cursed softly. "Not again!" His breath came in short gasps.

At that moment, as Ryan faced a massively superior force, he grasped why his grandfather wilted at the Battle of Vinegar Hill. He comprehended then how, in one second of overpowering doubt, that brave old man became a live coward instead of a dead hero.

A movement in the village distracted him. The two women who fed Heustis the previous evening bolted from the last occupied Newport house towards the British lines waving a white handkerchief. Muskets roared. Both women spun, dropped to the ground, and lay still. With one hand, the fallen mother held her teenage daughter's hand.

"You blood-thirsty cowards," Ryan heard someone call from below. He scanned the Hunter lines with his telescope and spotted Heustis shaking his fist at the British. Von Schoultz had promised all villagers safe passage. Ryan knew the deadly shots came from the Canadian militia.

"Eat dirt you buggers," Smith shouted as the Hunter cannon squad fired a salvo.

The well-trained civilian militia ignored the explosions of earth and wet snow and marched forward as a few of their fellows became the battle's first casualties. To Ryan, the only noncombatant, the battle below was savage theatre.

When two hundred yards separated the two armies, von Schoultz raised his sword and slashed the air downwards. The roar of Hunter rifles rolled across the river to Ogdensburg, where hundreds of spectators roared in support. Men fell in the advancing line, but the wall of soldiers kept coming. The Hunters fired a second volley. More attackers dropped. Acrid gunpowder smoke drifted into Ryan's windmill window. The faint hollering of officers and sergeants reached him between cannon concussions and rifle blasts.

The militia came within musket range and responded with a deafening volley of their own. Balls ricocheted off rocks and thudded into wooden fences. No Hunters fell.

As taught in countless drills, the Canadian militia reloaded while they marched and paused long enough to aim and fire as one. Several American farm boys and a Hunter officer toppled into the snow. In one coordinated action, every man in the British force pulled his seventeen-inch bayonet from a scabbard and clicked it into place. The metallic clang washed over the Hunter force. Goosebumps rolled up Ryan's back.

The militia charged en masse at a trot, their bayonets pointing forward. The Hunter line disintegrated as young men, who Ryan knew had no training in close combat, broke and ran. The screaming militia pursued them at a run through a haze of smoke and dust.

Ryan caught a glimpse of Lyman Leach, his comrade from the *Peel* raid, kneel to fire his rifle, and then bolt into the tavern. Ryan spotted William Gates running pell-mell from a squad of British militia towards the barn. His pursuers paused and let loose a musket volley. A musket ball tore his hat off and lead balls slammed into the barn's pine walls as Gates ducked inside it. Not safe in the barn, he sprinted the hundred yards to the windmill.

Ryan went below to check Gates' wounds. He slumped on the wall, panting but unscathed.

"Good thing the Brits can't shoot straight." He handed Gates a cup of water.

"It wasn't their marksmanship. I was so damn frightened, I outran their muskets balls," He laughed. Then his mood changed. "I'd like to shoot that lying coward Birge and feed his parts to my hogs."

"Ye are not alone in that sentiment."

Back at his second-storey window, Ryan found a marksman, Garret Hicks, hunkered behind a long-barrelled rifle. A farmer from Jefferson County, he was several years older and two inches taller than Ryan.

Unable to help, unable to scream a warning, Ryan and Garret squirmed as militiamen overtook fleeing Hunters and plunged their lethal three-sided bayonets deep in their abdomens. With a sharp twist, they yanked out the blades, tinged with blood and steaming slivers of guts.

"Them bastards are out of range, otherwise…" Hicks didn't finish the sentence.

The Hunter force retreated to the buildings and took up positions in doorways and windows. The attackers split into two groups. One group continued forward, pressing the assault. The other circled around to attack from the west through the butternut grove.

Von Schoultz observed the enemy movement and guessed the British tactics.

"Colonel Woodruff. Move your men to the grove. Hold that flank."

Four dozen Hunters raced to new positions behind the grove's rock fence. Oblivious to the musket balls whizzing through the air, von Schoultz ran between groups of Hunters, patting men on the back and pointing out strong defensive positions and lines of retreat.

The over-confident militia advanced aggressively from the north and west, finally bringing themselves within range of marksmen in the windmill, carriage house, homes, and the tavern. Hicks fired his first shot as Ryan watched.

"I think ye hit one."

Hunter marksmen raked the militia with lethal rifle fire. Raised on turkey shoots and similar marksmanship contests, the American farm boys were crack shots. The militia line wavered as their comrades fell screaming in pain. Their bravado crumbled and they retreated. Dozens of bodies lay in fields and draped over fences.

After a minute of eerie silence, the scream of descending cannonballs signaled the renewed naval bombardment.

"Quick," Heustis called to his men in the windmill, "get the wounded under cover."

Ignoring the cannon fire, Ryan and other Hunters rushed onto the cratered battlefield. The death of young Foster had prepared Ryan for the gore of war. He ignored the sight of bayoneted corpses, their dark bowels spilled onto the white ground, lightly steaming in the wintry air, as their blank eyes stared skyward. He stepped over puddles of dark blood next to bodies torn by musket balls and cannon blasts. His ears sought groans—the easiest way to find the living among the dead. Ryan hastily bound their wounds before others arrived to carry them to the windmill. The whine of descending cannonballs, a sound that hours earlier made him cower, no longer caused the merest flinch.

Seconds after Ryan settled the last wounded man onto a pallet of straw in the windmill's ground floor, a cannonball screamed in through a window. It smacked the inside wall with an ear-piercing boom, raising a cloud of dust. Instead of bouncing to the floor where the men huddled and the gunpowder sat in kegs, it rolled in circles around the windmill's round interior, like bug swirling down a drain, and settled on the floor, injuring no one. Heat from the eighteen-pound iron ball helped warm the frigid room. Everyone inside brushed moldy flour dust and particles of wheat chafe from their coats. Though unused for years, the windmill still held ample traces of a working flour mill.

The British launched a second assault. Ryan bandaged wounds, ignoring the war beyond. When the British retreated again, Hunters carried ten more bleeding men into the poor hospital.

Captain Heustis pulled him aside. "What is the state of the wounded?"

"Most have minor flesh wounds. A few are serious."

"How serious?"

"I expect one or two will die by morning. And 'tis lucky yer not among them, judging by the sight of ye."

"Pardon me!"

"Have ye looked closely at yer coat and trousers?"

Heustis removed his winter coat and examined it clinically. Light shone through three gaps where musket balls had ripped holes. The loose cloth of a pant leg revealed another hole. No wound marked his body. In typical Heustis fashion, he showed no emotion.

"How did we do in the second assault?" Ryan inquired.

"Not so well at first. They attacked from the east. We rushed men to that side of the village, a little too eagerly, I sadly admit. The British appeared to retreat at our assault. Thus encouraged, a score of men gave chase. It was a feint. The British circled our flank and forced twenty-five of our men to surrender."

"At least they'll be fed."

Heustis rolled his eyes at the remark. "We had better luck later. A British lieutenant led fifty men to capture our cannon. Our marksmen opened fire from the windmill and tavern. The officer and several of his men fell before they withdrew."

"How long can we hold them off?"

"Our force is reduced by a third between casualties and captures. I believe the British losses are greater."

"Yes, but they can bring more men and munitions. We can't."

"Yes, Ryan. But we fight better and harder than they."

"We have little choice."

"Your tone sometimes verges on insubordinate!"

"Ye have my permission to clamp me in irons, captain."

"Humph!" Heustis departed the windmill.

*****

In late afternoon, the British ships stopped their barrage and steamed to Prescott. Curious about the uncommon quiet, Ryan stepped outside and called to the windmill window where Hicks remained on sniper duty.

"What can ye see, Garret?"

"Some soldiers are marching to Prescott with their prisoners. The rest have formed a cordon around the village to hold us."

"What do ye think is happening now?"

"I bet they are waiting for reinforcements. Bigger cannon too, I wager."

Ryan meandered along the riverbank, enjoying the quiescent interlude after ten hours of roaring cannon. Snowflakes fell in increasing intensity and size. The silhouette of Ogdensburg—freedom and safety across the river—began to blur.

"Ryan," Daniel George called from beside the windmill. "We found a rowboat downstream. Find something to paddle it with."

Ryan salvaged four boards from roofs blown off by British cannon. With his tomahawk, he fashioned a rough grip at one end of each board. Not long enough for oars, they'd make passable paddles. When he arrived at the beach, George, Gates, and two men he didn't know waited by the rowboat. Nearby, riflemen under von Schoultz held a group of British militia at bay.

He handed over the crude paddles and scanned the river with his telescope. "There are no ships, Mr. George," he called down, "but I can't see far in this light."

"Let's give it a try," George said.

"Godspeed men," von Schoultz called.

The four men propelled the derelict boat at surprising speed, considering the poor paddles. Every minute or so, one man stopped rowing to bail water seeping in.

"They are nearing the border," von Schoultz said. "Success is within their grasp."

Ryan spotted a shadow moving in the swirling snowflakes upstream. He waited as the ship steamed closer. "Colonel! The *Cobourg* is coming."

"Maybe they British won't see them," the colonel suggested.

A moment later, the *Cobourg* with Captain Sandom in command changed course towards George's boat. The falling snow muffled her cannon's opening boom. A pale plume of water erupted near the little boat's bow. It sped up. No one paused to bail.

"I do believe they have crossed the mid-point," Von Schoultz called, smiling.

"I know from personal experience, colonel, that the British don't respect that border."

Without a pause, the steamer crossed into American waters and shot again. The men kept paddling. The cannon roared once more as the ship closed in. By the multiple splashes, Ryan knew the ship had fired a load of grapeshot. Still, the four Hunters paddled.

The steamer came within musket range and onboard marines opened fire. The fleeing men stopped.

"They've surrendered, colonel."

Von Schoultz cussed in a language Ryan didn't recognize and led a somber procession back to Newport.

*****

Ryan leaned on the windmill's dark bulk for an hour staring at the faints lamp lights of Ogdensburg across the river. He imagined how he might feel if he had stayed with Bill and watched the battle from Ogdensburg. He'd made the correct decision for him. Whatever battle wounds he might suffer, they were preferable to the permanent guilt that watching the battle from safety would inflict.

Heustis stepped from the silent dark. "Ryan. We have another enterprise afoot. Come with me."

Inside the tavern, von Schoultz conversed with a younger man by the hearth fire's glow. "This is Tom Meredith," von Schoultz said. "He spied for us in Prescott and joined us last night."

"Tom has an idea about crossing the river," Heustis said.

"I want to make a narrow raft. I need three or four fence rails and maybe a wide plank and something to hold it together," Meredith said.

"What will ye use for paddles?" Ryan asked.

"My arms."

"'Tis more than half a mile!"

"I'm a good swimmer. The raft will keep most of me above the water."

"'Tis worth a try. I know where there is rope we can use for lashing."

Ryan and Meredith scrounged materials from the wreckage of Newport and lashed the raft components together. With help from Heustis, they carried the odd craft to the river.

"If ye see Bill Johnston, give him our best," Ryan called.

Meredith waded to knee depth in the near-freezing water. With a cheerful wave, he lay on his raft and set off. He disappeared into the midnight gloom in seconds.

"What're his orders, captain?"

"The colonel wants someone to confront Birge and demand boats to take us off."

"Birge won't do anything."

"I know."

The sound of several rifle shots in quick succession came from the edge of Newport.

"I should investigate those shots," Heustis said.

"I'll see to the wounded."

*****

On the river, swirling snow created an odd miasma as it reflected the little natural light remaining. Paddling blind, Meredith struggled forward propelled by his rapidly tiring arms. He had not calculated on how fast frigid water saps strength. His water-soaked coat sleeves became dead weight. Halfway across the river, amid the hiss of snow hitting open water, he caught the whisper of men talking and stomping their cold feet in Ogdensburg. He moved glacially towards the murmur. His arm muscles became leaden mush in the frigid water. He could manage a feeble stroke once every five seconds or so. His weak effort nudged him forward. He did not waver—he had no choice.

Several men on the Ogdensburg waterfront spotted Meredith drifting semiconscious in the harbor. They launched a skiff and hauled the wet and hypothermic man off the flimsy raft. On shore, they carried him to the nearest all-night bonfire. Against long odds, he had made it.

The bonfire's heat, two shots of whisky, and strong tea revived him. Once he warmed sufficiently for his jaw muscles to work again, he growled, "Where's that bloody Birge?"

Several hours after midnight, Meredith awoke the sleeping general in an Ogdensburg hotel. Meredith, a man reborn, snatched from death and now afraid of nothing, hovered menacingly above Birge. "Do something for your men!"

Unable to resist Meredith's glaring eyes and intensity, Birge climbed from his warm bed. "I know just the thing," he replied in his most unctuous tone.

Birge composed a letter to Bill Johnston.

November 14, 1838

Dear Johnston,

The fate of the men on the other side of the river is in your hands. Nothing is expected of the British above Prescott; and if you can rally your men and go to Jones' Mills and kindle some fires, you will save the men and save Canada. Start fires also at Gananoque and the British will think Kingston is being attacked. Do, for God's sake, rally your men and start immediately.

J. Ward Birge

"Here. Go in haste and delivery this to Admiral Johnston."

With his letter, Birge created a publicly credible but militarily impossible solution to the tragedy unfolding at Newport. Simultaneously, he set up Bill to become a scapegoat for any failure. With Meredith gone, Birge poured a brandy, crawled into his warm bed, and chuckled at his brilliance.

Meredith stalked Ogdensburg until after dawn in an unsuccessful search for Bill. He neglected to search the rooftops near the river.

*****

On the river's Canadian side, Hicks entered the windmill, his expression tense and pained. Ryan passed him a tin mug of dandelion leaf tea. "Garret. What's wrong?"

Hicks blew gently and deliberately on the pale green water. "Them shots earlier?"

"Yes."

"We was shooting some hogs on the colonel's orders."

"Good. We could use the food."

"I'm not so sure. They was eating that dead British lieutenant we shot trying to capture our cannon. Is anyone that hungry?"

"Nay."

"When we gets captured, them Brits will blame the mutilation on us. I'm sure of it."

Several men sighed audibly. Some spat on the floor. Hicks' calm assertion of eventual capture hit the sullen men like a court sentence.

Wednesday, November 14, 1838

The battle's second day began with pelting snow that morphed into sleet as the temperature edged above freezing. The dead on both sides lay shrouded by wet snow in the no-man's-land between the Hunter and the British lines.

To clean wounds, Ryan boiled water over a fire fed by a dwindling supply of ruined roof lumber and the few sticks of cordwood found in local homes. For bandages, he tore cloth strips from dead men's clothes. He made more tea from shriveled dandelion leaves he found under the snow. The fire did nothing to warm the windmill interior. The heavy stone walls radiated cold.

His medic work completed for the moment, he climbed to the windmill's third-story and scanned the hamlet. Zak landed on the window ledge beside him. The raven wisely spent his nights in a spruce grove a mile away.

"Zaak!"

"Good to see ye too friend. I hope ye found yer own breakfast."

Not a single roof remained to protect occupants from foul weather. A pile of smoldering timbers marked the ruined barn's location. Hunter gun barrels poked from every window of the stone tavern and the four buildings closest to it. Canadian militia companies surrounded the hamlet.

"You know Zak, we could easily push through at any point, but where'd we go."

Zak flew up and circled the windmill. "Croc! Croc!"

Ryan glanced upriver and then called to men below. "The British navy's coming. Everyone take cover!"

A cannonball slammed into the windmill. Inside, it rang like a stone bell, shaking flour dust loose from cracks and wooden structures. Zak headed to the distant woods. Heustis joined Ryan at his window perch and watched balls streak past the windmill into the hamlet. The balls damaged men's nerves far more than they did the thick, limestone walls of Newport structures.

Ryan looked around. "Why do ye think men came here at such a risk? Was it the promise of free land?"

"That promise lured men to our cause, but most of them are in Ogdensburg drinking to their bravery." He paused at the roar of another British salvo. The rising shriek of descending cannonballs ended in a series of concussive thuds.

Heustis continued. "The men with us are true fighters for freedom. Their grandfathers fought with Washington. These lads are cut from the same cloth as those who flocked to Sam Houston two years ago. They dream to free Canada the same way their heroes Jim Bowie and Davy Crockett helped free Texas."

"So, is this our Alamo?"

Heustis quietly chewed his lower lip. Ryan changed the subject. "Captain, how did ye come to join the Patriots?"

"It was after I read news about British massacres of Patriots in Lower Canada. I had an epiphany where my comfortable life seemed cowardly in the face of such an abuse of justice. So, in January, I set out for Buffalo, hoping to join Mackenzie. He had already abandoned Navy Island, but I met him and Johnston at the Eagle tavern in Buffalo. I signed up for the duration of the struggle. Mackenzie is an intelligent reformer. Sadly, lesser men now seem to be running—"

"Look over there, captain," Ryan interrupted, pointing west.

British soldiers approached waving a white banner. The cannonade ceased.

"A flag of truce! I must alert the colonel. Come with me."

*****

Von Schoultz, Heustis, and Ryan trod through eight inches of new snow in dirty coats and boots not meant for winter to meet an immaculately dressed British officer on horseback and two infantrymen in scarlet tunics.

"I am Colonel Richard Fraser of the second Grenville militia regiment. Who commands your force?"

"I do. Colonel Nils von Schoultz."

"I propose a truce of one hour so both sides can recover their dead. Agreed?"

"Yes. I agree."

Colonel Fraser waved to his rear. Several dozen unarmed men came onto the battlefield with stretchers.

"Captain," von Schoultz began, "please arrange for the pickup of our dead. And direct our men to provide any assistance the British require."

"Yes, colonel." Heustis trotted to the tavern.

Von Schoultz approached Fraser. "Colonel, perhaps we can discuss other matters."

Fraser sneered at von Schoultz, spat on the ground, wheeled his horse, and rode away.

"Such solecism! I expected cordiality from a man of his rank."

"Colonel, that officer is one of the men we robbed on the *Sir Robert Peel*. He may have a grudge agin us."

"That is another problem for which I can thank that damn Johnston."

"Pardon me, colonel. What other problems has he caused us?"

"He abandoned us for one. He's a coward like Birge and Estes."

Ryan's face flushed at the untruths and injustice in that remark. The colonel's petulant tone acted as a warning; so, he kept his rebuttal to himself. "Perhaps, I should help gather the dead, sir." He departed without waiting for a response.

Minutes after the truce elapsed, a band of British militia launched a surprise attack.

"Colonel," Heustis shouted, "the militia has captured the furthest house east."

Von Schoultz borrowed Ryan's telescope and scanned the stone house. "Then we shall retake it immediately."

Led by the colonel, eleven marksmen advanced across Newport towing their three-pounder. Once within rifle range, the Hunters fired on the captured house aiming for any enemy soldier that showed himself. Two volleys from the cannon smashed in the front door and enlarged a window. The occupiers retreated out the rear door.

A smiling von Schoultz marched back with two wounded prisoners.

"Ryan. Give these men the best care you can. To be prudent, place a guard on them."

"Yes, sir."

That skirmish provided the day's only serious military action. Men on both sides shot at each other sporadically, with no effect. Cannonballs thudded like a bass drumbeat on Newport every four minutes. While the British regulars and militia fortified themselves with cups of tea and bowls of stew, the Hunters huddled in the broken buildings, dreaming of meals past.

From a windmill window, Ryan and Hicks watched night descend on Newport's shattered and cratered confines.

"I wish they'd attack," Hicks began. "It is all this waiting that's going to kill me."

"True. I nary imagined battles could be this boring."

"Boring but not without tension. I'm reminded of a steer waiting in an abattoir stall."

"'Tis so. Nothing to do but wait to die."

"Everyone is thinking the same, Ryan. I've seen men weeping in the shadows and others curled up in a ball like scared children."

"We are too cold, too hungry, and too fearful to find relief in sleep."

Hicks nodded, and then fired a shot at the enemy lines. It fell far short of its target.

The interminable bombardment ended as the long November night settled in. Looking for a respite from the groaning wounded in the windmill, Ryan went for a stroll on the riverbank. He was not alone. Hunter Vaughan, one of the last Sackets Harbor recruits remaining in the fight, waved him over.

"See that ship out there?" He pointed at the U.S. steamer *Telegraph* moving slowly downstream parallel to the shore.

Ryan nodded.

"That ship's skipper is my father, William. He's out there making sure no one comes over to help us or me."

"'Tis odd how things happen."

"When we set out, I expected better than this."

"'Tis not what any of us expected."

"We were grossly misled." Hands in his pockets, Vaughan shuffled away, watching his father's ship.

The surviving Hunters shivered away the night. Not a single candle or piece of firewood remained to provide light. Desultory whispers affirmed that Newport still held life.

Thursday, November 15, 1838

The first morning barrage from the British steamers jolted Ryan from his semi-consciousness stupor. He emerged stiff and shivering from the windmill. The prismatic glimmer of sun dogs in the deep blue sky promised a cold day. Hard snow crunched beneath his boots in subfreezing temperatures. His half finger throbbed.

Nauseous with acute hunger, he slid down the steep bank to the ice-free river. All available water in the village had frozen. Oblivious to cannonballs arching overhead, he lifted water to his parched lips in cupped hands. He thought of the pigs shot two days earlier. Desperate for food, he'd butcher them in an instant now, if he had the means to hack off frozen chunks and a fire to cook them.

Using a metal rod he'd carried from the village, he scraped aside snow on the steep bank and poked the ground. Frost had rendered most soil rock-hard. He levered aside a rotten log near the shore to expose the unfrozen dirt beneath. A sluggish earthworm tried to retreat into its burrow. With fingers so numb they barely moved, he seized the worm, rinsed it in the river, and swallowed it without chewing. Further digging uncovered a fat, white beetle grub with an orange head. He gulped it down. That meager meal only made his stomach beg for more. He searched between submerged rocks for any mussels lurking in shallow water.

A happy memory of feeding Zak worms, grubs and shellfish that first summer seeped into his numb brain. His arms akimbo, he flapped his elbows bird-style and cackled at himself. "Like a desperate chick, 'tis I today."

A subtle change in the background whine of British cannonballs snapped him from his hunger-induced reverie. The rising shrill meant one thing—the British gunners had targeted him. He dropped to his stomach and covered his head with his arms. The projectile hit half way up the slope above him. Dirt and pulverized bits of limestone rained down, pelting his body from head to toe.

Unhurt, he jumped to his feet and rushed uphill to the new crater. A quick search of the exposed soil yielded two earthworms. He dashed to the water, rinsed them, and ate both. He gave a sarcastic two thumbs up to the British ships. Another cannonball screamed its presence. It enlarged the previous crater and pelted him with earth and pebbles. He danced a little jig on the crater's edge and climbed up to the windmill, where two friends waited.

"Are you hurt, mate?" Smith asked.

"Nary a scratch."

"It looks like you were having fun," Hicks said.

"In a strange fashion, 'twas so."

"I think we should show them gunners the respect they deserve," Hicks added.

"What do ye have in mind?"

Grinning, Hicks began unbuckling his trousers. Ryan and Smith immediately understood his intention.

*****

On the *Experiment*, telescope to his eye, Lieutenant Fowell blushed and cursed as three Hunters turned their backs to the river, dropped their pants, and bent forward at the waist. Every British gunner set their sights on a triplet of wagging buttocks, glowing yellow orbs illuminated by the newly risen sun. Six screaming cannonballs smashed into the riverbank near the windmill, raising a cloud of dust and turning snow to steam. Fowell watched as the three men faced the ships and urinated down the slope. A second barrage of cannonballs greeted their cheekiness. They didn't flinch under a hail of explosion-driven sand and spray. They buckled up, waved at the ships, and sauntered into the windmill to a round of applause.

*****

The three steamers continued to lob iron balls into the ruined village until midday, and then departed for Prescott.

"Rrok! Cric! Croc! Zak called, as he landed on the last remaining windmill sail.

"My raven sees something Garret. Can you?" Ryan called from the ground.

"Good for your bird. There's a Brit gun crew sneaking up to the east."

Ryan swung his telescope to where Hicks pointed. Two draught horses were hauling a wheel-mounted field gun at the village edge. Four men in blue uniforms trotted beside it.

"Orrin," Ryan began, "can you see it, past the last house?"

"Yep! Help me with this."

With Ryan's help, Smith swung their relatively puny six-pounder. He loaded a double charge of powder and one of his last cannonballs. He hiked up the barrel for a long-range shot, aimed, and fired.

With uncanny accuracy, the cannonball arced across the hamlet and slammed into the whiffletree that connected the gun carriage to the harness. The big cannon flipped on its side. The steeds galloped away. A cheer rose from the Hunter ranks.

"Ye-haw!" cried Smith, as he pumped the air with his fist.

Zak called from the windmill roof. "Rrok! Cric! Croc!"

Ryan scanned the river. "Someone fetch the colonel," Ryan hollered. "The *Paul Pry* is coming across."

The ferry steamer stopped offshore. As lines of weary Hunters gathered in the cold along the bank's brow, a rowboat with two oarsmen and a single passenger dressed in a hooded coat pulled up on the rocky beach where von Schoultz, Abbey, Woodruff, Heustis, and Ryan waited.

The boat passenger threw back his hood. "Colonel von Schoultz. Glad I am to see you so well."

"General Estes! I didn't expect anyone to cross."

"We noticed an absence of warships and took a chance."

"What succor have you brought us? My men are in a desperate state."

"Colonel, you have two options, one glorious and one ignominious."

Von Schoultz scowled at the odious man's choice of words. "Please explain, general."

"We can take men off right now while the British ships are away. Or I can bring you six hundred fresh, armed men by morning."

Von Schoultz smiled. His face relaxed. "With six hundred men, we could fight our way home."

"Is that your decision, colonel?"

"Yes, it is."

"You choose honor. I am proud to know you." Estes saluted von Schoultz and then ordered the two oarsmen back to the *Paul Pry*.

"Colonel." Ryan tugged his sleeve. "There are no six hundred to come."

"Nonsense. Why would the general lie?"

Ryan looked for support from the other officers. Heustis shrugged. Woodruff and Abbey looked away.

"Colonel, please. We know the British are expecting reinforcements and bigger cannon. Tomorrow they'll pound us. If we had the six hundred, 'tis too late to land them and the necessary supplies."

"I have been in worse positions fighting the Russians. It is never too late."

"You told us you lost those battles, colonel."

"But we never lost our honor." Von Schoultz hurried away, signaling an end to the discussion. Everyone vacated the beach, except Ryan and Heustis.

"That little ship was our only chance, captain."

"I know. I know."

"Captain," Smith called from the bank above. "The rowboat's returning."

"Find the colonel," Heustis ordered.

The same two quiet men rowed a new passenger to shore as sleet began to fall.

"Colonel Schoultz, I am Preston King. The American authorities sent me to bring you home. What Estes promised cannot happen."

"Are there not hundreds of Hunters in Ogdensburg, Mr. King?"

"Yes, but—"

"Are they not armed?"

"Yes, but—"

"Then Estes may not be lying."

"The military impounded every vessel. There are no ships to carry the men, if they'd come, which I doubt."

"Our answer is no. We will wait for reinforcements."

"Then, what about the wounded, colonel?"

"Good point, Mr. King. Captain Heustis. Arrange to have them brought down."

"Yes, colonel."

Minutes later, one Hunter limped down the steep bank and climbed into the boat.

"T'others need to be carried, sir. It'll be a few minutes," Ryan explained.

"We'll take this man now and send the boat back for others. Agreed, colonel?"

"Agreed, Mr. King."

"Do ye have any food aboard that ship, Mr. King?" Ryan asked.

"I am sorry, no."

Seconds after King's rowboat reached the *Paul Pry*, Smith yelled from the riverbank. "British ship coming."

"Can you see it, Ryan?" von Schoultz asked.

He opened his telescope and peered into the gathering dusk. A steamer approached he knew all too well. "'Tis the *Experiment*, colonel."

"Damn that ship!"

The *Paul Pry* retreated into the evening gloom even as men carried wounded Hunters on rough stretchers to the windblown shore.

Officers and men, healthy and sick, huddled in the driving sleet for three hours, hoping the ferry would return. Finally, with a word from von Schoultz, they retreated to their chilled quarters to wait daylight and the final battle.

Friday, November 16, 1838

"How is our ammunition?" Heustis asked Ryan.

"We have three thousand cartridges. How many men have we?"

"One hundred and seventeen fit to fight."

"The gives us twenty-five per man.

"That will not suffice. Tell the men to shoot only when they have a clear target."

"They know to make—" The British gunboats fired in unison. A cannonball slammed into the windmill and deflected onto the road.

"—each cartridge count."

"What of our cannon?" Heustis asked, brushing stale flour and dust from his coat.

"We have powder but few balls remaining."

"Tell the men to gather up scrap metal and use it when the balls are gone."

"Already done, captain."

"Good."

"Captain! Someone said two men found an old canoe last night and crossed over."

"Yes. I wished them Godspeed."

"I heard they invited ye to go and ye refused."

"My duty is here. I cannot leave the men at such a time. Would you?"

"Nay."

*****

A new British army gathered in the fields beyond Newport. By midday, the Hunters faced over two thousand fit, warm, and well fed regulars and militia. The defenders huddled in the tenebrous ruins. Sleep-deprived, their empty stomachs now acidic knots, most verged on comatose. Only shivers indicated life continued.

Garret Hicks and other Hunter snipers at their window posts watched the distant soldiers form into four companies along the semi-circular perimeter. A lone soldier marched forward carrying a white flag.

Hicks called down from his windmill post. "Someone tell the colonel there's a flag of truce on the battlefield."

"I'll go see what he wants first," Lyman Leach yelled up to Hicks.

Ryan watched Leach stride across the battlefield like a man who'd eaten and slept well. An excellent act, Ryan thought, he's not a man to show the enemy any weakness.

Lyman talked with the British soldier for less than a minute, shook his hand, and returned.

"What do they want," asked von Schoultz.

"Their commander wants to talk with you, colonel."

Colonel von Schoultz with Abbey and Woodruff, all scruffy and haggard, trudged to meet the British officer in a tailored, red battle uniform.

"Are you von Schoultz?"

"I am. To whom do I have the pleasure?"

"Lieutenant-Colonel Henry Dundas, commander of the Eighty-third Regiment of Foot."

"How may I help you, colonel?"

"I propose a one hour truce. There are still some dead on the field. Are you in agreement?"

"We are. Please allow me to hand over your men we captured on Wednesday. We have no means to treat their wounds."

"Certainly. Bring them to this spot and my men will meet you."

Von Schoultz nodded to Abbey. He returned to the windmill.

"Colonel," von Schoultz began, "I propose we prevent further deaths and injuries."

"Do you surrender?"

"On the condition my men will be treated as prisoners of war, then yes."

"Impossible," Dundas replied. "I cannot accept renegades as valid prisoners of war."

"Please, colonel. Most of my men are naive boys. Show them some mercy. I take full responsibility and accept any punishment."

"I appreciate the commitment to your men, but I cannot grant your request. Your surrender must be unconditional. All must stand for court martial."

"I cannot accept such a diktat. Good day." Von Schoultz pivoted on one heel and marched with Woodruff to the tavern.

For an hour after the truce ended, the battlefield lay quiet. The British steamers in the river held their positions with silenced guns. The navy reinforced the blockade with three cannon-laden barges. On land, blue-coated British artillery crews guided two eighteen-pound, horse-drawn, field cannon in to position four hundred yards north of the windmill. Behind the guns came wagons loaded with cannonballs and powder.

From windows and doors throughout Newport, enervated and emaciated Hunters scrutinized their enemy's final preparation with the same fatalistic detachment that a condemned man studies the noose being tied around his neck.

The British land force stayed beyond range of Hunter marksmen. In the eerie calm, both armies waited for the British artillery crews to ready the big cannon. The militia fidgeted, eager for victory. The Hunters slumped against walls or window frames, too tired and hungry to care.

*****

At three in the afternoon, the silence ended when the British ships and barges commenced their final cannonade. Inured after days of siege, the Hunters no longer blinked or flinched at the boom and thump of cannon fire.

A half hour later, a new instrument joined the orchestra of weaponry. It reminded Ryan of a thunder burst overhead compared to thunder's rumble a mile away. Everyone knew without asking—the big artillery cannon had joined in.

Unlike the naval guns, the eighteen-pound cannon were long-range building-smashers. Though the same caliber as the carronades, they carried more punch. The first shot slammed into the windmill above the door and deflected into the river. The concussion threw Ryan to the second-story's wooden floor. His ears rang and he coughed as dust coated his nostrils and throat.

The second ball hit the two-story house nearest the cannon, blasting a gapping hole in the two-foot thick stone wall. For an hour, each eighteen-pounder hurled iron at the hamlet once every two minutes. The expert gunners never missed. Their projectiles steadily dismantled Newport. Only the windmill escaped damage.

*****

With the end clearly near, Ryan trotted with Heustis across the battlefield from the windmill to the tavern. They walked into a heated debate among the senior officers.

"Colonel," Abbey hollered over the cannon roar, "our situation is hopeless. We must surrender."

"I agree with Dorephus," said Woodruff.

"I most certainly do not," said Heustis. "The British have not yet made a final assault. There still may be opportunity for an honorable surrender."

"I agree with the captain. There will be no surrender yet. "Von Schoultz put an end to the debate.

"Colonel Woodruff," von Schoultz commanded, "I want you and Captain Heustis to hold the windmill as long as you can. It is our best fortification."

"Yes, colonel."

"Ryan! Stay here. I may require you to run messages to the windmill."

"Yes, sir."

In the darkened room, as all eyes watched the Canadian lines, Abbey silently bowed to the assembled men and slipped outside. With arms up and waving a white handkerchief, he trotted to the militia and surrendered.

Colonel Richard Fraser spotted Abbey and galloped over on horseback. Leaning down, he smacked Abbey's buttocks full force with the flat of his sword. Abbey howled and dropped to his belly. Fraser grinned at Abbey's pain.

As daylight faded into November twilight, a British bugler sounded the advance. At the instrument's martial notes, every able Hunter moved into position by windows, doors, and gaping wall holes. Newly battle-hardened boys and young men prepared for the final fight they knew they could not win.

With bayonets fixed, British regulars and throngs of militia marched towards Newport and the Hunter defenses. The naval cannon barrage continued, keeping the Hunters pinned down.

Through a cleft in the tavern's stone wall, Ryan watched the British captured one house after the other and set each afire to drive out their occupants. The evicted Hunters fled. Soon, only the windmill and tavern remained in the Hunters hands.

In the flaming orange glow, Ryan spotted Heustis and Woodruff marching from the windmill waving a white handkerchief. The militia opened fire. The Hunter officers retreated to the windmill.

*****

A red-faced Captain Sandom also witnessed the Hunter's foiled attempt at surrender. Firing on a flag of truce tarnished the reputation of every man in the field, including himself. Turning to his adjutant,

Sandom said, "If that militia company fires on a flag of truce again, have our marines fire on the militia."

"Our militia, sir?"

"Yes. Their actions dishonor us all. And someone bring me Lieutenant Leary."

Minutes later, on Sandom's orders, Lieutenant George Leary approached the windmill waving a white banner. Lyman Leach returned with Leary to parlay with Sandom.

Before Leach said a word, Colonel Richard Fraser appeared on horseback from the evening gloom and smacked Leach's buttocks full force with the flat of his sword. He dropped to his knees and grit his teeth to stifle a scream.

"Colonel! This is an outrage," Sandom roared, reaching for his sword. "He is under a flag of truce."

"Captain, that's how we deal with brigands in my county." Fraser rode away.

"Are you prepared to surrender?" Sandom asked the gasping Leach.

"Yes."

"Then go bring them out. My marines and the Eighty-third will protect you," said Sandom.

The windmill emptied as sixty Hunters, including Heustis and Woodruff, marched out with the hands on their heads.

*****

"Colonel, the windmill has surrendered," Ryan said.

"Men," Von Schoultz called. "The cause is just, but the battle is lost. You are free to make your own decisions. You may fight, surrender, or flee. My choice is to take to the night and trust God's grace."

Of the dozen other men in the room, the majority exited the tavern under a white flag. Von Schoultz, Hunter Vaughan, and three others climbed out a side window and headed to the river.

Alone in the tavern, Ryan stared into the night. A band of blue twilight hugged the western horizon. It reminded him of the hem on Kate's favorite summer skirt. The blue band also told Ryan the direction to travel to where he imagined her lips waited for his.

A full moon rose over the eastern horizon in a clear sky, its light magnified by the reflective snow. Removing his coat, he pulled it inside out so that Ann Johnston's pale flannel lining was on the outside. He dropped out the window into the soundless snow. Shouts came from all directions, but he saw no silhouettes of nearby men in the eerie moonlight.

Staying low, he trod deliberately, as if stalking game. Though the prey now, not the hunter, the elements of being unseen hadn't changed. Do not rise any higher than nearby objects so that your form does not stand out. Flow through the environment. Blend your shadow with other shadows. Be patient. Stop often and listen.

Moving among the eldritch shadows of the blasted butternut grove west of the tavern, Ryan charted a course from tree to tree along the stone wall. He headed north towards the British cannon crew, towards the enemy. No search party would expect a sane man to choose that direction.

The Road's Fork

Ryan approached a bonfire around which the British artillery crew and infantry toasted their victory with mugs of tea laced with rum. Sparks rose into the night sky like flaming insects. He moved towards the light, not through bug instinct, but native cunning.

The bright flame warmed the British soldiers, but Ryan knew it ruined their night vision. Their world stopped at the edge of the fire's glow on the winter landscape. Concealed in shadow, he passed two hundred feet west of the soldiers, unseen, unheard, heading north and west away from the battle and the search parties.

He paused at a narrow creek to drink from unfrozen water trickling over a ledge of rock. The hollering of victorious Canadian militia had faded to a distant drone. Recognizing the slender silhouette of cattails growing by the creek edge, he removed a glove, rolled up his sleeve, and forced his hand deep into the chilling muck seeking the roots.

"Damn this cold."

Yanking out a tuber, he rinsed it in the frigid water and sliced off the skin with his tomahawk. His teeth sought and found the starchy pulp. However humble, it was food, and better than worms.

He flinched at the unmistakable click of a musket hammer cocked into firing position behind him. "Stand up and turn around ya Hunter scum."

He knew that voice. A familiar rage rose from his gut, flushed his cheeks, and rang in his ears. In the dark, he kept his tomahawk hidden from view while he slowly turned. Tiny's stout silhouette loomed twenty feet away. The snow-reflected moonlight illuminated both men's faces in a ghostly glow.

"It's the little Irish hothead." Tiny grinned a lip-parting, sneering smile. He raised his musket. "Too bad ya tried to escape."

Ryan faked a step to his right—a trick Bill once painfully taught him —and then leapt to his left, raising his tomahawk to throw in defense. Tiny followed Ryan's movements with the gun sights. Neither man noticed the black shape passing in the night until it struck the fat militiaman in the head.

"Zrok!"

The raven hung onto Tiny's coat with his talons and boxed the man's ears with his wings. Tiny toppled backwards, dropping the musket to guard his eyes with both arms. Zak stayed on him, pecking his bare wrists with his chisel-like beak.

Ryan pulled the weapon from the snow.

"Zak. Come."

The bird flew to his human's shoulder and cooed in his ear. Ryan held the bayonet an inch from the big man's heaving chest.

"How did ye find me?"

"I visited the gunners' camp and saw tracks. I followed 'em."

"Ye should've stayed by the fire."

"I suppose ya plan to kill me." Tiny snarled in defiance.

"I have the right, given yer plans for me."

"I won't ask for mercy, if that's what ya expect."

Ryan studied his old tormentor. The rage dissipated. He expected groveling but, instead, Tiny displayed sullen bravery.

He sighed. "I spent five days in a pitched battle and killed none. I'm not about to soil my soul with the likes of ye." He stepped backwards. "I'll probably regret this."

He trotted into the dark with Zak on his shoulder. A mile west, he tossed the gun in a creek.

For hours, he traveled on a snow-rutted road, hoping to make his tracks less obvious. In the moonlight, he spied a log barn north of Prescott. Slipping across the barnyard through moon shadows, he climbed into the hay mow. Wind blew between the gaps in the barn's cedar logs. He burrowed into the loose hay and slowly warmed.

Lying awake, Bill Johnston's parting story days earlier swirled in his mind. Was it a tall tale or had Bill meant it as a prescription for repatriation?

*****

He awoke to Zak chatting a warning in his ear. Fingering his tomahawk handle, Ryan peeked from the mow to the threshing floor below. A girl of about seven in a simple homespun coat stared up.

"My daddy says you must come in the house for breakfast."

"How'd ye find me?"

"We saw your feet marks in the snow and the cows are restless. You talk funny. Where are you from?"

"Ireland originally. America recently."

"My daddy is from America. I like your bird."

Zak cooed.

"My bird likes ye, too."

"Breakfast is ready. Mommy cooks good."

He entered the farm kitchen by the side door. The trickle of sunlight coming through narrow windows illuminated a typical pioneer setting. A stone cooking hearth, food preparation tables, and washbasins covered the wall to his left. Doors led to bedrooms. A table and chairs dominated the center. A baby boy babbled gibberish in a handcrafted cradle. A woman and man greeted him with curt nods. Ryan recognized the man as one of the silent farmers who picked up loads of smuggled tea that summer.

"I know ye."

"And I you. How's Johnston?"

"He was well last I saw him."

"Sit. There's tea, eggs, fried potatoes, and toast, if that suits you."

"Sir. I've not eaten a decent meal in five days. It suits me like a feast suits a king."

He consumed the plate of food with esurient zeal. Then another. He requested more tea. Colonial people commonly refrained from talking during meals. Finally, the moment came to answer questions. The farmer sent his daughter out to play.

"Can I play with your bird, mister?" she asked.

"Yes. He knows simple words. Speak to him as ye talk to yer baby brother. Take these." He passed her toast crusts. "Throw each in the air for him to catch."

The girl departed laughing.

"I guess you were at the windmill." The farmer had his hand on the table. His index finger kept beat like a metronome as he talked.

"Yes." Ryan found no advantage in lying. "I tended to the wounded."

"Those Hunters were fools to promise our land to their fighters." Tap. Tap. Tap.

"I know."

"That turned most people against them." Tap. Tap. "It fired up the militia." Tap. Tap.

"Bill said that would happen."

"There are lots of patrols." Tap. Tap. "It's dangerous to travel and to have you here." Tap. Tap.

"What do ye suggest?"

He lifted his hand to point to his right. "I am heading north to deliver hay and other provender to a neighbor. I pass a big woodlot. You can hide in the wagon and jump off by the woods."

"Thank ye. I'll do that."

"From there you are on your own. We wish you good fortune." He rose and extended his hand.

"Ye've been very kind, and I don't know yer name."

"Best we keep it that way."

*****

Ryan traveled through forests and secluded valleys by day. Remembering Bill's story, he fed himself and Zak on raw mussels and crayfish caught in streams where the current kept the water ice-free. A freshwater mussel's texture resembles leather soaked in fish brine: not something to eat unless starving.

By night, he camped in thick wood lots beneath the sheltering boughs of spruce trees, tending a small fire to keep warm. In the cold, sleep was rare and slumber fitful. His feet went from chilled to numb.

After forty miles through snow that deepened daily, he emerged from scrubby forest late on the third day. Before him lay a familiar village on the St. Lawrence River. Ryan had eyes for just one establishment—the trading post. Concealed, he crouched and watched.

Daylight faded. The village residents finished their business and headed home. He trotted across the road and entered by the rear door. Stalking his prey, Ryan approached the front room where the proprietor was locking his door. Ryan slipped behind him and pressed his tomahawk blade to his throat.

"Ye owe me the value of a pack of furs and a pair of snowshoes."

The man started to tremble.

"And ye owe me for calling the British to kill me."

"I didn't do it."

"Sure, how else did Bonnycastle know I bought a telescope in this store?"

The man swallowed and stayed quiet.

"Have ye a boat?"

"My skiff is in the shed."

"Ye will drag that skiff to the shore, give me the oars, and wish me on my way. In return, yer debt to me'll be repaid. Do we have a deal?"

"Yes."

Ten minutes later, Ryan began traveling back to a better life. Once again, he rowed a skiff on the great river, moving his enervated muscles to the oarlock rhythm. Zak perched on the bow. Somewhere ahead in the familiar, dark distance lay Clayton—and Kate.

*****

On a foggy morning in late November, Ada set out to buy fresh eggs from the market for breakfast. Passing the family wharf, she spotted a scruffy man in a filthy coat standing on the dock. He appeared confused. She crossed the road, intending to tell the vagabond to cease trespassing, when she noticed the handsome raven sitting on a piling nearby.

"Ryan!"

Ada grabbed his shoulders, kissed his smudged forehead, and gazed into his eyes. "You are a mess but the loveliest mess I've ever seen."

He blinked. His knees trembled. The horror of war, days as a fugitive, poor nourishment, frigid nights, and inadequate sleep had taken a toll. The nervous energy that sustained him for days died like a doused flame. The numbness he'd ignored in his frigid feet made balance difficult. Dizziness and weakness washed over him. He passed out and crumpled to the wharf, his fall broken by Ada's strong arms.

*****

Ryan's troubled dreams faded as slumber slipped away. He lay on something soft, his body covered by sweet-smelling fabric. Dwelling for a time in that grainy but convincingly real oneiric state on the edge of consciousness, he dismissed the horrible images floating in his memory as a nightmare. Battle scenes had no reality at that moment in this cozy and safe place.

Someone entered the room. That little noise brought him fully awake, eyes open. Kate smiled weakly at him. He sat up, realized he was naked, and slipped beneath the down comforter.

"I have never seen someone slumber for twenty-four hours. How do you feel?"

He wiggled his toes and fingers. "I feel well. I'm hungry. Was I really in bed a whole day? Am I sick?"

"You had a difficult week. Do you recollect being in a battle?"

He jerked up, gasping. "So 'twas not a nightmare."

"No, Ryan. You are lucky to be well, alive, and free."

He lifted the covers to view his body. Somehow, all the grime and sweat had vanished—along with his clothes.

"I recall arriving at Clayton, but don't remember bathing and climbing into bed."

"You fainted. My brothers carried you to the house, removed your filthy clothes, and put you in the bath. Ada cleaned you up and the boys put you to bed."

He blushed.

Kate laughed. Her peel of mirth brought Ryan the first joy in weeks.

"Such a face, Mr. Pine. We could not let you go to bed filthy. Would you prefer my brothers had washed you?"

"No." Of all the possibilities, Ada was his first choice to bathe him.

"She said you had nothing she had not seen before." She paused and cocked her head. "I suppose she's referring to her sons or husband."

He swallowed in a dry throat. "I suppose 'tis so."

"Dress and come down for lunch."

"I will. So, how have ye been? I can see yer not happy."

"Let us talk at lunch."

He found clothes, clean, pressed, and folded on a chair. He dressed, combed his longish hair, and descended to the dining room. Ada and the family waited around the table. He eyed the plates of boiled eggs, bread, fried potatoes, and boiled cabbage. His stomach ached for food.

"Where's Bill?" He motioned to an empty seat.

"Father is in jail in Auburn," John began. "He was arrested two days ago for his role in the windmill battle."

"What happened that I missed?"

"I joined him in Ogdensburg on Wednesday of the battle," John explained. "He spent two days and nights on the roof in Ogdensburg observing the fight. He hardly ate. Twice he scoured the town in a vain attempt to encourage men to cross in boats, not to join the battle, but to take men off. He rowed out Wednesday night, but couldn't penetrate the blockade. It tore at him cruelly to be safe while you, Captain Heustis, and others faced peril.

"He was a forlorn man by that Thursday. His friends were dying. People excoriated him for not fighting at the windmill. He confessed to me he was tired of fighting and hiding. He agreed to turn himself in and ask for clemency.

"Father suggested he surrender to me so I could claim the reward. We were rowing into Ogdensburg, but the marshal's men found us first. Father was heavily armed and ready to fight. After some dickering, he stood down and I took his weapons. His trial begins in three days."

"John and I are leaving tomorrow morning to be with him," Kate said.

"Yer leaving?"

"I must, Ryan."

"I hoped we could—"

She held up her hands. "I must do my duty. You of all people should accept that." Her eyes urged him not to argue further.

"Yes, I do."

Ryan joined Zak on the covered veranda, trying to lose his thoughts among the flakes falling on the river. The raven perched on the railing and eyed his human. Both reveled in the quiet, but peace eluded Ryan. The bird sensed his restless mood and cooed in support.

Kate stepped outside wrapped in a woolen shawl and ran her fingers through his red curls. "I do believe you require a haircut."

That touch, that single act of affection disguised as a grooming assessment, calmed his inner turmoil for the moment. The exorcised bad energy escaped in an audible sigh.

"Still learning to relax?"

"I guess so."

He pulled her delicate, long-boned hand to his lips and lightly kissed her palm, and then held it to his cheek. Kate leaned against him.

"Rrok! Cric! Croc!"

"Someone's coming out."

Decatur stepped onto the porch, smiled at the two people obviously trying to avoid being obvious, flipped up his coat collar, and headed out on an errand.

"Come into the parlor. I will fetch the scissors. What about your beard?"

"Shave it off, please."

*****

On the day Bill Johnston's trial started, Ryan and Zak again rested outside, seemingly oblivious to the damp November chill. Ryan's foot tapped repeatedly on the wooden porch, while he thought of Kate far away and fretting for her father. Ann called him odd for preferring a cold bench to a cozy sofa near the hearth. Ryan's summer with the Algonquins changed his habits. Homes, no matter how comfortable, sometimes became a cage. Besides, being outside meant he could be close to Zak, the one friend that never let him down or judged him.

Since Kate's departure, he'd kept busy caulking Bill's fleet of boats and repairing oarlocks. When not working, he read upstate newspapers. Stories of the windmill prisoners—local men and boys—facing possible execution in British prisons dominated the news. The papers listed the known Hunter dead, missing, and captured.

Jim stopped on the porch on his way home from the store. "Whatcha reading?"

"History."

"In newspapers?"

"Most news is history. Not ripe yet. Not well aged like good cheese. But history still. Ye know what's different?"

Jim shrugged.

"Young history has more power to shape the future than old history."

"Ryan. You've always been an odd duck. Today, you take the cake."

"Can ye row with me to Wolfe tomorrow?"

"Where on Wolfe?" said Jim, unwinding his scarf.

"Near the south ferry dock."

"You have business in Kingston?"

Ryan nodded.

"Can I talk you out of it?"

"No."

"Meet me at dawn on the wharf."

Minutes later, Ada stepped outside and slammed the door. She pulled a chair close to Ryan and leaned into his face.

"Jim told me you are going to Kingston."

"Yes."

"You told Kate you'd settle down when your business with the Hunters was over."

"Yes. But that business is not finished."

"Why not?"

"I can't bear that Captain Heustis and Colonel von Schoultz may die."

"What can you do?"

"I want to speak to the lawyer fellow. If I ask Macdonald, I'm sure he'll defend them."

"Why not write him?"

"Writing can be ignored. I need to look him in the eye. I have to see him agree."

"You stay. I will go to him."

"'Tis my duty. I can't send a woman in my place."

Her forehead furrowed. "Men are such infants."

He ruffled at the word infant and frowned at Ada.

"Have you forgotten what I told you concerning Kate?"

"Ada, thoughts of her kept me going. At the worst moments, when cannonballs smashed buildings around me, when I shivered alone at night, when I paddled through the islands, I imagined bending on one knee and asking for her hand."

"What stopped you?"

"The timing's wrong. She's in a bad state. And it wouldn't be proper to ask her with her father in jail."

"You can't keep running off on new crusades if you intend to keep Kate."

"She's not home. If she was, it might be different."

"I'm not sure her presence would make a difference."

"What do ye mean?"

"It is not easy to explain." She paused, searching for words. "I've studied you since you arrived. You seem to latch onto men with strong personalities, men who lead you into trouble against your better judgment."

Sensing the direction of her words, he moved to stand up.

"Sit and listen." Ada pushed him firmly back into the chair. He could not resist her superior weight or moral tone.

"First it was Bill, then it was Captain Heustis, and now it is Colonel von Schoultz. These men are not replacements for your father. They do not deserve such loyalty. Walk away from them. Find your own path."

He stared into the distance. A solitary tear rolled down his cheek. Ada acted on pure instinct to kiss the glistening droplet, and then pulled his head to her chest. He accepted the loving gesture. He rocked in her arms, inhaling the lavender scent rising warmly from the gap between her breasts.

"When you were off fighting, did you think of me, too?" she whispered.

"Often."

*****

Ryan joined Jim at first light, his skiff waiting by the wharf with two sets of oars. Ryan stowed a pack under his seat near the bow while Zak perched in front. The men rowed in silence, which was typical of most river men. Ryan had nothing to say anyway.

Their route followed the American shore west until they came to Cape Vincent. The gap to Wolfe Island was less than a mile: a twenty-minute trip for two men in a fast boat. They rowed to a position near the border in mid-channel. Seeing no British ships, they completed the crossing and beached the boat east of the ferry.

"How are you getting along from here?"

"I'll walk to Marysville. Tis not far. From there, I'll go by ferry to Kingston."

Jim shook his hand. "Take care of yourself."

"I will Jim. I'll see ye soon."

Ryan pushed Jim's boat off and started walking. Typical of a November thaw, the air was damp and a fraction above freezing. Intermittent drizzle dampened his face and neck. The sticky snow clung to his boots.

He pushed Zak off his shoulder and swept his arm skyward. Zak drew too much attention. The raven seemed to understand that Ryan was not angry. He followed his human at a distance.

At the hamlet of Marysville, Ryan waited by the ferry dock, sheltered from the wind behind a wide elm. Across the bay lay Kingston, a jagged wall of limestone buildings. On the far eastern shore, Fort Henry loomed.

A steam ferry tied up at the dock, dropped its ramp, and disgorged a sullen mob of farmers returning from the market. Most trudged home on foot. A half dozen rode horses. They carried unsold goods: sacks of potatoes, crates of cabbages, and cages with damp chickens. One man led a pig on a rope. The pig seemed happier than the man.

When the ferry docked in central Kingston, Ryan headed up Brock Street past the Steamboat Hotel to Wellington Street. Zak circled high overhead. In front of Macdonald's three-storey brick office, Ryan contemplated his welcome. Would the lawyer still accept him as a client or call the British to arrest him? Would he defend von Schoultz and other Hunters? Ryan pushed open the wooden door into a lamp-lit room. A well-dressed young man of Ryan's age peered up from behind a pedestal desk.

"May I help you?" The clerk ran his eyes up and down Ryan's rough woolen clothing.

"I came to see Mr. Macdonald."

"He is busy at present."

Ryan dropped into a large stuffed chair. "I can wait."

The clerk's nose twitched as he caught the musky scent of wet wool. "What is your business with Mr. Macdonald?"

"He's my solicitor and I need his services."

The young man snorted in surprise, but deftly converted it to a convincing sneeze. Reaching for his handkerchief, he continued: "Whom may I say is calling?"

"Ryan Lone Pine."

He responded with another hastily converted sneeze.

"Better see to that cold, sir. Tis a poor season to be ill."

"Yes, by all means. Please wait while I see if he is available."

Shortly, the lanky lawyer emerged smiling from a back room.

"It is so good to see you once more, Ryan. You look thin and worn. How are you?"

He rose to shake the lawyer's outstretched hand. "I'm fine, John."

"What have you been up to these ten months?"

Ryan paused and raised his eyebrows.

"You have some legal issues to discuss, I presume?" said Macdonald.

"Yes."

"Everything you say to me and Oliver Mowat here is private and confidential."

"How would ye feel if I've been involved in matters some may feel are illegal?"

"We are not constables. We are lawyers."

"Well then, I'll answer yer question about the past months. After I nearly froze to death thanks to Bonnycastle, I moved to America and smuggled tea and rum with Bill Johnston. I helped burn the *Sir Robert Peel*. Last week, I fought the British army from a windmill near Prescott. Other than that, I've been quiet."

Mowat, mouth gapping, dropped into the chair Ryan recently vacated and mopped his brow with his ever-present handkerchief. Macdonald puckered his lips and examined his client with clinical interest.

"Did you kill anyone?"

"Nay. I tended the wounded and ran errands."

"So, legally speaking, you are a pirate and a traitor, but not a murderer. At that, they have grounds to hang you twice if such was possible. My best advice to you is to leave for America immediately. I doubt I can do anything for you."

222

"'Tis not for me that I came."

"Oh!" Macdonald clearly did not expect that.

"I want ye to defend some men captured at the windmill."

"Whom?"

"Nils von Schoultz, our leader, my friend Captain Heustis, and others if ye can. I can pay. I have three hundred dollars."

"I spoke to a man today on a similar mission," Macdonald remarked. "He claimed to be the brother-in-law of one Daniel George. Do you know him?"

"Mr. George was our paymaster."

"I asked him to return in the morning once I had opportunity to consider the case."

"Defending those invaders puts Mr. Macdonald's reputation at risk," explained Mowat, "so great is the ill will against them."

"Thank you, Oliver. I am of a mind to accept this challenge."

"Sir?"

"No, Oliver, I appreciate your concern. However, I feel this is the just thing to do. Those men have little hope and no allies."

"Can ye help?"

"I shall go to the fort tomorrow. Keep your money. If any payment is required, we shall discuss that in proper course. In the interim, we require a safe house for you."

"Perhaps, I can suggest a location."

"Please do, Oliver."

"An elderly friend of my father has a cabin up the Cataraqui past the end of Rideau Street. He is frail and needs someone to cut his firewood and put it under cover. I am certain he will exchange food and lodging for labor. He is a man of equanimity and not known to pry into another's affairs."

"Old man Naylor's place! Splendid plan. Ryan, please accompany Oliver. Tomorrow evening after dark, come to my home and I shall tell you all that occurs in court. Does that suit you?"

"Yes. Thank ye."

Mowat, being a young gentleman, hired a cab for the journey in the gloaming light. Bundled under blankets in the open carriage, Ryan drifted to the edge of sleep, lulled by the rhythm of hoof beats on the streets and the muffled thump of Zak's wings beating above.

*****

Naylor was Ryan's height, but boney thin. He had no immediate family, said little, and asked no questions when he accepted Mowat's proposal.

Next morning, with a hearty breakfast of eggs, toast, and smoked ham under his belt, Ryan assessed the woodpile lying near the old man's barn. Naylor's friends had unloaded a generous supply of logs and stumps. Raw wood was a common commodity in the new colony, but the labor to cut it for the fireplace was harder to come by.

He rolled a log from the pile with a cant hook and cut it into eighteen-inch stumps with a crosscut saw. He split each stump with an axe, or with wedges and a sledge when the wood was too large or too knotty for the axe. Lastly, he stacked the split firewood in the summer kitchen at the house's rear. He processed each log—cut, split, carry, pile—before moving on to the next.

He stripped to a light undershirt and let the energy of labor warm him in the frosty air. He hummed songs to the beat of the saw's raspy rhythm. He smiled at the way the blocks of wood exploded into sections when the splitting axe hit perfectly.

Zak perched on the barn roof and cawed encouragement.

The old man fed his woodcutter a hearty midday meal of rabbit stew, heavy with carrots and potatoes, washed down with large mugs of tea. Outside, Ryan fed Zak bits of stewed rabbit, potato, and bread crusts he'd saved.

With a file, he sharpened the crosscut saw's teeth and attacked the woodpile again, sawing and splitting until dusk. After washing, changing into his other set of clothes, and eating a generous meal, he excused himself and hiked to the two-storey stone house Macdonald shared with his family. He slipped through the side garden and knocked at the rear door. Macdonald answered.

"Come in Ryan. This is a splendid evening to converse. Everyone is out tonight."

Ryan removed his boots and hung his coat on a peg.

"Come into the parlor. Whiskey?"

"Thank ye, no.'

"Really! Didn't a métier of smuggling, piracy, and war give you a thirst for spirits?"

"Not yet, John."

"I have some sweet cider."

"Twill do nicely."

Macdonald returned with a glass of chilled cider for his guest. He nestled into a plush chair, crossed one long leg over the other, gulped a third of a large whiskey, and lost himself in the ceiling for several minutes. He drank another third of his whiskey and began talking.

"I met with Daniel George and agreed to accept his case. His trial was scheduled for tomorrow, but I convinced the solicitor general to postpone it until the twenty-eighth so that I can prepare. I also agreed to assist two other men on the docket, Nils von Schoultz and Dorephus Abbey on the twenty-ninth and thirtieth, respectively."

"And Captain Heustis?"

"He is not scheduled yet. That can wait."

"Can ye help those men?"

Macdonald shrugged. "They are charged under the *Lawless Aggressions Act* and face a British court martial. The act is an absolute abomination. It mocks the great tradition of British justice because it allows flimsy evidence from the prosecution and few avenues of defense for the accused. This law seems written for no other purpose than to wreak revenge on aliens that terrorize British subjects. It applies to attacks by citizens of a country with which we are at peace and it applies, albeit somewhat differently, to British subjects who aid them. The distinction between subject and non-subject is moot, as punishment in both cases is death by hanging."

Macdonald finished his whiskey and rose to pour another. "The rules restrict my role in the proceedings to the background. I cannot speak in court. I can only coach my clients on how to ask questions and present evidence. They are all bright men, but the facts and the law that apply to them make success improbable."

"What can ye do?"

"I may be of some aid to Messieurs George and Abbey, but not to von Schoultz, I am afraid."

"Why?"

"He has decided, as a matter of honor, to plead guilty. He assumes full responsibility for the invasion and does not intend to deny it. Such a plea means the gallows."

"Can I do something?"

"No! Your best recourse is to return to Clayton. You are at risk in Kingston. I shall write when I have news."

"Can I attend the court martial?"

"Are you mad? The trial is at the fort. You may be recognized. Besides, all public seating is already assigned."

"Can ye get me in as one of yer clerks?"

"Absolutely not. I could be disbarred. Do not arrogate the role of savior. Go home!"

"I'll not leave until the old man's wood is cut."

Macdonald eyed his client, weighing the veracity and intent of his last statement. "How much longer do you calculate that wood pile shall keep you busy?"

"A week. Maybe two."

"Why are you taking such risks for a condemned man?"

"'Tis hard to say, John. The colonel believed in the cause he fought for. 'Tis why I joined him. He meant well and risked his life for others. Just because he picked the wrong battle, doesn't make him any less great a man. If he'd battled the Mexicans in Texas instead of the British in Canada, he'd be a hero."

"In war, the winner dictates the rules." Macdonald finished his whiskey. "If you insist on staying, do not leave Naylor's unless I send for you. Oliver shall deliver any messages."

Ryan rose to go but Macdonald stopped him. "Stay a bit longer. You have neglected to tell me about your time with the Algonquins. I am curious and would be grateful, if it is not a painful story."

"'Tis a happy story." Between sips of cider tea, Ryan told Macdonald about his first summer in Canada.

Macdonald listened quietly and slid into whiskey-induced slumber as Ryan neared the end of his tale. He slipped out of the house without stirring his host.

Back at Naylor's cabin, Ryan took a chair by the hearth. Belatedly, he noticed the wooden rack holding his freshly washed work clothes, already dry. He smiled a thank you to his host. The old man smiled in return and passed him a mug of tea.

*****

The next day, Ryan started cutting wood before the lazy sun rose. To use the limited November daylight to its fullest, he worked all day, except for a brief lunch break. With woodcutting, the body does the work. Thoughts can wander freely. The months since he first arrived in Canada played through his head. He recalled his best moments hunting with Nick, watching Zak grow from a clumsy chick to a graceful lord of the sky, rowing with Bill, walking with Kate, and flirting with Ada.

At night, he read by the hearth fire from Naylor's collection of books. One, *The Pickwick Papers* by a new author named Charles Dickens, caught his fancy.

A knock on the door on November 29 interrupted his reading. Naylor answered the door and waved Mowat towards a seat by the fire. He accepted a mug of tea from his silent host. After exchanging pleasantries regarding the weather, Mowat said, "I have a cab waiting; so, I must be brief."

"Have ye news of the trial?"

"I was there. Sixteen officers sat at the head table in dress uniforms. Guards lined the back wall. The Hunter flag taken from the windmill and a pile of weapons lay on display.

"Mr. George's trial consumed all of yesterday and this morning. Solicitor General Draper—he is the judge advocate—spent much effort presenting his evidence. Being the first case, he was thorough in covering the three key points under the act."

"And they are?"

"To convict an alien, the Crown must prove he is a citizen of a peaceful foreign country, he conspired with British subjects to bear arms against the Queen, and actively participated in the hostilities."

"How did Mr. George do?"

"He followed Mr. Macdonald's instructions perfectly. He endeavored to show he did not participate in the hostilities. He insisted he was merely crossing from the United States in a rowboat when arrested. Do you know a fellow named Chipman?"

"Not well. He was with us at the windmill. Why?"

"He has turned Queen's evidence. So did two French-Canadian refugees captured at the battle. Chipman identified Mr. George as an active combatant. The court martial adjourned his case until December first. Therefore, we have to wait for the verdict.

"They tried Colonel von Schoultz next. As expected, the colonel pleaded guilty. He remained dignified, stoic, and courageous. He accepted full responsibility. He told the court other men induced him to take command under false impressions, and he now admits he was deluded. He agrees with the facts in the case and said it is no use to say anything in his own defense, and that he would persist in his plea. Draper warned him that a guilty plea meant the death penalty."

"No defense at all?"

"On one point, yes. Draper accused his men of mutilating the body of a British officer. The colonel denied it vehemently. He claimed it was hogs. I am not certain the court believed him."

"What now?"

"Sentencing is tomorrow and Mr. Abbey's trial begins."

"'Tis not sounding good."

"No, I am afraid not."

Naylor wordlessly collected the law clerk's empty tea mug. Mowat gazed at the old man expectantly as Naylor set the mug upside down on a saucer and rotated it three times clockwise. He peered at the pattern of tealeaf fragments in the mug.

"What do you see, Mr. Naylor?"

"Same as always, young Mr. Mowat: a long life, a happy family, and professional success."

"No specifics?"

"No. The leaves give trends, not details."

Ryan was impressed, not so much with the tealeaf reading, but at hearing the usually silent old man converse.

*****

Ryan lost himself for days in the comfortable routine of cutting wood. The effort made sense and the end product had value. It broke no laws and hurt no one.

On the evening of December 2, Macdonald visited the isolated cabin. Naylor knew him well. "Something to drink, Mr. Macdonald?"

"The usual please," he replied, sitting near the hearth. "I came in person, Ryan, because the news is bad." He silently accepted a mug of tea from Naylor.

"I wasn't expecting much."

"Colonels George, Abbey, and von Schoultz were all, sadly, condemned to die by hanging. George and Abbey presented their cases well, but the Crown had several Hunters testifying against their fellows. That was their undoing, I am certain."

"Why did they snitch on our men?"

"I assume Draper has offered clemency for testimony."

Ryan paused, chewing his lower lip. "When are the executions?"

"The colonel's is on December eighth."

"What about t'others?"

"The Abbey and George executions shall be four days after. In the meantime, the trials continue. Draper plans to try the remaining prisoners in large groups to speed things up."

"Any word on Captain Heustis?"

"His name is not on the docket yet." Macdonald locked his eyes on Ryan. "It is time for you to go home."

"Where will the hanging happen?"

"For the colonel, they plan to build a special gallows at the fort outside the walls. It is the only concession to his rank. The others shall be hanged in the town jail." The lawyer paused. "He is an extraordinary man, your colonel. British officers lavished encomiums regarding his sense of honor. He not only accepted full responsibility, he is leaving money in his will for families of British soldiers killed at the battle."

"That doesn't surprise me. Where's he being held?"

"All the condemned men are kept in the jail. He'll be escorted from there on that morning to Fort Henry."

"I'll go home then. He'll have nary a friend in town. I must be there for him."

"You are mad!"

"No. I expect the crowd'll be large. I can blend in. None'll see me."

"Done with that, Mr. Macdonald?"

Macdonald handed the mug to Naylor. Repeating the ritual of turning the mug upside down on a saucer and rotating it three times clockwise, he peered into the mug.

"Any change?"

"No, Mr. Macdonald. It's the same: long life and fame, professional ups and downs, and a difficult personal life."

"Is the future set in stone?"

"No sir. However for some men, the path is deeply engraved."

Three days later, Ryan finished cutting and stacking Naylor's wood. The following day, he patched Naylor's roof. With a mallet and froe, he split a pile of shingles from round stumps of cedar. Methodically, he tore out patches of rotten or damaged shingles and fit in new ones. The next day, he applied his carpentry skills to the cabin, making doors and windows fit more snuggly. Old Naylor's home would not only be warm that winter, it would stay dry and draft-free for years.

The last evening with Naylor, Ryan couldn't focus on reading. Instead, he sipped tea and stared into the fire. Plans for the day ahead swirled in his mind. He wanted to silently salute the colonel in Kingston when his final journey began, and then take the ferry to

Wolfe Island and on to Clayton and Kate. By bidding farewell to von Schoultz, he would also end his support for the Hunters cause and finally be ready to commit to a life with Kate.

Ryan retired. Naylor added wood to the hearth fire, and tidied up the cabin. Taking Ryan's empty tea mug, he turned it upside down on a saucer and rotated it three times clockwise. Holding it with both hands, he squinted at the dregs. He wiped away a tear and went to bed.

*****

After two weeks with Naylor, the day came for Ryan to say goodbye. With his bag packed by the door, he thanked the old man for his hospitality. To his surprise, his host hugged him with his scrawny old arms. Leaning back, he held Ryan by the shoulders and whispered, "Be brave. You have a good heart. You will prevail."

"Take care of yerself too, sir. Stay warm."

Naylor smiled.

With Zak flying overhead at a discreet distance, Ryan followed the cold Cataraqui River towards town. The morning of December 8, 1838, was below freezing, with misty clouds and a light wind. Ice clung to the stalks of cattails that edged the river, but the main channel remained open. Leaving the shore, he ambled up Rideau Street, past Macdonald's stone house, and made his way to central Kingston.

Along Wellington Street, at least fifty people had already staked out spots along the road, shuffling their feet for warmth, and waiting. From every direction, the curious assembled. People spoke in funereal whispers. Dozens of men wore white strips of cloth tied to arms or hatbands, marking them as militia. Ryan assumed they came to deliver a message to Colonel von Schoultz.

He found a spot at the market square across from the jail, and pulled his wide-brimmed hat over his red hair. Zak waited on a roof across the road.

At eight that morning, six redcoats marched from the grim jail and opened a path in the onlookers, by then numbering in the hundreds. A dark, four-wheeled wagon emerged from the jail courtyard pulled by a pair of black horses. A dark-suited man held the reins. A burly man dressed in a kilt rode beside the driver. Both man ignored their cargo standing behind them. Wrists bound in front, von Schoultz wore a clean uniform and a ceremonial military hat. Two dark-frocked priests steadied him against wagon jolts.

Von Schoultz locked eyes with each passing spectator closest to the road. Most looked away. When the wagon reached him, Ryan raised his right hand and brushed the top of his ear with his index finger. Von Schoultz caught the Hunter sign and recognized him. The colonel placed his bound left hand over his right with the fingers aligned, and bowed his head so slightly no one else noticed. Ryan squeezed his eyes shut to force back tears.

The wagon rolled along Wellington past the market towards Macdonald's office. When the bystanders closed in and marched behind, Ryan moved with them. He intended to follow for two blocks and turn down a side street to the ferry dock.

*****

Zak leapt from his perch and followed unseen by the people below —except for one. A stout militiaman, one with a hate on for a particular raven, grasped the significance of the black bird drifting high over Wellington Street.

Rounding up two soldiers he knew, Tiny edged into the strolling throng behind the wagon, searching. He had to be gentle and patient. The silent entourage included influential families, people who would not stand for rough treatment.

A hundred feet above, Zak recognized the big man closing in on his human and began a steep, deliberate descent.

Hearing the familiar song of wind in wings, Ryan swiveled his head in Zak's direction, exposing his face. Before he could react, the two redcoats tackled him to the stone road. His forehead scraped the rough cobbles. Onlookers hooted and moved aside.

Tiny grabbed the private's bayoneted musket. People gasped, half in terror and half in blood lust, expecting to see a prisoner shot or impaled on the spot. Tiny surprised everyone by turning around and firing at a fast moving black bird streaking towards him. The shot missed and shattered a window down the street.

"Zrok!"

Tiny ducked as the Zak swooped at his head. Several onlookers staggered back at the whoosh of air. Zak climbed high on the momentum of his dive without flapping, banked, and descended once more. Tiny held the bayonet high in front, his eyes fixed on the approaching bird.

Zak pressed his attack. Observers gaped awestruck. No one had witnessed such an odd struggle. The new colony had a legion of tales about men fighting cougars, bears, and wolves, but not a determined raven. Zak closed in. Tiny deftly swung the bayonet in a narrow arch and nicked a wing.

"Zrok!" The raven veered off and climbed to roof level. A single, black flight feather drifted to the sidewalk.

"Zak," Ryan yelled. "Danger! Go!" A punch in the mouth—delivered by Tiny—stopped further warnings.

"Zaak!" The bird sailed above the roofs and disappeared.

The redcoats hauled Ryan to his feet. Blood from a split lip dripped on his coat.

"Let's take him to the fort," said Andrew, the corporal. "I wager he is not going home this time."

With a British soldier on each side of Ryan and Tiny behind, they tailed the hanging party towards the fort.

Macdonald and Mowat stepped from the office as the crowd passed. Macdonald picked up Zak's feather and watched the throng dwindle down the street. "This exigency requires I visit the fort again tomorrow, Oliver."

"Yes, Mr. Macdonald."

Trial's Pawn

The death wagon rolled through the streets of central Kingston to the waterfront and across the causeway and bridge to Fort Henry. On the high plain before the fort, a new gallows silhouetted against the sky. Ryan's guards ordered a halt.

Ryan never intended to watch von Schoultz die. He turned away. Tiny jabbed the bayonet into his rear just enough to pass through the woolen pants and pierce the skin. Ryan jerked forward but made no sound.

"Watch the show or I'll ream yar arsehole."

The driver stopped the wagon beside the gallows. A hooded hangman guided von Schoultz off the wagon and up the steep steps to the platform, followed by the priests. The colonel knelt and said a short prayer.

While the kilted man read the warrant for the colonel's execution to the crowd, the executioner removed von Schoultz's hat, slipped the noose over his head, and placed a cap over his eyes. Von Schoultz adjusted the noose with his bound hands. The priests gave their final blessing and climbed off the wagon. Von Schoultz stood with dignity —calm and ready for his ineluctable death.

For ten seconds, the scene froze. The air lay still under an opaque white sky. No one spoke or moved. The horses' tails hung limp. Then, at a word from the burly man in the kilt, the hangman pulled the bolt on the trapdoor. Von Schoultz fell, convulsed three times as he dangled, trembled and was still. The crowd stayed hushed. Ryan saw a few people look away, their faces twisted by internal emotions.

"That's what awaits all ya Hunter scum."

"Eternal damnation awaits ye, ye fat bastard."

Tiny drove the musket butt into Ryan's kidney. He dropped to his knees gasping.

"Easy there, Tiny," said the corporal. "It's a lot easier for us if he can walk."

"Sure, Andrew—I mean, corporal."

With the private half carrying Ryan, the corporal barking insults, and Tiny prodding his posterior with a bayonet, Ryan half walked, half stumbled his way along the fort's western side, through Fort Henry's gate, and onto the advanced battery's familiar cobbled ground. His captors marched Ryan down the ramp, through the dry ditch surrounding the main fort, across the equipoise bridge, through the inner gate, and onto the lower parade square.

Once again, Ryan admired the portico's seventeen stone arches and its symmetric perfection. He'd prefer to be a tourist or a visitor instead of a captive, but one couldn't be immured in a nicer prison in Upper Canada.

"It could be worse."

"What did ya say, scum?"

"I said yer mother cursed the day ye were—"

Tiny jammed the musket butt into Ryan's back, knocking him to the stone ground onto his face. The corporal threw an exasperated look at Tiny.

"What is this?"

Ryan, semiconscious on the ground, heard that question in the clipped tones of an English officer.

Ryan's three captors went silent. A scowling Lieutenant-Colonel Bonnycastle strode over and confronted the quivering corporal. "Did you hear my question, corporal?"

"Yes, sir."

"Then, explain why this bound man was beaten to the ground."

"I had nothing to do with it, colonel."

"Are you not the highest ranking non-commissioned officer in your detail?"

"Yes, colonel."

"Then, you are responsible. Help him to his feet."

With a nod from the corporal, the private and Tiny pulled Ryan to his feet. Bonnycastle reached out his wooden swagger stick and raised Ryan's chin with its tip. Bonnycastle looked him over, noting the split lip, the face lacerations, and the bleeding wound on his buttocks.

"I see you are back with us, Lone Pine."

Ryan grunted in response.

"Why is this man in custody, corporal?"

"He was a combatant at the Prescott windmill, colonel."

"Really! Where was he arrested?"

"In Kingston, colonel."

"Then, how do you know he is one of the invaders?"

"He told me, colonel," he said, pointing to Tiny.

Bonnycastle stepped in front of Tiny. "Were you at the battle?"

"Yes, colonel."

"Can you place him there if I call you to court martial?"

"Yes, colonel."

"Are you also responsible for this man's injuries?"

"Yes, colonel. That's how our regiment treats invaders."

"Who is your commanding officer?"

"Colonel Fraser, sir."

"That explains a great deal. The militia must be desperate for recruits to arm ruffians like you." Bonnycastle scowled. "Remove yourself from this fort immediately. I intend to report you to your commanding officer, though I expect it will be a waste of effort. If you come here again without permission, I'll have you arrested."

"Yes, colonel."

Bonnycastle focused his anger on the corporal. "You are aware, I am certain, of our regulations regarding the treatment of prisoners?"

"Yes, colonel."

"Explain all his wounds? Did he resist? And before you reply in the positive, be aware that I will ask for a full report and witnesses."

"He did not resist, colonel. He received one facial wound when we arrested and bound him. The others were inflicted by Tiny."

"Under your watch!"

"Yes."

Bonnycastle glared at the corporal.

"I mean, yes, colonel."

"I apologize for the rough handling," Bonnycastle said to Ryan. "This is not the way we normally treat prisoners."

Ryan's head throbbed painfully, but his tongue still worked well enough. "Pardon my confusion. The last time, ye almost killed me by cold and now yer sorry for a few scratches."

"What is this about the cold?"

Andrew inhaled sharply.

"I was dropped off outside the fort with no money or gear, and nearly froze walking home." He held up his left hand. "It cost me half a finger."

Bonnycastle breathed deeply as one who is trying to remain calm. When he spoke, the words came out sharp-edged and enunciated. "My orders were to return you by sleigh to the trading post. I apologize for your discomfort." He glared at Andrew.

"Sergeant!" Bonnycastle called to a stout soldier nearby.

"Yes, Colonel Bonnycastle?"

"Arrange shot drill for the corporal. When he's done, demote him to lance corporal."

"Aye, colonel."

Turning to the private, Bonnycastle added, "Take the prisoner to the infirmary. Stay with him. I'll arrange for someone to relieve you soon."

"Yes, colonel," the private responded, snapping to attention. He led Ryan away.

Crossing the parade square, Ryan asked the young soldier, "What's shot drill?"

"See those piles of cannonballs on the ramparts?"

Ryan looked up at the pyramidal stacks of large, black iron balls. "Yes."

"In shot drill, you carry each ball with your arms stretched out in front. You go down the stairs, across the square, up the other stairs, and place it on the ramparts. Once you move the whole pile, you then move it back. If you drop a ball, you do the whole drill again."

"Sounds grueling."

"Each ball weighs twenty-four pounds."

"Suddenly, I don't feel so bad."

*****

Ryan gently pulled on his boots in the fort hospital. The military doctor had cleaned his cuts and scraps, pronounced him not seriously wounded, and released him. The jittery private would not leave.

"The prisoner is released," the doctor barked. "What are you waiting for?"

"Sorry, captain. Colonel Bonnycastle told me to wait until relieved. I have to wait, sir."

Before the captain could yell again at the twitching private, the door burst open and slammed the wall. A muscular man of Ryan's height and far heavier entered the room as if he owned it. Good-looking, gray-haired, with thick white sideburns and ruddy complexion, he was the same burly man in a kilt that rode in the death wagon that morning. He looked over the three occupants and stepped over to Ryan. "Yah be my new prisoner?"

"That is him, sir," said the private.

"Did I ask yah to speak, yah little catch-fart?"

The rough, vulgar language—a familiar slang from poor urban neighborhoods back home—surprised Ryan. He felt sorry for the young, cringing private. "I'm the man ye want, sir."

"I hear the tongue of an Irish clod hopper."

"Tis a compliment coming from a Highland dimber damber."

Both the private and the doctor-captain gasped.

The big man glared at Ryan from inches away. "Do yah know who I am?"

"Some Scottish upright man come to make my life miserable?"

"Well, Carrot," he said glancing at Ryan's hair, "yah got the last part right. I'm Colonel Allan Macdonell, sheriff of the Midland District, and yar jailor and maybe yar executioner. From this moment on, yah will not eat, sleep, piss, or shit unless I give yah permission."

"Ye sound like our landlord speaking back in Ireland."

Macdonell's faced darkened. "Shut yar potato trap, Paddy, and spare me yar whining pillaloo. The land clearances drove plenty of good Scots to these shores. I've no interest yar petty Irish troubles, yah little bog-lander."

Ryan knew from the dark tone he had gone too far. "Yes, sheriff."

"Come with me. Yar not bound. If yah run, notice the brace of barking irons on my belt."

"I'll not run, sir. I'm no dunghill. I'll face my fate."

Ryan followed Macdonell across the parade square and into one of the barrack rooms converted into prisoner quarters. Stepping into the dimly lit cavernous casement, Ryan winced at the fetid mixture of body odor, wood smoke, and outhouse stink. When his eyes adjusted to the gloom, he recognized unshaven old friends.

"Heustis!"

"Yes, colonel."

"I have a new man for yah. Before yah start complaining about overcrowding, stuff it." Turning to Ryan, he added, "Each casement has a captain. Heustis is yars, scab. Follow his orders like they were mine. Got that?"

"Tis my favorite order from ye so far, sir."

Macdonell scowled and left. Hunter Vaughan, Lyman Leach, Orrin Smith, Garret Hicks, William Gates, and others Ryan knew well stepped forward.

"Ryan," Heustis began, "we thought you escaped. What happened?"

"I made it back to Clayton, but had to see Colonel von Schoultz off on his final journey. Someone recognized me."

"That was foolish, however noble," Heustis responded.

"Are we not all here for being noble and foolish," asked Vaughan.

"I'm here for the food," Hicks quipped. Everyone laughed.

Ryan looked over the room. It was twenty by forty feet with a low ceiling. Straw-filled mattresses covered most of the floor. Wooden stools provided the only seats. A crude wood stove squatted at the rear with a stovepipe leading through the wall. Beside the stove rested a large wooden bucket that served as a group chamber pot. Two barred and glassless windows faced the parade square.

"Where are t'others, captain?"

"All our men are kept in five such casements as this, with about thirty-five men in each. We have only nineteen beds, so we sleep two to a bed or in shifts. We are confined except for one hour of exercise outside or for work parties."

Ryan scrunched his nose. "Tis why it smells like a barn?"

"Yes. We must use that foul vessel at the rear except for our exercise period when we can use the latrine. Many men hold themselves until then."

"So, yer still my captain."

"I am afraid so." Heustis smiled weakly. "Each casement's captain speaks for his group. Macdonell gives his orders to the captains and we relay the men's needs to him. If you have a problem or request, ask me."

"That Macdonell is a hard case."

"He is loud and crude, but fair. Keep your sharp tongue to yourself, if you can."

Ryan noticed Dorephus Abbey sitting alone by himself writing a letter by candlelight. "Is Dorephus not well?"

"That is putting it mildly," Heustis responded in a low voice. "The bloody British have condemned him to hang in four days. He is writing letters to his three children. Poor things will soon be orphans."

"Do the bloody Brits plan to hang us all?"

"We do not know, Ryan. Most have not gone to court martial yet. God willing, the British will show some mercy."

The thick wooden doors opened. Macdonell entered with two armed guards. The big Scot walked softly to where Abbey sat, squatted and looked the condemned man in the eye.

"It's time to go down to the Kingston jail, Dorie," he began softly. "Take a few minutes to say good-bye to yar companions. I'll wait outside. Knock twice when yar ready."

Macdonell and his guards left, closing the door quietly. Abbey struggled stiff-jointed to his feet, folded his letters, and slipped them in a pocket. He circled through the casement and shook hands solemnly with every man, stopping last by Heustis. Abbey grasped Daniel's outstretched hand using the Hunter's handshake.

"Farewell. May God be merciful my friend." With that, Abbey pounded twice on the door, which opened with a push from outside. Abbey walked out, head high. Heustis pushed the door shut. The outside bolt clunked into place.

"There is a melting power in the word 'farewell,' when spoken for the last time," Heustis said to the quiet room. "It opens the fountains of the heart and sends tears of sorrow trickling down the hardy cheeks of all who hear it."

Damp-eyed, Ryan sighed at the grim truth of that statement. The words also revealed a side to Heustis he'd not seen before. In his stolid captain's breast beat the heart of a poet.

Ryan peered through the window. Outside, one guard bound Abbey's hands. Beside him, also bound, stood Daniel George, pale and shivering. Ryan shuddered—he could be next.

*****

At noon, Ryan had his first prisoner's meal and grasped the meaning of Hicks' earlier sarcasm. They ate over-boiled beef and potatoes from a common pot. Their meager and barely edible bread ration seemed to contain wood ashes or other grit.

After lunch, Macdonell again burst in. "Alright yah brigands. Outside now. Get some air. Heustis! Show Carrot how to clean the latrines. And have him empty and clean yar piss tub," he called back over his shoulder.

"I see you have made a good impression," Heustis said.

"Stink is not to fear. Neither is dirty work."

"Garret! Fetch us a bucket of hot water from the kitchen, some soap, and a scrub brush."

"Yes, captain."

Ryan heaved up the heavy tub, making sure none of its foul contents sloshed over. He followed Heustis gingerly across the parade square. The enlisted men's privy was a narrow, stone room with an open trench without seats. Men leaned or squatted over the pit to do their business.

Ryan carried his noisome burden into the privy. Its two occupants hurried out. Heustis waited outside. Ryan poured the foul slop into the four-foot-deep trench. The stench from the churning liquid excrement filled the air. Despite his best efforts, Ryan gagged. Back home, he'd shoveled out animal pens and buried dead livestock crawling with maggots, but nothing smelled this loathsome.

Hicks arrived with the water, soap, and brushes. Under Heustis' direction, Ryan scrubbed down the stone trench's sill and the entire floor, and rinsed the piss tub. Heustis showed him how to open the latrine's hidden sluice gate. A great gush of rainwater, collected in a cistern, flushed out the trench and washed the mess into channels that flowed into the bay.

Next, Heustis guided Ryan to the officers' privy. There, a wooden platform with proper latrine seats covered the trench. Ryan scrubbed down the wooden parts and the stone floor. Once finished, Heustis led Ryan back to the casement. His clothes stank and his reddened hands stung from the harsh lye-based soap.

Macdonell waited near their casement door. "How was yar exercise break, Carrot?"

"Grand, sheriff. It made hanging seem merciful."

The big Scot burst out laughing. "Aye, Carrot. You've a fine wit for a bog-lander." He strode away, still chuckling.

"It is the first occasion I have observed him laugh."

"Tis that a good thing?"

*****

Supper fare was a repeat of lunch. Lamps-out came shortly after dusk.

Ryan lay awake in the dark, sharing a thin straw bed with another man. For months, he'd slept in quiet cabins or campsites in the pines, not a room full of stinking, snoring and farting men. Though tired, he could not sleep until he let his imagination wander. He visualized hunting in forests with Nick, and rowing through islands with Kate. Soon, he recalled the cave at Fort Wallace with his snoring comrades of summer. He slept finally, but morning came early.

Several thick slices of the gritty bread and a cup of weak tea with a hint of sugar served as breakfast.

Hicks said the food never changed. "We complained about the food," he said, "but Macdonell says we have the same rations the enlisted men eat. We asked the cook, and it's true."

"Still something is wrong with this bread, I'm sure," Heustis added.

Midmorning, Macdonell made his standard stormy entrance into the casement. "Carrot! Yar lawyer's here. Follow me."

With Ryan in the middle and a guard behind, Macdonell led him past four identical looking ground-level casements, up a set of wide wooden stairs to the covered portico above, and into a six-by-ten room.

"These are my quarters when I stay at the fort. Yar lawyer is inside. When yar done, clean the latrines and dump yar piss pot. The guard will keep an eye on yah."

Inside, Macdonald paced between the bed and the wall in the narrow room. He stopped when Ryan entered. "You look rough, but better than I expected. I was certain that big thug intended to kill you."

"I'm well, sir. Just a few scrapes."

Ryan eased his sore rear onto the room's only chair. Macdonald parked his long frame on the bed.

"I brought you this." Macdonald pulled a long black feather from his leather bag. "Have you seen your bird?"

"No, but I'm sure he's well." Ryan took the feather. "I thank ye for this."

"Let us discuss your case. I'll help you represent yourself."

"Yes, please."

"Here is what you must remember. The Crown needs to determine your citizenship. That does not matter in the end, so do not think much of it. The Crown needs to prove you conspired with British subjects bearing arms against the Queen. Since several British subjects were at the windmill, including several informants, the Crown cannot fail there if you can be identified. Lastly, the Crown needs to prove you actively participated in the hostilities. If you can win that argument, you can save your neck."

"That is what I figured after talking with Mr. Mowat, but I appreciate yer confirmation."

"Is there anything else I can do for you?"

"Yes. Please write to the Johnston family in Clayton, New York, and tell them where I am."

"I cannot write to Bill Johnston. That is tantamount to treason in this town."

"Well then, address the letter to Ada Burleigh. The Clayton postmaster will know to take it to the Johnstons. Tell them I'll write when Macdonell allows it."

"When you do write, send your letters to her and not the Johnstons. Trust me on that."

"I'll follow that advice. Thanks ye."

"Anything else?"

"Yes." Ryan pulled money from a pocket. "Buy a bottle of good whiskey and send it to Sheriff Macdonell with best wishes from Carrot, and buy one for yerself. Send a big packet of tea to old man Naylor."

"I will."

"Do I owe ye a fee?"

"No. Save your money. It will buy you better food, some writing materials, and maybe a few favors."

"Is there a date for my trial?"

"Yes. You, Heustis, and eleven others face court martial in just over a week, December 17."

"All of us in one day?"

"Yes. Draper wants all trials completed by month end."

"Do they plan to hang us in groups too?"

Macdonald stared at the air above Ryan.

Ryan changed the subject. "Will you defend Heustis, too?"

"No. He and two comrades hired their own lawyer. Is there anything else I can do for you?"

"Not now. Thank ye."

"I will stop by when I can."

*****

Ryan lurched from the officers' latrine, smelly and sore again, and collided with John Counter, his former shipyard employer.

"Sorry, Mr. Counter! Surprised I am to see ye."

"You should not be. I own a bakery and supply this fort." He paused and eyed Ryan. "I have to say, I am not surprised to see you a prisoner. I assume your temper landed you in trouble."

Ryan saw no reason to be polite. "I hope ye are a better shipbuilder than ye are a baker. That bread of yers deserves to be at the lake bottom."

"Such cheek. The bread is better than your kind deserves."

As Ryan returned to the casement under Macdonell's watchful gaze, Zak drifted over the ramparts and dropped onto his shoulder.

"Zaak!"

"Zakkie boy! Good to see ye, friend."

Macdonell came over. "What the bloody hell is that?"

"He's my companion, sheriff. I raised him from a chick."

Macdonell stepped close and looked Zak in the eye. Zak looked back. Macdonell tilted his head. Zak tilted his head. Macdonell raised his chin. Zak raised his beak.

A group of enlisted men gathered to watch, keeping a respectful distance—Macdonell's temper was famous. Macdonell slowly raised his right arm and pushed his wrist lightly on the raven's chest. Zak stepped from Ryan shoulder to Macdonell's arm. He brought Zak close to his face and made a series of faint whistling phrases.

"Zrik! Zrok! Crik!" Zak responded.

Macdonell caught Ryan's baffled look. "Surprised yah didn't I, Carrot."

"Yes, sheriff. He's nary done that before."

"Years ago, I raised a jay chick. They are smart and talkative too. What's yar bird's name?"

"Zak."

"Does Zak do any tricks?"

"He plays games, sheriff. If you throw up a bit of bread, he'll catch it."

"Yah think we have bread to spare?"

"Kach! Kood!"

Macdonell looked at the raven with growing respect.

"There's a fair bit uneaten in our casement, sheriff."

"Go fetch some."

Ryan fetched a slice of the gritty bread from the casement and broke off a piece. "Zak! Catch!"

Zak launched from Macdonell's arm, caught the bread as it began to fall, and returned to the sheriff's arm. The raven bit into the crust, and to everyone's amusement, spat it out.

"Zaak!"

"I told you that bread was foul, colonel," Heustis began.

"Carrot. Give me that last piece." Macdonell nibbled the grayish food and followed Zak's lead. "Pah! That's coarser than a crofter's arse. Is Counter here?"

"In the cookhouse, colonel," Heustis replied.

Macdonell passed Zak to Ryan and strode off, arms swinging and barged into the cookhouse. The entire fort heard his raging billingsgate, complete with the most vulgar expletives.

"Counter is a devout Methodist," Heustis whispered to Ryan. "He must think the devil has descended on him."

"Serves him right."

The day ended well. For supper, they had fresh, wholesome bread for once. Macdonell made Zak a fort mascot and appointed himself the bird's guardian, promising to supply slices of bread or bits of bully beef for the daily catch-food game.

The next afternoon, a package sent by Macdonald arrived for Macdonell. The peace offering worked—he relieved Ryan of latrine duty. William Gates, ever querulous, seemed to delight in annoying the sheriff. He became the new piss tub custodian.

Two days later, Macdonell entered their casement at the midday meal. His entrance was uncharacteristically quiet. He told them Dorephus Abbey and Daniel George had hanged at the Kingston jail at sunrise. He departed to visit the other casements.

"He seems saddened by the news," Ryan stated.

"As sheriff, Macdonell must arrange and witness every execution. I doubt the task rests lightly on his shoulders," Heustis explained.

*****

In Ryan's casement, men prepared for their trials and wrote statements to read in court. Hunter Vaughan sulked as Heustis and Orrin Smith rehearsed the stories they constructed at their lawyer's advice.

"That foolish story won't save you."

Everyone in the casement looked at Hunter in surprise.

"It doesn't matter what you say. They'll find you guilty and condemn you to die anyway, like they did with us. I claimed I was a reluctant recruit like you plan to do."

"Easy there Vaughan," Heustis said.

"You know what they asked us?" The pitch of his voice rose. "They asked us, 'if you were so reluctant, what prevented you from laying down your weapons and surrendering before the fighting began.' I had no answer. Do any of you?"

Vaughan rolled over on his mattress and hid his face.

*****

Monday, December 17, Ryan, Heustis, Smith, Hicks, and nine others, marched into the court martial chamber led by Macdonell. Flanked by two British flags, fourteen regular and militia officers in gold braid-encrusted dress uniforms—red for the infantry and blue for the artillery—frowned while the prisoners filed in. A row of armed sentries in red or blue stood at attention along a wall behind the officers' table. The invited observers and witnesses occupied the room's opposite side. At the rear, Ryan saw Macdonald standing a half head above most others. Levi Chipman, the former Hunter who had become the principal witness against them, fidgeted at a small table near the officers.

A dour, heavy-set man in a colonel's uniform stood up. His long side burns covered his neck, leaving only his chin and mouth area shaven. The room went quiet as he cleared his throat.

"This court martial is now in session. I am Colonel William Draper, Solicitor General of Upper Canada, and Judge Advocate. I am both prosecutor and chief law adviser to this court martial. I am not the judge. These officers are your judges. I am in charge of these proceedings and am tasked with adhering to the relevant British laws." He scanned the defendants to let his words sink in.

"While the *Lawless Aggressions Act*, under which you are charged, does not grant you the right to speak, I have decided, in the name of justice, to allow each prisoner to cross-examine prosecution witnesses and address the court martial directly.

"There is no appeal to a conviction under this act. The lieutenant-governor will review each conviction and may change a sentence or offer mercy."

"Sounds like they've already convicted us," Ryan whispered to Heustis.

"We shall now swear in the members," Draper said.

Each uniformed officer swore to God and the Queen to be true and honest. Next, Draper read the charges.

"Between the twelfth day and sixteenth day of November in the second year of the reign of our Sovereign Lady Victoria, by the Grace of God ruler of the United Kingdom of Great Britain and defender of the faith, with force and arms at the township of Edwardsburg in the Province of Upper Canada, being citizens of foreign states at peace with the United Kingdom, that is to say, the United States of America, having joined themselves to divers subjects of said Lady the Queen, who were then and there unlawfully and traitorously in arms against our said Lady the Queen, the defendants did then and there make war on our said Lady the Queen, armed with guns, bayonets and other warlike weapons, and did kill and slay divers of her Majesty's loyal subjects."

Ryan shook his head. The British are masters of longwinded blather, he thought.

"How do you plea?" Draper asked.

Each prisoner replied not guilty.

Draper called his first witness, a solicitor who had interviewed the prisoners before the trial. He testified that each man claimed to be an American citizen, except for one.

"I did not interview the prisoner named Ryan Lone Pine. He arrived after my interviews."

"Thank you. You may retire." Draper looked at the prisoners. "Which of you is Ryan?"

Ryan stepped forward. "'Tis I."

"Do you not have a proper Irish surname?"

"My family's all dead. I took a name given by my adopted Algonquin family."

"What was your old family name?"

"I forget," he said, shrugging at his interlocutor.

"Of what country are you a citizen?"

"'Tis difficult to say, being I'm not a lawyer."

"Do not trifle with this court!"

"Begging yer pardon, but I don't know the law in this matter. I was born and raised in Ireland. I lived about eight months in this colony and eight months in the United States."

"If someone were to ask you to which nation you bear allegiance today, what would be your answer?"

"The republic of the United States of America."

"Let the record show that prisoner Ryan is a citizen of a foreign country."

Next, Draper called an infantry sergeant. He testified that he recognized all the prisoners as among those he captured on the last day of the battle.

"Did you see significant stands of arms at the battle site, sergeant?"

"Yes, colonel. I saw rifles and bowie knifes in large numbers, and three cannon."

"Are there any questions from the prisoners?" Draper asked.

"I have a question," Ryan responded.

"Go ahead."

"Sergeant, ye say ye saw me among the prisoners?"

"I am certain I did."

"Colonel Draper, I doubt the reliability of this man's words. As many can attest, I was not arrested until three weeks after."

"Sergeant! Do you have a written list?"

"Yes, colonel."

"Please consult it now for the name Ryan Lone Pine."

The nervous sergeant unfolded a sheet of stiff paper and examined each name. He sighed. "His name is not on the list, but the other twelve are, sir."

"Thank you, sergeant. You may retire. We will find other evidence to put this man at the battle."

Next, a portly magistrate read statements written by each prisoner. In their defense, Heustis, Smith, and others painted themselves as reluctant or kidnapped participants. The magistrate folded his papers and rose to retire.

"Have you another statement to read?" Draper demanded.

"No, colonel. Only these."

"You read twelve statements. How many prisoners do you see in this court?"

He gulped. "Thirteen, sir."

"It seems we have neglected the eponymous pine again."

"Let me go and I'll cause ye no more trouble."

Draper fumed until the laughter subsided.

"You may ask questions when I give you permission. One more interruption and you will be removed to your cell and tried in your absence." Turning to the officers, Draper continued. "We will proceed without a statement from this witness. I now call Lieutenant George Leary to the stand."

The young naval officer came forward. Ryan stiffened at the sight of the man who sent all his family's goods to the river bottom.

"Lieutenant! You were present for most of the battle. From your observations, do you believe these prisoners were active in the hostilities?"

"I cannot point to specific men in specific places. However, I can assure the court that any man captured on the last day had to be involved in the hostilities. It could not be avoided. We had the battlefield surrounded for five days."

"Thank you, lieutenant. Are there any questions from the prisoners?"

"I have one, sir."

"Of course you do, prisoner Pine. Please continue."

"What opinion do you have of men arrested weeks after the battle?" Ryan stared at Leary, wondering if the lieutenant would recognize him.

"My testimony could not apply." Leary looked at Draper, not Ryan.

"Lieutenant, you may retire. The court calls Levi Chipman."

Chipman slunk forward avoiding the prisoners' murderous stares.

"You are a citizen of what country?"

"Upper Canada, sir."

"Did you dwell in the United States?"

"I was there for ten months, sir."

"Under what circumstances did you return to Upper Canada?"

"I came with an armed force to establish a republic in this country."

"Look at the American prisoners and tell us who helped you in that armed attack on British soil."

"I saw lots of Heustis. He was wearing a sword. Smith there was a gunner. I cannot be so positive about all the others, but I saw those ones for sure." He pointed at five other prisoners.

"That fellow there," he pointed to Hicks, "was a sniper."

"Prisoner Hicks," began Draper, "as a sniper, how many men do you estimate you killed?"

"Well I don't know. I guess I killed as many of them as they did me." Several spectators chuckled. Draper waved him back in line.

Draper pointed at Ryan. "Did you see him at the battle?"

"No, sir. Sorry."

Draper looked angry. Ryan smiled.

"Advocate," Bonnycastle called from the gallery. "May I suggest you call Private Campbell of the second Grenville militia regiment to the stand."

Draper nodded at Bonnycastle. "Private Campbell, identify yourself."

Tiny strode to the officers' table. Ryan's smug smile vanished.

"Lieutenant-Colonel Bonnycastle, please do me the honor of questioning this witness."

"My pleasure," Bonnycastle replied as he paced towards Tiny.

"Private Campbell, you helped arrest prisoner Pine in Kingston on December eighth last, correct?"

"Yes, colonel."

"Did you see him at the battle site near Prescott in November?"

"Yes, colonel."

"Did you see him at the battle?"

"No, colonel."

"Tell us then, where and when you saw him at the battle site."

"Yes, colonel. I paid a visit to the artillery crew north of the battle site late on the last day. I saw footprints in the snow and followed them. I found the prisoner drinking from a creek."

"How far from the battle site was he when you found him?"

"A mile and a bit, colonel."

"What evidence do you have that the prisoner participated in the battle?"

"He told me, colonel."

"Tell the court martial what he said."

"Colonel, the prisoner said 'I spent five days in a pitched battle'."

"Anything else, private?"

"No, colonel."

Bonnycastle nodded to Draper.

"Thank you, colonel. I believe that completes the evidence conclusively against this prisoner."

"Advocate, may I question the witness too?"

Draper seemed startled that Ryan dared speak. With a shrug, he said, "It is your privilege."

Ryan stepped forwards. "Gidday, Tiny! You don't mind if I call ye Tiny? That's what most calls ye, isn't it."

Tiny's eyes narrowed.

"On the day you mention, were you armed?"

"Yes. I had a musket."

"If you were armed, why didn't ye arrest me then?"

Tiny expelled an audible hiss.

"Answer the question properly," Draper snapped.

Tiny tried to speak but gagged. Ryan knew Tiny's pride might be too great to tell the court a bird defeated him.

"Sir," Ryan began. "This man's words don't ring of truth. If I was where he says, I'd either be arrested or shot."

"Is that true, private?" Draper asked.

The officers and guests began to murmur their disapproval. Tiny remained mute.

"Private! Have you anything else to say?" Bonnycastle barked.

Tiny stared narrow-eyed at Ryan, clearly wishing he had his hands around the younger man's throat.

"Private, you should be arrested for perjury," Draper said with malice.

Tiny glared at Ryan, who smiled back.

"You have wasted this court's time," Bonnycastle added.

Tiny's mouth began moving, but no words came out.

"Leave this court immediately," Draper motioned to a sentry to remove Tiny.

"Wait." He spoke in a whisper. The courtroom went silent.

"Wait, what?" snapped Draper.

Tiny ignored the protocol demand. "I have more to say."

"Speak up, man," Bonnycastle ordered.

"I apologize to this court martial," Tiny began hesitantly. "It was pride that forced me to hold back, but I'd rather be the town clown than let that Irish scum go free."

Ryan no longer smiled.

"I did attempt to arrest the prisoner the last night of the battle. His bird—the same raven that is now a fort mascot—attacked me like a demon in the night. It took me by surprise and I stumbled in the snow. The prisoner stole my weapon and escaped. He was there that night. He was with the invaders. He slipped my grasp."

The court martial was silent. Bonnycastle broke the spell.

"I am confused, private. The prisoner captured your musket?"

"Yes."

Bonnycastle glowered at Tiny for the lack of proper address. Tiny held firm. He'd found his courage. "Why did he not shoot you, I wonder?"

Tiny shrugged.

"May I speak?" Ryan said.

Bonnycastle looked at Draper for permission. The latter nodded. "Please do!" said Bonnycastle.

"Private Campbell, ye told this court martial some of my words after the battle, but no more than suits yer story. Please repeat my entire statement."

Tiny saw the trap Ryan had set. He hesitated, not wanting to give favorable testimony.

Captain Sandom stepped from the ranks of observers, "Private Campbell, I will have fifty pounds of your corpulent flesh flogged from your bones if you do not tell this court the whole story. It is imperative these proceedings be honorable."

Tiny showed no reaction to Sandom's threat or renewed glares from Bonnycastle and Draper. Needing to break the impasse, Ryan moved to within inches of Tiny's face. Speaking softly, he said, "I know ye hate me. For the good of yer own soul, ye cannot lie before God and this court."

Ryan stepped backwards and waited in the silent courtroom. He observed Tiny struggle with his conscience and hatred.

"When the prisoner stole my musket," Tiny began, "his whole statement was, 'I spent five days in a pitched battle and killed none. I'm not about to soil my soul with the likes of ye'."

The spectators and officers exhaled as one. Some men shouted bravo, but Ryan was uncertain who they meant it for.

"Is there anything else you wish to ask the witness?" Draper asked Ryan.

"No, sir."

Draper nodded at Tiny and he hurried from the court.

"Is there anything else you want to say to this court?"

"Yes, sir. Yer witness can place me at the battle, but ye have no witness to say I was involved in the hostilities. Like the witness said, I killed none. I joined Colonel von Schoultz on condition I wouldn't be asked to bear arms. I volunteered to tend the wounded. Tis how I passed my time."

"Do you have a witness to support this story?"

"Sir, Colonel von Schoultz handed over two wounded militiamen on the last day. I tended them. They can support my story."

Draper seemed stunned and unsure of his next move. Bonnycastle came to his aid.

"Colonel Draper, I believe this young man is telling the truth and we should not compel the wounded militiamen to relive their horrors."

"Quite right, colonel," said Draper sounding defeated.

"However, I have one more question for the prisoner."

"Please proceed, colonel."

"Prisoner Ryan!"

"Yes?"

Bonnycastle slapped his swagger stick against his pant leg. "You have not once addressed me by my rank at our several meetings."

"'Tis correct, colonel."

The timing of Ryan's response in the tense room set all laughing. Bonnycastle smiled.

"One question. In the heat of battle, did you ever carry powder or shot to infantry or artillery? Or perhaps help position cannon?"

Ryan had not prepared for that question. He glanced at Macdonald, who shrugged in response. For a moment, Ryan thought that his lawyer had no advice; but, then he caught the message hidden in the shrug.

"Colonel, I don't remember. Those days were a blur. I was cold, hungry, and afraid. Perhaps you have a witness who saw me carry powder or shot."

Draper shook his head and asked, "Are there any other questions for this prisoner?"

No one answered.

"Then, this court martial is adjourned. The prisoners will be informed of verdicts and sentences soon."

Fort's Inmate

With the mass trial adjourned, Sheriff Allan Macdonell led the prisoners to their cells. John Macdonald intercepted the sheriff on the fort's parade square.

"Pardon me, good sheriff. Can I have a word with my client, please?"

"Do yah need a private room, Mr. Macdonald?"

"No, sheriff. This spot is perfectly adequate."

"Carrot, I trust yah can find yar own way back to the casement."

"Yes, sir."

"Right then, off with the rest of yah bandits."

Ryan and Macdonald conversed a foot apart. Men in the infantry and artillery went about their duties leaving an oasis of peace around the two men.

"I am offended by that court martial. The evidence against several men was entirely circumstantial and bordered on hearsay and conjecture. In any proper court, half the accused would be released."

"It does seem more like revenge than justice," Ryan replied.

"I must say, your defense was brilliant. You show a knack for legal gamesmanship."

"Was I good enough to go free?"

"You would have exculpated yourself, if not for the testimony of Private Campbell. As it is, they certainly cannot hang you on the evidence presented."

"Tis freedom I want. If not, I risk losing everything that is dear to me."

"I will make representations on your behalf to the government for clemency based on your youth and noncombatant role."

"Thank ye."

"Also, I have some interesting news. Captain William Vaughan arrested Bill Johnston."

"I thought Bill was in jail. Ye can't arrest a prisoner."

"Correct. A court acquitted Johnston of that first charge shortly after you arrived in Kingston. The marshal promptly re-arrested him on an outstanding warrant related to the Hickory Island affair. Bill escaped. Vaughan recaptured him about two weeks later."

"I'm sure he won't be in jail long."

*****

Macdonell slammed his way into the casement at noon two days later. By that point, everyone knew Martin Woodruff hanged that morning. By all accounts, the execution was botched and poor Woodruff struggled long in agony.

"I have matters to inform yah of. Listen carefully."

The room went silent. Everyone knew the document he unfolded held their verdicts.

"For all those at trial on December 17, the court martial has found you guilty."

He let the words sink in. The men looked at each other and then at their feet.

"In every case but one, the sentence is death by hanging."

Every man sucked in his breath. Macdonell unfolded another official document.

"Hunter Vaughan! Come forward."

Hunter went pale and began to tremble, thinking the sheriff held his execution order.

"On December 10, yar father captured the notorious outlaw Bill Johnston. To show its gratitude, the colonial government has decided to commute yar death sentence to a full pardon. Yah will be released and shipped home at public expense."

The men next to Hunter shook his hand or patted him on the back as color returned to his cheeks. The condemned men's spirits rose knowing one of their own was going home.

"Carrot!"

"Yes, sheriff."

"Yah are the one man not condemned to death. Yah will be held until they determine an appropriate punishment."

As men shook his hand, Ryan smiled weakly—he remained in prison.

*****

Christmas, 1838, lacked any hint of good spirits, even with bread pudding added to the evening meal. Two more Hunters hanged four days earlier. Only days into the New Year, the British hanged four men in one morning. With one hundred and thirty-four Hunters sentenced to hang, and only ten dead so far, no one believed the dying would end soon.

However, the days that followed began a period of calm. For the rest of January and into February, no one made the one-way trip to the Kingston jail. In contrast, the British sent several wounded inmates home to America without trial. Every day, life improved. Heustis bought a cake for Ryan's twenty-first birthday.

Macdonell allowed longer exercise breaks. Families, friends, and whole communities in America raised money to pay for better food, warm clothing, and more firewood—whatever the prisoners needed. Other than keeping the casement clean and shoveling snow, the prisoners' assigned duties were few. Each man had free time to lose themselves in thoughts and memories—the single private refuge in the fort.

*****

In mid-February, the sheriff brought Ryan a letter. "Carrot! This arrived today from yar lawyer. Judging by the handwriting, 'tis from a lass. Have yah a sweetheart at home?"

"I hope so."

"Do yah need writing material?"

"Yes, sheriff, if 'tis possible."

"Don't be so damned daft. Yes, 'tis possible. You'll be needing postage too."

"I planned to have Zak fly it back."

"That might work, yah bloody slipgibbet. But let's save him the labor."

Ryan stepped closer to the casement windows and read the letter.

To Ryan Lone Pine
Fort Henry, Upper Canada
February 9, 1839

Dearest Ryan,

Such crazy times I have had since I last saw you. Father is imprisoned in Albany awaiting trial. I moved into his cell to make sure he is well taken care of. Father has daily visits from prominent men and their wives. Some men held benefits in his honor to raise money so our family can survive in his absence. The papers carry regular stories about him and letters from people both favorable and critical. Father is famous. Until now, I never realized how far his reputation had spread.

I am in weekly correspondence with Ada. She is home in Portland, Upper Canada, and is much in turmoil over your incarceration, as am

I. Father is livid. He was prepared to lead a gang of his men to storm the fort. Fortunately, my brothers' clearer heads prevailed.

Prominent men in Jefferson County are pleading with the British for release of our men and boys. They have promised their bond against any further trouble along the border. So far, the British have not relented, but I believe some good may come of this effort and we can once again stroll the Clayton shore and row off to some secret place in the islands.

Lovingly yours,

Kate Johnston

Albany, New York

Ryan read the letter twice and then lay back on a rough straw mattress. He pictured Bill holding court in an Albany cell, his feral stare taking in every deceit and conceit of his visitors. In his mind, Kate accompanied him, in a clean cotton dress—flattering but not fancy—turning eyes and hearts. In another room far away, he imagined Ada pacing and fretting over him. Ada, a formidable woman, feral in her own way, a woman often in his thoughts. Ryan sighed. His cellmates glanced his way. He ignored them and reread the letter.

The next day, Macdonell brought Ryan a quill, some ink, paper, and envelopes. After an hour composing passages in his mind, he wrote two letters. He related the days leading up to his capture, his trial, his life in the fort, and his plans for the future. To Kate, he wrote like her suitor. To Ada, he tried to write as a friend.

*****

Everyone's high spirits evaporated when the British hanged Lyman Leach. Following five death-free weeks, the execution brought the inmates' spirits crashing to earth and destroyed the growing goodwill towards their captors. Macdonell related Leach's last hours. Still eating breakfast when the Kingston guard came for him, he kept the hangman waiting until he finished his final meal. He met his death in peace.

Ryan remembered Lyman before the *Peel* raid—cheerful, idealistic, and fatalistic. He recalled Lyman's bravery at the windmill.

"You know why they hanged Lyman, Ryan?" Heustis asked bitterly.

"Because he attacked Canada?"

"No. I believe the British are finished with hanging us for that. I am certain they always intended to execute the leaders to make an example, and now have other plans for the rest of us. They killed Lyman because he is the only man they ever caught that helped attack the *Sir Robert Peel*."

"Lyman nary set foot on her."

"He was part of the plot. That is all they care."

"There's another here who was on the *Peel* that night."

"That man should keep quiet."

After a pause, Ryan added, "I hope for your sake that the hangings have ended, Daniel."

"You believe I may be next?"

"Yer the most senior Hunter officer still alive."

"Oh!"

*****

Heustis correctly predicted an end to the hangings. The following week, Macdonell entered the casement, a smile beaming on his usual taciturn face. He announced that Queen Victoria had commuted all remaining death sentences to transport for life at the Van Dieman's Land penal colony. While no one liked the thought of hard labor in an antipodal region, relief showed on every man's face when imminent death vanished.

"Pardon me, sir. Is there news about me?" Ryan asked.

The sheriff answered without turning his way. "Yar name's on the transport list."

Ryan slid down the wall, propped his arms on his knees, and hid his face. No spot on Earth was further away from Kate than Australia's island neighbor.

*****

With the threat of hanging gone, prisoners again relaxed. They received regular visits and gifts from spouses, friends, and relatives.

One unexpected visitor surprised everyone. When Macdonell escorted her into the casement, only Heustis recognized the young woman with the heavily bandaged face.

"Eliza! I thought you were dead."

It was Eliza Taylor, the teenager shot by the militia the first morning of the windmill battle when she fled with her mother. A musket ball that morning shattered her jaw knocking her unconscious.

"No Daniel, though I sometimes wish that were my fate."

Ryan pulled up a stool for her.

"Please, have a seat, miss."

She smiled at Ryan as best she could through her disfigurement.

"Daniel," she began, speaking slowly, "I came as a witness for the truth. Men in the militia are lying. They say it was you Americans who shot us. I tell anyone who will listen that Colonel von Schoultz's men held their fire. The musket balls came from our militia."

A sullen Macdonell ordered tea brought in. For an hour, Eliza and Heustis exchanged stories about their lives before the battle. The reunion ended in tearful farewell. They hugged like parting siblings.

*****

Ryan and Kate wrote each other weekly. He related his life in prison and described his cellmates. She told him how, in New York State, committees had formed in a dozen towns to organize efforts to free the men. Every influential British colonial figure had received letters and visitors pleading for the Americans' release.

When spring arrived to warm the thick stone fort, the American repatriation campaign started to pay off. On April 8, Ryan and the other inmates applauded while Macdonell marched twenty-two unshackled prisoners, boys and men in their teens and early twenties, out the fort's gate bound for America.

The next week, Ryan read newspaper accounts of their arrival by steamer at Sackets Harbor. Well-wishers and sobbing, happy family filled the wharf. Politicians and marching bands greeted them. Prominent town leaders shook hands with Macdonell and thanked him for the British generosity.

Reading the news, Heustis interpreted the events. "Our community leaders in Jefferson County clearly understand the required protocol. They will happily toady before Macdonell or any British officer if it means bringing more men home."

Ryan read the letters published in the Watertown *Jeffersonian* from the freed inmates. Each author expressed gratitude to the British colonial government for its mercy. Each confessed that Hunter leaders had misled them regarding the poor condition of Canadians and each now regretted the harm he'd caused. The letters, many from men Ryan knew could barely read, were remarkably similar. A guiding hand was evident.

In the final week of April, Macdonell accompanied thirty-seven more young men to Sackets Harbor. Ryan waved good-bye to several friends. Again, a flurry of letters in local papers applauded Britain's kindness and disowned the Hunter cause.

The day after the sheriff returned from his second trip to Sackets Harbor, he tacked a paper to the door of his quarters. It named twenty-five men to be sent home in the next group, including Ryan, Heustis, and William Gates. That night, their casement celebrated. They pooled funds and bribed the cooks for better food and a cake.

*****

The next morning, the first of May, Macdonell entered the casement after breakfast.

"Carrot!"

"Yes, sheriff."

"Clean yarself up. Yah have a visitor"

"A visitor?

"A fine-looking lass. Yar betrothed she called herself."

"Where is she now?"

"Outside playing with your raven. He spotted her the moment I escorted her into the fort and fussed over her like a lost puppy finding his master."

"Anyone have a clean shirt?" he called to his casement mates.

"I do," Orrin Smith called.

"I'll escort her to my room. Come up when yar ready," Macdonell said.

Ryan scrubbed himself as clean as possible using cold water and rough soap. He shaved, combed his longish curls, and put on a clean, light-colored cotton shirt and dark brown linen pants. Fifteen minutes after getting Macdonell's message, he stepped into the bright spring sunshine. The sheriff waited on the parade square with Zak on his shoulder. He smiled at Ryan and tilted his head towards his quarters on the second level.

Ryan ran up the wooden stairs two at a time and stopped in front of Macdonell's door. It stood ajar an inch. Lamp light from inside reflected on the doorframe. He rapped twice. Kate opened the door, smiling like sunshine at Ryan. She wore a sleeveless, white summer dress, tight at the waist to show off her slender figure and without her usual modest, high collar. The sweeping décolletage revealed the upper edges of her petit breasts. Her tied-back hair accentuated her long neck and high cheekbones.

Dazzled by her beauty, Ryan hovered on the doorsill, his eyes locked on hers. He dared not blink for fear of missing a moment of her. She grabbed his sleeve, tugged him into the room, and swung the door shut. She pushed Ryan to the wooden door and pressed her body on his from shoulders to pelvis.

Her light brown hair lay beside his cheek and wisps tickled his nose. He inhaled the fresh, light floral scent of good quality soap on her smooth skin. His hands rested on her hips. She leaned on him, eyes shut. Her breasts pressed his chest. He held her close, feeling her heart beat through their clothes.

He broke the spell with a joyful whisper. "I have some very good news."

She stepped back smiling. "Tell me!"

"My name is on the list for shipment home. I'll be free in a week or two."

"Oh-h! I am so happy. I have this vision of us rowing in the islands again."

Ryan grinned. "The sheriff says ye called yerself my betrothed."

"I had to. Before I came, I visited my uncle James and his family in Bath. They said I might not be allowed a visit unless I was a spouse or direct relative. So, I lied that we are betrothed. Though, I do enjoy the sound of it."

"How's yer father?"

"Fine. They released him on bail. Why do you ask?"

Ryan grabbed Kate's hands. "When I return to Clayton, I'll ask Bill for permission to make ye my bride."

She let out a peel of laughter that sent a wave of goosebumps up his spine. Kate bit her lip to stifle her mirth. "You never met my older sister Maria. She lives in Detroit now. Her beau did not ask Father for permission. Father does not dwell on formalities. All he cares is that we choose a good man. You surpass his expectations."

She tilted her chin down and gazed up into his face. The effect was to widen her already large eyes. Ryan knelt on the floor in front of Kate, still holding her hands. He had no training or advice on proposals, but he'd read somewhere you should kneel.

"Kate Johnston, would ye please consent to be my wife?"

Her mouth twitched while she searched for the best words. He started to quiver with anticipation. He envisioned an instant positive reply, a hug, and a kiss. She sighed and replied, "Maybe."

"I don't— I thought—"

She pressed a finger to his lips. "Sh-h-h. I did not say no."

"What did ye mean then?"

"I need you to prove you are not another loveable rogue like Father. Life has been hard for Mother. I do not desire the same. If, for one year, you stay away from affairs that can bring us trouble, I will say yes."

"Then ye are as good as my betrothed, because I can do that easy."

"It will not be so easy for me." At a questioning expression from him, she added, "because…ever since that day we swam together, I have dreamt of our wedding night."

"Ye have!"

"Part of me wants to let you take me now."

"We could, but part of ye would always regret it. We must wait."

"If we must."

"'Tis for the best."

"Kiss me."

Oblivious to the passing minutes, they kissed and talked, each imagining the farm and children they would have someday, until a discreet knock on the door reminded them of another world.

Outside, Kate played the catch-food game with Zak for five minutes before the sheriff escorted her out the gate and beyond Ryan's sight.

For the next week, no one saw Ryan without a smile. He whistled while he worked. He laughed often. He greeted Bonnycastle with a sincere 'Gidday, colonel,' whenever they passed.

*****

A week after Kate's visit, Ryan and Heustis lounged on a bench enjoying the spring sunshine. They discussed their futures and swatted mosquitoes that had breached the ramparts. Ryan planned to join a shipbuilding firm in Clayton and put aside money for a farm. Heustis intended to return to the Watertown store where he and his cousin sold groceries and West India goods. Zak stood on the bench to Ryan's right, his eyelids half closed in a raven nap.

Macdonell ambled towards them from the officers' quarters. He picked a spot on the bench and pulled a metal flask from an inside breast pocket, took a drink, and passed it to Heustis.

"Take a drink Daniel and pass it to Carrot."

Heustis hadn't tasted whiskey in months and did not hesitate. He tipped the flask, guzzled deeply, and held it out to Ryan.

"No thank ye. I don't drink."

"Make an exception this once."

Ryan shivered. "What's wrong, sheriff?"

"I have a sad tale to tell." He cleared his throat. "Two days ago, one of my sheriff colleagues released seven Patriots, held at a different jail, to New York officials at the border north of Massena. My superiors expected them to show the same respect and gratitude we experienced in Sackets Harbor. Yar leaders in Jefferson County understand that appearances are important. They are to be commended. I never believed they were sincere, but the kind and polite words were essential to the continued repatriation of American prisoners."

"Damn it, colonel," Heustis snapped. "Get to the point."

"In my own time, Daniel." Macdonell sipped from the flask. "A pudding-headed American judge accepted the prisoners. A brazen-faced fool he is with the wit of three folks: two fools and a madman. Someone should shoot his ballocks off. Instead of taking the men and departing quietly, he gave an inflammatory speech. He lambasted our sheriff for holding the men so long without proper trial. He said the Patriot cause was noble. Worse of all, he accused the British of tyranny in Canada."

"What's this to do with us?" Ryan mumbled, not wanting to hear an answer.

"Everything. Sir George Arthur, our Lieutenant-Governor, already faced much criticism for granting pardons. Now, he has no footing. He rescinded all release warrants. None of yah jailbirds is going home, except maybe Zak. I am terribly sorry."

Not since a simple question from Grandfather drove Ryan away from homesteading two years earlier had the young man experienced such an avalanche of grief. A stabbing pain seared his stomach. Bending double, he rolled forward off the bench onto the stone ground and curled into a fetal position. His body twitched with silent, tearless sobs.

Zak dropped off the bench and stood beside his human's anguished face. "Zaak! Croc! Rrok!"

"Give me a hand, Daniel."

Macdonell and Heustis hauled Ryan to his feet. With their shoulders under his armpits, they dragged him to a mattress in the casement.

*****

For weeks afterward, Ryan resembled a dying man. He ate little. He lost weight and grew pale. He slept as many hours as the prison schedule allowed. When he spoke, he used no more words than needed. He became a master of monosyllables. Zak sat on the nearest gun carriage to Ryan's casement, cawing, "Kach! Kood!" Other men answered the call in Ryan's absence.

Macdonald came to visit after the sheriff sent word of Ryan's poor condition.

"Come now, Ryan, buck up! Sir George Arthur may have a change of heart."

Ryan shrugged.

"Is there anything I can do?"

"Yes. Write to Ada. I can't. Tell her what happened."

Minutes after Macdonald bid farewell, Macdonell slammed into the empty casement and halted above Ryan, his arms akimbo.

"Alright, Carrot. On yar feet or I'll have yah cleaning latrines again."

The memory of the stink injected some life into him. He pushed himself to his feet.

"Where's yar bog-lander spirit? Yah'll go all beetle-headed if yah don't snap out of it."

"I feel like a caged animal, sheriff. I grew up on a farm. I lived in the woods. I hunted with the Algonquin. I hiked the deep forests. I lived on the river. I haven't seen a green growing thing for months. Living in this stone pit's killing me."

"H-m-m-m! I'll see what I can do."

The next day, Ryan sat outside, gazing mindlessly at the cobbled ground. Zak perched beside him, half asleep.

"Rrok! Cric! Croc!"

"On yar feet, Carrot." Ryan jerked awake at Macdonell's bellow. "I've a new job for yah. Take yar hick arse to the cookhouse. The assistant cook has a broom and a brush waiting for yah. Get it and come back."

Ryan did as ordered.

"Right. Follow me."

He led Ryan up the stairs to the second floor near his room. On this occasion, he continued up the set of narrow stairs beyond—a route that fort rules forbid prisoners to go. Made of stone, the steep flights followed a curving, domed passage barely the width of a man's shoulders.

They emerged from the shadowy stairwell to the wide, pale limestone ramparts bathed in sunlight. Eighteen monstrous cannon perched on semi-circular stone platforms. The wheels of each gun carriage fit into a curved track to let gun crews swivel the multi-ton weapons towards the enemy. A stone ledge linked the platforms. Infantry mounted the ledge to fire over the wall.

"Carrot! Prisoners are not permitted on the ramparts. Seeing that yah've been a model inmate, Lieutenant-Colonel Bonnycastle agreed to let yah work up here."

"Work at what."

"Look at yar feet. See all them little cracks between the stones?"

"Yes."

"They must be kept free of dirt. A little dirt is an invitation for some errant seed to sprout. Plant roots have a way of carving tiny channels into the stone. Them tiny channels can fill with water. When winter comes, the water freezes and cracks the stone. This whole fort will crumble to rubble if we let those seeds get a toehold. So, yar job is to clean the cracks with the broom and that brush."

"Is this some new form of punishment?"

Macdonell smiled. "Stand on the ledge for a minute. The parapet needs cleaning too."

Ryan stepped up, glanced over the parapet, and gasped. A spectacular panorama stretched from the fort's walls down the earthen bank to the St. Lawrence.

To a man starved of color, Ryan feasted on a rainbow. White and yellow wild flowers sprinkled the dazzling green spring grass carpeting the slope. The river shone bluer than he remembered. To the east, pink and white blossoms of an apple orchard added a pastel touch. Tears welled up. Zak flew to the parapet and cooed in his ear.

"Yah know, Carrot. I'd send yah home if it were up to me. This is the best I can do for yah. Avoid trouble and this is yar job as long as yar here. Yah are allowed on the ramparts anytime between reveille and roll call. Don't forget to drink water. The heat from this stone will fry yar nob."

He began to walk away and stopped. "Don't overheat yar knowledge box figuring out how to escape. Ever since Montgomery and his crew tunneled out, we take extra precautions. It won't happen again."

Ryan peered over the parapet at the outside wall. The drop into the dry ditch below would kill or cripple him. If it did not, there was no place to climb out of the ditch. There was no escape.

Zak launched from the parapet and flew towards nearby Cedar Island. In his imagination, Ryan extended the raven's flight. He pictured flying across to Wolfe Island, then soaring along the island's southeast arm, across to Hickory Island, then to the west end of Grindstone Island, and on to a home on the Clayton shore, a wood-sided house with two upper windows like owl's eyes.

*****

For the remainder of spring and the hot months of summer, rain or shine, Ryan passed his days cleaning the ramparts and parapet, always with Zak nearby. He silently acknowledged the gift Macdonell gave him. He worked methodically and relentlessly. No dirt could accumulate to nurture a stray, fecund seed.

He spent long periods gazing out at the islands, the river, and the bay, dreaming of another life. At such times, he fingered the Algonquin medallion and tried to find strength in the lone pine image. Daily he tossed food for Zak to catch. The monastic simplicity and order brought him some peace. Ryan came down for meals and extra water on the hottest days.

During their regular meetings discussing prisoner affairs, Heustis and Macdonell remarked on Ryan's change from a gregarious youth to a quiet loner. From his vantage point on the ramparts, he often spotted the two officers looking his way and chatting. Not a sound reached his ears.

There was little Heustis could do for Ryan, and he had his hands full trying to keep up morale in his casement. For the Fourth of July, Heustis had the men sew together pocket handkerchiefs into a crude facsimile of the Stars and Stripes. That evening, they toasted America's birthday with lemonade and sang the anthem. Ryan slid down the casement wall in a dark corner so the cheering men could not see the wetness under his eyes. Memories of the previous summer's famous celebration on Fort Wallace Island, of kissing Kate and flirting with Ada, drove home how much he had sacrificed for the Hunters' futile cause.

*****

Families continued to visit and bring news and gifts, but their optimism had faded. All the beseeching of politicians, influential men in the military, and Family Compact stalwarts failed to soften the British resolve. No other men went home.

A letter arrived from Ada.

To Ryan Lone Pine
Fort Henry, Upper Canada
July 29, 1839

Dearest Ryan,

I write this at Kate's request. She has been unable to complete any attempt to write you personally. The poor distraught girl breaks into sobs after a few words. She asked me to tell you that she thinks of you daily and prays for you nightly. She still hopes for your return.

Bill has been in a terrible temper about you and the other men imprisoned in the fort. He is back in the islands with several boats and crews. I do not know what he intends, but his sons worry.

Kate informed me that you proposed. Such joy! Then days later, I received the letter saying they revoked your release. Such sorrow! I do believe I shed as many tears as dear cousin Kate.

We will continue to work hard for your release.

With affection,

Ada Burleigh

Portland, Upper Canada

He read the letter twice, placed it in the casement stove, and set it on fire. He wanted no information on Johnston to make its way to Macdonell.

Ryan now had something else to ponder while he swept the ramparts and brushed out cracks in the parapet. He had to write Kate —there was no honorable alternative. He waited weeks, trying to compose the truest words to put to paper. Finally, he did.

To Kate Johnston
Clayton, New York
August 27, 1839

Dearest Kate,

The rumor is we will leave the fort in September for the penal colony. That way, we depart afore winter and arrive in the South Seas in its spring. I hear 'tis the best schedule for sailing there.

We prisoners are now resigned to our fate, to years of hard labor on the other side of the world, far away from family and friends.

I am sorry to disappoint ye. I was wrong to go back to Kingston. I suppose there are other things I might change too, but 'tis too late.

I am glad I asked ye to be my wife. Though this may never come to be, it was the happiest day of my life when you said 'maybe.'

I do not know how long I will be incarcerated. If may be for life. So, I must free ye from any promise made and any bond built in love between us. If the right man comes along at the right time and asks for your hand, say yes.

When opportunity allows, I will write. Though it be several years, do not despair. You will hear from me.

Give my best to your father. Tell him it was an honor knowing him. If ever he thinks some of my misfortune is his fault, tell him that is nonsense. I made my own choices and my own mistakes.

I worry about Zak. He may try to follow the ship. I told him to go find you, but he ignores me. He is stubborn.

Best wishes to your mother and brothers. Hug Ada for me.

Your friend forever,

Ryan Lone Pine

Fort Henry, Upper Canada

*****

"He's gone all cork-brained," Macdonell said to Heustis as they stood on the parade square staring up at Ryan brushing the inside edge of the ramparts wall.

"I really do not believe it is as bad as that, colonel. I admit he does not seek anyone's company, but he will chat and listen if someone initiates the conversation."

"Yah know he sent a letter his betrothed yesterday. There was nary a smile on his muns, so I know the words be sad."

"Most of us are in the same boat, colonel."

"Aye. But yar all guilty. That one should be acquitted."

"It is a moot point now, sir."

"He hasn't been the same since losing a place on the parole list. I blame myself. I should have sent him with an earlier group."

"Short of letting him escape, what can you do?"

"Don't be daft, Daniel. There'll be no escaping. I have my duty. Maybe I can cheer him up. His aunt has enquired about him. Perhaps I can arrange a visit."

"His aunt?" Heustis knew the story of Ryan's lost family.

"Yah. A Mrs. Burleigh. Do yah know her?"

"No," Heustis lied.

*****

On a hot mid-September morning, Ryan worked alone on the ramparts with Zak for company. High above the bustling fort population below, his mind drifted though the Thousand Islands.

"Zaak! Zaak!" The raven recognized someone and glided into the great pit that is the fort's parade square. Snapped from his daydreaming, Ryan's gaze followed his bird's flight.

Below, Ada sashayed on the proud sheriff's arm. Macdonell sported his formal military jacket and highland kilt, including a sporran of gleaming white fox. Ada wore a shape-flattering, bosom-reveling yellow summer dress. Every man in sight stopped whatever pastime or duty occupied the moment, and watched her pass. The sheriff escorted her into the officers' mess.

The young lance corporal, Tiny's unfortunate friend Andrew, ran up the two flights of stairs. Panting and sweating in the heat, he sputtered, "Colonel Macdonell ordered me to clean you up."

"Why?"

"To meet your aunt. She's having lunch with Colonels Macdonell and Bonnycastle. When they are finished, she expects a private visit."

Ryan stared impassively at the poor sweating soldier.

"Come on, Ryan. I've been in enough trouble lately. Please cooperate. I need you washed and barbered."

"Ye have nary called me by name afore, Andrew."

The lance corporal blinked. He had no answer.

"Why should I help you, Andrew?"

"Because I know Ada is not your aunt. I was in Kingston when you met. So far, I have kept my mouth shut."

Ryan fixed his eyes on Andrew's face, for the first time seeing the man behind the soldier.

"Fair enough! Here's what I want, Andrew. Take me to the river to bathe. Bring soap, a towel, a change of clothes, and the barber. For a moment, let me pretend I'm a free man on the banks of the river I love. Can ye do that?"

"I can."

"Then, let's go."

*****

Washed and shaved, Ryan paced Macdonell's narrow, windowless room, waiting. His heart raced and his palms sweated. He sipped water to ease his dry throat.

A single rap on the door announced Ada. Bending under the low doorframe, she filled the room with her immense femaleness and the scent of lavender. She dropped the latch into place and leaned her back on the door, her gaze on Ryan. Unconsciously, he rose on the balls of his feet.

At that moment in the candle light, he thought her the most attractive mature woman he'd ever seen. One could not fairly compare her beauty to the fresh, teenage prettiness of Kate. Nor, could Kate fully measure up to Ada, a naturally beautiful woman at the peak of the prime of her life, still vibrant, youthful, confident, and experienced.

"Whatever criticism we might rightfully level against the British military," she began, "bad manners is not one of them. Never have I met finer gentlemen than the colonels Bonnycastle and Macdonell. And that Allan—such a handsome fellow. If I thought it would help your case, I'd happily bed him in a second."

"What about yer husband?"

"You are too young to know how a married couple changes over decades. Twenty years after leaving the altar, you cannot expect to have the same ideals. I respect my husband, but I am my own person."

She smiled and held out both arms at waist level, a signal for him to step closer. He hesitated. A quick twinge of anxiety jolted his gut, while an erection stirred in his pants. "Pardon my confusion," he began, "ye so often pushed Kate at me and now ye want to pull me to yer bosom."

She kicked off her shoes to reduce her height. "I always wanted you two to marry. I mean that. That can no longer happen; so, now is our one chance to be together," she whispered.

Ryan stood entranced.

"That is a pleasant tune you are humming. What's its name?"

"I don't know. Tis just a wee bit of song that comes to me sometimes."

She half-turned. Smiling sideways over her shoulder, she asked, "Do you see that button below my neck."

"Yes."

"Be a dear and undo that for me. It is impossible to reach."

Ryan froze. He knew where undoing that button would lead. "Well?"

He stepped close and undid the fabric covered button.

"There are three more. Please undo them too."

He complied. She twisted around to face him, now inches away.

"So. Are you going to put your arms around me?"

For a second, an image from his teens flashed in Ryan's mind. He trembled on a ledge of rock, working up enough nerve to dive into the cold lake twenty feet below. He remembered leaning forward until he passed the tipping point and how he then relaxed and gave into gravity.

He stepped forward into her grasp and buried his nose in the gap between her breasts. He luxuriated in the scent of warm female skin. As he kissed the mounds of her breasts exposed above the neckline. Ada ran her fingers down his back and squeezed his buttocks.

Ryan relaxed and leaned his weight on her. Lust and loneliness conquered fear and guilt.

Gently, she kissed his forehead and sniffed the fresh scent of his sun-dried hair.

"I believe I'd be more comfortable sitting on the bed."

Ryan, whose legs wobbled from the flood of hormones in his blood, happily stepped backwards and plunked down on the narrow mattress.

Ada dropped her shoulders and lightly shook her torso. The shoulder straps dutifully slipped off and her dress dropped in a heap at her ankles. Lightly brushing each shoulder with her finger tips, she sent her silk slip to the floor next to the dress. Wearing only a red silk, overbust corset, she sat thigh-to-thigh beside Ryan. She caressed his knee.

Ryan forgot to breathe. His head dizzied and his lungs started to burn while he studied her half-naked body, from her elegant feet, up her shapely legs, over the row of six buttons on the front of her corset, slowly past her barely contained bosom, past her full lips, to rest on her green eyes. The gold iris flecks sparkled.

He exhaled slowly. His jitters dissipated. He smiled.

"Why are you smiling?" she asked softly.

Leaning on his left arm, he ran his right hand across her nearest shoulder. "Tis embarrassing to say."

"Nothing that happens in this room can embarrass either of us if we are honest about our feelings."

"I'm smiling because I know how lucky I am that ye'll be my first."

He studied Ada's reaction to his confession. Her eyelids relaxed into a sultry stare. Her full lips parted, exposing the tip of her tongue between pearly teeth. He raised himself on his arm to give himself a tiny height advantage, and lowered his lips to hers.

Her tongue darted into his mouth and he responded in kind. She ran her hand to his waist and tugged his shirt loose from his trousers.

With both hands she pulled the garment towards his head. He reluctantly broke free of Ada's lips to let her lift the shirt over his head and off his arms. She dropped it to the floor.

His fingers touched her shoulder and moved with the delicacy of a butterfly to her neck and then to the top corset button. He rested his finger on the button and scrutinized her face, making sure he had permission. She ran her tongue across her upper lip. His thumb and index finger undid the first button.

"I recall that hungry look from the day we rowed together last year."

"Do you?" Ada ran her hand up Ryan's leg from his knee and rested it on his groin.

A mild shiver ran up his spine from the sensation of her touch. Ryan undid Ada's other five buttons and pushed aside the corset halves. Before him lay the most talked-about bosom in Kingston and upstate New York, firm breasts that titillated men and stirred envy among women.

"Not bad for a woman that has suckled four children!" she boasted.

Ryan ran his hand from one breast to the other, stiffening the nipples as he grazed them with a fingertip. He bent forward. She twitched when his lips contacted the nipple. With his free hand, he caressed the other breast.

"For a first-timer, you are good at that."

He smiled in response. "Tis amazing how young yer skin feels. Ye look in yer twenties."

"You will find most women are the same. Time is crueler to our faces than bodies."

He tilted his head, forming a question.

"What are you thinking, now?"

"Ye want the honest answer?"

"I do."

"Earlier, I was terrified by the size of ye."

"I noticed."

"Tis not so now."

"Women are much the same on their backs," she said in a salacious tone.

"Tis not that. Stand up by the door as ye were afore."

Ada's eyes widened. She leaned towards him and lightly bit his nipple. She jumped up, removed her corset, and leaned on the door facing Ryan.

For a moment, he forgot his cockiness. This was his first unobstructed view of a naked woman. What exactly lay hidden between the legs, he could only speculate before. He glimpsed a patch of dark, curly hair partly concealing a fleshy fold that looked like it should be kissed.

He rose, still dressed in his trousers, slipped his palms up her torso and rested one on each breast.

"I now see great advantage in yer height," he whispered.

Without needing to bend his head, he kissed each nipple twice. Ada slid her fingers through his curls.

"Earlier ye said nothing that happens in this room can embarrass either of us. Did ye mean that?"

"Yes. Why?"

"Because there is something I want to try." He dropped to his knees and began kissing the mysterious fold between Ada's legs. She gasped.

"Am I hurting ye?"

"No!" She grabbed his curls and pushed his head closer. Her breathing deepened while the pace of it quickened to match the rhythm of Ryan's probing tongue.

Ryan never knew such sensory intoxication. Her smell, her taste, her sounds, her touch, and the sight of her made him giddy.

She let out a bellow and sank to the floor knocking him sideways. She slumped beside the door, panting.

"Is something wrong? I didn't expect ye to fall." He lay on the floor propped up on his elbows.

"You have…no idea…what just…happened to me?"

"No, but ye seem pleased."

"I am. I will show you why."

He gawked with gathering awareness while she undid the buttons of his trousers and pulled them over his ankles. She twirled a finger in the red hair of his testicles and then slowly wrapped her hand around his erection.

"You feel like you are ready to explode. This won't take long." She bent over, her breasts touching his legs, and took him in her mouth. True to her prediction, Ryan soon arched his back, emitted several grunts, and flopped backwards onto the floor, quivering.

"Does that happen to women too?" he mumbled.

"The details vary, but the pleasure is equal."

Ryan's penis began to droop.

"We will have none of that," she blurted. "Quick. Up on the bed. We are not finished."

Dutifully Ryan lay on the bed. She stroked him back into rigid form. "That was easy." She smiled as she straddled across his knees.

"Technically, you are still a virgin."

"I am?"

"Yes. I intend to change that…if you don't mind."

"I'd be daft to mind."

"One thing."

"Yes?"

"This bed is too short for me, so I must be on top. Can your male pride take that?"

He grabbed her ass in both hands and pulled her forward.

"My male pride can take it as much as ye want."

*****

As Ada prepared to leave Macdonell's room, Ryan held out his lone pine medallion.

"Keep this for me, please."

"Yes, but why?"

"We are leaving in two days. Last night I had a vision. I know if I leave it behind, someday I will return to claim it."

"Of course, Ryan. I will wait patiently to return it to you."

She put the medallion in a leather bag. From the same bag, she removed a silk handkerchief embroidered with the initials KJ.

"Kate sent this so you will not forget her and return someday."

Seeing a tear in her eye, he leaned forward on pure instinct to kiss it away.

*****

On Ryan's last day cleaning the fort's ramparts, his broom remained idle. Part of him hoped a billion seeds would fill the cracks, grow to tree size overnight, and reduce the fort to rubble with the suddenness of an avalanche.

His pulse thumped hard enough that it echoed in his ears. His half finger throbbed. He couldn't eat and had skipped breakfast. It wasn't the memory of yesterday's sexual awakening that had him tied up in knots. In fact, he tried to focus solely on those two hours because it soothed him. He ran through every second of his liaison with Ada, every touch, every scent, every curve of her larger-than-life body.

All the joy and thrill of losing his virginity to Ada could not hold down the angst building up in him like a summer storm. He paced the ledge along the parapet trying to work up a sweat. Despite the warm day, a chill crept up his spine. Ryan recognized the warning sign—fear waited impatiently to grip him in its icy hands.

"Kach! Kood!" Zak called from a parapet perch as Ryan strode past.

Ryan halted, yanked from the edge of his pit of fear by his raven's needs. "What am I going to do with ye?"

"Kach! Kood!"

"Zakkie boy. Ye can't stay with me. Go find Kate." With that, Ryan nudged Zak off and swept his arm in an arc. Zak understood the command to fly, and swooped from the parapet only to bank around and land beside Ryan.

Ryan stepped forward intending to push Zak off. The raven hopped from his reach. Again, the man moved closer, and again the bird moved away.

"Kach! Kood!"

"No more catch-food. Go away."

"Kach! Kood!"

"Go away!"

Zak flew down below the wall out of sight and didn't return.

After half a minute, Ryan's curiosity forced himself to look over the parapet to see if Zak had flown away.

Ryan spotted the bird circling a familiar gig drifting in the gap between the fort and Cedar Island. The boat's lone occupant scanned the parapet with a telescope. Seeing Ryan, he waved.

Ryan could not see facial features at that distance, though he recognized the lanky silhouette in a heartbeat.

Jim Johnston pulled a length of cloth from a canvas bag, tied it to one oar, and waved it like a flag. Ryan recognized the green pennant that formerly flew over the Johnston warehouse when it was safe to come home.

Ryan climbed onto the parapet and waved both arms over his head with ecstatic energy. Ryan wanted Jim to have no doubt that he understood the message.

*****

The next morning, a gang of blacksmiths arrived to shackle the American prisoners in pairs at the wrists and ankles. The sheriff wanted no one bolting for freedom. After ten months in captivity, the day had come for the long journey away.

Bound together, Ryan and Heustis waited on the parade square watching other pairs of men shuffle from the casements and form a line.

John Macdonald arrived to deliver a sullen good-bye.

"Don't take it so hard, John, ye did the best ye could," Ryan said.

"The Canadian public wants revenge," Heustis began. "There has to be scapegoats."

"I am so angered at the colonial government's intransigence, especially in your case, Ryan. They failed to prove you were a combatant at the windmill. I have endeavored on multiple occasions to obtain your pardon. Colonel Macdonell and I have beseeched Sir George Arthur to at least downgrade your sentence to a few years in prison. He refuses."

"Macdonell took up my cause? I did not know."

"Yes. We have done all we can. Your fate is now in the hands of New York politicians and community leaders. They plan to petition the Queen for clemency. It is too late to stop your transport, but they may be able to bring you home in three or four years."

Macdonald rose to leave. "I guess this is good-bye, then," he said, extending his hand to Ryan and then Heustis.

"Thank ye John for all yer efforts. I'll come visit ye again someday. I promise."

"I hope you do." As Macdonald departed, Ryan waved over the young lance corporal.

"Andrew, I want ye to have this." He handed the startled soldier a roll of pound notes. "I'm told 'tis of no use to me where I'm going and 'twill only be confiscated."

The corporal stared dumbfounded at the money, the equivalent of six months pay.

"Do me one favor."

Still tongue-tied, Andrew's cocked eyebrows asked for an explanation.

"Buy Tiny an ale or two. After he drinks it, tell him the ale's on me and I hold no grudge. Say that I know he had a hard life and I forgive him."

"That will drive him mad. He may not talk to me again."

"Tis that so bad, Andrew?"

He shrugged and replied, "I will do it. And, take care of yourself as best you can." He extended his hand. Ryan accepted the peace offer and Andrew marched away.

"Your remark about confiscation is untrue. That money might have come in handy," Heustis said.

Ryan laughed. "Don't worry. I have much more. Twas worth it. Tiny'll go to his grave knowing I bested him."

"You seem uncommonly chipper for a man awaiting imminent transport to a penal colony," Heustis said.

"'Tis an odd way to be, I grant you, but I have not given up hope of deliverance from that fate."

"Alright yah brigands," Macdonell shouted. "March!"

With sixty shackled men, Ryan passed through the gates of Fort Henry. He carried nothing with him but the clothes and hat he wore. Inside his shirt, wrapped in a silk handkerchief was a single raven's feather. The feather's former owner followed the men a hundred feet overhead.

They marched in short shackled steps down the hill towards Navy Bay. Spectators lined the route to the water and shouted insults. In the bay itself, a fleet of private craft and naval ships crowded the water. Sailors and marines watched the prisoner procession. Ryan recognized the square-shouldered form of Lieutenant George Leary near the bow of the *Bull Frog*. "Damn him and his ship," he muttered.

"It seems our adversaries have come to revel in our poor predicament," remarked Heustis.

Ryan scanned the flotilla for another familiar craft. He found it—a gig at rest among the throng of private boats past the bay's mouth. A lanky man sat amidships. From a narrow mast at the gig's stern, a green pennant fluttered in the faint breeze.

"What are you smiling about?" asked Heustis. "I have not seen you so jubilant since the day Ada visited the fort."

"'Tis a grand day to sail upon the river."

Macdonell marched his prisoners into the windowless hold of a wide, flat-bottomed canal boat. As soon as the guards secured all prisoners, the boat departed, towed by a small steamer. Ryan welcomed the gentle side-to-side rocking and waited for it to turn to port at the mouth of Navy Bay and head into the St. Lawrence River.

Instead, the barge swung starboard.

Ryan grabbed his companion's arm. "Daniel. Why are we going this way? Aren't we going down the St. Lawrence?"

Heustis pried Ryan's fingers from his bicep. "Easy there, Ryan."

"Tis all wrong. This ship's going the wrong way."

"Macdonell told me yesterday that we are headed up the Rideau Canal to Bytown first, then down the Ottawa River to Montreal."

"Why? Tis much further."

"It was Bonnycastle's suggestion. His spies think Bill Johnston is waiting in the Thousand Islands to attack any vessel carrying Hunter prisoners."

After a long pause, Ryan let go his last faint hope in a long exhale. He said, "Do you know that Bill and I once nearly blew up Bonnycastle and his ship?"

"No. Why do you mention it now?"

"Because I wish to God now we had succeeded."

*****

Zak kept pace with the steamer for the four-day journey and often rested on the pilothouse. At first, the captain objected to Zak's presence, claiming black birds were a bad omen. After sharp words from Macdonell, the skipper kept quiet. In Montreal, the sheriff oversaw their transfer to a large river steamer for the trip downriver. Zak followed and again the sheriff protected him from suspicious sailors.

On September 28, they docked at Quebec City. Macdonell escorted the Hunter prisoners in groups to the *Buffalo*, a large, three-masted sailing vessel moored at a naval pier. When each pair of transportees boarded, Macdonell's assistants removed their shackles. The grim-faced sheriff spoke words of encouragement and shook their hands. Armed guards escorted them to cells in the hold already packed with Hunters and Patriots shipped to Quebec City from other prisons.

*****

When Daniel and Ryan came aboard, Macdonell personally opened the padlocks on their ankles and wrists.

"Good luck to yah, Carrot. Follow the rules on this ship and at the penal colony, no matter how harsh they may be. After some years of hard labor, yah'll be given some freedom of movement and lighter work if yar record is good?"

"Yes, sheriff. Thank ye for being such a good friend to Zak."

"Aye. I am worried about yar bird. I cannot protect him any longer. He'll not be welcome on this vessel."

They both looked up to where Zak circled high overhead.

"I think he knows to be careful, sheriff. But I worry for him too. He won't leave me and can't fly around the world."

"Aye. He has the spirit to try. Do yah have any last letters?"

"No. I've already said my good-byes."

Heustis removed a letter for his wife and a fob watch from a pocket. "Colonel, I have had this timepiece for years. I wonder if I am permitted to keep it. If not, would you be so kind as to convey it to a friend in Watertown."

Ryan saw Macdonell's stoic visage crumble. The tough old Scot started blinking away tears. "Yah can keep it." A little sob escaped from his throat. His assistants looked away in embarrassment.

His hands on the sheriff's shoulders, Heustis said, "Take care, sir. It was an honor knowing you."

Macdonell shook their hands and hurried down the gangplank. Guards led Ryan and Heustis to the cramped, windowless cells below.

*****

For three days, they sailed down the ever-widening St. Lawrence. The captain allowed the captives on deck in groups of ten one hour per day. During each deck visit, Ryan searched for Zak. Always, he quickly spotted the raven as he paced the ship beyond rifle range to starboard.

Seeing him, the bird called out, "Kach! Kood!"

Ryan could not answer the bird's requests.

On the fourth day, the ship entered the Gulf of St. Lawrence and ran into a gale. Wind and rain whipped the wooden vessel until its ropes and timbers groaned under the load. She tossed and rolled. Seasickness confined most other prisoners to their bunks.

Ryan, already a veteran of an Atlantic crossing, was unaffected by motion sickness. On his next shift on deck, he found himself nearly alone. Dense clouds, wind-driven sea spray, and wet snow reduced daylight to a false dawn. He searched for Zak on the starboard side. He was not there. He ran to the port railing. No Zak.

"Are you looking for that bird?" asked the bosun.

"Yes, sir. Have ye seen him?"

"Is he special to you?"

"Yes, sir. I raised him from a chick."

"Follow me."

The bosun led him to the aft starboard rail, and handed him a telescope. "Look to the stern. He's there, but not visible to the unaided eye."

Ryan scanned the gray expanse. He found Zak, a bird-shaped black spot struggling in a harsh head wind. He could see the raven bravely fighting to keep up while steadily losing the battle.

"Zakkie boy," he whispered into the wind. "Give up. Go home to Kate."

The wind and snow intensified. The black spot vanished. Ryan dropped to his knees, sobbing. He'd seen the last of his faithful companion.

Letters

To Kate Johnston
Clayton, New York, USA
March 10, 1842
Dearest Kate,

    I am sorry it took two and a half years to write. My circumstances did not allow it until recently.

    Ye are on my mind daily. In the darkest moments of my travails, I drew strength from memories of our times together.

    Over these thirty months, we have endured physical trials and oppression so severe that I am amazed most of us are still alive and healthy. I was fortunate that Daniel Heustis was my group captain on the ship and in this wretched penal colony. He always worked to keep up our morale and he used his keen wit to defend our limited rights.

    We left Canada on the Buffalo with 142 Hunter and Patriot prisoners. Except for an hour or so on deck each day, we lived in cramped quarters too low to stand straight in, without windows and with poor air movement. In the tropics, the heat was oppressive.

    After 140 days at sea, with one stop in South America, we arrived in Van Diemen's Land on February 12, 1840. We presented ourselves to the governor, John Franklin, the former polar explorer. He must have insulted someone badly to be posted to such a God-forsaken place.

    Franklin told us we were bad men who deserved to hang. He put us to work constructing roads with common convicts. That chafed Heustis severely. He said we were prisoners of politics and conscience, not common thieves and scoundrels. Heustis always insisted they house us separately, and for the most part, he had his way. I respect him and love him like a brother.

    They took our civilian boots and clothes and gave us poorly made shoes and uniforms colored half yellow and half black. We called them magpies because of how we looked. The workmanship was poor. Our clothes and shoes fell apart in two months. We received new gear every six months. Many of us worked nearly naked and barefoot for months at a time in all manner of weather. At night, we had a mattress stuffed with grass and two rough blankets.

    For making roads, we had only crude tools and no horses to draw wagons. We became the beasts of burden, pushing carts and wheelbarrows loaded with rock. For two years, we worked sunrise to sundown, five or six days a week, winter and summer, building their damned roads.

Our overseers were all hard, mean men. At least two came from slave plantations. Guards regularly flogged men for minor infractions. On Daniel's advice, we Hunters made a pact that, if they attempted to flog any of our group, we would all rise up and resist to our deaths. Once the overseers realized we were serious, they nary laid the lash on any of us.

My greatest suffering, next to missing ye, was the poor food. I dream often of meals with your family in Clayton. The food at Fort Henry was poor, but every meal since was far worse.

On the road gang, our daily ration per man was one pound and five ounces of coarse bread, less than a pound of poor meat, a half pound of potatoes, some salt, and a thin skilly. The diet nary varied. We always boiled the meat. That made it easy to spoon the dead vermin from the broth. We nary had enough food to maintain our bodies. We all became dreadfully thin. Disease took a few brave comrades who were too weak to resist its ravages.

Our guards usually freed us from labor on Saturday afternoons and Sunday. On Saturdays, we washed our clothes and bodies as best we could. On Sundays, we were forced to attend an Anglican church in the morning. Sunday afternoons were ours to do as we wished.

Some men took jobs on the sly outside of camp in their few spare hours. With their meager earnings, they bought food, soap, and tobacco. I found a small creature, much like our crayfish back home, living in the rivers. I often boiled up a meal of the wee beasts. I also occasionally snared small game or a strange creature called a kangaroo and roasted it over a fire. At such moments, I always thought of Nick and his grandparents. I wonder where they are now.

Cruel and strange as it sounds, rules prohibited us from buying food or obtaining it by any means. If caught, it meant a flogging or more time at hard labor before obtaining a ticket to leave. Still, we needed extra food to survive.

After 14 months, Governor Franklin visited our work camp. He told us that men sentenced to transport for life normally must work eight years for a ticket to leave. But since we were not common criminals, he reduced the period to two years. He said, if we be of good conduct for another 10 months, he would grant our tickets.

Two weeks ago, the governor kept his word. We are not free, but are no longer slaves. We can now accept payment for any work we find. We must now buy our own food. The law confines us to six districts and we cannot go near any port because they fear we may abscond on one of the American whalers that stop for supplies.

Heustis, myself and others found work with farmers. We have clean and comfortable lodgings, good food, and a modest income. The farmer lends me books, of which he has many.

Life is better, but far from what we had. I miss ye. I miss Zak and often wonder at his fate. I miss your father, mother, brothers, and Ada too. She was always so kind to me.

Give my love to your family. Write me as soon as ye can. It takes five or six months for a letter to travel one way.

Forever yours,
Ryan Lone Pine
Hobart Town, Van Diemen's Land

*****

To Ryan Lone Pine
Hobart Town, Van Diemen's Land
August 28, 1842
My dearest Ryan,

I received your letter yesterday and cried with happiness. You cannot believe my joy at reading your words, at knowing you are alive and among friends.

Your recounting of terrible food and harsh servitude left me in tears when I thought of you living in such diabolical conditions. How cruel of the British to send you there.

Enough of such sadness. I have some happy news. Your raven returned two weeks after you departed. He stayed with us for many weeks and we played the catch-food game every day. Since then, he has taken up with a lady raven and now lives on Whiskey Island. Father purchased the island and warned everyone on the river that they face his wrath if they harm those two birds.

I also received a letter from our dear friend Hugh Scanlon. He used the money Father gave him to set himself up in business. He operates a store buying and selling used goods in New York City. He was always shrewd. I am certain he will prosper. I will write him soon to tell him you are well.

These last three years, Father has been up to his usual antics. Just before you departed, he was arrested in New York. He escaped, as always. The Hunters offered him another commission, but he did not accept. He is finished with them. Their influence has thankfully faded.

At my brothers' urging, Father surrendered voluntarily to the jail in Albany just weeks after you left. I joined him in his cell. The man needs taking care of. But his restless spirit prevailed when the spring came. He made a key, escaped in May, and returned to the islands.

In August 1840, he became a Mason, and then took up a petition to ask the president for a pardon based on his heroic efforts in the last war with the British.

Martin Van Buren was defeated in the 1840 election. We soundly trounced him in this state for not stopping the transport of our boys. Father took his petition to Van Buren in the final days of his reign of cowardice. Van Buren met with Father, but refused the petition and stated he would sooner see him shot or hanged.

A few days later, the new president, William Henry Harrison, happily signed the pardon and Father was a free man.

Father is now an honest businessman again, or as close as he gets to honest. He still has a smuggling crew. I help him and my brothers at their various businesses and give Mother a hand around the house. Ada visits often. She is such good company and comfort when my sorrow over losing you gets the best of me.

I will end with some interesting gossip.

The Queen knighted Father's old nemesis, Lieutenant-Colonel Bonnycastle, six months after he helped send you and the others to that terrible place. Colonel Dundas from the windmill battle was also knighted. Father says he has now helped at least three British officers obtain knighthoods. He jokes that, with a little more time and effort, he could have assured every British officer in Canada a knighthood.

Upper and Lower Canada have combined into one colony simply called Canada. I hear your old lawyer, John Macdonald, was elected to office.

That is all. Write soon.
Love always,
Kate Johnston
Clayton, New York, USA

*****

To Kate Johnston
Clayton, New York, USA
February 9, 1843
Dearest Kate,

    I was overjoyed to read your letter, to hear news of your family, and good news about Zak. As I read it, I imagine your sweet face as ye wrote these words to me and your delicate, lovely hands on the quill.

    Heustis and I continue to roam this island working for farmers, sheering sheep, cutting wood, and making shingles. Tis like my labors in Ireland, Canada, and America. The work is familiar and not burdensome, though our pay is meager. This is not a wealthy island and many are willing to work for little.

    I now see beauty in this harsh land. The plants are much different from back home and here lives the oddest of creatures. The weather is terribly hot in summer, but temperate in winter—nary as cold as Canada. It has rugged mountains and beautiful rivers, not as majestic as our St. Lawrence, but they satisfy my restless soul.

    Sometimes I see the original people. They are dark skinned like Negroes, but otherwise different in appearance. They live off the land as hunters, but are landless, like my Algonquin family. The English have not set aside a place for them and the white settlers drive them away.

    I turned 25 two weeks ago. I feel older. I suspect the harsh conditions aged my appearance. Heustis will soon be 37. I have known this dear man for 5 years and I am certain he has aged 10 or more.

    I am no longer resigned to being away forever. I will find a way off. I am certain the years will peel away like the skin of an onion if I hold ye in my arms again.

    Forever yours,
    Ryan Lone Pine
    Hobart Town, Van Diemen's Land

*****

To Ryan Lone Pine
Hobart Town, Van Diemen's Land
July 24, 1843
My dearest Ryan,

    You spoke of age in your last letter. In two months, I will be 24. I do not feel physically old yet, but I am aging socially. Most women my age are married with children. I stand out as being different. Many attribute this to my "wild years" on the river with Father. They explain my reluctance to marry as "not ready to settle down yet." What they do not know is that I wish to be a wife and mother, but my heart is not yet whole.

Ada is 42 this year. She still turns heads. I hope I age as elegantly. We are quite a pair. We spend time together without the company of men either walking in town or rowing on the river. Whispers eddy around us wherever we go. We both have our suitors. Ada discourages hers easily by showing her wedding ring. I must resort to saying no often enough to discourage mine.

Ada and I often talk briefly of you. Your fate saddens both of us so harshly that we dare not speak of you for long. I do think Ada loves you as much as I.

Father is 61 now, and still hale and hearty. He finally met Bonnycastle. Sir Richard was in our county looking for British deserters, which I am told is his legal right. The Hound and the Fox chatted down by the Clayton wharf for several minutes. I was present and saw respect shown by both for the other.

We also had a visit from yet another British knight, this time a fellow named Sir James Alexander. It seems Brits can receive a knighthood just for putting their boots on correctly. He too came to Clayton in search of deserters. Since Father is our Knight of the Thousand Islands, the townsfolk sent him as head of a delegation to meet Sir James. He asked Father what he gained for all his efforts fighting the British. Father responded that he took great pleasure in knowing the British spent at least four million dollars chasing him or building defenses against him.

I will post this letter in a few minutes and head out on the river to visit your bird. We are still good friends. You are godfather of sorts—Zak and his lady have three chicks in a nest.

Love always,
Kate Johnston
Clayton, New York, USA

*****

To Kate Johnston
Clayton, New York, USA
January 9, 1844
Dearest Kate,

Tis good to hear Zak has a family. Someday I hope to do the same. By the way, I still have a feather of his. I keep it wrapped in that handkerchief ye sent me. I hid it from the guards those years on the road gang.

Sadly, Heustis and I went our separate ways. Last I saw of him was at our annual Fourth of July party in 1843. Daniel had a fair helping of spiked lemonade. It was the first occasion I've seen him drunk.

The governor conscripted Heustis and forty other ticket-to-leave men to hunt gangs of bushrangers—escaped convicts who rob and murder settlers. It seems odd to me that our captors now give us arms to hunt for other prisoners, for, without full freedom, we are still prisoners.

Most men willingly agreed to hunt the bushrangers, since the reward can be generous. The governor pardoned four of our fellows and sent them home after they captured the most notorious gang of bushrangers. One lucky man was Stephen Wright, a casement mate at Fort Henry.

I now live on the north coast outside of George Town. I found employment with a man who is a shipwright, cooper, and wheelwright. I have a great opportunity to extend my skills beyond shipbuilding. Many opportunities in this world await a man that can make boats, barrels, and wagon wheels.

I am more certain everyday that I will not be on this island forever. Governor Franklin left here last August after six years. I pray that the new governor will work to have us all pardoned soon.

Forever yours,
Ryan Lone Pine
George Town, Van Diemen's Land

*****

To Kate Johnston
Clayton, New York, USA
October 29, 1844
Dearest Kate,

I have such good news that I decided not to wait until I received your reply to my previous letter of January 9. Word arrived that Queen Victoria has pardoned all the Americans prisoners. We will be free when the governor receives the pardons in writing.

By the summer of 1845, I will be back. Our dreams of walking again on the streets of Clayton and rowing to some secret place in the islands can come true. Wait for me.

Forever yours,
Ryan Lone Pine
George Town, Van Diemen's Land

*****

To Ryan Lone Pine
George Town, Van Diemen's Land
July 5, 1844
Dear Ryan,

In your letter of January 9, you mentioned Stephen Wright's good fortune. It was not news to me. He published a letter in the Northern Journal in February after his return. He told how he and three others were rewarded after catching bushrangers. It is too bad you were not with them in their hunt.

I have some news, which I impart with great reluctance. You remember Charlie Hawes. Of all my suitors over these years—and there have been many—Charlie was ever vigilant. Where other men gave up the challenge easily, he did not. Each time I turned down his invitations, he waited a respectable time and then approached me again. Yesterday at our Fourth of July party, I agreed to be his wife. He is a good man. He came at the right time. I said yes. We plan to wait a year or so to marry. Charlie wants time to build up his shoe business before we start a family.

Father was not happy to hear of my engagement, but he did not refuse me. Ada was furious. Both still hold out hope you will return soon. Alas, that hope has faded in me.

If you ever do come home, please visit. It would be so nice to lay my eyes—though, alas, not my fingers—on those red curls of yours once again.

Your friend always,
Kate Johnston
Clayton, New York, USA

*****

To Ada Burleigh
Portland, Upper Canada
March 1, 1845
Dear Ada,

I received Kate's last letter in January telling of her betrothal to Hawes. As ye can imagine, the news was a cruel blow coming so soon after news of my pending freedom. I cannot write her at this time. Tis too hard.

I left a sum of money in Ann's keeping. Please use it to buy Kate a wedding gift. Relay my best wishes for her future.

My pardon is official. I am now free, but like many of my long suffering fellows I must find my own way home. None has enough money to buy passage and the American government refuses to provide for us.

In January, Daniel Heustis convinced the captain of an American whaler to take as many men as possible on their bond, with payment to come once they got home. Heustis had men spread the word to distant towns. Word did not reach me in time. Daniel Heustis, Orrin Smith, and 25 others left on January 29 bound for California via the Antarctic whaling grounds. Many Hunters remain here yet, including 28 of the windmill group, if ye do not count those buried in these dusty hills. My casement mates Garret Hicks and William Gates remain, though I see them rarely.

I am glad now that I did not travel on that whaler with Heustis. If so, I would have missed Kate's last letter and sailed home with impossible expectations.

I'll be leaving for Australia tomorrow and plan to explore that land for a time. I will return to the Thousand Islands someday.

I think of ye often. Farewell, my special friend. I will send an address once I have one again. Give my best to Bill, Ann, and their sons when ye next see them, and John Macdonald too.

Lovingly yours,
Ryan Lone Pine

Epilogue

The salt tang of the sea reached inland as Ryan pushed his newly built rowboat off the narrow Tasmanian beach into the briny Tamar River. Glancing up at the antipodal summer sun, he tightened his wide leather hat's chinstrap. He secured his food sacks and water jugs in the stern compartment.

Into a clamp on the bow, he inserted the black feather he'd hidden for so many years. Taking his seat, he set the two long oars into their locks and began to row north towards Australia. He'd be at sea at least a week—more if the weather went bad. Plenty of time, Ryan knew, to ponder the currents that took him so far off course and the best route home.

###

About the Author

Shaun J. McLaughlin maintains two history blogs: one on the Patriot War and other Canadian/American border clashes; and, one on William Johnston, the Thousand Islands legend. A researcher, journalist and technical writer for over thirty years, with a master's degree in journalism, he lives on a hobby farm in Eastern Ontario. Now a semiretired freelance writer, he focuses on fiction and nonfiction writing projects.

Made in the USA
Charleston, SC
11 March 2012